PRAISE FOR
PRYOR RENDERING

"Wow, can Gary Reed write! *Pryor Rendering* dazzles with
its wildly original images and vivid characterizations. . . .
A vivid, unforgettable picture of what it's like to grow up
queer in small-town America."   —*Island Lifestyle*

"It boggles the mind to think this could be Reed's first
novel. It is as well written as anything I have read in years . . .
a reading experience you will never forget."
                                        —*Pryor Daily Times*

"Lyrical and hauntingly forthright . . . offers poignant
insights into the soul of a youth desperate for acceptance
in a world filled with rejection."   —*Publishers Weekly*

"Colorful . . . rich . . . a near-perfect tale, and a compelling
alternative to the spate of gay epics that have lately inundated
readers."   —*Kirkus Reviews*

"*Pryor Rendering* wins with its stylish, poetic writing."
                                        —*Lambda Book Report*

GARY REED grew up in Oklahoma and now lives in New
York City. *Pryor Rendering* is his first novel.

GARY REED

PRYOR RENDERING

A PLUME BOOK

PLUME
Published by the Penguin Group
Penguin Books USA Inc., 375 Hudson Street, New York, New York 10014, U.S.A.
Penguin Books Ltd, 27 Wrights Lane, London W8 5TZ, England
Penguin Books Australia Ltd, Ringwood, Victoria, Australia
Penguin Books Canada Ltd, 10 Alcorn Avenue, Toronto, Ontario, Canada M4V 3B2
Penguin Books (N.Z.) Ltd, 182–190 Wairau Road, Auckland 10, New Zealand

Penguin Books Ltd, Registered Offices: Harmondsworth, Middlesex, England

Published by Plume, an imprint of Dutton Signet,
a division of Penguin Books USA Inc.
Previously published in a Dutton edition.

First Plume Printing, April, 1997
10 9 8 7 6 5 4 3 2 1

℗ REGISTERED TRADEMARK—MARCA REGISTRADA

The Library of Congress has catalogued the Dutton edition as follows:
Reed, Gary.
Pryor rendering / Gary Reed.
p.   cm.
ISBN: 0-525-94102-9 (hc.)
ISBN: 0-452-27797-3 (pbk.)
1. Teenage boys—Oklahoma—Fiction.   2. Gay youth—
Oklahoma—Fiction.   3. Family—Oklahoma—Fiction.   I. Title.
PS3568.E36487P38   1996
813'.54—dc20   95–41849
                                                      CIP

Printed in the United States of America
Original hardcover design by Julian Hamer

PUBLISHER'S NOTE

This is a work of fiction. Names, characters, places, and incidents either are the product of the author's imagination or are used fictitiously, and any resemblance to actual persons, living or dead, events, or locales is entirely coincidental.

BOOKS ARE AVAILABLE AT QUANTITY DISCOUNTS WHEN USED TO PROMOTE PRODUCTS
OR SERVICES. FOR INFORMATION PLEASE WRITE TO PREMIUM MARKETING DIVISION,
PENGUIN BOOKS USA INC., 375 HUDSON STREET, NEW YORK, NY 10014.

PRYOR
RENDERING

· Part One ·

■

I WAS BORN IN A BEER JOINT IN PRYOR, OKLAHOMA. THE JOINT was called Chick's. It belonged to a gnarly old cuss named Charlie Bash—"Chick" to his friends—who built it with his own sweat and know-how out of the aggravation of having to drive seventy-five miles from Pryor to the nearest barstool and cold keg in Tulsa.

"Hell," Chick said, "I'd have a few too many in T-town and couldn't find my way home at night. After dark, my eyes ain't what they used to be. One mornin' I ended up in fizzlin' Arkansas. Oh, hell, yes! I asked a ol' feller there on the road, 'Where the hell am I, Buddy?' He says Arkansas. I said, 'Arkansas? Oh, shit!' Well, I figured I could build a piddlin' joint in Pryor cheaper than gas money for Arkansas and back. 'Sides, ain't no fun for an old peck-erwood just drinkin' at home. Hell, I like a little bullshit with my beer."

Chick was my grandpa. I got his name and my mother, Ida, got his bar.

Even though he died of drinking, I never saw him touch a drop outside of a bar. It's the truth. On Sundays, when county law pre-vented him from selling beer out of his place, he'd spend the day sober rather than drink at home. Of course, more Sundays than not, he'd take off for Tulsa and hop the bars there. Sometimes, when I was still just a boy, he'd take me along.

We'd hit a slew of places with names like Jack's, the Beehive, Jewel's. Seedy places that smelled like piss. Rooms with painted windows and so dark that, once inside, the light would burn your eyes when the door opened.

"Who's your drinking buddy, Chick?"

"My little grandson," Chick would announce, lifting me to a stool. "Give us a cold draw and," giving me a wink, "a bottle of Coke, I guess. And fill that ol' peckerwood's glass down there with whatever the hell he's drinkin'."

"Thanks, Charlie."

"Put 'er there, Chick."

"Hello, you old dog."

In every bar my grandpa sauntered into, someone was glad to see him. Big perfumed bosoms pushed up against his chest, lipstick smudged his earlobes. I watched his hands cup around fat girls' butts in tight pants and slap the bent backs of crusty old men in undershirts. Woozy faces opened up around huge yellow teeth and boozy laughter at the sight of Chick Bash walking through the door. Blood-red fingernails stroked Charlie's smooth head then scratched at the bucks stacked next to his beer.

Chick liked a little bullshit with his beer and was willing to pay generously for it. He'd lay out a twenty or fifty on the bar top, and if there were more than us and a bartender in the joint, the bullshit would flow.

"Hell, that boy's too civilized to be a relation of yours, Chick."

"Oh, goddamn! If I knew they let SOBs like you drink here, I'd sure as hell gone somewhere else. Better pour that ugly shit something to hush him up, Jewel. And don't forget to take a little somethin' for yourself now, Honey."

Jewel, or whoever, would pull the taps and pour the drinks and help herself freely to Chick's money. The more the register pinged and slammed, the faster the ashtrays filled to the rim. Insults boiled to steam, then evaporated into a dingy haze. Old cronies rehashed lost nights, cursed the cost of living and drinking, teased the whores, and scouted for rides home to bitched-about wives.

Chick would hand me a stack of quarters to put in the jukebox. I'd plug the machine and push random buttons until the dusty

speakers warbled and whiny steel guitars finally outblasted the 45's
scratchy static beneath the needle. The whole clink and clatter and
babble of drinks and drinkers would be submerged momentarily in
the syrupy lyrics of some sad barroom tune.

"How come you always pick such sad ones, Honey?" Jewel
would ask.

"I don't know," I used to answer. I hadn't yet learned that the
odds of pushing random buttons in such a bar were usually in sorrow's favor.

The novelty lamps advertising brands of beer evoked Bavarian
snowcaps and cascading waterfalls. They created a rhythmic rocking light in the dank atmosphere, gave me an underwater sensation.
I just drifted on the drunken current.

I was a listener, a bug-eyed witness in a room of giants. I
watched them, the men especially, humpbacked over the bar, lips
clinched to highballs or bottles, sucking the amber out of the afternoon, sucking the afternoon out of Sunday.

I can't clearly remember a single face, only certain features.
They rarely had names. Chick called them all "Buddy," "Feller,"
"You ol' Peckerwood." They came and went, almost always alone,
each out of and back into the same blinding light of the open bar
door. Some were pot-bellied and old, others young and lean. Some
wore workshirts pasty with sweat, dirty jobs wedged into the
creases of their necks. Others talked bitterly of no work at all.

As they drank, their sighs and belches loomed, wildfires burned
into the whites of their eyes, their shoulders merged up near the
ceiling.

My eyes bumped against their jaundiced tattoos: a dagger-
pierced heart bleeding on a bicep; a hawk, claws spread, stalking
the birthmark on a shoulderblade; the lewd splay of a chesty
woman on a hairy forearm; a cobra coiled around a wrist like a
venomous Bulova.

I peered through the gaps of their teeth into the black caverns
of their conversations. Bigoted slurs and expletives banged against
my ears. I dodged the stumble and stagger of legs slung like car-

casses through the dim light, heard thunder in blubbery paunches, and bladders behind locked doors splashing the urinals with their forceful streams.

My grandpa fell apart when he drank. The tough old leaning-post whose middle-of-the-night footsteps padded through the house in Pryor as reassuringly as the creaks and moans of the old house itself crumbled before my eyes. He drank himself to pieces and blurred into all the other men. He was interchangeable fragments among the tattoos and sideburns, the weedy nostrils and Adam's apples that bobbed like sinkers.

Because I never had a father, my heart was always cocked toward the affections of these men. Again and again I went with Chick to the bars to guzzle the brawling sights and sounds, the scents and ways of men; each Sunday hoping to find some masculine crook or hollow where I could lodge.

But inevitably Chick deserted me for the realm of drunkenness I could not yet enter. I lost him in the jigsaw puzzle of men I could not work. I was abandoned to the attentions of barmaids and whores. Hard-faced women with sour breath and throaty voices hugged me to their pillowy chests, played with my hair and gave my forehead repeated moist kisses.

Often it was the attentions of these women that brought Chick back to my side, for he was a notorious womanizer. Chasing pussy, he said, kept him young, and he laughed at that as if quietly sobbing.

Occasionally, we'd leave with a woman, usually only to end up in another bar. But more than once, some gal scooted into our car and pointed out directions to the driveway of a run-down house or hotel in an even shabbier part of Tulsa. Those afternoons, Chick flipped me a silver dollar or promised a barbecue dinner if I'd wait in the car while he helped out his girlfriend with something important inside.

I sat behind the steering wheel of the parked car and pretended to drive. I drove all the blacktop and backroads out of Tulsa, past the Pryor turnoff, farther than Arkansas, never slowing to ask fellers along the road, "Where the hell am I, buddy?" Not even caring to know.

One of those times, sitting at the wheel, a husky set of bare shoulders and the crew-cut head of a retarded boy appeared in the window of the passenger door.

"Where you driving to?" he asked. His jaw jutted forward like an open drawer exposing the wet interior of his mouth. His hair was waxed stiff as nails and accentuated the blockiness of his head. His eyes were cornerless and so glassy dark they mirrored what they saw. Until he spoke, I was unsure of his seeing me at all, because his eyes stared not at but disturbingly beside me.

"Nowhere," I told him. "Where'd you come from?"

"Down there." He tilted his head back, awkwardly indicating the deep ditch behind him. "You want to fight?" he asked.

The slowness of his pronunciation took the emotion out of his speech. Maybe because he seemed to be looking at an invisible image beside me, I felt unthreatened by his question. "No," I said, like I'd been offered a piece of gum.

"How old are you?" he asked.

"Seven and a half," I answered.

"I could pick you up good. I'm thirteen. No. Fourteen, I mean. Come on." I watched him through the windshield walk around the car toward my door. He moved unsteadily like a tightrope walker with his arms floating out from his body for balance. He stopped a few yards from the door in the middle of the empty street. Not only shirtless, he was naked except for underpants and cowboy boots with high slanted heels. They were so prominent on his exposed legs my first thought on seeing him full-view was not of his lack of clothes but that those boots must account for his odd walk.

I pushed the heavy door open and slid down to the blacktop. Then I was lifted off my feet in the glare of sunlight and flesh. He had swooped down on me with crouched legs, locked me to his chest, and launched me off the ground by simply unfolding his height. His arms crushed my own to my sides and my legs dangled

like a scarecrow's as he swayed back and forth in his black boots
rooted to the hot gluey road.

Because my ear pressed into his sweaty face, my own voice
sounded deep and muffled inside my head. I said, "I'm waiting for
my grandpa," watching the baggy screen door of the house pass
back and forth across my vision.

I'd never been held by a man before; he was as big as most men.
Pressed to the sturdy trunk of this boy, I was keenly aware of my
own body and I felt solid and very real. His flesh gave way only to
a degree because beneath his flesh was an impenetrable density, like
packed earth beneath thick grass. His hardness was a border I
wanted to squeeze through, but it was tightly sealed and I only
sprang back into myself.

When he put me down, I felt unsteady, the way you feel stepping out of a boat onto solid ground, but also I felt awed by a kind
of instant trust that, perhaps, comes only from being plucked out
of a lonesome drive to nowhere and lifted into the sky.

"I told you," he said. His droopy lower lip overlapped his top
one, and he turned his off-kilter gaze to the house. "They're
fucking," he said in a matter-of-fact tone.

I nodded, staring at the house also, but without any idea as to
the meaning of it all.

The boy reached into his underwear, fidgeted with himself and
asked my name.

"Charlie Hope," I told him, and he said he was "Buddy."

I asked him where his pants were. He looked toward the car,
maybe at the vacant lot beyond it—I wasn't used to his crooked
eyes—then down at his feet. His hand slid lazily up his belly and
opened palm-up under his nose. He stood for a second with his
head bowed, breathing over his outstretched fingers. "Hot," he
said, then "I'll show you something," and I followed the creak of
his boot leather across the tarred road to the edge of the steep
gully.

The ditch was freshly unearthed for a new water or sewage

line. Man-size sections of concrete piping were strewn across the bare lot.

Buddy dug his slanted heels into the slope and with his arms flapping like wings made his way to the bottom. I didn't have his weight with which to dig footholds into the loose decline, so I slid most of the way by the seat of my pants. The ditch bed was flat and muddy, spotted with puddles of water, and though the sun beat down into the hole, the high embankment of damp earth was almost cooling.

Seeing Buddy's jeans hanging from a root that poked through the gully wall tempted me to undress, just because nobody would ever know. The deep dirt walls amplified our privacy. The rest of the world seemed to be buried behind their high embankment.

The ditch was full of frogs. Buddy's pants pockets were full of firecrackers. He grinned, said he had a beebee gun in his garage. His crooked eyes fell upon a toad climbing out of a puddle inches from his toe. He gutted it by grinding his sharp heel into its back. He squatted over the flattened body and picked it up by one leg. He grabbed the other hind leg and ripped the thing apart down to its skull. It took a concerted pull to split it, and I heard a snap and a small splash as some part of it fell into the puddle between his feet.

I stood to his side, stunned.

Buddy tortured or killed every one of the frogs. The first few he simply smashed with his boot or slammed against the embankment. Then he began inserting firecrackers into their mouths or the gashes in their bellies, lighting them and tossing them into the air like hand grenades. He did this without expression. At most, he tilted his squarish face in an approximation of curiosity about the innards of the exploded bodies. As he slit open the underside of a live one with a pocketknife, there did finally register across his face a look of total engagement.

The frog was kicking in his hand, even as Buddy pried its belly open with his knife. "Look at it," he said. Obediently I moved close enough to see into the frog's guts. The knife must have cut something vital, for the thing was suddenly still. The tip of Buddy's knife gently poked around the throbbing heart, trying to loosen and dislodge it. It was an engrossing and almost tender surgery. Buddy sat down against the dirt wall, knees up, holding the frog between his legs. I squatted beside him, rested my chin on my hands, my hands unconsciously on his wide knee. The frog's organs gleamed in the strong light. Buddy severed the delicate strings that held the heart in its cavity. He picked it out with his fingernails and tossed the body to the side, into the open grave of toads where we crouched.

"Oh!" he said. "Look at it," holding the purplish frog heart in front of his eyes, which seemed to repeat "Oh!" with their perfect roundness, not to the amazing little pump between his fingers but to the off-center invisible image of the heart only they could see.

The moment Buddy separated the heart from the frog, time became transformed. The dread and repulsion I had been holding to me seemed worthless and in the way. I flung them aside like the lifeless toads. It's impossible to say how long we admired the heart or what happened to the heart, for eventually it was just gone and what was left was the pumping motion and Chick's car horn honking for me and an altered field of vision that took in the act of the boy's masturbation, not head-on, but off to the side, behind the raised knee. My eyes rested on his pink ear, illumined by the sun like a flower curling inward from harsh light.

■

CHICK BASH WAS SIX-ONE, THIN, AND STURDY AS A LEAD PIPE. HE wore soft felt fedoras that protected his bald scalp from the sun, but the short sleeves he wore year-round had left his hands and forearms leathery brown, as if he'd spent his whole life plunged elbow deep in scorching labor. His breast pockets sagged with a pack of Winstons and a briarwood pipe. He carried his tobacco and stripping-lady Zippo in the side pockets of his gray trousers that were so long in the crotch and roomy in the rear that his buddies wisecracked it looked like somebody had moved out of the seat of his britches.

"Really?" Chick would say, taking an exaggerated look behind him. "Oh, hell, no. My ass has just been chewed out so many times, there's fizzlin' nothin' of it left."

Charlie had a laugh like a choked motor, all heaving breath and wheeze. After a few seconds it churned up a croupy cough, but it always stalled with a long sigh and an exclamation. "Oh, shit!" summed it up.

Charlie's nose bloomed out of the shadow of his hat brim, pink and porous as a strawberry. It dwarfed the size of his head and gave him the silhouette of a fierce bird. He said his nose was so big because he kept it out of everybody else's business and just let it grow. His other features paled by comparison, especially his small, weak eyes.

I was born in his bar because Chick had taken off for Tulsa on an August Sunday and hadn't returned to Pryor by Monday night. Fay Rose Savory, a local widow and a reluctant retiree of the rendering plant and Chick's steadiest lady friend, spent most of her time at the bar. When she found it locked up on Monday, Fay Rose came by the house to find out why.

Ida was always weird about answering the door; company made her nervous. When Fay Rose got no answer to her knocking, she used the key from the mailbox and walked right in.

She hollered when she saw Ida sitting in the dark. "You scared the tar out of me! I knocked and knocked. Where's Chick?" she asked, fanning herself with both hands.

Ida said she didn't know, "probably drunk." She asked Fay Rose who she might be.

"Oh, I beg your pardon, Hon. Fay. Fay Rose Savory, friend of Chick's. He's run off again? Well, I help keep things runnin' over at the joint. I come by for the keys. You must be Ida. Well, well. Ida Bash, a growed woman, I swear! Where do the years go?"

"Ida *Hope*," my mother corrected. "I *was* married, but I'm widowed now. I came a few days ago from Tulsa." But, Ida said, she knew nothing about any bar keys. She was a Christian.

Fay Rose always did a good impression of Ida, softening her voice to an indignant whisper and saying, "I'm a Christian, you know."

"Of course you are, Hon. Chick told me. I know all about *that*. I just plumb forgot you was here. Lordy, it's hot!" Fay fanned some more. "Why don't you have that water cooler blowing?"

"I did, for about a minute," Ida explained, "but it blew a fuse. I couldn't find any spares and the fusebox must be in the basement anyway. I can't manage those stairs—not in the dark—not in my condition." She sighed, dropped her head back against the rocker. "It don't matter. The dark is cooler."

Ida was pregnant with me, and Fay said the house was like an oven. "You poor thing. You're sweating to death in here. You've got to come with me. I'll grab the keys and the two of us gals can get acquainted down at the bar."

"No, ma'am," Ida refused. "I've never in my life set foot in a bar," nor into the company of a woman quite like Fay. "I don't tolerate drinking. It's against my religion."

"But this is your own daddy's bar," Fay Rose cut in, "and it's got the coldest air conditioner in Oklahoma. Besides, Sweetheart," Fay said while heading for the keys, "everybody around here is a Christian, Hon. Even the drunks."

I was born that night in Chick's joint. Ida thought it was God's way of humiliating her and would never talk about it. Fay Rose said it was the heat and the titillation. She retold the story a million times. Chick said things just fizzlin' happen.

Chick and my grandmother separated when Ida was just a girl.

"It was *her* decision," he said, "but I can't say it wasn't for the best. Esther, that's your grandma, didn't have a religious bone until Ida got born. Well, maybe she did, but she was average about it, I mean. Then all at once, she joined up over there at that Pentecostal church in Purley. Hell, I never paid much mind. Women do go to church. Eventually it come between us though. Your grandma turned into one of them fizzlin' Holy Rollers, speakin' those tongues and such.

"I reckon it was my drinking all along. She never could abide it, and that church business just egged her on. It got to be the shits after a while.

"Finally one day out of the blue, she just packed up Ida and took off for Tulsa. I tracked her down; I begged her to come home, got on the wagon for a while. I tried sending her money, but she wouldn't take it. Said the Lord provides! Well, I knew for a fact it was her fizzlin' Aunt Mabel providing for 'em. Anyways, I put something aside each paycheck, figuring I at least owed Ida. But she grew up against me, brainwashed by her mother. Esther's nonsense and those fizzlin' churches is what turned Ida into a tight-assed old spinster. Poor girl didn't stand a chance, that's for sure. I'll take some blame, if somebody's dishin' it. Hell, I wasn't never around much, even before they left; working double shifts at the rendering plant, trying to stay ahead.

"I reckon I wasn't much of a daddy, but I swear Esther was too much of a momma. She held on to that girl like a third titty. No wonder Ida's so odd. You know, they slept in the same bed for nearly forty years. Never worked a job her whole life, didn't know a kiss-my-butt about life.

"When your grandma died, she left Aunt Mabel's money, what was left of it, to the Assembly of God in West Tulsa. Now ain't that the shits? Didn't give Ida a thought. I offered her the money then to start out on her own. Even asked her to come back to Pryor and live with me. I couldn't picture her getting by on her own. But she wouldn't have nothing to do with me.

"She stayed on in T-town. Moved in with some old church-woman who'd got bedridden and took care of her for a while. Less than a year, I think, till that one died, too. Then the pastor's family took her in. She lived and kind of worked for them up to the time Garl—your daddy, that is—came along."

Garland Hope was a godly husband, Ida told me, and a Christian missionary who had received the Lord's calling and followed it far away from Pryor.

"How far away, Momma?"

"Oh, some place so far away, it has no name really."

"Farther than Arkansas?"

"Gracious, yes. Much farther than Arkansas."

He'd followed the calling into heathen lands and lived in un-named jungles with the most savage of God's unwashed. "It's a hard life converting savages, Charlie." In spite of his charity, devotion, and faith, the heathens would not be saved, and in their sinful lack of grace, because they were Satan's children, they had set fire to my father's mission. God had called him home to heaven from out of those flames.

"How far is heaven?"

In miles she couldn't say. "Yes, Charlie, farther than Arkansas."

It pained Ida to tell the story. If I prodded too deeply for details, she seemed to retreat further into her sadness, and I feared that the place my questions sent her was so distant and the journey so dangerous that she might never return. So over the years, her telling receded to memory and I tended the details myself. And yet the strongest bonds between my mother and me were built of those early moments we had shared in a far-off jungle, fabricating the myth of Garl Hope, whose absence haunted our relationship like a holy ghost.

Our house was very quiet. We kept our noise bottled up. It was unnatural, but that's how it was.

Chick was a mouthy bastard in a barroom, but he was as quiet as pipe smoke at home. He somewhat guarded his cuss words around Ida, and even the volume of the ball games he watched on TV was low enough to lull you to sleep. Fay Rose would burst through the door, a loud bundle of gossip, but even she would eventually fall under the spell of silence that hushed the house like a deep snow. It was Ida.

Life was thick, and she waded through it slowly. She could sit in absolute stillness for hours and dim light suited her. Sometimes I had to reassure myself of her presence in the house by looking for her.

In the dark living room, I'd find her sitting in the same sag of the couch, staring into space as if patiently waiting for something to happen or resigned to nothing ever happening again. I'd say, "What are you doing, Momma?"

Waiting for the bread to rise. Waiting for the floor to dry. Waiting for the mail to come, the iron to heat. Waiting.

At bedtime, her hair fell to her waist like a stream of mercury. She seemed to travel the same hundred miles every night without leaving the edge of her bed, each brush stroke returning her full circle to where she began. From my bed across a narrow hallway, I fell asleep hypnotized by the bureau mirror's reflection of her silent repetitive motions.

Then, as if her long silver hair were just a dream, I'd open my eyes in the morning to the sight of her face bent over me, blank

like the sky without its color or clouds, offering nothing with
which to judge its weather. Her hair was darker in the morning,
tightly braided and wound in a bun, the color of pewter that had
tarnished overnight.

Her skirt hems hung midway between the floor and her knees
and seemed to cover layers of underclothes. Somehow her dresses
never fluttered or swayed when she moved, her sleeves ended at
her wrists, her legs were thickly stockinged and her heels, low to
the ground. My mother was thirty-nine when I was born, but she
always looked old enough to be Chick's wife.

Her expressions were fragile; even a smile strained her passive
face. Beneath her white skin was a tense embroidery of blue
threads that unraveled into pink frays at the corners of her eyes.
Those eyes, almost colorless, were such a pale and watery gray, I almost felt too garish a sight for them to bear. Her eyelids fell heavily
on all vulgarity and coarseness. She would straighten her back and
clasp her hands in a prayerlike pose. At such times, she seemed as
far away as heaven, yet she was there, listening, just resting her eyes,
she said.

She never attended church. She said the Lord knew her reasons,
and I never doubted that. But she spoke aloud to Jesus all the time.
"Good Lord," "Praise God," "Blessed Baby Jesus," she would call
out from another part of the house. I'd run to answer her calls, find
her hands sunk in dishwater or curled around a stationary broom,
her head flung back, oblivious to the chores of her body or to me
standing in the doorway listening to her carrying on with heaven
in biblical tongues.

Ida's Bible sat beneath the rabbit ears on a crocheted doily atop
the console TV. It absorbed stripes of sunshine through the venetian blinds of the picture window during the day and soaked up
the warm embers of the television tubes when the set was on at
night. Its cushioned cover was usually warm like a spongy cake
cooling from the oven. It was a large family Bible and as heavy as
a baby spread open across Ida's lap. I was jealous of the attention,

silent and somber as it was, that the book received from my mother, and I coveted the place on her lap that it stole from me.

Its seared onionskin pages and their faint smoky odor seemed appropriate to the book's constant warmth and holy aura. The Bible was the only surviving possession Ida had of her mother's.

"This was your Grandma Bash's, Charlie."

"You mean Chick's wife?"

"Um-hm. My momma. She passed on before you were born. She's in heaven now."

"With Daddy."

"Well . . . with Jesus for sure. Sometimes, though, when I'm with the Scriptures, it's as if Momma's still here with me. Praise God, the Good Word survived the fire." She rubbed the pages like a loved one's cheek. "About the only thing I have left."

"Was Grandma's Bible with Daddy when those savages burned his house?"

Her eyelids fluttered shut. Her posture became rigid.

"Momma?"

"Yes, son." She barely spoke, resting her eyes. "Momma's Bible was with your daddy . . . in the fire . . . when he died."

It was a hard life converting savages, and Ida had given it up. She never really preached or testified. She never read to me from the Bible. My mother seemed disturbed by my religious interests, as if she resented the intrusion upon her private relationship with God, when all I sought was another bond to her. I wanted to be the Bible spread across her lap. I wanted to speak her Pentecostal tongue. I was snagged on the threads of her imagery: those unnamed jungles of Godless souls, those lush landscapes of sin, the mirage of Garl Hope rising from a blaze in the mythic field.

My unmet prayers sailed toward heaven like little toy boats: Father, come home. Punch a time card at the rendering plant. Rattle your empty lunch bucket at quitting time. Be my diving board of broad shoulders in the lake at summer. Light the furnace. Be the appointed sayer of Grace.

Ida called Charlie "Daddy," but it sounded uneasy on her lips.

She was his "Baby." Charlie said "Grandpa" made him feel too old, so I called him Chick like all his friends. Ida was "Momma" when I addressed her, but she has always been the distant Ida when I thought or spoke about her.

■

"OH, HELL, I RECKON SO," CHICK MUMBLED WITH A PORK RIB BE-
tween his lips, "but I don't make myself miserable over it."

We were sitting in a booth at Inez's in Purley. We'd stopped for
barbecue on the way back to Pryor from Tulsa one Sunday, but I
was too bloated with Coca-Cola to really eat. Sopping hickory
sauce from my plate of ribs and beans with a slice of white bread
as thick as angel food cake, I'd asked my grandpa if he believed
in God.

He sucked the bone clean with a smack and added it to the neat
pile on his wiped plate. He seemed to ponder as he dug at his teeth
and studied the wet end of his toothpick. He said, "Well, way
back, I guess. Don't make much matter if Adam was a feller or a
half-ape. Think far enough back, it's all got to start somewhere.
You got to think a little bit about God. I'll give you that. But in
my opinion, He's kept his holy nose out of the whole mess once
He got it started. One thing I know for sure is I personally weren't
put together from dirt, and God ain't never had no say-so with
me—not once. Reckon I'd be a churchgoin' believer if He had.
No, I spent my whole life the best I know, and that is not looking
too far back or ahead, little feller. Looking back only gets you to
wondering, and wondering will get you nowhere. Regret is a private matter. A person's conscience is a very private matter. If God
comes grabbin' at the dead, it's the heart He's gonna grab for." He
paused and smiled in confidence. "Course, He's got most of 'em by

the balls while they's still livin'." His shoulders vibrated with a
hoarse, chesty laugh. "Damn peckerwoods!" he wheezed, wadding
a napkin around his greasy cough. He took a long sip of coffee, lit
a Winston, and sighed, "Oh, shit." His smoke hung above my red,
soggy bread. "I ain't too afeared of dyin' really," he almost
whispered.

Chick's mention of his own death cut me as sharply as the sound
of silver scraping the plates all around us. My grandmother, Fay's
husband, my father, had all died before I was born. They were
ghosts in Pryor. Their actual dying was as unreal to me as heaven,
where they lived on as if simply relocated to a big city. Heaven was
up the road a bit in my mind, like Tulsa, but out of state, farther
than Arkansas.

I sat in the booth facing Chick as he contemplated his death,
and I felt a burning sorrow swarming to tears. I saw God's hand in
the breath of smoke Chick drew and exhaled. It reached deep into
Charlie's chest, as if merely unbuttoning a worn torso, and by the
unseen heart snatched him away.

Over the booth where his face had existed a word ago, deeply
lined, swollen about the nostrils, half-drunk, and sighing, "I ain't
too afeared of dyin' really," now only blinked "INEZ'S" backward
in neon, buzzing in the sweaty window.

Only a few dirt roads and mailboxes called Purley lay beyond
the pickups in the gravel lot, bearing off into other roads in limited directions: some to dead-end fences overgrown with guinea
beans; some winding toward Pentecostal sermons; some stretching
through the Indian graveyards, past feedlots and fields of grain-
sorghum, past the black ponds astir with crappie, into a string of
low-slung towns with electric stoplights at intersections where a
Dairy Queen or a Laundromat glared as brightly as the all-night
gas stations on the highway. The here and now coursed through
me like the gaseous light through the neon tubes of "INEZ'S." A
flash of doubt concerning the existence of heaven placed me smack
in the middle of where I was, and it was a hard and desolate place
for me to be.

I intuited a sudden connection between my grandfather's drinking and his dying, how each beer in the Tulsa bars was just a short foray into death. I'd always felt abandoned by his drinking self, but his death would leave me stranded in one foggy place or another, with no man at all to take notice, to lift me down from the high stools, to eventually drive me home. I'd be left with women who would pat my head forever while the juke moaned on; while Ida sagged deeper into herself beneath the weight of Esther's Bible or else waded off into her dreamy jungle following her Jesus, following Garl, untethered from Pryor and Chick and me at last.

"Oh, some people need that bullshit I reckon," Chick said, eying me. "What's wrong, soda pop up your nose? Look like you might bawl."

"I was just thinking," I said.

He stared a little harder. "Well, I know it's your mother that's got you thinking this kind of crap. Women are taken in by that stuff. Hell, I don't know. Them ol' church broads, they think their shit don't stink, I know that." He raised his coffee mug toward the window over his shoulder. "That fizzlin' tabernacle joint your grandma hooked up with, just up the road there a ways . . . I guess it's still in business." He thought a moment as if adding up the years. "Oh, hell, they're probably shakin' up a sweat this minute! Anyways, Esther used to nag on me about all that stuff—testifyin', she said—about the healin' and whatnot where some ol' cripple got his bowlegs straightened out for a minute. Oh, shit, they used to wash one another's feet on Wednesdays, I think it was. Some rigmarole every night of the week. And what'd it get her?

"She got fits! You know, when the Spirit come into the joint there and knock 'em all around, down on the floor? They'd get to floppin' and jabberin' like fools or somethin'. Ida peed her pants in a fit one Sunday. She wasn't even as old as you but old enough not to wet herself. Esther drug her home to change her drawers, then rushed her right back again for an evenin' service." He licked his lips and shook his head. "I see nothin' in that sort of believin'.

"Some bunch of fools at one of them joints—I don't think it

was over here, maybe those Nazareens in Adair—I hear tell march around with snakes! Big ol' mocs and copperheads crawlin' over theirselves!

"Now, how has mousin' around with snakes got any more bearin' on God than a open bar on Sunday? Hell, every one of these churches got their own kind of nuthouse rules. They all think they's the only ones gettin' in heaven—whatever that is—and anxious as the devil to shut the gate on everybody else. Belief in heaven just makes it hell on earth, buddy.

"You should have heard the ruckus when I first opened up the beer joint. Damn churches preached up such a stink. Let me tell you, Baptists got more pull in Oklahoma than common sense. Hell, ain't enough they go breakin' up marriages and spookin' younguns. They gotta vote against hard liquor all together and beer on Sundays, goddamnit!"

More calmed, he said, "No, feller, your momma cain't help the way she was brung up. She's odd, I know, but innocentlike. Try not to hold it against her.

"He ain't hungry, Inez. Wrap up those ribs and give us a check, sweetheart."

Chick confused me with the picture he painted of Holy Rollers carousing on the dark side of Pryor's stained-glass windows. He discounted with a wholesale sweep that God was any cause for concern. He paid tithes to the honky-tonks of Tulsa and seemed to find a kind of redemption in beer and the laying of hands on women.

I steeped my mystical imagination in Ida's jittery silent religion and sanctified those vaporous barroom scenes. The essential atmosphere of vice that the churches so fundamentally damned became in my mind—for Chick's sake and, I guess, my own—a version of spirituality.

Racing the sunset back to Pryor in Chick's car, I pressed my nose into the shoulder of my shirt, permeated with the smoke of a hundred cigarettes, and the odor was "biblical" to my childhood sense of smell; it was the air stirred by the turning pages of Ida's heavy book. The jeweled glass of bar lights, the painted windows, and shining jukes imbued those Sabbaths with a mosaical, ethereal beauty; churchlike, I thought. There was a reverent hush to the bars in the early afternoon, especially in summer, when the days were scorched with sunlight. Chick would pull open the bar door and the cold interior would gush out, the immediate darkness beckoning like a baptism by total immersion.

We were early customers, and the stools filled slowly around us. The first hour or so was quiet: Jewel sipping coffee, Chick nursing his first beer. No music, just soft voices, perhaps the click of pool balls on a clean felt table. But later, there were sermons to be heard. Tales of miracles or outright lies as the congregation gathered and the Spirit swept through the joint, raising the pitch, knocking some off their feet. Hands would slap the bartop in passionate fits. "That's the truth! You bet! Hell, yes!" The Spirit rebounded like a chorus of "Amen and hallelujah!" If possessed by a tune, girls would sometimes jig out of control.

Chick denied heaven, but liquor took him someplace similar that, from my small, sober perspective, seemed very high and far from earth.

The barhopping in Tulsa was something of a secret between my grandpa and me.

"We're goin' to a show," Chick told Ida, or "a rodeo in town." Ida was a hermit. Her skin seemed to envelop all she could calmly tolerate of the world. I respected her delicacy, her vulnerability and sensitivity, as my own. I clung to time in the house with her, accepting that proximity as love. Chick feared that I was a "momma's boy."

"Well, there ain't too much else for a fatherless boy to be!" I heard Ida snap back.

I suppose that was why he took me to bars and why Ida never questioned or objected. Her indifference struck me as a sort of relief to be rid of me for a while. I was an enigma to Ida, the same

as perhaps any son or daughter might have been, but at the time
I felt it was my failure as a son that kept her so distant. I had the
vaguest idea that it was Chick's gender more than his fatherly in-
eptitude or sinful soul that was the impenetrable wall between
them, and I felt uncomfortably barricaded in that same sex.

The only man Ida seemed comfortable with was Jesus. Men
were savages, drunkards, or worse.

For instance, one day the Turtle Man knocked on our door.
Chick was gone and Fay Rose was visiting, the only company Ida
ever had. They were drinking coffee in the living room and I was
on the floor, cutting paper into snowflakes and angel chains, eaves-
dropping on Fay's husky-voiced stories about the rendering plant
before they laid her off, four years short of a full pension because
she was a woman.

"It just riled me," Fay said, "that it was the women they let go!
Not that it was much of a job, hah!" she grunted.

Ida tended to nod slowly throughout Fay's visits, more like
keeping time to the radio than agreeing to anything being said.

Fay Rose Savory was worldly in my eyes. There was an earthy
sophistication to her diamond-pierced ears, bleached bright hair,
and pantsuits that gave her a speculative reputation around Pryor.
Chick called her the Savory Widow. Her gabbiness, general energy, and out-for-laughs mood made me question the role of widowhood in Ida's sad nature. Fay had a gut laugh that was rare for a
sober woman, and half of what she said seemed to be for her own
amusement. Something about her openness and directness invited
confidence, even though she told everything she knew.

"Got a pot on, Ida?" she'd ask, first thing through the door, not
bothering to knock since the day I was born. Fay Rose was an ad-
dict; she sparkled with caffeine. She drank bottomless cups of coffee all day long and into the night. "Oooh, that's a good fresh cup,"
she'd sigh, settling down with a percolator and ashtray.

"I told him off, right there on the floor in front of God and everybody," she said, "hollerin' over those roarin' melters, I says, 'Jim
Mack, you lard-ass so and so! You been sniffin' around my behind

since day one. You know good and well the only reason my name's on that layoff list is because I wouldn't give you a piece of my—' "

There was a screen-rattling knock on the door, loud as a cap gun. "What in the world!" Fay jumped, then laughed at her own loss of composure. "—scared the tar out of me. Hah!"

My scissor blades stuck in the paper. I was looking at Ida, like Fay Rose. My mother was rigid on the edge of the rocker by the window, her hands dug into the wooden arms, and she leaned forward from the waist, tilting the chair with her.

"You're white as a sheet. What's wrong?" Fay Rose asked. Ida didn't speak. She seemed to be perched for flight on the rim of the chair. I watched Fay set her coffee cup on the table and rise from the couch.

"Don't," I warned her in a whisper.

"Don't what? Someone's at the door, honey."

"I can see him," Ida said hoarsely, her lips trembling. "It's a *man*! He'll go away."

Fay Rose tiptoed to the window and peeked through the slatted blinds. "Yea . . . looks like Owen the Turtle Man," she whispered, nodding beside Ida. "Don't you know him?"

"I don't need to know him. I don't need no strange man on my porch," Ida whispered. Her eyelids twitched against the very thought.

Fay Rose peeked through the window once more, then looked back at Ida. "Just ol' Owen. He's harmless." She looked my way and said, "Probably peddlin' his shells is all, or maybe he's got some wood to sell."

The stranger knocked again, more determined to be heard. Ida bit her lip.

"I'll tell him no thanks." Fay took a step toward the door, but Ida jumped up and grabbed her by the arm, flipping the rocker into the wall, which filled the room with another loud knock. We all froze, listening to the man's shifting weight on the creaky porch boards.

If we had been alone, my mother and I could have ignored the knock at the door, as always. I would have continued through the paper with my dull blades, Ida would have sat still, neither of us acknowledging the intrusion, yet each of us inwardly moved by the violent boom a man's knuckle makes against a door.

"Baby, he's just sellin' turtle shells," Fay Rose smiled, patting my mother's white hands wrapped around her arm. Fay seemed amused by the situation, but I'd witnessed similar scenes before. Alone with Ida, the phone always rang unanswered. If later, Chick should mention calling the house and getting no answer, Ida would say she was napping or she'd been in the basement doing laundry. I never said a word about her hovering near the ringing phone, how she stood over it or eyed it anxiously from across the room as if it were a vicious animal making menacing noises. I worried that Fay Rose might now open the door and prove that callers were harmless, that men were not so dangerous.

Fay Rose was on the verge of messing everything up, making Ida say just what was so awful about a man and if that were finally said, some catastrophe would result, a quake in the heart so powerful as to render it wide open.

So as not to hear the unsayable, I screamed at the door. "Get out of here! Go away from here!" I startled Fay Rose with my rage. The scissors still squeezed in my hand, I screamed at the awful tension in the air, at my mother's craziness and Fay's interference with the way things were. I screamed like a small preacher casting out big demons. Men didn't belong in our house.

Then Ida hugged Fay to her chest. "God help us," she said.

"God what?" Fay asked, then saw what had spooked Ida into her arms. The man was pressed against the window screen, his hands cupped around his eyes, a threatening shadow in the parted venetian blinds.

"I'm gonna call the sheriff, you ol' coot!" Fay yelled, tired of playing around. She made a quick swatting motion with her hand, then patted Ida's heaving back.

There were a few muffled words from the other side of the window as the figure hurried down the porch steps. I joined the hud-

dled women at the window, and the three of us watched the man
shaking his head all the way to the street, where he climbed into
an old truck loaded with firewood. We didn't speak until the
grumbling of his motor faded off and he had disappeared from
sight.

"Lord-y, hon!" Fay Rose said, separating herself from Ida's grasp.
"That was a mountain out of a molehill, I guess."

Standing at the window with my back to the room, I heard Ida
smoothing her skirt, almost felt the waves of air her praying hands
made coming together in her lap. "Can't be too careful with *men*,"
I heard her say. I stared at the empty road, snapping the scissors
open and shut in my hand, heard a cup clatter against a saucer,
thought about the oily smell of old pickup cabs, the high springy
perch of their seats.

■

I DIDN'T PLAY BALL LIKE OTHER BOYS. I PLAYED MISSIONARY. IN THE verdant jungle of my childhood, I was both savior and savage. The savage, I called Bub.

He was an invisible heathen and a nudist. Nakedness was so wicked that you were arrested for it in Pryor. I'd heard Fay Rose gossiping to Ida about teenagers being arrested in the lakewoods: "Caught in the bushes, *N-A-K-E-D!*" she spelled in a whisper.

"Why were they naked?" I interrupted.

It was the kind of question a heathen would ask and I felt scalded by Ida's apparent shame. She closed her eyes, of course, then abruptly left the room. For the longest time, she wrung her hands in soap under the kitchen faucet. Fay Rose cleared her throat, lit a cigarette, and took a long, exaggerated sip of coffee to distract herself from my unseemly question, which loomed as uncomfortably in the air as Ida's reaction.

Buck naked and dark as soil, Bub was the queer demon I wrestled in my mind. I made him up because of Ida's sadness. I needed someone to blame.

Ida's yarn about a missionary in a jungle, the heathen natives setting him afire and all: Bub never bought a word of it. He could smell a lie. But it was the seed of him. He was Ida's creation as much as mine.

He knew everything I knew and more. Half of my thoughts were his, and he was the sole renderer of my dreams.

He used what scraps he found: the discarded piths of memories, bits of dialogue, the really gristly feelings. These things, melted by sleep, made the glue that bound us to one another despite our different tongues, our different minds like day and night, like truth and lies.

He told me right off, "Ida's crazy. She's bullshitting you." He said, "Jungles are places with names, and Garl Hope was a son of a bitch." He asked, "Who saved Grandma Esther's Bible from the ashes? How'd Ida get it back from the savages?"

He told me, "Ida don't love you." I spit at him for that. He told me, "Chick loves you some." I said Chick was a drunk. He said, "He don't lie."

I thought Chick was a sinner. I said, "He won't hold me."

"Ida neither," he said.

Bub wanted to hold Chick, wanted to kiss his big old nose and put his face under his hat brim against his shaved neck. I had to sit on him to keep him from it. I had to practically tie him up to keep him from doing all sorts of such embarrassing things.

He said living in my belly grew aggravating. He felt cramped and hungry for attention. So he climbed my interior like a snake inching up a tree. "Too much racket in your heart," he said. "You pray like you was God's own boy." My throat was dry; he needed a humid climate. He moved into my dreams, recklessly tinkered with the knobs in the back of my mind, acquiring his shape, increasing his volume, until he was a near-constant companion, a loud vision of all the hubbub in my head.

Somehow, I envisioned him so (though I'd never seen anything quite like him before): about my own size, but stronger; dark as shoe polish from his scouring pad of hair to his calloused heels; his bared teeth sparkled like a double strand of opals. Without clothes, the expanse of his skin was overwhelming, like a whole barn wall of skin. He chattered constantly in a foreign tongue, which always translated into the voice of my crudest instincts. It was a persuasive language, as expressive and emotional as a bad conscience. I trusted Bub about as much as my own prayers.

Being half savage, I only half believed in prayer. I felt widowed by God, as if He'd been called off someplace far from Pryor to tend other, more urgent souls and had left no memento of Himself behind. I thought it was the tragedy of desertion that had broken Ida's heart, and I blamed God for that as well as for my own unspecified desperation.

I used to wrestle Ida's Bible down from the TV and open it across the floor, pore over its fine print when I could barely read, staring page after page into gray rectangular blurs. At the time, I believed in miracles, as I believed in Easter rabbits and tooth fairies. I concocted religious spells over the Bible's pages, believing a concentration of will would invoke some image from the incomprehensible abundance of words. That image of God I expected to spring from the book was as concrete as it was unclear: flesh and blood for sure, but yet in some new, startling form. The truth is, I thought God to be as monstrous in shape as in deed, though that monster was probably jealousy of His romantic hold on Ida, for His stealing away of Garl, and His anticipated snatch at Chick's heart.

Although God had never had a say-so with Chick—not once—my ear was triggered to the blast of trumpets heralding His say-so with me. Ignorant of Scripture, unaided by doctrine, I looked everywhere for God in Pryor, in Purley, in the Tulsa bars.

Once at the Tulsa State Fair I thought I had seen evidence of God.

The arrival of the fair each September occasioned a school holiday. Fretful of crowds and the hedonistic atmosphere, Ida had an aversion to such fun. Chick said there were too many fizzlin' lines and too much fizzlin' noise. He gave me five dollars and said to ask Fay Rose. Fay said yes. Dressed up in a headscarf, high heels, and movie-star sunglasses, she said we were going on a date.

We strolled the stockyards, admiring the prize pigs and livestock through the fresh scent of hay and manure.

We walked through the home show armory, up and down the aisles of paraffin-sealed jelly jars, ribboned pies, and the produce of a hundred competing gardens. To rest our feet and because Fay

Rose said it was romantic, we went to a matinee of the Ice
Capades, where I was bothered by the sound of the skates scratching the smooth ice. The clank and slice of the blades scraped
against my utter entrancement with the slender men and beautiful
women whose even smiles and prancing glides formed an impression of what Fay Rose had called romance.

Later, after corn dogs and ring tosses, after a leisurely float in a
padded bucket along the high wires of the skylift, I spied the banners that, to me, hailed that God was afoot at the fair. On a narrow
trail of asphalt, away from the blurting sirens, bucking rides, and
candied apples shining like stoplights in the milling foot traffic of
the midway, these banners were stretched broad as billboards
against the dusky sky. They depicted amazing sights for the paying
curious. Here were mermaids, trolls, and bodiless heads telling
their tales. Here was a stallion so tiny it grazed in the field of a human palm. "Carpa the Fishwoman," a banner pronounced, and
there she was: an exotic beauty queen in swimwear, breaststroking
in a fishbowl, her aquabatics animated by the wind flapping against
her painted torso. "Tongo the Human Pincushion." A two-headed
gator, stuffed. The garish "Armless Wonder."

"Lord, no," Fay drawled when I begged for a ticket. "If that ain't
pitiful, it's a gyp! Ida would have a conniption if I took you to a
freak show. Hah!" But the idea of such sights tugged religiously at
me. So extraordinary and unearthly was God that surely only in
that form could He be seen. But Fay Rose yanked me away from
the confrontation.

I could never be certain of my mystical intuitions, if the God I
envisioned was pitiful or a gyp. I searched for His minute people
in the prairie grass and bluestem. I hoped fish would suddenly
bark. I consecrated a cigar box with sacraments of cloth and prayed
in vain for a lizard to crawl in, to rest its double heads.

Unable to snare such a freak to call my own in Pryor, I eventually dug God out of my own head. I rose from a soapy bath in
the deep claw-footed tub, the cold air unplugging the water and
the engulfing underwater silence from my ears. Shivering cold and

naked, the consuming drain whirling the water about my ankles, I
shook my head against a flutter in my ear. I was nearly deaf to the
sucking noise of the thirsty old plumbing and somewhat blinded
by the white dizzy brightness of the tiled room shaking before my
eyes. But I couldn't lose the clogged sensation in my ear. I heard
an amplified whispering, airy vibrations so deep within my head I
could almost swallow them but not silence them.

I pressed my palm like a plunger against my ear. I hung my
head, twisted my neck to undamn my hearing. I would have
scratched my very brain if my finger could have reached through
to it. For a long time, I was absorbed in the immense feeling of my
finger digging against the shifting whispers, the folding and unfolding phantom wings brushing the narrow walls of my ear's canal.

When I looked at what I finally pried into my hand, I thought
I had scratched a scab from some painless sore, but it was so perfectly round, about the size of a dried pea with a strange crusty
hide. Practically weightless in my palm, it felt hollow like an empty
pod, delicate, ancient looking and when closely examined, covered
symmetrically with dull nibs like a burr. I reacted with a hot blush,
fearful I had damaged myself, removed some inner component of
my ear. A word rushed out of me for the sake of testing my ear or
even my speech, and for some reason—perhaps wonder—the word
was *God* and maybe it was the mere chance of that word or maybe
my private obsession that produced that word and then the con-
ception itself, that what I held in my hand, what had fallen from
my ear, was a piece of, or a sign from, or maybe, somehow, God
Himself.

Bub suddenly appeared to prod me on. "Show Ida. She'll have
to love this for sure."

She napped in the parchment light of windowshades drawn
against the afternoon. Home from school, I often unsealed the
hushed house with a beam of daylight sneaking through the
opened and quickly closed front door as I let myself in, walked
quietly past the room where she reclined on top of the made bed,

retreating to my homework or my bath while Ida rested her eyes
before supper.

"Momma," I said too suddenly, too loudly, shaking her shoulder.
She rose drowsily, as if sleep were still holding her in its arms.

"The Lord's called me, Momma. Look, the Lord's called." Self-
awareness settled over me in the darkened room as I saw the reaction that settled over her face.

"Lord have mercy! Where's your shame? Cover yourself up,
Charlie! What are you doing?" Her head turned from the sight of
me, which sent a shiver of humiliation up my backbone. Bub's im-
modesty fled my body, exposing the momma's boy with everything
to hide.

"Hurry up! What is it?" Ida said to the window.

"I want to show you, Momma."

"I think you've shown me enough already. Put some britches
on, Charlie." One hand lay between her breasts. It rose and fell
with her anxious breaths. Her turned head offered me her neck,
painfully tense in its effort to hold her face away. She was only half
raised off the pillow in a contorted semi-levitation.

With a tentative and self-conscious effort, I opened the fingers
of her fist, embedded in the mattress with all her weight, and
placed the mysterious pocked bead in her hand.

"What is that?" she asked without even looking.

"I found it," I said, hesitated, added, "I think it's a calling from
God."

Ida rolled over heavily, sat up on the opposite side of the bed
with her full back to me now.

"Why would you say that?" Her head bowed over her lap where
her hands rested. From my side of the bed, she looked deflated,
caved in, even further away. "Is this a joke? Why would you say
that? To me? Tell me." Each word stiffened her, until she sat erect-
ly, awaiting an answer, her face turned to the side in profile, her
eyes closed as if concentrating on the waiting.

"I don't know . . . I didn't mean it. I'm sorry."

"You're sorry?" she mocked. "Do you know what blasphemy is?

Do you know what taking the Lord's name in vain is?" She spoke so seriously, still in profile, her eyes still closed. I didn't answer. I didn't know what she meant, and I was ashamed that I was naked with her and I didn't know what either of us actually meant.

"This," she declared, "is just some dirty . . . I don't even know what this is . . . a bug? A hull of something?"

"It was in my ear." I began to cry.

"You put this in your ear?" She turned and faced me, looked at me directly, sadly.

I took a step back from the bed. The floor was cold on my feet. It sent chills to my scalp. I couldn't hide my body from her. I used my arms to hide my tears. "It came out of my ear . . . I didn't put it there. I don't know what it is. I thought . . . I thought God put it there . . . 'cause . . . 'cause He was calling to me, like my daddy, like Garl. . . ."

I surrendered to the floor, my arms still wrapped around my face. I gave in to the tears, and I gave up forever on God for causing me such humiliation.

After a while, I felt Ida's skirt slide across my skin, felt her hands on my arms, unfolding them to my sides. I let her move me. My sobbing had changed my breathing; I felt lightheaded and limp. My eyes rested, and I gave myself to Ida as a loose heap. Black space seemed to sink around me as I was lifted, then lowered, into a warmer place, turned on my side. A blanket settled over me, seemed to creep warmly around my neck, tucking itself around my shoulders. I felt a light breath on the side of my neck in regular, predictable intervals. I remember the feel of her fingers tracing, stretching, probing my ear.

■

I WAS SMART. I KNEW IT FROM SCHOOL AND THE PATRONAGE OF MY old marmish teachers, their red plus marks and oversized As in the neat margins of my papers. I slipped into the ideals of those harried, prune-faced women as effortlessly as Chick, sliding his head into his satin-lined hats, but without the same comfortable fit.

The fuss and praise of teachers meant nothing to me because they were women, the same as the bar women adoring my hair with their taloned fingers, cooing abstractly about my face. Whereas the barmaids and whores repelled me with the voluptuous spill of their flesh, their engulfing curves and rolls, I disregarded the clucking teachers for their bony figures, their dehydrated faces like withered fruit. They were powdered brains, wrinkled with fusty facts. The feathery edges of their lipstick bled outward from their prim mouths like puckered incisions. Miss Guthrie, Miss Stanberry, Mrs. Lord. They seemed to swallow, day in and day out, some bitter grudge against the less smart children boxed into the desks of their airless rooms. This they revealed in stern recitations and in their distaste for restlessness or the innocent wanderings of the imagination.

They were easily infatuated by my docility, my calm resignation to silence, my malleable attention and will. I was a listener, and that was the measure of smartness. I heard what they said and could remember what they wanted to hear, and if the cumulative effect of my correct answers somehow thawed their icy boredom and quieted their shrill edges, their appreciation of my sensitivity, their nervous coddling of my so-called brightness meant nothing in return, because they were only women and they were not Ida.

In my most distracted states, I passed tests with the highest grades, but without pride or the least sense of superiority. I used to cringe in my desk when one of the old crones exercised what seemed a sadistic pleasure (though no evidence of pleasure ever flushed those chalky jowls). The pleasure was noted in the fingers savoring the smoothness of beads, twisting pearl necklaces into sensuous tangles over a sharp collarbone, while calling on a slow student for a comment or answer, usually one of the more athletic boys who reigned like a panting beast over the schoolyard at recess, but who seemed timid and dispirited, caged in a classroom, prodded into a corner by one of their questions.

When a teacher insisted that one of these boys stand and recite, to answer a question he invariably could not, her fingers dallying over her own jewelry in the tensely extended silence of his stammering effort, I empathized with the boy's stupidity. My soul squirmed with him. Though I was smart and he was not, though he was a type of boy who ruled Pryor with a bully's indifference or disdain for the likes of me, his situation brought me to the verge of tears.

My anxiety had to do with the gulf between me and these other boys. It teetered on the discrepancy between my inner world and the whole other world of Pryor to which brainless boys—the ballplayers and vandals—seemed better adapted.

I loved my masculine classmates, envied the casual slouch of their gender, loved them quietly, inexpressively from my own crooked perspective, ill-suited as I was to that identical sex. I suspected the teachers disapproved of what I secretly loved, just like Ida, and that was why they exposed the dumb boys to humiliation by calling on them for unlikely answers. Knowing those answers set me apart, sent me into the camp of women and girls, made me a stray dog adopted by barmaids and the obedient pet of spinster teachers.

I believe I was innocent in these roles, innocent as a born runt. I didn't strive to be smart, but I would have if Ida would have loved me for it.

Loving Ida was like trying to guess the answers to impossible questions, questions asked in another language with eyes sealed against the slightest clue as to what she wanted to hear. I cringed with compassion for a boy like Silas Jackson or Eric Armstrong, straining for the names of the Five Civilized Tribes. Miss Guthrie would deride their struggle as surely as Ida denied my interpretation of God's calling. I stammered stupidly for the answers to the questions I heard in my mother's disapproving silence.

I began to avoid the dark regions of my mind, the dense jungles and the poisonous thoughts that sprouted there. I was confounded by God before I ever found Him, and my mind refused to forge itself around Him. I more or less ignored the wavering missionary that occasionally flickered into consciousness. Around the age of eleven, I let go of Ida's Pentecostal skirts, tossed my rejected love for her into a ditch, like a frog with no heart in it.

Without seeing him, I saw more of Bub, began seeing through his heathen eyes. One thing I clearly saw was a photograph.

Fay Rose Savory had a great-nephew in Knotty Pine, Arkansas. "Lord, that's the sticks! Don't get me started on Knotty Pine!" she nearly growled. "I shudder to remember it!" The boy's name was Hunter, and his mother had sent Fay Rose a high-school portrait. She was waving the gilt cardboard frame in front of Ida, and I had asked to see it. Fay Rose held the picture so respectfully about the edges I was afraid to touch it, so I just looked while she held it out to me.

"Ain't he a doll?" Fay Rose proudly asked Ida. My mother nodded.

"What's that?" Chick asked, stretched on the couch.

Fay said, "Nyla's boy, Hunter."

Chick said, "Who?"

"My brother's girl, Nyla! Over in Arkansas."

"Arkansas!" Chick said. "Oh, shit." He raised his head off the sofa arm and twisted around to see. Fay aimed Hunter in his direction.

"Oh, hell, yea," Chick said, lying back down, "he's a looker, Fay Rose."

The patter continued back and forth between Fay, Ida, and Chick. Ida nodded, Chick occasionally mumbled, and Fay Rose got started about her stick beginnings in Arkansas, but their conversation retreated to the background of my attention. I was transfixed by the image still fused before my eyes long after Fay Rose had folded the picture's cover and latched it away in her pocketbook.

The nature of what this image made me feel was beyond my experience, and for the odd private pleasure of it I might once have called it sin. But such judgments no longer took root within me. Being Bub, I was now a savage idolater, beyond salvation. I was Hunter's captive.

That's how the picture made me feel: imprisoned, helpless, locked in the act of fondling my own emotions.

It was as if I walked inward toward that image. Perhaps this is what happened to Ida when the Spirit filled her. Those times I had spied her, entranced in the kitchen, or beneath the backyard mimosa speaking in tongues, she was like a vacant body, a marionette dangling on still strings. To the Pentecostals, God is an outward presence, real as light, external as the sun, and the heart and mind and human body can be literally filled like a vessel with His experience. I imagine such glory pouring into you would obliterate all sense of self. If that's the truth or not, I was filled with the image of Fay's great-nephew.

Against a backdrop as neutral as infinity, I remember the vivid comb marks in his dark hair and the white triangle of his shirt, the whitest white in the world, framed in a black suitcoat, sliced in half by the straight edge of a tie. It was as if he existed in that pose, within that rectangular border, all alone in a blank eternity and for that reason his veins coursed with more blood than one body needed, and the hand-tinted tones of his face and neck gleamed with its abundance. I thought he was beautiful, and I don't think that until that moment *beautiful* was anything I had ever really seen or felt before. I desired him, and although in memory I have idealized my desire beyond the sexual, to an eleven-year-old boy sexual desire is ideal enough. I didn't understand my attraction, but I was so caught in its wave, I felt no need but for the unspecified pleasure.

Lost in the picture of Hunter, I felt happy, as if in a wishful dream, but meshed within the pleasure was a certain sorrow, a filmy ache.

It reminded me of the special pain of uprooting a loose tooth, the consuming attraction of my tongue shifting, rocking, easing a tooth from its gum. The nagging ache, the palatable self-torture, teasing that nerve of pleasure embedded in the pain. The pain was something to be tested. At the point that it seemed unbearable was a desire to bear it a little further, to see how good it could possibly hurt.

Maybe this association was a premonition of desire haunted with sorrow, with loss. Perhaps I was yearning for some relief from desire. Unaware of the mechanics of sex and the nature of the wanting stirred by Hunter's image, I kept my desire private and as personal as that loose tooth.

I wasn't aware of Ida watching me. For a mysteriously lost period of time I wasn't aware of anything except the inner surging and swirl about the luminous icon of Hunter, but when the magic ebbed, when what I had come to know as the savage moment evaporated, and Bub crouched back into the low grasses of my awareness, I caught a real moment of righteous disapproval across my mother's face. Her forehead was pinched, her lips tight, but her look was direct and briefly piercing until I caught it, and then the cold silver returned to her eyes, reflected for a second by a slat of light as they darted nervously like minnows receding from the bright surface of a creek, netted from view by the downward sweep of her heavy lashes.

■

CHICK'S JOINT SAT ON THE OLD HIGHWAY, A QUARTER MILE OR SO on the Pryor side of the county line and, on gusty days, within smelling distance of the two tin-sheeted buildings straddling that invisible line separating Purley Slaughter from Pryor Rendering.

Purley had some good barbecue and rowdy churches, but mostly it was just cow pastures and feed lots, the biggest being next door to the processing plant where fattened steers were taken apart and changed into meat on a disassembly line.

Stunned by a hard blow to the head, they were hooked to a conveyor rail. The main artery above the heart was slashed and blood drained. Heads and hides were removed, carcasses opened, and the internal organs pulled out.

The carcass was split with a saw along the backbone. Sides were trimmed, washed and inspected, then chilled in a cooler for twenty-four hours. After chilling, they were packed off whole to butcher shops, and all the slaughter scraps were sent to Pryor through tin chutes.

Rendering recovered the fat from the scraps. Fay Rose said the plant didn't hire women until the war left them short of men and her, short of her husband, Gun Savory. Before World War II, when they switched over to dry-rendering melters, Fay Rose said the close-up stink of boiling steer scraps would have killed a woman. As it was, the stink was foul enough.

Fay was a cooker operator. The cookers built up a steam pressure that disintegrated the raw stuff and broke down the fat. Sterilization, digestion, and drying all took place in the cookers. Then you had cracklings.

The hard cracklings were milled into powders and sacked. The tallow rendered from cattle was used in soap, candles, and industrial lubricants. Meat, blood, and liver meals could enrich the protein of stock feed without increasing the volume. Bone, hoof, and horn meals made fertilizers and cattle licks. The piths separated from the horn made gelatin or glue. There was very little to a beast that was not good for something.

You couldn't get from Pryor to Tulsa without passing the rendering plant and could get nowhere in Pryor without, at least, the smell reminding you that this was a rendering place. Practically everybody worked or used to work at Purley Slaughter or Pryor Rendering. Not much choice, unless you were a rancher, because most of the farms had turned to gardens by the time I was born. The lake only supported a few bait shops. There was a Ford lot, a Dairy Queen, a Piggly Wiggly, a few stores and gas stations, a Boys Home in Strang, and a nuthouse in Vinita.

Since the plant was unionized, most boys considered the route from high school to Pryor Rendering a fortunate path, and the girls were anxious to marry and settle down with the good union benefits.

I could never stomach the smell and the violence of its associations. As far back as I could remember, I had turned up my nose at the thought of having to breathe it day in and day out for the rest of my life.

I couldn't much stomach the notion of being born in a bar, either, although it appealed to Bub. He liked those dark masculine joints and the raw excitement fermented by drink. He liked the company of men and had as little favor for women as he had for missionaries.

He eventually wedged himself between me and my odd mother. "Ida belongs in Vinita," he said. "She won't talk on the phone. She doesn't answer the door. She has those spells where she jabbers at the Lord, who's never talked back."

"She's devout," I said.

"Why doesn't she go to church like other religious people?" he provoked. I knew she had her reasons, but she'd never fully explained. He said, "Chick knows her reasons, I bet, and he won't lie."

Sure enough, Chick told all he knew when I finally asked why Ida never went to church. In the telling, though, Garl Hope fell from grace. His halo took on the amber light of hard whiskey. His jungle mission turned to ashes and smoke. His home wasn't heaven after all. It was just a fire-blackened garage lot in Tulsa, Oklahoma.

"Well," Chick said, "I guess it was while living with the minister's family in Tulsa that she met up with old Hope, there in the same neighborhood. Now, I can't say I knew that son of a bitch, but he was a hard drinker and I'd seen him around some of the joints before. Garl, that was his name. Hell, he was somewhere near my age, and I'll never for the life of me understand what Ida could've seen in him. He ran a shack with a gas pump in West Tulsa, and I hear tell once upon a time, wasn't too bad a mechanic, but by the time he met up with Ida, he was just a bum without a pot to piss in.

"I reckon he must have cleaned up long enough to marry her. Damned if I know why. Course, I didn't hear nothing about it at the time. It must have scandalized those Pentecostals, her takin' up with an old coot like Garland Hope, 'cause she up and left the church. I don't know what she had in her head, Charlie, this is your mother's story. All I know is I got a call in the middle of the night from some old gal I'd never heard of saying come into Tulsa right away and get Ida.

"Well, Ida and Garl was living in this garage apartment behind some other old widow woman's house. But by the time I saw it, it was fizzlin' burnt up. Seems they'd just married when Garl started hittin' the bottle again and then hittin' on Ida. I figure she put up with that shit for close to a year.

"Well, that night, he'd got crazy drunk and was beatin' on her pretty bad. Landlady said she'd heard the ruckus but was trying to mind her own business till Ida come pounding on her back door, stark naked and half-mad. Garl had locked her out of the apartment without a stitch of clothing. Then the bastard must have passed out with a lit cigarette or something, 'cause the next thing, the whole garage was up in flames and ol' Hope burnt to death.

"Ida was in some kind of shock, and I guess I was, too. I didn't know she'd got married, let alone pregnant, and at her age! I felt so sorry I could have died. But of course, I didn't.

"I was already retired, and I'd spent up my savings by then on the joint, so I didn't have nothing to give her but this old place. I brought her back to Pryor like a found pup. Took a day or two for her to even speak—so damn spooky it drove me out of the house—and you know she's never said a word to me since about Esther or Garl, none of it. After you was born, she snapped out of it somewhat—well, you know how she is now. I think in her head, it all happened different somehow. Hell, I hope! I've kept my nose out of it all these years, 'cause I figure she's been through enough. I don't want to stir up her nerves but, little feller, I reckon you've a right to know."

The truth that Chick revealed thundered through me like a sudden twister. I was knocked haywire by the tail of that storm. Before my wits had settled, I was in the kitchen doorway, facing my mother's back.

"Chick told me everything," I said. She was leaning over the sink, washing supper dishes.

"Chick don't know everything," she countered, continuing her chore. "What'd he say?"

"My daddy wasn't a missionary. You said he was burned in a jungle by . . . I know how he died."

Ida's hands turned to lead and sank into the china stacked across the bottom of the sink. I watched her head slowly unbow from the dishes to face the window in front of her.

"Chick didn't know him, Charlie." It was night and all there was to see through the window was her own face in the glass. Her reflection said, "Your father was a godly husband, a churchgoing man. . . ." It sounded dull as memorized Scripture.

"You lied," I said. I was determined not to cry about it.

Ida cried. In the black mirror of the window, I saw her panic melt to tears. "Oh, my Jesus," she muttered and turned, wiping her face with wet hands so that, instead of drying her tears, she left her face covered with dishwater. She looked hot and sweaty. She kneeled on the linoleum, reached out for me. I stepped back, leaving her hands hanging in the air, dripping water all over the floor. They fell to her lap and wound themselves up in her skirt. They burrowed into the fabric, wringing at the pleats, began bunching her dress into a wad between her knees.

"No," she said. "Honey . . . I didn't lie, son. I didn't lie. I think you're too young . . . too young to understand exactly. Daddy doesn't really know. He shouldn't have told you whatever he did. Your father *was* a preacher, he had a calling. . . ."

"He drank and he beat you," I stated, "because he was just a bum. I hate him. You hear me, Ida? He was a bum, and I hate how you made me love him."

"God help me!" Ida sank lower to the floor. She clutched her skirt to her face, not so much to wipe her tears, it seemed, as to smother her words. The gesture exposed long underpants that covered her legs to mid-thigh. The sight was shocking. "I hate him, too. I hate him, too," she moaned, swaying on her knees. "I hated the bastard. Hated! He was my husband and I hated him! But, Charlie . . . he wasn't your daddy."

I heard what she said without understanding. "Let's run away from here," I heard Bub urging in my ear. "Just run away." But I wasn't understanding him, either. I wasn't actually understanding any of it. I just looked at my mother, unmoved by her rocking posture. I looked at her hysterical disarray, listened to her muffled sobs. Inside, I was a blank screen. I had already erased my whole story, as if to start myself over from scratch. The thing was, I didn't want Ida to make a single mark on my clean beginning. I just turned away from her and walked into my room, closing the room's door for the first time, turning its lock securely behind me.

Because staying blank was such an effort, I couldn't exactly sleep. I felt welded to the pillow, trapped inside the nothingness in my head that I concentrated on sustaining. I could not think or feel anything to disrupt the fragile order in my blankness. So I was awake hours later, listening, when Chick stumbled through the front door.

"Oh, hell, Baby! You scared me," Chick said. "What're you doing up?"

He was talking to Ida, who was probably sitting in the dark. With the bedroom door closed, it was hard to hear her answer. But then the exchange of words could be made out within the general drone of their voices. Ida was speaking in a low voice that rose and fell in volume. Chick's voice was smoked-raw and gravelly, on the groggy side of drunk. Everything he said stumbled into Ida's words.

I remained blank. Not an extra heartbeat registered at the sound of my name or the mention of Garl Hope's. Chick mumbled, "Things just fizzlin' happen."

Ida mentioned Garl again. Chick said, "Why glorify a bastard?"

Ida clearly said, "He wasn't much different from you. . . ." Then softly, "God forgive me." Then paused, ". . . had no choice, Daddy." I heard her say "Sin." She was weak, she said. Weak with the preacher.

"Preacher?" Chick asked, his voice rising in a squeak.

Ida cried, and it was even harder to follow her words. "When Momma died . . ." she sobbed. Brother somebody, she said.

Chick moaned, "Brother? Oh, hell, Baby!"

"Man of God," Ida said. He was good to her. She loved him. "The only man who ever even *tried* to take care of me," she cried.

Chick mumbled, "Took care of Esther's fizzlin' money, didn't he? He took no care at all with you, Ida. Jesus Christ on a crutch!"

They hollered back and forth. I couldn't make out the exact words, only the tone. I could feel an emotion through the closed door. It had a sharp buzz to it, a hum like electricity. I kept looking at the door, expecting to see the feeling, like light, glaring under it.

Ida's crying sounded as if she were spitting tears at Chick. Chick's crying sounded drunk and reckless. His was a big clumsy cry, swinging fists at itself.

Late into the night, the emotion dimmed. It just ran out of fuel and collapsed. I unfolded my knees and elbows from my chest, rolled onto my back, and settled into a kind of stunned rest, soothed by the quieting sobs Chick and Ida shared in the other room.

Bub was lying with me in the bed, listening to the blowing of noses and to the eventual patter of kitchen sounds: Ida making coffee, unstacking saucers. It smelled bracing, strong and fresh.

The sun rose in a quartered rectangle of light behind the drawn curtains. My pulse relaxed. I heard Chick's irregular snores coming from the living room. He had probably passed out on the couch. I handed all the overheard bits of the night's confessions to Bub. "Keep these for me," I said, and this is Ida's story, pieced together by Bub while I then slept.

She'd felt abandoned by Chick when she was little and Esther had moved her to Tulsa. Esther never told her he had tracked them down, had tried to see her, had offered support all along. Ida thought he had just let her go, and when her momma died she resented his appearance after almost thirty years of absence. She said her only real memory of her daddy was the sour smell of beer on his breath. She said she was scared, being on her own for the first time. She had devoted herself to her mother, and her mother's church was all she had left for comfort. The church was the only kind of family she knew, and she entrusted herself into God's hands and the hands of God's people.

An invalid widow from the congregation offered her room and board to take care of her, and Ida felt thankful to be of use in the only way she knew: tending the needs of an elderly, religious woman.

Ida said when the widow died it was like losing Esther all over again, and she became nervous and sickly.

She thought the preacher was offering brotherly love and compassion by taking her into his home. When she regained her strength, which she attributed to the Lord's will and her Christian faith, she began doing the housework to pay her keep and then took on the church cleaning, too, freeing the preacher's wife from the menial chore. It was in the church that I was conceived, out of Ida's "foolish" trust, she said, and the preacher's insistence that divine love takes many secret forms.

When she realized her pregnancy, Ida left the church out of shame and guilt but mostly disgust. My father had called her a seductress and worse, had pronounced her possessed by demons even to imagine himself as a party to her sinful condition.

Garland was old and half insane from drinking. He lived, carless and alone, in the same neighborhood and had always made vulgar flirtations with Ida as they passed each other walking along the streets. Ida said he wanted sex and was too broke to buy whores. She sold herself to him for a marriage certificate and a name for me. Only Garl didn't know about me. When he found out, he turned mean. "It's how men are," Ida said.

He had tried to force himself on her in her last month. He passed out drunk in the struggle but left her badly beaten. She saw the lit cigarette in the bed but locked the door behind her, and not until the flames ate the curtains from the window did she start pounding on the landlady's door.

I bolted upright in bed. The box springs screeched like crickets.

"Charlie Hope," Bub reassured me. "Chick's feller. Ida's boy." I didn't know who I was. Bub had to tell me more.

Of course, nothing was quite the same after that. Ida's story had rendered our lives to the bone. We could have refashioned the tallow into anything that morning: the heart of a family, a candle for the dark house . . . but we didn't.

We made only the feeblest of efforts toward acknowledging the exorcism of Garl. For one thing, Chick was at the breakfast table, a rare occurrence, since he usually slept late. He looked red-eyed and crumpled, hungover, either from drinking or his short nap on the couch, but he was there, moaning over each slurp of coffee. For her part, Ida had made biscuits and chocolate gravy, something I used to love. And she offered such a brief and feeble grace, she seemed only to be clearing her throat. "Bless us all. Amen," she prayed, staring at her lap. Then we ate, listening to our own smacking and swallowing.

I couldn't stand it, couldn't stand the quiet, the way we stared at our plates, even as we chewed our breakfast, we just stared at our plates. But I couldn't stand to say whatever it was that needed saying, either. Just when I thought I might choke on the silence, Bub asked for a cup of coffee.

"What?" Ida asked, as if startled awake from a sound sleep.

"I'll have some coffee," I repeated.

"When did you start drinking coffee?" Chick asked.

"This morning, I guess."

"It'll stunt your growth," he declared, "and it turns little boys black, you know."

I resented being treated like a little boy just then. "Does not," I stated defiantly.

"Well, hell," Chick sputtered and coughed, turning to Ida. She just stared through him. "Give the boy some coffee, then. Why the hell not?"

Ida objected, "He's too young to . . ." then hushed before finishing exactly what I was too young for. She sighed, rising from her chair, reaching for a cup from the hutch.

"I like it black," I said, pushing away the milk she had put down beside my cup. Something manly in liking it black, I thought.

Ida wearily filled my cup and sank back into her chair.

She and Chick sat in a conspiracy of silence, watching me drink the black coffee, which was bitter and left a swampy aftertaste on my tongue and that took a conscious effort to swallow without a grimace. But the warm cup was something to hold on to, a reason to linger over the sopped plates with Ida and Chick. It was a grown-up gesture that put us on more equal terms. The three of us, quietly blowing and sipping, avoided the revelations we shared that morning, embarrassed to be any more honest than we'd ever been.

Maybe Chick had been dead wrong when he said there was no harm in knowing the truth. I'd heard the anger and deep pain with which he and Ida had handled it the night before, and this morning they seemed to be nursing secrets with a pair of martyred hearts.

Bub made me jittery with those same black secrets.

It's the coffee, I thought at first.

"Nope," Bub said, "it's just the truth."

Chick fumbled with his Zippo and his pipe until he drew smoke. Ida buried her jaw in the crook of one hand.

"She deserved better than Garl Hope," I told myself. "She took all she could take."

"Then she let him burn," Bub echoed back.

"He hurt her," I said.

"Tried to hurt you, too," Bub said.

"I didn't feel it."

Bub said, "You do now."

"I was all she had left," I thought. "She loved me as best she could."

"Not enough," Bub thought.

I wondered about that, studying Ida over the rim of my cup. "It's true," I thought. "She loved God more."

"She's afraid of God, after what she did," Bub said. "Afraid of what He might do next to get back at her." My head began to hurt with all of Bub's excuses.

I drained the cup and carried it to the sink, needing some distance from my darker half. I stood there for a minute looking out the window, feeling nauseous.

"Charlie? You all right?" Ida finally asked.

"I guess so," I answered with my back still to her.

"Last night—" she began to say.

"Just let it be," I interrupted, still looking out the window, until the chair's legs scraped across the linoleum and I heard her leave the room.

"I'm late for school," I sighed, walking past the table and through the kitchen door. Chick followed me into the living room, fumbling with his billfold.

"Here, feller," he said, shoving a bill into my hand. It was a wrinkled twenty.

"What's this for?" I asked him.

"Oh, hell!" Chick croaked, rubbing his head. "I don't fizzlin' know! Just take it. Hell, I'll only drink it."

I pulled at the front door, then pushed at the screen. I looked back at Chick standing in the middle of the room, both hands searching his pockets for his Zippo, pipe bit between his teeth. "Bye, Chick," I said, then the screen door slammed between us. I poked the twenty into the back pocket of my jeans that felt tight and outgrown that morning as I ran up the dirt road toward school.

Maybe it was the coffee that fueled me. I ran hard and fast, plowing up dust and twigs, as determined to get somewhere as Chick's Impala soaring at seventy on the turnpike to Tulsa.

School was only a halfway place between the house and the rendering plant. It was still Pryor. It was almost the summer when I'd turn thirteen and then start the next grade at the high school in Strang. Strang wasn't such a somewhere, either, but I hoped to be a totally different boy in the bigger crowd there. Since he'd pried me away from Ida and her bullshit about Garl, I figured Bub owed me someone to fill the empty place, someone to help me do the time. He was my buddy, but he wasn't real. I needed someone. I needed a half-savage flesh-and-blood friend.

Part Two

■

FRIENDSHIP HAD ALWAYS SLID RIGHT OFF ME. TIME WITH PEOPLE just didn't stick. I was too bookish and soulful for a Pryor boy and some called me even worse. I scrutinized the routine of boyhood as if stranded on a barstool in a raunchy joint, feeling sober and forsaken on the fringes of both situations, blind to exactly what kept me on the outside, feeling inferior.

That poorly fit feeling started at home, but it resurfaced in school, in something the kindergarten teacher called "House," shepherding us into a corner of a room outfitted with miniature appliances and pint-sized furniture.

"You're the daddy and I'm the mommy," a bossy girl named Vaughndean Harper declared, orchestrating an invisible meal with a plastic spatula over a cardboard stove about the size of a few stacked cases of beer. "Well, kiss me, stupid," Vaughndean said, offering me a puffed cheek. I just stared at her shoes.

Leon, who was playing the baby, wormed in his seat at a small table and began making slobbery smooching noises. Vaughndean told me, "Honey, make that baby behave hisself, while I fry up these fish." I couldn't, and Leon only smooched louder. Vaughndean spun around from her frying and told the baby to hush up. He was giving her a migraine, she said.

Leon's house had different rules than Vaughndean's because he didn't shut up. He jumped on the table instead and started a spastic smooch-dance, pumping his armpit and making fart sounds, to boot. Vaughndean gave me a stern look, then walked up to the table where Leon was hunched like a monkey and slapped his puckered face. Leon grabbed hold of her ponytail and nearly succeeded in yanking the smug expression off her face.

I backed away from the violence of Vaughndean's spatula beating Leon's legs, which were about to kick her in the apron when the teacher pulled them apart.

"You all are supposed to play nice together," she scolded us as a unit.

Vaughndean said Leon was acting like a wild goober and she just *had* to slap him. Then she whined that Charlie Hope wasn't playing right, either.

"I don't know how to play house," I guiltily confessed. And who'd want to, I privately thought. But just a few years later, Vaughndean Harper and Leon Hurt were making out like movie stars behind the winter coats in Mrs. Lord's cloakroom. Instead of breaking apart when I walked in on them, Vaughndean just giggled and Leon smirked without breaking the suction between their lips. Before turning away from this other game I didn't know how to play, I watched Leon's tongue slide over Vaughndean's open mouth. The girl's eyes rolled beneath their delicate lids, but the boy's eyes challenged me from the woolly shadows with their unflinching sideways glance.

I was certain that Leon's exploring tongue and Vaughndean's acceptance was a sexual act, but Leon had looked away indifferently from the act, looked at me, as if its triumph, for him, were in its being witnessed. I thought of Chick and wondered if he took me along to his girlfriends' houses in Tulsa just to be witnessed by me after he'd had sex.

Although it was something that happened between men and women, it seemed some aspect of sex was only finished up between men. I suspected that girls spoke differently, if at all, about sex—I'd never really heard—but what I heard in the boys' room at school was only a more doubtable version of barroom bullshit. For what I noticed, the thrill was somewhere in the filthy boast and jokes. Sex was just a game of roles, like playing house. If I stood back and watched for a while, studying the pose and slang, perhaps I could learn the rules, get the joke, and someday play the daddy right.

■

THAT AUGUST BEFORE HIGH SCHOOL WAS A MANGY BEAST PANTING over Pryor with the stagnant breath of the rendering plant. What breeze there was couldn't even sway the dandelion puffs from their stems.

Our house became a wind tunnel, with fans draped in wet towels humming to one another in their nervous oscillations from corner to corner and the old water cooler, bulky as the cab of a semitruck, grunting and drooling over the edge of the sill.

Ida was as cloistered as ever. Her wardrobe lost no weight from winter to summer, so what her high-buttoned dresses did lose in the heat was their starched and static crispness. They wilted and stuck to her stooped shoulders, clung to her hips and legs. She was even more withdrawn in her silence because the religious wind had been socked out of it. She no longer had fits or spoke in tongues. I don't know if she had banned the Spirit's entrance into her or if it had simply abandoned our house altogether after her confession, but she had also forsaken our mealtime prayers with a look of dog-tired weariness. Even the Bible gathered dust.

She wandered from chore to chore as if propelled by no more will than the directional draft of the fans. The artificial breeze flapped her dresses like the broken wings of a bird too bottom heavy to fly away.

Chick extended his hours at the beer joint for the summer boaters and fishermen the lake attracted to Pryor. Having the coldest air conditioner in Oklahoma and being one of the few places in town where you could loiter in such cool comfort for a fifty-cent draw, even a few Baptists wandered in on the hottest days. The world seemed so static and fixed in Pryor that summer. I saw both Ida and Chick as more heeled-in than ever to how they would always be, while I felt myself to be evolving, second by second, and cell by cell into an entirely new and different kind of animal, a teenager. I felt like a sideshow freak in a cramped cage.

Everything I felt was a battle between two opposing emotions, or more, if you counted the everpresent boredom that weighed on me like the damp towels on the bedroom fans.

My body developed a fragrance in the heat it never had before, concentrated in my sweat and strongest at the jointed places of myself, at least in all the body hinges my nose could privately reach. Scrubbed clean, I could detect this scent within or seeping from somewhere beneath my skin, as if I were molding. I couldn't decipher the strange pleasure from the disgust that this smell invoked. I sometimes lost myself in my own odor, wondering where such a smell might lead and fretting that something so intimately me might ever be discovered by anyone else. I secretly rubbed Chick's deodorant stick under my arms. Even the sensation of that was perplexing, for I could not help the naked images that such a personal sharing with the old man brought to mind.

Nakedness, itself, became an irresistible urge that summer. I took to the lakewoods to strip and swim. The lake and its woods were the only place I could feel comfortably alone. It also seemed a fitting background for my growing sensations. The way my bones were thickening and jutting, muscles tightening, feelings frothing to an overflow, made me feel claustrophobic in the house as well as in my clothes. The density of the trees provided privacy without containment. In the woods, things grew and fell, ugly weeds thrived, roots spread out, jays squawked, and branches stretched where they did. The sky was no roof holding anything down. I was feeling as wild as the woods and at home in all kinds of jungles.

Of course, it was all child's play at first, just Bub and me in the
woods, naked, smoking cigarettes filched from Chick's stray packs.
In that buggy glade, we shooed at the gnats and the emptiness of
the long dull hours between waking and sleeping. We wrestled in
the lake, napped on warm rocks, and teased one another into the
slick cool grass.

I discovered masturbation, dispassionately at first, testing the
feeling, not quite trusting the few quick spurts that so brilliantly, if
briefly, obliterated the boredom. And then I rediscovered it almost
daily. It seemed about the only thing to do. Then I'd wade into the
lake and just float. Soon, the urge would swell again, so that the afternoons stretched into a period of time that was gauged by the
number of obliterations reached and by their intensity or disappointment in altering my life.

"Where do you run off to every day?" Ida asked. "What have
you been doing?"

"Nowhere," I'd answer. "Nothing." And that was, in hindsight,
the truth.

Bub was my lookout. From the corner of my mind, he played
that sexual aspect I'd served for Chick and for Leon Hurt, the witness or some such bullshit as that. But I wasn't really connecting to
sex. I was learning the pleasure, but inside the pleasure was a dull
ache and an unrelieved sorrow. In this pleasure was an aggression,
an anger, a so-called self-abuse. It was a dead pleasure. No heart in
it, nothing worth watching.

Then, something just fizzlin' happened.

It was Fay's photograph of Hunter, or the memory of it I had
filed away. It slipped through my thoughts in the commotion of
coming and purged the innocence from my pelting drops of
semen.

Like that, in a flash, the idle pleasure of that summer became
distilled with its sexual nature.

He was a real teenager, I mean he had muscles. He had a man's
arms, those thick arms your hand can't quite wrap around. They

were the kind of arms that for some reason reminded me of horses. The flanks of brown horses.

He was older than me and heavier. Not so much bigger, as heavier. If density can be determined by looks, I'd say he was more dense than I was. There was more to him. He looked like someone who drove well. He looked like he would drive fast, not to show off, but because he drove well. He had the kind of arms that could really handle a car.

He also looked very clean. This had something to do with the seamlessness of his skin. He was naked and his body was smooth and he was very clean looking.

The most arousing thing was this cleanliness. It made me swoon in a corny, sexual way. My knees buckled and my stomach sank. I had a convulsion of pleasure, more than pleasure. It was a fit.

The idea of something, someone, someone's body being so clean; the idea of anything in this world without a trace of disgust, not even hidden inside. Even his guts were clean, his blood clean as spring water, the deepest recesses of his ears absolutely clean, the pitch darkness there was clean. The idea seized me, so filled me up with its revelation I couldn't contain the force of it. I boiled over with the feeling, ejaculated in astonishment at the light it awoke in the core of me.

Who could resist anything like it? It just drew me to it. It was like plunging into the scent of a rare blossom, wallowing in clean sheets flapping on the line. Who could resist touching the wind with your whole body that way?

This picture of Hunter made such sense to me, more sense than anything had ever made to me and my heart ached that it was just a picture in my head, that I couldn't touch it with my hands. It was just chemicals and imagination, just a new idea, another emotion. And it wasn't real sex. I was naked with my own hand and my sperm in the air and my brain on fire and I knew it was connected to this picture but it wasn't what it was supposed to be. I knew it was queer. I didn't quite get it all, but it just didn't matter enough. Matter enough to stop the feeling, I mean. All those words didn't exactly fit. They were too big, those words, too stupid, too much of a joke to exactly fit, but they were the words I thought of. They were the only words I knew and the closest to my gut vocabulary.

I'd always avoided those words, pushed them out of my mind when they'd been thrown at me. They'd been thrown at me many times like they were thrown at a lot of boys at a certain age. Most boys threw those words around at each other because they didn't mean much, didn't stick or hurt most boys. They didn't really stick to me. I was just more wary of them than everybody else seemed to be. It was a premonition I had about those words. They had the ability to mean something more to me.

Truth is, I thought those words were invented by schoolboys. I thought those words were one of childhood's conspiracies against its own. I thought those words were something you grew out of and not into. I thought those words didn't exist in manhood. I thought adults weren't able to see those words on bathroom walls. They were written in the invisible ink of childhood and they vanished after a length of time. Then they didn't apply to anyone anymore.

The picture of Hunter I saw in the lakewoods when I was almost thirteen, when I was naked, when I was masturbating and feeling sexual for the first time didn't scare me because it was connected to words like queer. It was just that those words were hovering around the atmosphere of the picture. I was used to their hovering, used to ignoring them, keeping myself locked up against them, waiting out their vanishing time.

I haven't gotten to the scary thing about the picture of Hunter. I haven't gotten to the picture at all, just the impression of the picture: its cleanliness. I guess I was so used to the privacy of my feelings, keeping my noise bottled up, that I wasn't scared by too much that passed through me. I had concocted my own father and gotten him all wrong, God and gotten Him all wrong, all kinds of cockamamie versions of things and gotten them wrong. I wasn't threatened by getting this sex thing wrong. It was easy enough to keep such mistakes secret. It was easy enough to live with yourself in secret and pretend you understood everything and go on about your days like you were normal. I mean, after all, I'd walked all over Pryor for years with a naked savage inside me without being arrested, noticed, or even suspected. So, if this picture of Hunter was a queer way of looking at sex, it didn't bother me too much. I could live with secrets.

But there was an aspect to the picture that did frighten me. There was an aspect that I raged against, that I so much hated that I wanted to kill off the part of myself it came from. I wanted to wipe out the part of me that saw such things so clearly.

It was a still picture, like a photograph, only it was not framed in gilt cardboard. It was a still pose that filled the center and circumference of my inner vision. It was an insight.

He was dead or asleep. He was very still. Life or consciousness was gone from him. He was laid out across my mind like a banquet across a table. He was defenseless, naked, still. He was mindless. He had no say-so with me. I could have done anything I wanted. I could have swallowed him whole. I thought of him in terms of what I wanted, what he would allow me to do with him, to take from him. And that was the thing. That was the sad, frightening thing.

What scared me was his stillness. My sexuality was born in his stillness. That's what was wrong. It was a one-way desire, nothing no one else could be awakened to. Only the sleeping, the still, the dead or dead drunk could tolerate what I wanted. That's how alone I was against that infinite gray backdrop with Hunter; I didn't want to want him, I wanted him to want me. It wasn't the nature of the desire I wanted to kill; it was the one-sidedness of the desire.

The absolutely essential thing about this picture of Hunter was its heartlessness. I mean, there he was, so clean, so still and possessable, but there was no heart in it. The picture of Hunter had no heart in it.

■

Bᴜʙ ʜᴜɴɢ ʜᴀɴᴅsoᴍᴇʟʏ ғʀoᴍ ʜɪs ᴄʀoss. Tʜᴇʀᴇ ᴡᴀs ᴀ ᴠɪᴠɪᴅɴᴇss to his flesh he'd never had before. He was no longer just a sliver of my imagination. It was his otherness that I'd nailed down.

I did it at the lake one summer night. We were almost thirteen. I had my reasons.

At first, I was far away, looking down, and he blended into the cross: a slender X on the bare shore. Then everything shifted and I was in the water, gently rocking below his feet. Gazing up from the lake, I saw him suspended in the night against a dark curtain of pines, scattered with the tiny sparks of fireflies mimicking the stars overhead.

The scene was as beautiful as I could make it. All things considered, it was a fine crucifixion. I felt peaceful, enveloped by the warm water, my feet firmly planted in the mud. I was shoulder deep in the lake and the distance between Bub and me was good. We were calm with one another.

Until that night, I'd never let my eyes dwell on Bub. He had roamed the wilds of my thoughts, vague as an urge. His voice was doubt, ruffling through my feelings like a foreign wind. He built fires in all the dark places of my heart, only to bask in their deep shadows and smoke.

There was no place for Bub in Pryor. Whenever he appeared, I turned my head or squinted my eyes. I liked him blurry, in quick glimpses. I colored him dark and hazy as a dust storm.

In death, wickedness seemed to have drained from his nudity and my eyes took in every angle, arc, and jut of him.

There was almost a man beneath his boyish skin, but the bones pushing through the slim muscle seemed too vulnerable to bear the full weight of masculinity. The languid slack and swell of his sex belied the childish pout of his lips, his smooth jaw. He was delicately shy of manhood. It was myself I was seeing for the first time.

I rose from the water, approached his face. How passive he was with my betrayal. I searched his eyes for spirit. I wondered how I would live without this cannibal gnawing on my heart. I kissed him. His lips parted with a slight breath. He bit, held me in the air by my lip pinched between his teeth and then released me. I fell slowly, weightlessly to my feet, sucking a trickle of blood.

Then minnows appeared. Schools of minnows flew out of the water, swam through the air. The swarming minnows spiraled the cross, encircling Bub in a silvery flame of flicks and fins.

His body, spangled with minnows, ascended the stake, soared upward, was arrested for one still moment in the brightening moonlight before toppling and shattering the surface of the lake. The water swallowed him with a deep gulp—then silence, but for the dim, wet smacking against the cross.

"Minnows."

"What?" Ida asked. Her voice was sleepy, hoarse.

I didn't know. She sounded frightened, confused. I stood at the foot of her bed. The room was dark.

"What is it, Charlie?" she asked.

I couldn't find my voice. I had no explanations. I had been yanked from one world into another by her question and I couldn't decide which place was real and which was the dream place. The brightness of the lamp hurt. I had to close my eyes and squeeze them to soothe the sting of the sudden light. Ida got up and held my face toward the bedside lamp. She asked many questions: Was I awake? Did I have a bad dream? Was I hurt? I fell back to sleep with my mother patting my chewed lip with a cool damp cloth, asking many questions.

★ ★ ★

The sun wasn't visible yet, but it was more dawn than night. The kitchen window let enough of the approaching morning into the room that she hadn't turned on any light. The kitchen was soft and peaceful, the cabinet corners still rounded and fuzzy.

I'd only awoke minutes before, next to Ida in her bed. Her hand was lying across my forehead, a cloth folded over my mouth. The numbness of my lip was my first sensation. My second was the awareness of my mother's body so close to mine and the connection between her palm and my head. It was like some of the tension had been punctured and the space between us was a softer place, someplace I'd felt so long ago I'd never remembered it until I suddenly found myself there again. I woke up trusting.

"I'm gonna make coffee," Ida said, and she slipped off the mattress, already in her robe, into cloth slippers and left the room in a hushed shuffle down the hall. Those words brought my situation to focus. I drink coffee, black. To that thought everything else latched like needles to a magnet.

Suddenly I was ashamed to be my age and in my momma's bed. Because I was and because I was confused by the time of day—the dimness of the room suggested the middle of the night—I assumed for a moment that my dream was part of the room, that I had killed Bub on a cross only minutes before and with a blank time between that crucifixion and Ida's hand on my brow; I thought she knew everything.

When she asked, "What in the world is happening?" across the kitchen table, the coffee perking on the stove, there was a real soul behind her questioning eyes. But I turned to walk away from where I'd only just arrived because the question knocked me straight. Day was instantly distinct from night, life from dream, me from her. Then she surprised me. She asked, "You know what my worst dream ever was?"

I stopped, sat back down. Her hair was loose, a straight tail down her back. She looked so tired, ancient beyond her fifty-some-odd years. "No," I said. "Tell me."

"Your grandma," she calmly began. "I always slept with her, at least as far back as I can recall. I couldn't even dream in privacy."

"What kind of dreams are you talking about?" I was curious but afraid. I was scared by the confessional tone, by her sudden opening up, yet I was compelled to know by the history of being her son.

Ida looked at the rattling pot on the stove. She got up and turned off the burner, then lifted the pot with the hem of her robe wrapped around its handle. She filled the empty cup that had been sitting in front of me, an act that had already become natural, and then her own, before easing the pot out of her hand onto the tabletop.

"Well," she began again, nervously, watching the spoon that stirred the heavy stream of milk to the surface of her cup, "being pushed up a flight of stairs. Some endless and steep steps that wound around in circles so tight I couldn't see the top, could never see where they were going. I recall I was wearing a church dress, because it was long and swept the floor. I caught my shoe in the hem and tore the cloth. I tried to hold my skirt up as I climbed, but it was such a long skirt and the steps were so steep. All the while, Momma was pushing me on up these awful stairs, "Go on, Ida! Go on!" And there was other voices, below, like schoolkids laughing and playing and I knew they was laughing at my long torn dress. I wanted to cry, and I was so tired. But Momma wouldn't let me rest.

"Then the stairs started getting rickety, you know, loose and creaky and I was so high up I just felt like I couldn't take another step. Couldn't go any higher. Couldn't breathe. I just stood. Held onto Momma so I wouldn't fall, but she kept pushing at me to go on, to go on. Well . . . finally, I pushed back. You can't imagine how high it was and how far she fell. It was horrible to watch, but I did. I watched her get farther and farther away. And the awful thing was, I felt so light and unburdened the whole while I watched."

She looked at me, embarrassed. "I never told a soul. Except

God, of course. For the longest time, it was the only sin I could find to pray about. All my prayers were for forgiveness for that one dream.

"She scared me, Charlie. Filled me up with the fear of hell and damnation. Kept me plain and so different, always laughed at by other girls. No boys, no makeup, no movies, no dancing, no haircuts. Everything was the devil's temptation. She was savin' me from her own mistakes, she said, meaning Daddy, of course.

"Well . . . ," she paused. "Is that the kind of dreams you have? About . . . me?"

It was a simple question. I wanted to answer it for myself more than for Ida, but for Ida too. I wanted to list all of my sorrows right there in the kitchen, every shortcoming and failure, confess everything I was so tired of holding in. I wanted to tell all, but I didn't have faith in forgiveness. It was funny that after all of her years in the church, after all of her fits with the Spirit, talks with Jesus, hours with the Holy Word, she'd never seemed as good a woman as she appeared to me right then, because she'd never been so down-to-earth human with me before, never asked such a heart-to-heart question.

I suppose she felt like she had nothing left to lose by honesty. We had lived so far apart in the same house for so long we may as well have been foreign relations meeting for the first time. I was on the brink of what I'd always imagined death to be about. Only it was not the gauzy hand of God reaching into me for my heart. It was my own fingers hesitating at my breastbone, drumming with indecision. What will she do with it if I hand it over? Carry it to the window to turn it in the light? Stare at it in wonder? Or drop it like a compost scrap?

"I feel bad," I said.

"But, why? You're such a good boy."

"I'm not a boy and not so good. I'm practically grown. Oh, please don't cry!"

"Oh, Lord," she sniffled, "I've done everything wrong. All this time, I've let you alone feeling the way you do and I thought the whole time: Dear God, I thought, I don't deserve such a blessing. Thinking I would only mess you up with my own mistakes. You've always looked at me like you was seeing right through me, like you were counting up every mistake of my life."

"I was only looking for you. You never saw that?"

"No," she said. "I stopped looking for me long ago. I'm eaten up with regrets, Charlie, and I don't know how to fix any of it."

"Tell me about my daddy," I said.

"Garland?" she asked, with disgust.

"No, ma'am. I already know everything about him."

"I pray you don't," she said.

"I heard you telling Chick that night."

"Dear Lord! You heard all . . . I thought you was sound asleep."

"I heard."

Tears welled up in her eyes. "No wonder you have nightmares."

"I don't care about what happened to that man, Ida. I don't think you should either."

"My judgment will come, for sure," she said.

"I don't believe in God," I confessed.

"I know. I'll take the judgment for that too."

I didn't respond. The knot of her faith was too tightly drawn for me to slip so much as a word through its twists.

"What was his name?" I asked.

"Luke," she told me. "Luke Marable."

"Is he alive?"

"I wouldn't know. He couldn't have died of old age yet."

"Do I look like him?"

"Yes. He was a handsome man." This she said with tenderness, whether for me or Mr. Marable I couldn't tell.

"You must have loved him, once."

Ida sat like a statue with one faraway thought carved into her face.

"Did you, Ida?"

"Yes," she quietly said, "with all my heart and a whole lifetime of pent up . . ." She stopped, as if the honeyed memory had turned to vinegar. "A lifetime of ignorance, is all. That's how much I loved him. So much I turned deaf, dumb, and blind to common dignity. Blind to the Lord's house as I profaned it; dumb in my heart for any Lord at all but Luke Marable. Every time we came together, I thought, Thank you, Jesus. Thank you, God, for letting me be a woman. Can you imagine the shame? Well, I guess not—I ought to be ashamed for even saying such things to you. In the church itself, in the act of adultery, thanking God for that very sin . . . 'cause . . . well, 'cause I finally felt alive, I guess. Part of the earth I'd always been outside of. I was noticed for myself and not because I was a body on a pew or an obedient daughter, but because I was Ida Louise Bash, a woman. Not Sister Ida, but Ida, and I had precious eyes. He said I had precious eyes.

"Yes," she said. "I loved him. Until the time came I needed just a sip of love myself and found I'd only been pouring it away like water down a dry well. The ladle came up empty for me. Worse than empty. Rusted and full of dust.

"Momma always said that's how men are. Said men don't love nothin' but takin', least of all giving. I've only known three in my time: my daddy, your daddy, and Garland Hope. Loving the first two killed the hope in me of ever being loved back. God knows, killin' Garl has killed whatever remained of love I had left to give, including me and I guess you, too."

We sat silently. She let go of my fingers, and, as if to replace the warmth of touch, we both cupped our coffee and sipped. Then I asked, "Don't you think Chick loves us?"

"I reckon we wouldn't be here now at his table if he didn't. In his way. Lord knows where we would be. Sometimes, I think he pities me like anyone does a lonesome old maid. Me and Daddy are as far apart as two can be. What love there is has so thinned out over the years, it's hardly love at all. And I don't think he loves a thing more than his drinkin'."

"That's the truth," I said, and we both almost smiled.

"Charlie," Ida said, "I'd like to be different, but I'm getting to be an old woman. Starting over is like switchin' heaven and hell.

I can't undo the way I am and the things that've happened. I don't blame you for any grudges. It's too late for me and Daddy to reach any further than a truce, but is it too late for me and you?"

"No, ma'am. I hope not."

"Can you forgive me?" she asked.

"Yes. Can you do the same for me, right now?"

"Tell me what, Charlie. I'm ashamed to say I'm too simple to know what it is."

"Forgive me."

"For what?"

"Because it's what I need."

"I don't understand," she said.

"I don't either, Momma. I'm sorry I can't say what it is, even though I didn't choose it and can't change it. I'm still sorry. It'd help to feel that one person in the world can forgive me, even without understanding. It has nothing to do with you. But, please forgive me."

"All right," she said weakly.

"Will you always remember?" I asked.

"Well, you ain't going to rob no gas station or nothing, are you? Ain't going to kill nobody, are you?"

"I might," I said, trying to smile. "What if I do?"

She shook her head. "God knows, each of us might. If it comes to that, my forgiveness won't mean nothin' compared to your own. But, I'll always remember, Charlie."

We drank our coffee without another word. There didn't seem to be another word of any use. Then the hot rim of the cup blistered open my scabbed lip, and I left Ida in the kitchen to go tend it myself.

■

IT WASN'T EXACTLY MY BIRTHDAY; CHICK HAD RUN OFF FOR THAT. But a Sunday or two after, as if jarred by the sight of me, he said, "Let's git to T-town."

It'd been a long while since he'd dragged me through the bars in Tulsa. I didn't much cherish the idea of another tour, but the boredom of Pryor made me compliant.

Chick had been scarce around the house ever since the night Ida told him all about Garl and my true daddy. He'd been drinking more than ever, taking off on two- or three-day binges in Tulsa or thereabouts, leaving the Pryor joint in Fay's hands. He'd wander home later, sometimes after sunup, and sleep for fifteen- or twenty-hour stretches. When I saw him, perhaps at suppertime with Ida, as he was just stumbling fully dressed from bed, he worried me with the pallor of sickness that clung to his complexion like the sour odor to his breath. He would settle into a chair at the table as if his bones were dried out sticks being snapped into pieces, groaning, panting, gargling phlegm. Ida fixed him plates, but he rarely ate more than a bite of this or that before lighting a cigarette and coughing up its smoke. Something was eating him up from the inside out.

"Daddy, you're gonna drink yourself into the ground," Ida would sternly warn.

Chick would look at her uncertainly, his eyes yellowish as if still awash in beer, deep pouches sagging his lower lids, peeling back their raw gumlike inner sides.

"Naw," his gravelly throat would grumble until a damp cough avalanched from the denial, and Ida and I would try not to stare at the painful hacks he spilled into his handkerchief. "Oh, shit!" he'd moan, burying his swollen nose in the wad of linen.

"For pity's sake," Ida'd say, patting him between the shoulder bones.

"It's just old age," Chick would say, rubbing his belly as if smothering a fire.

He shook a pack of Winstons in my face, across the car seat, keeping his eyes glued to the road. I looked at the profile of his head against the prairie land, so monotonously flat and endless that it didn't seem to be moving at all past the window behind him. I was looking for a sign of permission or a reason, until I remembered that permission or reason was not and had never been an aspect of our relationship. I silently accepted a cigarette and punched the lighter into the dashboard. Chick bit into the pack and pulled out one for himself.

Watching the wide mouth of the Impala suck up the dividing lines of the highway, I fiddled with the cigarette, thinking hard about how to hold it nonchalantly. Smoking was something I'd studied my entire life and had earnestly practiced in private for the past year, but had never dared attempt in public. I saw it as a prop in my performance of adulthood and a kind of front for my insecurity. My smoking act was modeled on the ritualized lighting up, deep dragging, and cool, taut-lipped unraveling of smoke by my school's most masculine heroes and hoods.

The lighter popped, and I imitated the serious gestures of those teenaged boys in my mind, but Chick paid no heed to my smoking and we traveled another ten miles or so in a contemplative silence, shielding the ash-ends of our Winstons with our palms from the wind that loudly vacuumed our smoke out the open windows.

"I was probably just half your age," Chick finally spoke, "when

I first started stealing smokes from my daddy." He hacked and spit into the wind. "Or, we'd roll cornsilk out in the goddamn barn," he laughed. "Got switchin's for it. Son of a bitch! I remember that fizzlin' plain as yesterday. We chewed us Sen-Sen to cover the smell, and then got switched for suckin' Sen-Sen. Shit!" He smiled and shook his head.

"I guess Ida wouldn't approve of my smoking, either," I said.

"Oh, hell, I reckon not," Chick agreed, "but then with Ida, who can tell."

"You think she killed him, Chick?"

"Jesus Christ on a crutch!" he said. "She told you that?"

"I heard her telling you. Do you think it really happened like she said?"

"Well, she says so. Wouldn't nobody know one way or the other but her, and no fizzlin' reason I can think of to say so now if it weren't the truth. I reckon it's what she believes happened, true or not, and I can't see who'd blame her, really. Goddammit! Ain't that the shits?"

I tossed my filter out the window.

"You don't blame her none, Chick?"

"Why, Christ no."

Then why do you leave her so alone, I wanted to ask. Why have you been gone ever since she told you, I wondered. What is it you're trying to drown with all your drinking? I could feel the change in my grandpa since that night he'd cried himself to sleep, mumbling, "Baby, Baby, Baby. I didn't know. I didn't know." I could feel the changes in myself since that same night and the days and nights since, but I couldn't feel changed enough, or man enough, to actually question Chick about his secret pain or his drinking secret.

"Me, neither," was what I said.

He turned in my direction. "That's good," he said. He held his gaze on me for a second more, before returning it to the road.

"Speakin' of your mother," he said, "she's got a notion that you're in some kind of trouble."

"What kind is that?" I asked.

"Hell, I don't know. Are you?"

"I had a dream, is all. I guess I worried her some by walking in my sleep. I woke her up."

"A dream?" Chick said. "Is that all?"

"She thought it was about her and Garl and all . . . but it wasn't."

"Well, what was it? Some little gal?" Chick adopted a falsely confiding tone with this question. I'd heard it before in the bars when I was too young to understand his innuendoes, but even then I sensed the veiled tease in his voice and felt patronized, a bit ridiculed for my innocence.

"Yes," I lied to his suggestion. I lied because I was no longer innocent about his implications and I wanted him to know it. I lied for my own protection because I knew I had to, to maintain a smoke screen between my inner and outer feelings. I lied, in the hope of breaking my grandpa's mocking tone, in the hope that he might teach me something about women and sex that would add credence to my future lies. I lied because, in spite of the wrong I felt about my sexual stirrings, I sensed a wrongness in my longings that reached way beyond the sexual. I wanted Chick to explain what sex meant, what love meant, and why the two just slid off one another. I wanted to know how Chick could have sex without having the love of which he never spoke. I needed to know what love was. I lied because it was easier.

Still conspiring, Chick grinned. "Well now. Ain't that the shits! I sure as hell can't remember the last time I dreamed about a piece of tail."

Chick lit another cigarette off the filter of his first. "You're still a virgin, I take it."

"Hell, Chick, I'm only thirteen!" I cursed in my own defense.

Chick laughed up a wad of spit and blew it out the window. "Well, that's old enough for a hard pecker and a wet dream, ain't it?"

I blushed. I turned my embarrassment to the open window and let the wind cool the fire in my cheeks.

"I know me a few younger ones," Chick boasted. "Pretty, too, and eager . . ." I closed my eyes to the wind.

"I can guarantee, a piece of pussy is money well spent. Best cure in the world for whatever the hell's ailin' you. I believe I owe you a birthday present, Feller. What do you say to the two of us gettin' us some . . . ?"

I turned to Chick with a calm mask on my dread. "Some other birthday, Chick," I said. "I don't think I'm ready for a whore."

"What's that? Oh. Oh, well. OK then." His tone was different, fallen, maybe a bit shamed, certainly apologetic. "You don't think bad of me for the idea, do you?" he finally asked.

"No, Chick."

"I'm just a dirty old cuss, I reckon. I don't mean nothin' by it. You know that, don't you?"

"I know it."

"Hell," he said, easing the awkwardness, "you got plenty of time to do it all, Charlie. Ain't no rush for you, no fizzlin' rush. And don't let no fizzlin' ol' peckerwood push you toward nothin' you ain't rearin' to do, hear? A feller's dreams is his own business, I guess. Ida or me shouldn't butt in. If you got eyes for some nice little gal, well . . . that's fine. That's real fine."

"OK," I said.

Ten minutes later, with the city skyline encroaching on the lack of conversation, I could have sworn Chick said, "Oh, Esther." But the wind whistling over flat land through a fast car can sometimes play tricks.

We pulled up beneath a pawnbroker's sign on the north side of the old train tracks in downtown Tulsa.

It was a jailhouse of junked pistols, accordions, and cameras. There was even a ventriloquist's dummy strung up from one of the ceiling fans like a hung child dangling in the draft.

A man peered through glasses thick as beer bottles from behind the iron bars separating the cash safe and gun racks from the rest of the deep, narrow room.

"Uh-oh. Here comes trouble!" he yelled the full length of the store as we walked through the front door of glass and more iron-work and set a cowbell to clanging from its thong around the in-side hinges. "Oh, hell, here comes a big screw in the ass!"

"I heard that, Browny, you ol' four-eyed peckerwood!" Chick yelled back, squinting at the far end of the room. As Browny ap-proached from his side of the cell and Chick actually caught sight of him, Browny shook his fat head and extended a hand, beefy as a ball mitt, through the bars. Chick grabbed it with his own and the two men, one short and stocky as his lead safe and the other lanky as a fishing pole, held hands through the black railing, smacked their lips and nodded at one another like two convicts with pieces of the same crime in common.

By thirteen, I'd shot up to Chick's shoulder, but I still felt like the waist-high boy who needed a boost to a barstool, and I hung back from my grandpa and his friend who, like all of his buddies at first, made me feel invisible and overlooked in the long shadow of a character like Chick.

The pawnshop smelled like a basement crammed with dusty old things too ugly to be used but too useful for the dumpyard. I ran my finger over the worn spots of purple velvet that lined an empty carrying case of some sort. It was laid open like a black leather cas-ket on a countertop, robbed but for the indented outline of its one-time contents.

"It's the kid's birthday," Chick said.

"Well, what do you know," Browny replied, giving me a thor-ough look over through the bars.

"Ain't old enough for a blow job apparently, so we're a-shoppin' around," Chick said as seriously as an undertaker.

"You crazy bastard!" Browny laughed, and Chick burst into a smile himself that faded to seriousness as the two of them looked me over together.

"Well, I've got some goddamned deals on shotguns," Browny

said. "What's he hunt?" he asked Chick. "Coons? Squirrels? Birds?" His artificially brown eyebrows rose a fraction higher with each guess. "Niggers?" he laughed.

"I don't think he does, Browny," Chick answered with just an edge of shame in his lowered voice.

I hated this feeling of being talked about like I wasn't in the room and the feeling that I was being sized up for something other than a stupid gift from a pawnshop.

"I don't want a gun, Chick," I spoke up in my own defense, though still lingering in the shelter of the aisles.

Chick seemed indifferent to the mean-hearted remark of his buddy, but Browny had set off an interior alarm in me from the moment I spied him behind those bars. The warning felt like a fever in my cheeks, forehead, and hands. I didn't understand what it was exactly about him I didn't like and wasn't certain what it was about him that felt so dangerous that my heart seemed to be turning around in my chest so as not to face him. He was the first man I'd ever encountered as a boy that I wasn't either drawn to or indifferent toward. I'd never disliked someone so superstitiously or with such disgust except for, at times, myself.

I had already made up my mind to speak as few words as possible. This seemed like a decision in favor of my own safety. Browny was paying too much attention to me with his froggy eyes, studying me too closely, I felt, for my own good. But, of course, he was managing all this in Chick's presence and was doing it casually and with a sinister confidence. I wanted to be as separate and private and different from him as possible.

I eyed him cautiously with careful glances from one piece of merchandise to another.

Browny was sucking a match fire through a big cigar, gnawing the mouth end of it, making it dark and slippery with his slobber. From the moment he caught me watching, his relish seemed to increase as he turned the huge smoldering thing in a slow circle with the muscle of his lips.

I withdrew my gaze but I thought about how he reminded me

of an old woman who is commonly ridiculed behind her back for trying too hard to look young. Hair dye, makeup, jewelry, even clothes, all the materials women were allowed to use, but not abuse, to look prettier, softer, even sexier, seemed shockingly grotesque on a man, and Browny appeared as artificial as a hussy. His eyebrows were unnaturally arched and dark, perhaps penciled in to perfection. His matching hair was thin but long-stranded and somehow matted into a stiff tangled resemblance of hair hiding his scalp and crown where it was evident none had grown in many years. Digging into the fat flesh of each pinky was a flashy diamond ring, one or the other of which he unconsciously but daintily stroked. He was an ugly man made uglier by his attempts at good looks. Even his baby-blue knit trousers, visible behind the glass display, were offensive to me as he jiggled his stinking cigar with more boisterous statements peppered with words like *nigger*, *cocksucker*, and *cunt*.

The aggression in his fartlike speech maddened, but frightened, me. Such masculine, but foul, boasting belching out of such an effeminately powdered-over man was eerie. I was on such thin ice with my own insecurities, I felt dread at the twisted rage of his opinion should he see through me, and I only wanted to get out of there as quickly as possible.

"How about these?" I said to Chick, distracting his attention from Browny with the pair of ice skates I'd unthinkingly grabbed off the shelf and now held up for his approval, purchase, and quick departure.

"What's that? Oh. Skates. Well," Chick stuttered with a cigarette in his mouth. "They look kind of big, Feller. What's their size, anyway?"

Browny pulled the cigar out of his mouth, kept his elbows on the glass counter and said, "They're 11½'s." Then, snidely, he said, "That's a man's 11½. What's your size, exactly, boy?"

I dropped the skates back to the shelf, as if I'd never touched them, and strolled to the end of the counter Chick leaned against.

Browny popped the cigar back in his mouth, which smirked around it.

I looked at the boxes of jewelry in the glass case below my hands. "How about a ring," I said. "That one," I pointed.

Browny slid open the door and pulled out a woman's frilly ruby. He held it under my nose on the fat tip of his dirty-nailed finger. "This one?" he asked suspiciously, puffing smoke out of each corner of his lips.

"No," I said. "Never mind. Let me see that knife."

"Hey," Chick whistled, "now you're talkin'."

"Switchblade," Browny said, laying the pearly cased blade on the glass top. I picked it up carefully, turning its smooth cold heft in my hand.

"No tellin' whose throat that blade's cut. As I recollect, some pimp brought it in. Yes, sir," Browny said, pulling the cigar from his lips, "that was one nervous nigger."

I slid the button that flung a shiny blade no longer than three inches from the mother-of-pearl handle, then folded the knife back together.

"I like it fine," I told Chick, laying it down.

He picked it up and inspected it, springing it open a few times, running his thumb along the blade's edge. "Dull as shit," he said to Browny. "But I reckon I could sharpen her up. That's a pretty little fish gutter," he said, looking at me. To Browny, he said, "How much you want for this, you old crook?"

"What's the matter? You need glasses? It's got a tag."

"Sixteen, my ass," Chick griped. "Poor old blackie you robbed probably only got five."

"What if he did?" Browny smiled. "All right, tightwad," he bargained, "fourteen, but that's a steal. This ain't your neighbor's garage sale!"

"I tell you what—I'll give you twelve," Chick said, pulling out his wallet.

"Goddamn!" Browny grabbed his butt like he'd been poked.

"All right, buzzard. I reckon I'll make it up on the next nigger, but I'm being fucked. Only 'cause you're so good at it."

Chick ignored the joking around, which had embarrassed me, and laid out the money on the counter. Browny pawed it over the glass. Chick pocketed my birthday present and I walked hurriedly toward the door. Chick said, "I owe you a cold one."

Browny said, "You owe me a fuckin' bottle."

"I'll see you around." Chick extended his hand.

"So long, Chick." Browny took his hand, then, "Hey, boy!"

I turned back from the door. "This is one hell of a old man. Y'ought to be proud of the relation." He and Chick finished their handshake.

"Yes, sir," I said, clanging the cowbell on my exit.

"It was there when I got up," Ida said, looking to me for an explanation. Chick had pocketed the knife at the pawnshop the previous afternoon. Now it lay beside my breakfast plate.

"Chick bought it for my birthday," I told her.

"That figures," she said. "What are you going to do with that?" She'd set the table around it, as if it were too dangerous to touch. She jumped back when I unsnapped the blade and it sprang open with an oiled *whoosh-click!*

"My Lord!" she gasped, clutching a potholder to her chest. "That'll hurt you for sure, Charlie."

Chick had honed the blade to a stunning gleam sometime between Browny's and this morning. In close light, the flint marks were as precise and artful as the fine grain in mahogany. The steel spine and cap on the butt of the handle, even the tiny screw caps flush in the pearl, were polished like a mirror.

I don't know what my grandpa's careful restoration of the switchblade meant. Aside from his home, his money, and his uncensored, erratic company, it was the only real present he ever personally gave me. Christmases and birthdays before, he'd absentmindedly doled out twenties as if paying a tab. If sober enough to anticipate a holiday, he'd say something like, "Oh, hell, is it that time again?" and slip Fay Rose fifty bucks or so on the sly, saying, "Buy the kid and Ida something from me." I'd annually unwrapped boxes of school clothes and predictable packages of underwear and socks.

"What's that? Oh," he'd say. "What'd I get you?"

"Underwear," I'd tell him. "Thanks." Or, I'd hold up a new shirt by the shoulders and he'd feign interest for a second, then, "That's sharp, ain't it?" he'd whistle, or, "Oh, hell, I guess you must've needed that."

"Everybody needs a knife," I told Ida, closing the blade.

"I can't think what for," she worried.

Finally I confessed that I really couldn't either. "It seemed more useful than a shotgun. Chick sure cleaned it up."

"Well, I wish you'd just put it away somewhere. Clean or not, it makes me nervous."

Something about it unnerved me too, perhaps the threat of that unleashed blade at the command of such a small sensitive button. But I was attracted at the same time to the elegance of the thing and the sensual feel of its fit to my hand.

But I did put it away. It was too long and weighty to carry around comfortably in my pocket. I put it in the cigar box where I kept the accumulated twenties I'd saved from Chick over the years, along with the silver dollars he'd given me for waiting in the car while he made love on Sundays. It was a box lined years ago with scraps of red flannel from Ida's ragbag. I'd covered it with butcher paper and lettered it with carnival banner headlines in Elmer's and glitter. "Amazing Sights," it boasted in an arc across the lid. The sides exclaimed one after another, "Behold to Believe," "Astounding Miracles," Wonder of Wonders," and "Astonishing Bazaar of Mystery." This treasure chest exhaled a weak breath of old tobacco as I opened it to place the switchblade atop the scattered bills and coins. I closed the box and studied it, suddenly shamed by its outgrown intentions. I'd made it to house a leprechaun or fairy, some blessed freak of nature or manifest holy spirit. I was going to trap a piece of God in this cigar box and present

Him to my mother, but all I'd managed to collect was a hundred and thirty dollars and a pimp's pawned switchblade. I opened a drawer and hid the bank beneath my abundant supply of underwear and socks.

I opened the door of Chick's room, knowing he'd be asleep till at least noon. It was a back-of-the-house room at the end of a hall, the second largest next to Ida's. I'd seen it, of course, but was never invited in or tempted to spend more than a minute at the door. It was not the kind of bedroom one would expect of a retired renderer and barfly like Chick Bash.

It was a very private world, somehow detached from the rest of the house, not particularly clean if you looked closely enough, but neat and kept that way by Chick himself. His irregular sleeping hours kept its doors closed during the day when Ida did the housework. She didn't trespass on his sleep, and when Chick was up or out, she was on to the laundry or supper or sleeping herself. The door at the end of the hall might as well have been the locked gate to another house.

It contained Esther's furniture. That is, she'd picked it out for the large room they once shared, Ida's room now, and of course had deserted it like Chick when she left Pryor for good. For some reason, Chick had crammed it all into the smaller back room, even before Ida returned to live with him. So the space was cramped by too much furniture, a coffin-size cedar chest at the foot of a high double bed, whose headboard, like the giant double dresser and mirrored vanity, was a honey maple carved with droopy garlands of bluebells. The wood tops were covered with yellowed linen and lace cloths, which gave the room its tidy feminine look. The only arrangement upon them was a woodshop project of my own, a crude pine rack for six darkly mellowed pipes whose incense was ingrained in the oval rag rug and the windows' satiny blue drapes, faded as smoke.

Slid into the ornate frame of the vanity table's tall mirror, which I faced through the crack in the door, was a sepia-toned wedding picture of two young strangers, my grandparents, and an old-fashioned portrait of my mother as a girl. On the dressing table itself, framed in dime-store gilt, was my most recent school picture. My forced chromatic smile was as vivid as a night-light in the dim room.

It was through the mirror that I saw Chick hunched on his side in a bony curl beneath a sheet. I'd never pictured his body as so bendable. He was folded up small in the bed, his curved back to me. His spine poked at the thin sheet like the knuckles of a tight fist. In the mirror I saw his face bent toward his knees, his hands bunched the sheet beneath his chin, like he was freezing to death with the recent loss of August. The door didn't creak. He didn't stir. I closed it with the decision to thank him later for the knife.

We couldn't bury him until five days later. It was the Sunday before Labor Day, and the doctor and undertaker were off together bow hunting in the Ozarks. It wasn't until late the following night that they pulled up to the house in a pickup with three wild boar heads and cleaned carcasses piled in the bed. It didn't seem at all right, the two of them leaning over Chick's drawn-up frame with the reek of campfires, moldy woods, and hog blood still fresh in their hunting jackets, but at least they came quick as they heard and had the good manners to scrub their hands before examining the body.

The doctor told Fay Rose a heart attack was his best and only guess. He was willing to leave it at that unless Ida wished an autopsy performed in Tulsa, "which would further delay a burial," Mr. Knickerbocker, the mortician, said. Ida mumbled that she had no such wish.

Fay Rose spoke for us when she refused to let them take the body away that night. "You mean to throw him in that pickup bed with pig heads like more raw meat! No," she said. "Leave him be. Another night ain't gonna change nothin'. Come back in the morning with a proper hearse, for Pete's sake! We'll be down to the funeral home in the afternoon and make our arrangements.

Now pardon us please, but it's late and the two of you are stinking up this poor woman's house."

"Well, I—" Knickerbocker objected.

"Jed," the doctor interrupted him, "Mrs. Savory's right. Let's go." Fay Rose ushered them toward the door where the doctor paused to offer his sympathy to Ida and me and his regret for the troubling delay.

"Thank you kindly," Ida said from the couch. Fay locked up behind them and fell into the cushions between us. I stared at the untouched cups of cold coffee on the TV tray before us.

"I'll make a fresh pot, Fay Rose," I offered. She wrapped her arms around my shoulders and pulled my face next to hers. I just closed my eyes and breathed against her neck, counting each of her slow trickling tears against my cheek.

Ida had barely moved from the couch since the Sunday she'd found him dead. I'd gone out a little later that morning after peeking into his room, thinking he was asleep. I'd walked down to the lake for a swim and had spent most of the day in and out of the water and sun. The end of summer and start of high school was on my mind.

I'd fallen asleep on the bank of the lake sometime around noon and was awakened by the feel of bugs crawling over me, which was only the trickle of my own sweat. Brushing my hand across my skin I felt the sting of a sunburn and at the same time heard the distant strain of a choir. My head ached from the heat and my eyes were dazed in the September light.

I saw the angels across the glare of the lake, a band of them, lining the opposite shore of Purley. Their white robes waved, their wings spread and closed as they clapped and swayed. Some swooned to the drone of their hymn. Their tambourines shimmered in the light. In twos and threes, they stepped away from the wooded bank, their gowns billowed like sails. I thought they would hover over the bright sheet of water. I thought they were singing to me. I thought they were coming to Pryor.

But they only waded into the lake until their robes floated in fans around their waists. My vision adjusted to the brightness and I saw their black faces and hands, the mistaken halos of their swimming caps. The congregation on the shore commenced a heartier gospel as the baptized were lowered backward, submerged, and reborn with violent, happy shouts.

Thinking about them later, I wondered if the angels were not a mirage of my own premonition that Chick was not just asleep but submerged in something much deeper forever, in that folded-up position in bed. Folded up as that switchblade he'd revived from hock and left on the kitchen table. Chick didn't believe in angels and neither did I, I thought, but my heart had leaped at the sight of them.

I waded into the lake to cool off, to wake myself up. I estimated at least a thousand swim strokes between me and the black congregation on the other side, a feat beyond my strength and yet their joyful noise called. If I had been able to swim across to Purley, I would only have disrupted their ritual, appearing in the midst of their baptism, about as welcome, I reckoned, as a red demon. And so instead, I stood in the lake and smeared myself black with the cool soft mud, which soothed the pain of my skin if nothing else, before I dunked and came up clean.

"Daddy's gone," Ida said flatly as I walked through the door. She sat on one end of the couch, her feet together on the floor, her hands overlapped on her skirt. Her eyes were closed and she said it as if speaking from a nap. I thought she meant he had gone off to Tulsa or somewhere and saw no importance in the statement. It was Sunday, after all, and he couldn't get a beer in Pryor.

Fay Rose then appeared through the kitchen doorway. "Honey," she said, as our eyes met, "looks like he went in his sleep— sometime last night or early this mornin'. There's no way of tellin' yet."

I didn't understand Fay, her nor Ida's somber concern about Chick's whereabouts. My confusion must have shown upon my face, because Fay studied my reaction, and before I could ask where they thought he might have gone, she set the coffeepot she was carrying on a tray before the couch.

"Don't be scared, Charlie," she said, placing her palm flat against the side of my face. With that gesture and simple order, I knew he was dead.

"I know it's a shock, Sweetheart, but he was bound for it like we all are. He was old," she said dully, "and even last night was drinkin' like no tomorrow. Well, here's tomorrow, Honey, here it is."

"I couldn't stop him," Ida said. "I couldn't stop him when I was little. I couldn't stop him when I was growed."

"Of course not, Ida," Fay said soothingly. Her fingers stroked the back of my hair before she dropped her hand and turned to my momma. "It was a waste of breath to even try. Don't go takin' on blame for this."

"I told him it would kill him. I knew it would," Ida continued.

"He wasn't stupid, Hon. He knew it, too."

I left Fay tending Ida's nerves with sympathy and coffee and approached the door at the end of the hall. It was closed but opened smoothly, with a wide swing.

There he was, curled in bed just as he had been that morning. The sheet had been pulled from his hands and spread out smoothly up to his neck. The window had been opened, though the curtains were still drawn. They expanded and deflated with the irregular breeze like a pair of pale, wheezy lungs.

"Don't be scared," Fay had told me, and I wasn't. I don't think I was anything at all except certain that Chick was dead. I circled the big bed to get closer to him.

I remembered him saying once that he was not too afeared of dying, and his expression did not betray the claim. I read no fear, no pain, no change at all upon his face. I looked directly at him and told myself over and over, "He's dead, he's dead," not because I needed to be convinced, but because I felt obliged to react to his death in a certain way. He's dead, I told myself, and I waited for my sorrow to arrive. I thought I should feel sad, but I didn't. I thought I should cry, but I couldn't. I only felt ashamed that I felt no more than I did and I apologized out loud for that. I said, "I'm sorry, Chick." Then I added, "Thank you for the knife."

His skin looked so dry against the pillow, some important feature of it seemed missing so that it resembled an inanimate fabric stretched around his skull. I couldn't resist touching him. My fingers were stunned by the coolness and absolute stillness but did not retreat. I ran my fingertips across his bare head, smooth as a lake stone. I stroked the prickly stubble of his jaw and put my forefinger on his sealed lips. I pressed gently but far enough to feel the rock-like clench of his teeth. I hesitated only briefly, still with no feeling in my heart, before I traced the rest of his body with my fingers. I was compelled as if an opportunity of some significance had presented itself and there was no time to figure out its consequences. I touched his hard frame and curled length. I guess I caressed him as if I knew him. I felt all that there was left of him; then I re-smoothed the sheet and turned to leave. But I stopped myself, before my first step away from the bed. I bent over him and put my cheek for a moment against his neck. I breathed a few breaths into his ear. My arms were folded tightly across my chest, and I didn't close my eyes for fear of losing my balance in the vertigo as I leaned over and kissed him dryly and quickly in an awkward contortion to meet his turned lips, and then I left the room.

Fay Rose stayed over because Ida seemed incapable of managing. She didn't know who to call or who should be informed. She kept insisting that we needed a preacher.

"Honey," Fay Rose finally told her, "your daddy needs an undertaker, and we need a houseful of neighbor women with casseroles and pies to keep us going, but I'll go get you a preacher, if you think that you need one. Just tell me who you want."

"I don't know," she said as if scolded.

"Well, I don't, either," Fay Rose admitted.

"When Momma died, the preacher knew what to do, is all. I just don't know what to do." She broke into a frightening wail. And for the next two days, until the hearse backed up to the porch steps and he was carried out of the house on a stretcher with the bedsheet finally concealing his face, she continued to disrupt the hush of death with that surprising wail. It was the most lonesome sound I had ever heard. It seemed to tear itself out of the tissue of her throat and just shred itself to pieces in the air. Hours after it had faded away, its vibrations could still be sensed just as surely as the presence of Chick's body could be felt in any room of the house.

The atmosphere was so strange for those few days, with his corpse closed off in the back room and Ida withdrawn into her trance of inactivity. Sometimes she'd begin humming bits and pieces of church music; other times she'd come to life with a low moan, and then there were those piercing, haunting wails.

The three of us didn't leave the house until our trip to the funeral home in Purley, and there were long periods of just sitting together, each of us wrapped in our own kind of quiet. Fay Rose and I would talk in the presence of Ida as if she were not even there.

Fay said it was natural and good for Ida to mourn any way she could. "You're being a man about it though," she also said. "You're being real strong."

At one point I asked her if she loved him. Yes, she said, she did. "How could you?" I wanted to know.

"Well," she smiled, "it wasn't easy. I guess I understood him, Hon. That's the biggest part of it."

"Why didn't you marry him?"

"Why should I? 'Sides, he never asked me, and marriage is foremost a question and a answer."

"He had other women," I said, "in Tulsa." I wasn't trying to hurt her or to disparage Chick. I was just trying to understand what Fay Rose now meant to me. I was trying to be adult about an adult situation.

"I know that," Fay said, lighting a cigarette. "Whores mostly. They meant about as much to me as they did to him. Now, don't think there wasn't a time when I couldn't have snatched him bald-headed over some of his monkey business! Ha! But, oh," she said, her cigarette smoke mingling with the sentiment of what she recalled, "that was a long time ago, Charlie. I got beyond all that with Chick Bash. Thing is, he was good company. I can't say that was true of Gun Savory or too many other men I've known and—pardon my sayin'—it sure weren't the case with your grandma, who I knew a little of. We both married young and wrong, I reckon. Charlie, don't ever underestimate the comfort of good company." Her face was rocking back and forth, tilted back a little on her neck, her eyes closed with furrows between the brows. "One thing I do know." She paused to snuff out the cigarette, then pinched the bridge of her nose, somehow taking the tremor and sweetness out of her voice, as she said, "I'm gonna miss that ol' peckerwood's company more than I'll ever miss a husband."

Time became as irrelevant for the three of us as it was for my grandpa's body. We wandered in and out of the various rooms, sometimes meeting up with one another in the kitchen by pure accident, which would seem indication enough to fix a meal and eat it, whether it be two or eight in the morning. We slept in shifts wherever and whenever the urge overtook us, sometimes all together sitting up in the static and light of the TV fuzz, but more often, one at a time, wandering off to beds of brief and fitful rest. The weirdness of those days and nights was in the lack of anything but waiting to be done. The waiting seemed hardest on Ida. She couldn't keep a grasp on what we were waiting for. She'd walk dazedly out of her bedroom and would seem caught off guard at the sight of Fay and me, already up and dressed before her. She'd ask confused questions.

"Did he come in yet?"

"Who, Honey?" Fay would counter.

"Daddy," she'd say. "I fell asleep listening for him."

"Chick's dead," I'd remind her.

"Oh, yes. I knew it," she'd say, pouring a cup of coffee and joining us at the table, but before she would bring the cup to her lips, that howl would start seeping out of her. I'd just have to bow my head to at least erase the sight if not the sound of it and an unconscious prayer would rise up into my throat. "Please don't let my mother be crazy. Please, somebody, just let us bury him and go on."

The funeral was simple and brief with the cheapest minimum of ritual. His retirement policy from Pryor Rendering paid for the grave and a plain casket. Fay wrote a check for a bronze nameplate, since no headstone was included. There was no preacher, although Mr. Knickerbocker had recommended a few. With all the details finally arranged, Ida decided her own silent prayer would do as much for Chick's soul as a Baptist stranger's. Two retired work buddies and a couple of regulars from the beer joint, including the Turtle Man, showed up. Nobody cried, except maybe Fay Rose behind her dark glasses.

Knickerbocker had rigged some ropes to a crank that lowered the box into the grave. Its rusty gears made an awful squeal, and the only thing I wondered was if they'd been able to straighten him out for the casket because it seemed too short for his long frame as I remembered it, but maybe I was just trying to remember him taller than he was as I stood there looking so far down, still trying to miss him.

A middle-aged black man in short sleeves and tie filled the hole with dirt. We all stood around until he patted the grave level with the back of his shovel. That was that, it seemed.

Ida's wailing fits ended as abruptly as Chick's life, once the body had been removed from the house. There was something undefinably different about her from that moment on, as if the three days of mournful bellowing had relieved her of a welled-up sorrow that had more to do with living than dying. She seemed lighter and almost normal.

Like Fay Rose, she was dressed in black that afternoon, but somehow the color enlivened her. Fay looked somber and restrained in her tight suit. Her makeup was heavy and cakey, her

face powder dusted her dark shoulders and collar. She looked unnatural and as artificial as her brass-colored hair.

I was struck by the comparison of the two women, arm in arm,
at the graveside. Even in the sunlight, the blackness of my mother's
plain dress seemed cool next to her skin. It accentuated the clear-
ness of her complexion and was as flattering as dark velvet to jewels
in the way it lured the beautiful aquamarine from within her gray
eyes. At one point in the proceedings, she returned my studious
gaze, for we stood on opposite sides of the grave. We held each
other for a moment with our eyes, and then she gently patted Fay's
hand resting in the crook of her elbow and smiled at me with a
knowingness I felt down to the soles of my stiff new shoes. It was
a smile I'd given up looking for and it surprised me in the context
of her father's burial, but I grabbed it in the muscles of my own
lips and held it there, upturned and slightly open for her to see. I
think we both felt somehow free.

"Fay Rose, is there any money?" Ida asked across the front seat
as Fay drove us home from the cemetery.

"Well, no savings to speak of," she answered. "Course, there's
the insurance to hold you over. I showed you, remember?"

Ida sighed and turned her face toward the window. We were approaching the rendering plant, whose smell was beginning to filter
through the air-conditioning vents of Fay's old Cadillac.

Reflexively breathing through our mouths, we passed the processing plant in silence. "At least the house is paid for," Fay reassured. "And the bar, too. But there's taxes and upkeep. Maybe you
could sell the bar," she thought out loud, "though I don't know
to who."

"Is that beer money what we been living on, Fay?" Ida asked.

"He drunk up his pension. There ain't nothin' else, Hon."

"Ain't we near it?" Ida asked.

"What?"

"That cussed bar!"

★ ★ ★

The car tires crushed the loose gravel as we pulled into the lot, stirring up a gray dust that we watched settle across the hood as Fay killed the engine and we sat for a moment in the ovenlike enclosure of the Cadillac. Ida was the first to open her door and step outside. Fay and I followed.

"Leave the winders up," Fay Rose said, slamming the driver's side door. "I don't want this powder blowin' all over my seats." She'd trekked up to the entrance and was rooting in her pocketbook for keys before she looked back and asked Ida, didn't she want to go in.

"I reckon I got to, Fay," my mother answered, still standing next to the car, holding on to the open door. Finally, she swung it closed with a deliberate push that also propelled her a step or two across the pebbled ground toward her new bar.

We entered through the back way, a padlocked wooden door atop a concrete ledge of a step. There was a sealed up mildew odor to the dark room we stepped into.

"Lord! What's that sour stink?" Ida complained from behind her own hand.

Fay Rose chuckled as her backless high-heels click-clocked across the linoleum. "Just pure-D beer joint I reckon, Hon." She flipped a few switches along the wall and lit up the place, then set the room to vibrating by another switch with the roar of the air conditioner starting up.

"She's grouchy till she gets to goin'. But so am I," Fay said, motioning her head toward the bulky ducts of the cooling system sprawling around the perimeter of the ceiling. As if responding to the insult, the racket suddenly died to just the whir of a fan, and blasts of cool air began scattering the sickly odor.

Fay Rose stationed herself behind the bar, pulling a Chesterfield from her needlepoint cigarette case. She lit up and threw back her head to exhale with a deep sigh.

Ida walked over to one of the two booths and sat down slowly on the very edge of the brown plastic covered seat as if she wouldn't dream of sliding her legs beneath the table. She rested one arm on the Formica top, then jerked it swiftly aloft. "Sticky," she frowned, resting both hands palm up on her lap.

Fay held the elbow of her bent smoking arm and stared out the front window, a long horizontal pane of grimy glass that framed the flat highway it looked out upon.

"I ain't been able to bring myself over and clean up since . . ." She cut herself off with another deep drag.

I took a stool at the bar halfway between the two of them and tugged at the knot of my tie.

"Hmmph," Fay suddenly shrugged. "This is about the sorriest party of sadsacks this joint's ever seen!" She reached over the bar and jokingly yanked me toward her by my loose tie. "Why not have us a cold one, since we're here," she said, winking at me over the top of her black sunshades. "What do you say, Handsome?"

"Sure, Sweetie," I played along.

"God almighty, Fay Rose Savory!" Ida exclaimed from the edge of the booth. "Why, don't you talk silly!"

"Oh, why not, Honeypie?" Fay answered, slapping the bar and then spinning toward the refrigerator. She dislodged three mugs from the frost-encrusted freezer and, with her cigarette dangling between her lips, filled them with beer from a tap she maneuvered like a semidriver shifting an eight-wheeler.

"Fay, dear," Ida said, slowly approaching the bar where Fay Rose had clanked down the three mugs, one of them foaming right beneath my nose. "I think the heat and all has done somethin' to your senses, Honey. You know I'm a Christian and don't abide drinkin'. And here you go settin' a mug of liquor within Charlie's reach! Now, let's git on out of here. This was a bad idea. Drive us on home and I'll make us some coffee."

"Well now, Ida, dear," Fay Rose snapped back, raising a mug. "You know I love you like you was my own blood and I got the patience of I don't know what when it comes to your ways, but, little girl, you got to come down off your high horse one of these days."

My mother was taken aback. "What?" she asked.

"You can stay hidden up in that old house till you die. One day you'll be sniffin' daisies from the root-end, girl, and regrettin' all of these 'shalt nots' of yours. If God is so almighty, He's got more to fret over than every little drink of every fool child. And that means you too, Ida Bash."

"Hope!" my mother cried out.

"Oh, Hope my ass!" Fay snapped bitterly. "All right then, Mrs. Hope, don't that prove the point of it, you fool? Honey, you ain't nothin' better or different to God than you was to your own daddy, and that's just Chick Bash's spooked girl, run off and married to some old crazy coot named Hope 'cause she was foolish enough to git knocked up Holy Rollin' with a even bigger fool between the church pews."

"Fay Rose, what is the matter with you?" Ida pleaded. "Take me home."

My face burned as I kept it bowed over the head of my beer.

"I've had a pot a coffee already. Now I need a drink is all that's the matter with me. I just come from buryin' a man I cared very much about. I'm standin' in a place that he built from the worthless ground up with his own two hands, and it may not be much of a place but it was about all he had and we spent times here, some good, foolish, and careless times in this dump, and drinkin' beer in this joint has kept you and Charlie in food and walkin' shoes. So walk on home if you want on the two good legs God gave you. I feel too lousy to go home, Hon. I feel so goddamned lousy I don't know what to do with myself except what we always did here before. I want to drink me a mug of cold beer and maybe even another one and try to forget that Chick is gone and his only flesh and blood is standin' here turnin' up her nose at the very idea of drinkin' a fizzlin' beer."

I grinned at the familiar sound of Chick's favorite word.

"What?" Fay Rose turned to me, the mug still perched midair in her hand.

"Fizzlin'," I said, smiling at her serious expression.

With her free hand she finally removed her sunglasses and

looked back with puffy eyes. Then her face exploded into deep gutsy laughter.

"It's just a fizzlin' beer," she growled at Ida as I heaved a heavy and slippery mug toward Fay's. We clinked the glasses together and held them up over the bar long enough to see what Ida's response might be. She was standing erect, holding her purse in front of her skirt.

Slowly she slumped onto a stool beside me. "I don't know what to do, Fay. I just don't know anymore."

"Me, neither," I said, taking a cold drink.

She reached for a mug. "Oh," she smiled as she lifted it, "that's heavy, ain't it? Lord knows where I'll end up," she sighed to Fay as we touched our glasses together, "if you get me to fizzlin' drinkin'."

Fay took a gulp, I drank and Ida tasted. "It's kind of bitter," my mother said, wrinkling her nose between small consecutive sips.

"Like medicine," Fay responded.

"Charlie!" Ida scolded, then changed her tone, "Honey, slow down now. This ain't Coca-Cola. Mercy!" She put her glass down and puckered her forehead. "I feel tipsy already."

"Good night, Darlin'," Fay laughed. "You barely wet your tongue. You can't be feelin' nothin' yet."

"Cain't help it. I feel dizzy."

"Well, open your eyes then, Honey," Fay told her, while closing her own, tipping back her head and draining her beer. She slammed the empty mug down with a grin. "Charlie knows what to do with it, don't you?"

I peered meekly at my mother over the rim of my mug. Her eyes remained pinched as she rubbed her forehead. I returned Fay's encouraging grin and killed the glass.

Ida got drunk, more on the violation of her own inhibitions than alcoholic imbibing, because she never even finished her first draw. I had two and most of a third. Fay Rose drained four or maybe five. I lost count once she turned on the radio. I began smoking one of Fay's Chesterfields to Ida's tongue-tied surprise, but eventually shrugged at the situational confusion of right and wrong, and then Fay Rose distracted us from the issue altogether by doing a boogie-woogie dance to a jazzy radio tune and was so funny Ida said she might bust a stitch if she didn't stop. That egged on Fay's hopping and wiggling until sure enough, something broke loose in my mother and she jumped up laughing and wild-eyed, shimmying with arms flung in the air, her fingers just a blur of hootchie-kootchie motion. She and Fay cut up around the room while I clapped and hooted until the music abruptly switched to something slow and bassy like a warm deep thumping in the chest and they collapsed against one another in a tight bear hug. Ida's hair had shaken loose and fallen over Fay's shoulder, her hands lightly tapped the lonesome tempo on Fay Rose's back, and they began to rock back and forth in each other's arms until they were swaying in a gradually evolving dance among the empty chairs and stools.

The next thing I knew, my head was nuzzling between the black fabrics of their mourning dresses and my arms were embracing their waists. I was breathing deeply in a half-willed struggle to swallow an emotion strong as a fist around my throat. We huddled and swayed to the radio's music. The closer I held and was held, the sweeter was the release within me. Though I finally cried then thinking about the whereabouts of Chick, it was the comfort of the leaning and the giddy shifting of our weight, the giving to and taking in of one another's consoling warmth and salty smells, the hands soothing and rubbing my back that eased the choking tension from my throat and all the dead weight from my chest.

"Hold on," I think I said among other forgotten and crazy things about the glory of drinking, feeling loving and drunk and dizzy and able to just hold on.

· Part Three ·

■

DEWAR DREW ON A CIGARETTE THAT HAD NEARLY TURNED TO ASH between his fingers. He inhaled the last of it, flicked the butt toward the lake, and exhaled a heavy sigh into the still night air of the woods. "Me and my brother were twins," he began. "Our momma died the night we were born, and our daddy went crazy. He snatched us up by the ankles like two plucked birds.

"He hauled us out to a lake just like this and threw us back at God, yellin' that he never even wanted a baby nohow, not even a boy, not even two goddamned boys. All his cussin' and hollerin' spooked a couple of fishermen in a boat way out on the water.

"The two fishermen were young and good lookin', both married and feelin' a little pinched by it. They had their rods cast into each other that night. Their bodies were trawlin' for satisfaction and they were close to it when my daddy's commotion brought 'em up short and nervous in the boat as he hurled us into the lake and then ran off rantin' and ravin' into the woods.

"So, they came in toward the shore and began searchin' the muddy water, scoopin' the lake with their arms and a paddle, until they touched our bodies here," Dewar stroked the side of his rib cage and hooked his hand under one arm, "and were able to grab hold and lift us out, one by one.

"They figured us for drowned, but tried anyway to bring us back, squeezin' the water out and forcin' their own air down our throats.

"They were kinda proud and pleased with what they finally managed to do and for a while just sat in the boat, happy, warmin' us in their arms until a guilty shame came over 'em in the quiet and ruined it all.

"They started talkin' low and serious about the crime—the one they'd seen and how the law might see through their own—two buddies who were really strangers, you see, far from home, alone together out on the lake in the middle of the night with no tackle or poles. They argued the different angles of what to do—talked theirselves way around the law. They talked till what they began to talk about seemed like a natural thing to do.

"They decided that each one would keep the boy that he'd saved and agreed that me and my brother be reared apart, that the two of them had never even met and they wouldn't ever meet again. So, that mornin', in towns on far sides of the lake, they each brought home a baby and a lie about how they'd found it."

Dewar held his tongue for a few moments, looking far off over the lake where the black sky met the dark water. He was giving me his story in slow doses. I held my breath in the pause, feeling baited, lured.

"I always knew that I'd been found," he finally began again. "It wasn't said. I wasn't told. I couldn't exactly *remember* it.

"And it didn't really mean nothin' till the whippin's started—tree switches usually, a few times his belt. His hand always hurt the most.

"You know how some kids cling to their mommas like as long as they keep a hand or a finger on her, they're not gonna die?" His arm whipped up and hurled a small stone toward the lake. It made a hollow plunk sound in the dark. "God, I hate kids," he spewed. "Whiny, snot-faced, bed pissers. Dickless, needy little . . ." His lips came together tightly, withdrew between his teeth. It was an unconscious habit I'd noticed before, a restless tension in his mouth muscles, the way he sometimes chewed his lips or gnawed his inner cheek.

"Well," he went on, "I was like that with him instead. Small enough to climb him like a tree, I dug into him, clung tight, hung on . . . kid stuff. Then one day I kissed him, or tried to, like I had a hundred times for years before. He was in a chair and I was in his lap. I thought he was sleepin' and I just put my face where his breath was coming from and got knocked to the floor. 'Don't do that!' he said—like it was a law.

"After that, I couldn't get near him. Almost anything I did broke another law. All of a sudden, he didn't like the way I laughed or cried, the way I looked at him, the way I ate or walked. It felt like he was tryin' to beat every little thing about the way I was out of me.

"My mother was miserable about it, but acted helpless. He was angry, and it spilled onto her. 'Don't aggravate him,' she'd say, like I was to blame. 'Watch your step, Dewar. Stay out of his way.'

"So that's what I did. I snuck off to hidin' places around the house, out of his way. The cellar, the yard, other people's barns, anyplace where I could be alone and figure out what had gone so wrong with me.

"That's how I figured all this out—made it up, the whole thing. Lyin' in bed in the dark, kind of dreamin' with my eyes open, I used to think about another man or a brother, a twin, with a different kinda life, someone I could've been. Sometimes I wondered what it would be like to find him, wondered if I'd know him if I ever did, if he'd like me. I was always curious about . . ."

He turned his face to me, finally. I could feel myself appearing before him as if I hadn't quite been there until just then. His eyes seemed to be looking for something, maybe a reaction. I hoped that I appeared neutral and unphased.

"About what?" I asked.

"Other men and other boys," he said, his eyes drifting to the ground where his fingers idly combed the grass and scratched at pebbles lodged in the dirt. "I just never fit in enough.

"I wasn't good at being pals and pitchin' balls or catchin' fish or ridin' bikes. I was weird. I wanted to share blood with someone, my daddy how he used to be or my lost brother however he was.

"When I was just ten or so, a boy let me kiss him once, like a game. He liked talkin' about girls. He was dyin' to know how they looked and felt down there, what their titties felt like. He didn't know nothin'. So I said I'd show him. He only played along 'cause a practice girl was just a horny joke for him. Wasn't so funny when my old man found us like that, though. The boy took off runnin' for home, and I got the shit beat out of me for the last time."

Dewar leaned back on his arms, stiffened like stakes, his legs outstretched, ankles crossed. He let his head drop back between his shoulders, arching his neck as if all he'd said had cramped his throat. His tone shifted with his posture as he lowered onto his elbows and raised his head to continue.

"I was twelve the first time I ran away for real. Got picked up, though. Tried again a few months later and got caught again. But I kept at it till I was fourteen and made it all the way to Tulsa with a trucker named Jack.

"He picked me up off the Lawton highway one night, this slick lookin' full-blooded Indian with hair down the middle of his back. He was kinda tough but relaxed, quiet but cool; didn't ask nothin' past my name. I was bein' careful. Told him it was Dean. I kept quiet, too, grateful for the ride and especially the speed, didn't ask what he was haulin' or how far he was headed. I didn't care.

"A few miles along, he starts pullin' on a bottle, offers it to me. First taste of whiskey I ever had, and the rush felt good. A few towns streaked by and then nothin' to see but the empty road.

"A little further on, he pulls a joint out from behind his ear, fires it up, tokes on it awhile, then sorta hands it out to me, just enough that I had to reach for it.

"I hit on it a few times but choked and coughed it up worse than my first cigarette. I was a little loose on the whiskey anyway—didn't get nothin' from the pot. Jack says, 'Don't fuck with it, Dean, if you don't know what you're doin',' so I handed it back, and he finished it off down to a pinch of paper. He released that to the wind with a low mumble about 'sacrament to the fathers.' I took it for an Indian thing.

"Am I puttin' you to sleep?" Dewar asked, squinting at me in the dim night. Barely a sliver of a moon lit the woods or the lake despite the sky's thousand stars.

"No," I answered, "I'm listening."

He sat up, pulled his feet in and resettled against the tree. I rested my head atop my knees and studied his profile, as I had since he began. I'd doubted his honesty even before he'd admitted inventing at least half of what he'd already told. It was his sincerity I was looking for now; his reason for lying interested me more than the truth.

"Well, the way my body was hummin' with the road, the dashboard lights in the dark cab, the whiskey and everything put me half to sleep. With my head against the door and my legs up on the seat, I drifted off on the sound of the wind through the windows and every once in a while the swish of Jack's bottle.

"Then, Jack starts yellin', 'Mother fuck! Mother fuckin' hellshit!' and before I could really get my eyes open, the truck was spinnin' and screechin', the whole eighteen-wheeler tiltin' like a fuckin' house about to slam over on its side. There wasn't time to think about pissin' or dyin'. It was over like a jolt of thunder. Jack was thrown so hard and fast against me, it felt like my chest bone had crushed my lungs. I was too stunned to breathe. Everything was so upside down in the pitch black and quiet. Jack was pressed into me like we were froze solid.

"When he finally did stir, I felt it like an ice-crack rippin' right through me. It made me heave, and the more air I gulped in, the more it all turned back to normal.

"Jack started moanin' and crawlin', killin' me 'cause I was like the ground he was tryin' to stand up on. But all I could do was laugh. I started laughin' loud and crazy and couldn't help it. 'Shut up!' he says. 'What's so fuckin' funny?' I wasn't able to tell him, just kept laughin'. But the first thing I remembered after comin' to was the last thing I thought as the truck was rollin' over. I'd seen this big black bird whippin' toward my face, divin' right into my eyes, felt the tip of it slappin' across my face. I thought Jack's hair was some kind of mighty raven about to sweep me up in its wings.

"I could smell the whiskey all over him. 'You hurt?' I asked. I figure it was the booze that saved us. Bein' as loose and limp as a couple of sleepin' cats instead of scared stiff, we were just banged up and bruised, sore as hell, but able to climb out onto the road and take in the sight of that dead truck on its side.

" 'Christ-shit!' Jack said, stompin' around. 'This is bad!'

" 'What happened?' I asked him, already figurin' he'd just nodded off at the wheel. He was still so high he could hardly stand still. 'I saw a baby,' he says. 'A little human baby lyin' in the road right in front of me.'

"There was nothin' one way or another all around us, not a single car or light. He was just stoned crazy, I thought, but we walked back a long way, lookin' everywhere for a fuckin' baby. We didn't find nothin', but that didn't change his mind about it. 'What're we gonna do?' I asked him. 'You get the hell out of here,' he says. 'This is as fuckin' bad as it gets. I got to CB the patrol, no way out of it. I'm gonna fuckin' waste in jail.' He was pacin' around the highway, cussin' like I'd never heard before. 'Where'm I gonna go?' I asked him. 'Wherever the hell you want to go. I don't give a shit. Just get the hell away from me. I ain't doin' time for some punk shithead runaway. You don't know nothin' about this. You don't know me, hear?'

"He climbed up the belly of the truck and crawled back inside the cab. He pitches the empty bottle down to me, then a whole bag of pot. 'Take this shit with you. Throw it away, but not around here. And stay off the highway at least till mornin'. Tulsa's no more than twenty miles ahead. There'll be gas stations before then. Fuckin' go, man!' he yells. 'You don't know me!'

"So, I ran off up the road, hidin' from any cars that came by. Found a rest stop with a crapper and a picnic table, where I slept a little. I ditched his bottle down the shit hole, but I stashed the bag down my shorts.

"Daylight came and I hitched to a station and got another ride there into Tulsa. I was let out at the bus station downtown."

"I've been there," I said, as if latching on to a thread of truth. "What'd you do?"

"Everything, Charlie. It's a big city."

"I mean where'd you stay, how'd you live?"

"I hung out in parks and all-night cafés, the bus station, too. I found a hundred stores to steal what I needed. I bummed spare change and cigarettes. Found a library as good as a hotel. There are so many runaways in the city, there's even somethin' of a church just for them—just an old house, belonged to a feisty ol' woman, who bragged about bein' some kind of preacher even though she never preached at me, and her husband, who was just about the most decent man I ever met. They were like foster parents to who-ever walked in. I could always go there for a cup of coffee and a doughnut, free clothes, people to talk to who didn't bullshit, who sure wouldn't turn me in. Plus," he said, "a bag of dope in Tulsa will get you about anywhere you want to go, Charlie. You want to know about the place where I stayed the most?"

"Sure," I nodded.

"It was a garden—big public place, acres of grass and trees and fountains and flowers. Trees of flowers and bushes of flowers. It was . . . beautiful," he said, as if embarrassed by the word, but I heard sincerity in it, absolute and undoubtable.

"With the sun shinin' and the air warm, there was just no better place to be," he sighed. "It was free and wide open every day and all day, but never crowded; felt like all of it was mine. Time there was the only time in my life I ever thought about God. Thought good about Him, I mean.

"In the middle of it was a big, fancy, clear house with a lot of silos or bell towers." His hands tried to model the vision for me out of the air. "A greenhouse it was called even though it was built of glass. But it was so full of plants and trees that the color green is all you really saw practically bustin' through the panes. It was a glass mansion built around a jungle. It was the most incredible place I ever saw.

"Hot and muggy, like every leaf was a wet tongue, some as broad as doors, just pantin' with life. And off to one side in a bright private corner was the orchids.

"Don't laugh," he said. "They made me want to cry."

"The flowers?"

"It's hard to explain, but they were more than flowers. I don't know any words to describe those colors or those big-headed . . . like beautiful monsters. Some were small though and huddled up like a bunch of butterflies on a tall reed. They were kinda like orphans, each one a weird accident—all brought together cause there was no kind of real garden where they could survive. I thought they would've had a perfume strong and ripe enough to make you drunk. Did you know orchids have no smell at all? I didn't, and I was so disappointed by that . . . until I finally turned on to weed."

"What do you mean by that?" I asked, raising my head level to his gaze.

"What I mean," he began slowly, like a teacher who has the attention of an innocent mind, "is that after the third time or so I tried Jack's pot—got used to it, I guess—and got high for the first time, it was like driftin' straight through any kind of disappointment in the world. Bein' high," he explained, "is like smellin' the perfume of orchids that just ain't there."

I thought I understood, nodded quietly as if I did.

"You ever been high?" Dewar asked.

"In Pryor?" I laughed. "There're no drugs around here. Not even beer on Sundays. We're Christians, you know."

"I'll turn you on sometime," he said as if making a promise, "and then I'll show you an orchid."

It was an unlikely guarantee, but I was warmly flattered that he was offering to share anything with me, especially something as exotic as orchids coupled with something as illicit as weed.

"There was another place, too, where I wound up a lot," he said. "My first stop in Tulsa was the bus station. That was just the end of my ride. I went into the bathroom there to take a leak and wash up and was followed in by a Coast Guardsman stuck between buses on leave from Galveston. He walked off from a duffel on a bench to follow me, came up to a pisser beside me, and started talkin' like he hadn't spoke in so long he had things stored up to say—about how many buses he'd rode, some game he had a bet on, a girl he was dyin' to see.

"The whole time not pissin' a drop but his pants wide open, pullin' and squeezin' his dick, stretchin' it out like taffy, like there was some problem with it or maybe he was tryin' to wring the pee out of it.

"It was weird the way he kept on talkin' while messin' with his dick like that—about how much he hated his whites and his clipped hair, how he'd joined the Guard at eighteen and wasn't even twenty yet, but all the places he'd been.

"I hadn't said nothin' to the guy, had just been listenin', eyein' him head-on, him bein' a sailor and all. I tucked myself in and went over to the sink. The perv turned around so I could see him full-out in the grimy mirror. Still waggin' it back and forth in his hand, says, 'Be a pal, man—help me out here.' I looked back at him, said, 'I don't know what your problem is, man. I'm just washin' up.' And he came a little closer, says, 'There ain't no problem, man. It'll feel good, I promise. Just take it out. Let me do you. You don't have to do nothin'. Here,' he says, layin' a ten next to the sink and diddlin' some more. 'Over here,' he says, backin' into one of the stalls.

"I took the money and thought a minute about just walkin' out. What was he gonna do about it? But, I didn't know shit about Tulsa or where I even was, where else there was to go.

" 'What the hell,' I thought—I'd fooled around some before. At least this guy was beggin' for it, even payin' for it. I let the faggot blow me. No problem."

Dewar fell silent. His lips were sealed tightly between the slow sawing motion of his teeth. The whole night seemed to come to a standstill in his sudden silence, as if he were chewing on the moment, holding time in his bite. I hated how life stopped, like now, and bore down on me for answers. I felt panicked by the pressure to respond.

Until Dewar's story turned so blunt and almost deliberately vulgar, I had listened patiently. The starlight and lakewoods' slight breeze, the time of night, and the low, steady course of his voice had cast a spell that had passed through my guardedness like fingers combing through my hair.

We weren't drinking, and there was no jukebox to score the tale with melancholy lyrics and slide guitars, but I had felt that obtrusive yearning once again, as if I'd not budged from my boyhood barstool, had become that same small audience of one mesmerized by the meandering stream of masculine conversation. I'd allowed his story to seep into me, and it had stoked embers of a smoldering longing.

It was Dewar's nonchalant coarseness, the crude and gritty notions he'd put words to and left hanging in the air with which I now felt blackmailed. The ransom that the thick silence seemed to demand was my own romantic vagary. His lurid recounting felt like spit on the faggy stars in my eyes.

"Bullshit!" I said, my stomach defensively stiffening, readying for a punch.

"What's the matter with you?" he asked.

"Nothing," I told him. "Nothing is the matter with me. It's you! Jesus Christ! I can't believe you could sit here and say something so . . ."

"So what?" Dewar challenged.

"Queer," I said.

"Fuck off!" His voice rang in the air. "What'd you want, Charlie, to spend the night at the lake with me fishin'? Smokin' cigarettes and singin' church songs to the moon?" Dewar kicked the ground, rose to his feet, brushed the dust off his jeans. "Don't pretend you've never . . . ah, just fuck it!"

He slowly turned away and walked toward the lake.

I stayed beneath the tree, straitjacketed by my own crossed

arms, breathing deeply, concentrating on my jumping heart. I studied Dewar's stance against the dark lake water, which broke and scattered the moonlight into shards across its rocking body, until the trick of the light on the water appeared to wrap Dewar in its spell and his body waved and rocked on the shore in the same rhythm.

We'd hooked up at the lake that night at half past twelve. Dewar had escaped out a window and over a fence of the Strang Home for Boys. I had snuck out the creaky back door of the kitchen, where Chick had come and gone at such ungodly hours for most of his life.

Our meeting was an intimate risk. Our friendship from school was recent and tentative. It had an edge like a switchblade. Nothing was settled or secure between us. I was compliant but careful with Dewar. I wasn't used to companionship and didn't trust its boundaries.

Of the person he was, I knew little except what he'd started to reveal that night. To question the boys from the Home about their background was not the thing to do. Such boys were privately pitied around Pryor and Purley, in Strang itself. They were segregated from the mainstream, patronized with a charitable smile, but shunned from the everyday acceptability of family life.

Bright or slow, boys from the Home were passed through school like a social obligation fulfilled. The Home in Strang was like another kind of rendering plant. It took homeless or hopeless boys from all over the state and processed them from the family scraps and discards they were into eighteen-year-old union apprentices for Purley Slaughter or Pryor Rendering.

Dewar was a reputed delinquent, unmanageable in high school terms. Having been thrown into Strang, both the Home and the school just that year at seventeen, he was too far gone to really tame. You could see the old chalkboard biddies pucker up and look right past him in the hallways. Too old and tough for them to sink their claws into, they weren't up for his kind of trouble for an extra term. As a senior, he was just coasting through, practically home free.

He was a year ahead of me, so we had no classes together. I'd first seen him in the library, where I'd elected an hour of advanced study hall to avoid another semester of gym. He was on detention for a schoolyard fight, smeared with dirt and sporting a shiner around a swollen eye. His good eye was scanning a *National Geographic* he'd slapped on one end of the long table before he flung himself down before it with the same violent disregard. He kept blotting the flow of a nosebleed with the cuff of his white shirt. I pretended to ignore him from my place three or four chairs away at the same table, but he was a provocative sight. The book before me lost its meaning in the racket of his vibrant colors—his blue eye, violet bruise, grass stains, and blood spots. Between stolen glances, his scent was a further distraction, like a breath of wildlife overpowering the smell of paper, leather, cloth tape, and ink pads; a strong, not unpleasant, odor seeped with iron, salt, smells of deep holes in rich earth.

He showed as much interest in me as in the pages of the magazine that he turned quickly, one after another, obliviously. I was unable to find my lost place in my own history text. I couldn't concentrate and couldn't find relevancy in the words or what they stood for. The pages of his magazine were more compelling, the shuffling sound of their rapid turning, the slow motion of their falling, their gloss catching the light, the lush colors of their pictures passing through his fingers. I felt hypnotized by the collage of ferns, forests, fauna, elephant hide, bared breasts, black feet.

Between and sometimes during classes he hung around the smokehole, which was whatever patch of gravel was left empty from day to day in the teachers' parking lot. Smoking allowed me a certain right, not into the company of the rather rough cast of boys who staked the claim on that daily space, but at least into their territory. I kept quiet and to the edges.

On the fringes himself, Dewar found me there. Completely without money, he began bumming cigarettes, and as I always willingly complied, the nicotine craving became a kind of gravity that initially drew us together and held us in a mutual proximity for as long as it took to finish a smoke.

As gradually as the dark ring around his eye had faded and finally disappeared, we had became companions of a sort, tolerant of each other's mostly silent company. We shared an intolerance for almost everybody and everything else around us. He made me laugh and I think he tried to. He was full of bitterness, which made him capable of violence but he wasn't a bully. He just didn't take crap.

We didn't push into each other's pasts, but I think we each sensed in the other some common wrong deep and tender inside.

To befriend a person such as Dewar Akins was somewhat of a familiar calling for me. He was not the imaginary demon of my childhood, and I was no longer the zealous missionary beating the devil out of my path. He was not Bub debating my conscience or conspiring with my anger to burn down all of Pryor. He was real life, flesh and blood.

His flesh is what made me tense and on guard every second with him. My attention to his body was like a vice I couldn't control, a strange desire in the back of my mind since I'd first set eyes on him.

The more time we spent together the stronger and more intrusive my feelings became. He seemed so comfortable with his own body as to be reckless about it. While, for me, the most innocent brush of our fingers while passing him a match or the accidental knock of our knees beneath a table as he lunged into a lunch tray of ice-cream sandwiches made me so self-conscious that I anticipated such chance connections in order to avoid them. I kept a safe distance. The maintenance or narrowing of that gap depended entirely on him. I had a craving, a curiosity, a passionate willingness for whatever Dewar was offering.

I'd accepted his dare to ditch school one day when the temperature was warm enough to be distracting and he'd suggested going to the lake instead of first class. Even though I'd led the way there, I was following his nerve.

We simply killed a few hours tramping through the woods, kicking stones, looking for arrowheads. He hadn't been to the lake before and I showed him around the various trails and paths, pointing out the ones that led to the boat docks, the most scraggly and hidden one that led to the Turtle Man's houseboat, and the one that I claimed as my own, which led us to my private place beneath a huge old elm tree with spoked roots spread out toward the water. The roots made several wide laps to settle back against. He paid close attention to the winding route, as if memorizing the land. The lake brought out a gentleness in him I hadn't seen so openly before. His sarcasm softened a bit and his humor lost some of its raunchy edge.

Without much detail, as we reclined beneath the tree, talking more to the broad stretch of the water than to each other, he had spoken a little about himself, that day.

"I'm *glad* I don't have family," he claimed. "That makes me troubled, you know—it's officially recorded. But, what about you? You only got half a family. I'd say you're at least half troubled."

"Maybe," I admitted, "but your opinion's not official."

He grinned. Dewar had a sly grin, tight and narrow, subtle on his mouth, less so in the squint of his eyes. "You're good with words. One thing I like is the way you talk."

"Can't help it," I said, "my mother spoke in tongues when I was little."

"See," he laughed, "you're as much a smart-ass as me, but you just come across smart. You're not as serious as you act."

"Nope," I said, surprised by the attention the comment implied. "And you're not nearly the ass you seem to be, Dewar."

"Punk!" he said, his face overwhelmingly close and unfocused. I could taste and smell the damp spray of his breath on my lip. He'd moved so quickly, I hadn't seen him coming. My whole body balled up in a tense reflex. His arms wrapped around my chest, his leg and hip swung over me and he knocked me to the grass on my side

with his laughter loud against my ear. The tighter he wrapped himself around me, the more I relaxed, even though I realized the point
of his bear hug was for me to hate it, to fight against the oppression
of it.

But, I liked the feel of him. I was grateful that it'd finally happened so easily and naturally. It would have been unthinkable for
me to have touched him so casually, under any pretext.

"You're not much of a fighter, are you?" he said, slipping loose
from me, stretching out on his back.

"You haven't made me mad," I told him.

"I could hurt you if I wanted," he bragged, staring lazily into
the sky.

I couldn't argue with what I'd never doubted.

My only inkling of what could transpire in the lakewoods in the
middle of the night was planted in my childhood by Fay Rose's
gossip of naked teenagers caught in the bushes by the sheriff's
flashlight. I had been too young in Fay Rose's opinion to overhear
such scandal then, and so she had lowered her voice and had
spelled the offensive "naked" to Ida. Her dramatics had only amplified the implications to my imagination well into my current
year. Of course, from the talk in Tulsa barrooms and then the
high-school smoke holes and ball-game bleachers, the full picture
of naked coupling in dark woods had been fleshed out for me.

I knew that such winked-about goings on should not apply to
Dewar and me, neither of us being the correct sex for sex, and yet
I was on edge with a nervous sexual arousal anyway when, just a
few days later, he'd dared me to meet him at the lake that night.

Amidst the familiarity of specific trees and the scent of pine and
the dank mud-bottomed lake so well known to me since I was a
kid escaping the oppression of summer in a house with Ida, I had
begun telling Dewar some of the stories from my life. He had listened quietly and that had urged me on. I avoided looking at him,
but had spoken to the woods themselves.

I felt confessional and somewhat relieved to finally put my voice
around such long kept secrets. I didn't feel any betrayal of Ida or

Chick by telling Dewar the story of my family. Their secret histories and outright lies were as much a part of me as their blood, and
I trusted Dewar with the truth that was, after all, mine.

I had told him all about Bub, about the weirdness of his death
and his death's-door kiss; about the naturalness of Chick's death
and how my only kiss of him was on his dead-cold lips; and about
how Ida had changed since then and had taken over a beer joint
where I was born, that she once called a den of sin. In essence, I
had left myself wide open for Dewar Akins as we settled shoulder
to shoulder against the ground that night, the soles of our shoes
facing the lake, our faces to the crescent moon beyond the elm
branches and leaves. With hardly a heart's beat of a pause, Dewar
had begun the queer tale of his own orphanhood.

My eyes were fixed the few yards ahead of me, on Dewar, still
rooted to the edge of the lake. The flickering water, the repetitive
rise and fall of the cicadas asserting their patience with the night
and the sporadic croak of bullfrogs cushioned the pathway to him
with a pulsing viscous sensation. One foot led the other through a
realm of feelings so slippery they were beyond my understanding.

His unbuttoned shirttail flapped around his torso in the soft
wind. His frayed jeans were too big and hung heavily from the
thick belt that cinched them low on his hips. His fists, burrowed
into his front pockets, dug the belt tighter into him and his elbow-
locked arms against his sides forced his shoulders up into arches
nearly hugging his ears.

"You're an absolute heathen, Dewar. Orphaned into the devil's
arms," I declared. "But, fear not! The salvation of the Lord is at
hand!"

He twisted around from the waist, his eyes somewhat reluctant
to leave the entrancement of the lake. I stood behind him, one arm
rigidly raised to heaven with a single finger pointing the way.
Dewar grinned slightly with a creased brow in partial apprehension
of my sudden possession by the Spirit. As he shifted his feet to

meet the vision of me full faced, I opened my arms outward in the wingspan of a grounded angel.

"You must empty your heart of its abundant sin. You must be cleansed in the waters of redemption. You must forsake all others . . . but me."

Our eyes locked. "Who are you?" he asked.

"Hallelujah," I howled to the moon. I grabbed him by the shoulders and shook him hard. I pulled his face close enough to kiss. "I'm the fisherman of men, you savage peckerwood. I am the savior of your hitchhiking soul. I'm Brother Hope, Dewar. Are you ready to get baptized tonight?"

"Hell, no!" he shouted.

His breath exploded against my face. I grabbed him in my arms and raised him off the ground. I felt the belly spasms of his laughter against my own chest but struggled to carry on with my mission. I staggered, heavy-footed, toward the lake. Dewar fought and struggled in my arms.

"Crazy fucker, put me down," he yelled. But he didn't mean it. He was happy where he was. I could feel that, too.

The lake was icy even through my shoes and socks. Mid-shin into the water, I lost my balance, what with Dewar's kicking and wrestling, and we crashed into its shallow freezing pallet. We jerked and twisted like two fish in a net. Our splashing about only intensified the shock of soaked clothes to skin, and the whole time Dewar was cursing and laughing and choking in a joyous fit of abandon. I wondered if this was love.

I kept my hands on him however I could, clutching at his shirt, latched around his belt. I grabbed at him like a prized catch I couldn't afford to lose.

The wind on our soaked clothes drove us into deeper water for comfort. We stopped wrestling and just stood in the lake up to our shoulders, face to face, while our arms floated freely into and off of one another.

I asked him honestly what had happened to him in Tulsa.

He turned his head away, said, "I told you," somewhat bitterly.

"I know, Dewar," I tried to assure him of my willingness to listen again. "But, how'd you get here?"

"I got picked up eventually," he said. "For hustlin' a cop.

"Hustlin' is a lot like hitchin'," he said. "A lot of standin' around in the middle of nowhere with your thumb out tryin' to look casual and harmless instead of like some kind of perv. After a while, you learn to read people from a far distance. You know who's cruisin' by how fast they're goin', how straight they're drivin', even what they're drivin'. You can just tell whether they're goin' to slow down for a closer look or speed on by like you're not even there. Sometimes a ride'll stop a ways off, make you walk a little 'cause they haven't quite decided to pick you up yet. They've still got the doors locked, and you can see by the brake lights that their minds are goin' back and forth, off and on as you come closer. You know a woman'll never stop; with men you can never be sure. They might peel out just as your hand reaches the door.

"I was always on the lookout for police, and sometimes that meant leavin' the streets. I was too young to get into the bars," he grinned. "Not the kind of joints you managed to get into at half my age, Charlie!"

"What can I say?" I played along. "I was mature for my age."

He splashed me with a face full of water. I sprayed him back with a hard shake of my hair in his face. "Oh, shit!" he screamed, "It's a bird! It's a bird!" and he ducked under the water, out of sight.

When he surfaced, he wiped the clowning from his face with the water that he rubbed away with both hands.

"I knew without even tryin' to know that the toilets could be a hustlin' place—and not just the bus station, Charlie. Almost any of 'em, anywhere.

"If I couldn't pick up cash, I'd settle for a ride across town or a joint or beer, maybe a drive-in hamburger or just a single night in a real house. It was like barterin' what I had for what I could get.

"Well, what it finally got me was busted for solicitation. You know that fancy word, Charlie? I know it from my official record. It means a fuckin' lyin' cop.

"But, since I was a minor and a runaway and my folks refused custody, I was sent here to the Home until they change their minds or until I'm eighteen or until I die of boredom."

"I don't think you can die of boredom, Dewar. I'm living proof."

"I ain't planning on it," he said, his body levitating to the surface of the water in front of him, his head sinking back until his ears were buried and he fanned his arms in a backstroke toward the clay shore. I followed him in a weighted trudge until we had returned to our spot beneath the elm.

We began peeling off our sopping clothes.

"I feel like I'm skinnin' a rabbit," Dewar complained with his pants inside out around his knees.

I couldn't help laughing at the sight of him struggling with the drenched denim. He sat, grunting and cursing under his breath, his underwear grass-stained where his butt rocked against the ground.

"These will never dry out by morning," I laughed, stooping down to pull the rolled socks off his feet. He leaned back on his elbows, kicking out one leg at a time until I'd inched the jeans off of him. I hung them over a low limb next to my own, picked up his shirt from the grass and hooked it on a twig of the same limb. Before I could turn around, Dewar's shorts hit me in the back with a cold wet smack. I spun around and stepped on them with my bare foot. There he was, flat out on the grass, one hand behind his head, ankles casually crossed, a hoodlum's smirk on his face, an erection not too well covered by the hand that loosely cupped it.

Defying my shyness and mustering a grin to approximate Dewar's, I stepped awkwardly out of my own wet shorts, twisted and wrung them out for a few nervous seconds and finally just tossed them onto the grass.

"Those are gonna be swarmin' with ants if you don't hang 'em up somewhere," he smiled.

"I don't think I'll be putting them back on," I answered.

I took a few strides toward him, my hand modestly hiding what swung freely between my legs with each naked step and sat down beside him. I removed my grandfather's retirement watch from my wrist, studied its watertight face in the moonlight, and placed it in the heel of my nearby shoe. "Two-thirty-five," I announced, reclining next to him.

"I used to come here all the time a few summers ago—for the privacy," I told him. "It's easy to feel like you're the only one in the whole world here, isn't it?"

"I don't much care for that feeling," Dewar sleepily responded. His head was next to my feet, and we each stared overhead.

"Me neither, really," I agreed. "I almost always do though—always have. Bub was usually with me here."

"He was kind of, for you, like the twin brother I dreamed up, wasn't he?" he suggested. "Except your Bub was as different as you could imagine him and mine was just the same as the me in a mirror."

"I don't even think I know what I look like," I confessed. "When I see my face in a mirror, it's like I can't quite see it, because the mirror is in the way. When I look away, the whole image goes. I can't remember my face like I remember anyone else's. It's a picture that doesn't hold together, you know? I can close my eyes and see you sharp as a knife, but I can't see myself."

My eyes were fixed to a particular star, one of the smallest and dimmest among hundreds of brighter, more obvious and sparkling points. I couldn't see Dewar at all, not even peripherally, yet I felt him looking up the length of me, sensed it somehow through my skin as if his eyesight had a weight that my entire skin prickled beneath. My dick swelled against my hand the instant he touched me.

His hand came down, soothingly cool, on my leg just above my knee. "You don't have to do nothin'," he said. "Just this once only, I promise, Charlie. You can pretend you're drunk, so passed out drunk you won't even have to remember. Just this once, I promise. It'll feel good. Say it's all right."

A couple of syllables of sound tumbled out of me. Dewar's hand remained motionless. "Go on," I said hoarsely, cleared my throat. "It's all right."

With my tentative permission, my life shifted forward with an energy much greater than my will and with a motion that made me dizzy, meek, and confounded as if born again. Dewar's hands defined my body, sculpted its vague boyish matter into an adult form that was surprisingly masculine and joyous in its manhood.

His hands touched me with liberty, unsatisfied to rest in any one place, concerned with a mission that eventually became my own. He touched me with his soft lips from my chest to my knees, leaving moist marks that ached in the air that wasn't his breath when his mouth lifted and moved away.

I deliberately contained my pleasure while Dewar expelled his in loud moans and sighs. My closed eyes became the only barrier between our mirrored figures meshed in their sliding and pressing efforts until Dewar's face fell heavily into mine and his mouth pried my lips apart. It felt as if the seal of the noisy self inside me was broken and a great energy rushed up to meet his tongue in the melding twin caverns of our mouths. The lids of my eyes rose up, Dewar's jaw rose in a taut point upward, his shoulders pulled back, my groin rose up against his, straining the ropy ligaments that bound its pleasure within me as the warm, fast spasms of our coming glued us at the stomach, face to face but for a breathless frozen moment that seemed, surely, to have been a second of God's eternity.

As my blood gradually retreated to its normal course, leaving my extremities unengorged and listless against the rested weight of Dewar, the whole environment appeared softened at its edges and throbbed like Dewar's heart, which I could feel through his ribs, now heavy and inanimate against me. The invisible crickets seemed to be applauding the transformation of their lakewoods with their rhythmic leg music. His weight upon me was the most alive sensation I'd ever held until my rational thoughts returned from their blood journey of my body's unmapped wilderness. Then I felt compelled to speak, to use words as a bridge back to reality from this strange ethereal glow of thoughtlessness, back to the comfort of my own discomfort.

Each second beneath him increased my self-consciousness. The trickling bead of perspiration beneath one arm. A pebble pressing into my buttock. The mingled scent of our ejaculate, spoiled-smelling in its coagulation, drying and tightening the skin like a thin scab around my hip.

Dewar ungently lifted and rolled off me.

"Sorry," he said, tossing the apology haphazardly from the side of his mouth while turning his face slightly away.

"It's all right," I said, sitting up, scouting the grass for the cigarettes. "I mean, don't be sorry." My false assurances belied my own creeping panic, the taste of guilt rising in my throat and my near-frantic search for the cigarettes. I was desperate to occupy my hands.

Dewar handed me the half-crushed pack, dropping it to the ground between us before I had a hold on it. "Sorry," he said again.

"It's all right," I repeated, irritated with his tone. I dug into the pack and salvaged the last bent and flattened cigarette. I stroked and straightened it between my fingers and lit it luckily with the only remaining match, inhaled as deeply as my lungs would accommodate, smothering my hurt feelings with the smoke.

"I never kissed no one before," Dewar confessed. "I didn't mean to do that."

It seemed the toll of what we'd done weighed as heavily on him as it did on me. But I chose not to be pinned down by it just then. I didn't want to talk about it yet. I smiled conspiratorially. I broadened my mouth and bared my teeth at him. "I was so drunk, Dewar, I don't really remember," I said.

"Don't do that," he commanded seriously. "I got to tell you something. I've never kissed nobody before, not a guy. I never did nothing before with a guy. And I ain't never been to Tulsa, either, or nowhere else really. I've been raised in foster homes my whole life, one after another. I've always been the new kid or the foster son or the orphan boy. I never knew my folks at all, and if I have any family, they've never stepped forward to make a claim on me. I feel like an asshole right now." He was almost mumbling, rocking a little, speaking as much to himself as to me. I wanted to gather my own wits together and escape before the same devil of confession possessed me. But some entity with the power of speech, already within me, spoke through my lips with reason and compassion.

"Dewar," I interrupted calmly, "it's all right. Truth is, I wanted this to happen. I'm not sorry about it."

"You don't understand, Charlie," he said desperately. "You don't understand. I ain't queer, I swear to God. I mean, I don't think it's the worst thing or nothin'. I know lots worse. I grew up around all kinds of boys everywhere. It's common and don't mean nothin'. It's not supposed to mean nothin'. I lied about it 'cause I don't really care. I lied to you about it 'cause I thought maybe you did care and 'cause I like you, Charlie. I never liked anybody as much. I don't know how to make somebody like me. I was just barterin' what I got for what I wanted. But this doesn't feel right now. I mean it did feel right—what we did, Charlie. It wasn't supposed to but it did, and that's fucked me up. I don't know how to lie myself out of it now." He sat, rubbing his arms, then pushed his hair back off his forehead. He finally met me eye to eye.

I handed over the cigarette and he took it. The smoke seemed to settle him. "You talk too much," I said. "Maybe it's best to just feel and wait about . . . all this, Dewar. You know you don't have to be a fag for me to like you. I liked you fine before you were."

A slight grin escaped his cannibalistic lip chewing. "So, are we friends?" he asked.

"More like brothers," I ventured, "maybe twins."

Our eyes remained locked for a moment more. Dewar was hunched forward over bent knees, hiding himself in his own shadows, but he opened up with a sudden relaxation, fell back into the grass with his legs splayed like a book. My gaze slowly traveled over his body then for the first time. If he felt my eyes the way I'd felt his, he didn't seem to mind or stir. His stillness in his naked body seemed completely honest. For nothing more than the appreciation of that, I moved and kneeled a little closer beside him.

"What's this?" I asked, touching the center of his chest where the breastbone was concave like a smooth empty nest. My fist would have fit there if I'd tried.

He remained dead still, calm and passive beneath my curious touch. "It's a fisherman's thumbprint," he said, "from when I was a day-old baby, still soft enough to dent. And then later, it got deepened by the chin of a fallin' Indian. Did I say his hair was a bird?"

"Yea," I smiled, "that's what you said." I slid my hand away and he sat up, began searching me up and down. I assumed he was looking for some such flaw in me to question, but instead he began scratching at my side, flaking away at the dried patch of our come.

"You need to wash up," he said, digging his fingers into me. It tickled, and I tried to pull away.

"Stop!" I yelled. "I've been baptized once tonight."

"But, you've had a relapse, brother. Come on."

Dewar rose to his feet and pulled me up with him. Now he had me by the waist with his arms and was struggling to heave me over one shoulder.

He waded deep enough into the lake so that I simply floated out of his arms. We cleaned ourselves with bare hands and swam around in separate spheres. We felt no need to further antagonize each other; perhaps we were tired of the constant attention. The engulfment of the cold lake was a stilling sensation that eased us back into our twin solitudes.

Then, once again, we found ourselves shivering like cold, wet dogs beneath the elm tree, this time already unclothed but our clothes more soaked than us and well caked with lake mud.

"Shit!" I cursed, bent over to retrieve Chick's watch from my boot. "It's after five!" I slipped my hand through the Twist-o-Flex band. "Ida'll be up in less than an hour!" I thought aloud.

"So will General Nuisance," Dewar said, stepping back and forth in place, hugging himself for warmth.

I looked curiously in his direction.

"That's what we call him . . . at the Home, behind his back, of course, as if he could hear it anyway. The old general who runs the place."

I'd begun yanking our clothes off the limb but they were all sopping, too wet even to pry ourselves into. With no time to actually ever state aloud or rationalize the decision, we rolled them into balls, worked our gritty feet into wet shoes, and began creeping back to town, stark naked. The way out of the woods itself was no problem. We stayed off the cleared pathways in case any pre-dawn fishermen might be heading for the lake, and we clawed through the thick brush, vines and trees of wild land that actually shortcut us to the edge of the old blacktop turnoff to Strang. Most traffic took the newer highway that looped past Pryor and Purley on the opposite side of the lake, bypassing Strang altogether. Still, we leaned out of the woods cautiously in search of any distant traffic.

The Home was less than a half mile down the road. Dewar could cut through the sorghum fields that lined the road all the way up to the Home's back lawn.

"Think you'll make it?" I asked.

"If I don't rip my balls off on the chain-link fence and some fucker hasn't locked the window."

"Go on then. I'll see you at school, I guess."

"Smokehole before first bell?" he asked.

"Sure."

"Well, good night then." The sun was rising on the other side of the highway, but it seemed the most appropriate farewell.

"Good night," I said.

We stood, hunched behind the leafy curtain of the woods, our cold outfits pressed against our crotches. "Well," Dewar said again. He extended his right hand, palm up. "Good night, Charlie."

I put my palm to his, and his fingers closed tightly. "Good night," I said again.

Then Dewar raised my hand to his bowed head until it reached his mouth and then kissed it.

Lifting his eyes, he asked, "Was that queer or what?" He grinned broadly but didn't wait for judgment. Tearing off across the highway with long-legged strides, he leaped the wooden railing of the pasture like a white-tailed buck. The golden sunrise on his naked back melted like butter into the crops.

I stood there alone on the edge of the woods for at least five minutes, waiting to turn back into myself before going home. But as the sun grew gradually higher, I remained unfamiliar and changed. I felt like I knew something, whose value I alone had any inkling of and, by its very nature, something that I would not share with the law and order of my external life.

I thought at first that Dewar had run off with the courage that had anchored me through the night, that the courage was actually his to begin with and he had only spared me enough for the course of the moon's sail across our nude backs. But a bit of it was my own after all, I found, and I felt it on me there, shadowed by the woods' brush on the side of the road in the peering sunlight. It seemed to cover the shamefulness of my nakedness like a garment of new skin and by the comfortable fit, felt like it would wear for life, that I'd be buried in that newfound brazenness.

A gnat buzzed around my ear. I slapped at it like an alarm clock, suddenly alert to my predicament. I glanced at my watch, quickly surveyed the road, then darted across it and the field opposite. I circled the trailer park, then the back lot of the Dairy Queen to the car lot where I zigzagged between the fenders and bumpers. I snuck through more fields and then residential alleys no more than wide footpaths linking the backyards of far-flung neighbors. Eventually I came up behind Mrs. Mosey's rotting garage. Her old hound must have smelled my sweat and began barking from within its half-collapsed walls. He growled himself quickly back to sleep, and I cut across the dirt driveway in front of our garage, climbed the back porch steps, and snuck through the screen door, which whined painfully on its unoiled hinges.

I'd moved into the back bedroom of the house a year or so after Chick's death. It was smaller than my first room across the hall from Ida's, but with half of Esther's furniture dismantled and stored in the basement, it was big enough and more private. Ida had not objected, had even helped with the transition, seeing it, I think, as one more change, among a slew of changes that had overtaken her so relatively late in life. She took to the idea stoically and was a good sport about my teenage proposal for more privacy, even though her time at the bar had separated us in time and space more privately than any bedroom walls and doors ever could. The entire house was mine alone from after school till after midnight, when Fay Rose drove Ida home from the bar. By then, I was in bed behind a closed door at the end of the hall and she retired noiselessly, shortly thereafter. She still managed to rise by six and prepare us both a breakfast while I bathed and dressed for school.

It was a silent meal, as it always had been. There was nothing about my life at school and, until that morning, nothing to my life at all, that I felt compelled to share with her. After three years in Chick's joint, her own life was as routine with the bar regulars, juke music, keg deliveries, and Fay Rose's constant companionship as it ever was as a widowed housekeeper to Chick and me. She was tight-lipped without being secretive about it.

Her initial shame about her fate as a barmaid had long ago been swallowed with the bitter dose of necessity, but I think she continued to harbor a certain shame on my behalf and what she assumed to be my feelings about her and what circumstances had made her into. Occasionally she related some funny incident from the bar, but it was always told without reference to the bar itself or to the circumstances of drink that inspired such outrageous stories. She

told these stories with the propriety of a receptionist sharing a
glimpse of her life at a respectable office. Many times she made the
point of our financial solvency, quoting Fay Rose, who kept the
accounts, about our profits and savings.

"We have a decent income, Charlie," she'd announce and
reannounce the first Tuesday morning of every month, "now that
it's not being guzzled and squandered. More than I ever dreamed
possible for me and you. Fay Rose says there'll be a college education for you by the time you need it. Praise be to God," she'd
add superstitiously, afraid to credit such blessings to her own hard
work and long hours.

My room was accessible by two doors, one directly off the rear
porch. I had barely unstuffed the pillow dummy of myself from beneath the covers of the bed when Ida's knuckles rapped against the
hallway door. "OK," I hoarsely answered, as if stirred from a decent night's sleep. I shoved my wet clothes far under the bed,
wrapped a robe around myself, and double-checked the sounds of
breakfast preparation through the back door before creeping out
the other, down the hall, and into the bathroom.

I leaned into the medicine-chest mirror. My hair was wind-
blown and tangled, my complexion still flushed from the hike. My
eyes were as clear as prized marbles. My prominent nose appealed
to my sense of handsomeness, and I turned my head in both directions to study my profile from objective angles. And as I untied and
shrugged the robe off my shoulders to the floor, I was surprised by
the sense of uprightness and outwardly presence that emanated
from my body. This particular vanity impressed me, not with any
vainglorious pride, but with the confidence that I was at least attractive enough to be memorable. I was impressed finally that I was
not invisible.

I closed my eyes and was able to see the mirror image of my
own face, which I held in my head for a moment while my hands
wandered down the front of me, recalling the touch of Dewar's
hands, and I thought of his face grinning on the verge of telling

before it vanished. I opened my eyes to the overhead bulb shining on the bathroom tile, the bathwater rocking near the rim of the tub, and I let go of my body to, once more, submerge, soak, and cleanse it of any queer traces of love.

Part Four

■

Fated as she seemed to be to passing the tail end of her widowhood taking in other people's ironing by the piece or, God help them, other people's children by the hour, Ida was the most unlikely barkeeper in the history of Oklahoma juke joints.

With Fay Rose Savory's advice and full-hearted assistance, Ida had Chick's joint reopened for business the week following his burial. In fact, over time, she became filled with the beer-selling spirit. Ida never acquired the taste for drink or for its effect, which perhaps was the key to her success as a barkeeper. She kept a sober, religious eye on the operation and, unlike Chick, lacked the fellow-drinker's sympathy for the thirst of regulars too broke to pay, so she also held on to a profit. "In God We Trust. All Others Pay Cash," read a placard she taped to the mirror above the tacklebox till. She swept the deadbeats off the books by cutting off all tabs. More than once, she literally chased a few freeloaders off the premises with a broom.

Owen the Turtle Man, a legendary, local hermit who lived deep in the lakewoods, in rambling scrap-built quarters, whose core was a houseboat as old as Noah's reputed ark, persistently riled my mother's broom-swatting rage with his routine raggedy-man appearances.

No one seemed to know for sure just where Owen had come from or who his people once were. He'd always just been a part of the Pryor landscape. The smokehole lore was that he'd crawled out

of the lake one night at the beginning of time, like some old snap-
per, and that he only appeared to be a man. He supposedly lived
on turtle stew eaten out of turtle shell bowls. He made all sorts of
things with turtle shells, which he peddled around town: ashtrays,
soup ladles, baby rattles, helmetlike hats for very small heads, as
well as a turtle oil love potion.

Ida's fear of men had eased up some, but something about
Owen, nevertheless, overrode her newly grown tolerance and in
the name of her right to refuse service she'd chase the Turtle Man
out the bar door and halfway into the road, calling him a heathen,
a scavenger, and once, according to Fay Rose, a fizzlin' peckerwood.

"That poor soul Owen came back today," Fay whispered to me,
one afternoon. It had become my custom to stop by the bar on my
way home from school. It was about all Ida and I saw of one another in those years following Chick's death.

My mother was just a few yards away, filling a clip-on display
rack with bags of pig rinds and goobers and chips. She removed a
bag of pistachios from its alligator clamp and slid it down the bar
like a shuffleboard puck. "Why don't y'all sample these and see if
they're as fresh as the secrets you're tellin'."

"No, thank you, Honey," Fay sweetly replied, pushing the bag
into my hands. "Nuts mess up my colon. I didn't know you and
Owen were no secret, though," she teased.

Ida turned her back. "You love to talk stupid, don't you, Rose?"

"Can't say that I do," Fay Rose replied. "Course," she kept on
with a widening grin, pouring herself a coffee refill, "a woman
chasin' a man halfway to Purley with a broom, like some kind of
old witch or tomboy. . . . Well, some *might* call *that* stupid, I
reckon. What do you think, Hon?" she winked at me. "You think
that sounds stupid, or what?"

"I'm not sure," I half-conspired as Ida cleared her throat with a
loud snort and pushed her recently bobbed hair behind her ears.
"Why won't you let the Turtle Man come in here," I asked Ida.
"Chick always did."

" 'Cause this ain't a bus station. Why should that white trash take up room to gawk and chew the fat with those who can afford to pay? I don't like his looks, and he smells like a bucket of fishguts!"

"Oh, I can't see how he can help that," Fay Rose said, adjusting the strap of her underclothes and smoothing the crease of her pants as she crossed her legs. "There's only so much a man can do. It ain't his fault he's ugly, but, of course, he could bathe, I reckon."

"I mean the way he looks at me!" Ida spewed with exasperation, her fists on her hips.

"Well, what do you mean by that?" Fay asked.

Ida shifted her weight and relaxed her fists, in which she realized she held two crushed bags of Fritos. "Oh! *You* should know," she said, tossing the bags into the trash can.

"Know what?"

"How men are," Ida answered heavily.

Fay Rose laughed under her smoky breath. "What I know about men and what you know, Ida Hope, are not necessarily the—"

"I am not a child, Fay Rose," my mother interrupted. "I don't know why you always talk down to me like I was one."

"Well, for pity's sake!" Fay sputtered. "I swear I don't know what you mean. Was I talkin' to her like she was a child, Charlie?"

Swerving around any involvement in this conflict, I asked Ida, "What is it exactly you don't like? About Owen, I mean."

"I don't feel like goin' into this with you, Charlie," I was told, as Ida hauled the now empty box of assorted snacks to the incinerator out back.

"Or nobody else for that matter," she added a few minutes later, once she'd returned. She leaned back against the mirror with her arms folded across her chest, looking peeved. Then she sprang to life again with, "When was the last time I went prying into your likes or dislikes? Some things don't need to be spelled out, Fay Rose. My life ain't no TV story for your entertainment. You know good and well how fresh that Turtle Man stares at me. I may pretend not to hear half the loose talk that goes on here, and maybe you think it's right funny to pass the day like a floozy just fannin' it on, but I won't be stripped down by no man's eyes and talked about to my face like a cheap you-know-what, not on my own property."

"Why, Ida Hope, you're talkin' like a crazy woman, or a crazy jealous one! Calm down, Honey! I've been knowing these men since I was a newlywed. I worked the renderin' line with half of 'em. They's just full of hot air when it comes to women. I can't help it if I got a sexy sense of humor and you don't, but I'd like to know when Owen or any other of these fellers ever looked crosseyed at you? Why, every one of 'em's scared to death you won't serve 'em lessen they say a prayer first."

"You are fibbin' for sure!" Ida said. "Hulon Turbo sure wasn't sayin' no prayer about my rear end the other night."

"Hulon? That ol' coot? What'd that rascal say?" Fay leaned forward as if finally engaged by the words she and Ida had been tossing back and forth.

Ida pulled her lips between her teeth as if she were biting down on the urge to say anything more. "I took him his beer over there to that table," she began, motioning with her head. "Remember he come in here with that Wiley what's-his-name from over at Strang?"

"Hazelle Gourd's old man," Fay Rose nodded.

"Well, whoever . . . He was decent enough," Ida continued, gathering her hair into a tail high on the back of her head. "I gave 'em their draws and Hulon handed me two dollars, so I was walkin' back here to the box for his change and I hear him talkin' some filth to that Gourd man about my rear end."

"Oh! What'd he say?" Fay squirmed on the stool and Ida grinned despite herself.

"Said, 'nice to see what's finally moved into the seat of Chick's ol' britches.' "

"Oh, shoot! Is that all?" Fay's posture deflated of all enthusiasm.

"I let on like I forgot his change," Ida added smugly.

Fay waved her hand and flatly stated, "Well, you're askin' for that kind of talk wearin' your daddy's old pants. I've said it before and now I've said it again."

"Fay Rose, you have been trying to nag me into pants for a dozen years."

"Yes, Honey, but those ain't just pants. Those is your deceased daddy's trousers! For pity's sake! It's not like you can't afford the Penney's catalogue."

"They're too good to throw out," Ida huffed, poking her hands into her britches pockets. Fay had been needling my mother about her "get-ups" since long before she began wearing Chick's pants, so now she sat wordlessly, sipping her coffee, assured that her opinions on the subject had been well expressed.

I cleared my throat in the pause. "So, what's it got to do with the Turtle Man?" I asked.

"He's been out there on the lake so long with nothin' but those turtles," Fay kidded. "Ha! Maybe he's turned on by a gal in men's pants."

"Would you hush?" Ida slapped Fay Rose on the knee.

Fay swatted my mother's shoulder, then her own thigh for emphasis. "Maybe he's turned funny and thinks you're some kind of sexy, long-haired boy. One of them hippie types."

"Abomination, Fay Rose!" Ida blushed. "Don't you know when you've gone too far?"

I lit a cigarette and turned my eyes to the window. Fay Rose continued to hum with her own laughter. Finally my mother's own version of a snicker broke through the damn of her tight lips. "You are just too mean to live," she told Fay Rose.

"Me? Honey, you're the one that chases him up the road with a stick."

My eyes were dulled by the view of the empty road through the bar window. The sky rose up from the flat pavement in tedious gradations of gray. From the gravel parking lot to the brittle weeds of the ditch along the strip of asphalt to the low clouds, sagging like fish bellies, everything was gray and dim and edgeless.

"Looks like snow," I sighed, but Fay and Ida didn't hear the comment. They were too tickled by the idle speculation that Owen the Turtle Man was "funny."

"I feel sorry for him," I said, a bit surprised by my own interest in his defense. It must have startled Fay Rose and Ida, too, for it silenced their clucking and they both eyed me somewhat suspiciously from behind the bar, where they now huddled shoulder to shoulder, at one end.

I muttered on, "I don't see what's so queer about him really," and nervously fumbled with the pack of Winstons in my shirt pocket. I lit a cigarette with Fay's lighter from the bar and tried to casually divert their eyes off me by gazing interestedly out the window once more.

"Charlie," my mother familiarly began to lecture, "you smoke too much for your age—or any age for that matter." She cast Fay Rose a sideways glance. "It is going to stunt your growth and that's a fact!"

If I were to have stepped off the barstool where I sat, I would have towered over my mother by nearly half a foot, despite the raised floor behind the bar. "I know it, Ida," I agreed, pushing my empty coffee mug toward Fay Rose. "When coffee turns me black."

Fay Rose smiled at the displeasure in Ida's tense huff and refilled my cup, as she rewarmed her own.

"Don't be fresh," Fay Rose winked. "You'll get your ears boxed or I'll go get the broom and swat that sass right out of you my own black stunted old self!"

I smiled at the false threat and the turquoise shadowed wink, sipped the coffee in front of me. "Yes, ma'am," I replied to Fay Rose. "Sorry," I said to Ida. "But, after all, he is harmless. Certainly keeps out of everybody's way, down on the lake. He's polite as a preacher and never stank when I was near him. Seems just because he keeps so much to himself, people laugh and pick on him as if he's a fool or retarded. Neither of those things could be his fault—even if they were true."

"Oh, he ain't retarded," Fay Rose affirmed. "But he *is* odd now,

Honey. You got to admit that he's odd. And he's pathetic, that's for sure. Selling those nasty shells and turtle oil potions. Course," she said as an aside to some invisible audience at the other end of the empty bar, "I always buy my winter wood from Owen. He sells it cheap and always stacks it for me. Not like that Hulon Turbo, that one year, who just dropped it in a pile all tiddly-winkly all over my driveway!

"I feel sorry for him too, Hon—Owen, now—but he *is* a hermit, which is not normal, and he doesn't know how to talk right or get along with average people. Why, even when he worked over at the rendering plant, he kept to hisself and had nothing to do with nobody. You wouldn't believe it now, but he wasn't too bad-looking back then—had a good head of hair and pretty teeth, as I recall. That broken nose of his ruined his face a smidgen, but you know what makes you interesting when you're younger usually makes you ugly when you're old. I've noticed that.

"I asked him once how he got his nose broken, and he said it come from a fight when he was a kid in the Home. I said, 'Well, Owen, I hope that other rascal got some permanent damage out of it' and he said 'No, it weren't no other boy. It was a general.' This wasn't too much after the war, so I thought he meant some kind of army general of course, and I said, 'Owen, I thought you said you got your nose broke in the boys' home. You mean the service?' Even though he wasn't in the war, 'cause he was working in the rendering plant with me all through the war and that was suspicious right there, 'cause, Honey, we was all women then and just the oldest or somehow damaged men—and I don't mean broke noses—and he says, 'No, Mrs. Savory, I mean the Strang Home. The old feller in charge of the boys, he was called the General,' and that was that, of course. He turned and walked away like he still does if you try to be conversational."

"I didn't know he was brought up in the Home," I said.

"Oh, mercy, yes. His whole growing-up life till he was big enough to start a rendering job, which only lasted till the soldier boys come back home and they laid him off along with the women—that riles me still!" Fay's indignation flared like heartburn. Even Ida's eyes began to roll upward in a silent plea for mercy from the oncoming diatribe.

I attempted to spare us both the familiar monologue. "There still is a general at the boys' home," I said.

"What?" Fay Rose asked, confused by the shift of tracks beneath her wheels just as her conversational steam was rising.

"They call him General Nuisance," I casually commented with a smile. Both women stared blankly back at me. "The boys," I clarified, "behind his back. The orphans call the old man in charge General Nuisance. He must be a hundred if he was there when Owen was a boy."

Fay Rose suddenly hopped on this train of thought and said, "No, Sugar, not really. Owen's not so nearly as old as he looks. Probably about your momma's age. It's that poor nose of his and those hand-me-down clothes." She cast a sly glance of comparison toward Ida before completing her thought. "And living so primitive out there on the lake, I reckon, that just makes him look like Methuselah." She slowed to a rolling stop for a sip of her hot, black, and sugared fuel, and then continued.

"Course, I don't know diddly about the Strang Home, but if they got a General Whosit over there and he's the same one that broke the Turtle Man's nose, he could be well shy of a hundred, Darlin'. Maybe in his seventies," she frowned momentarily, as if lured by an inner doubt. "Or early, early eighties," she added with the positive composure of someone sure of their calculation.

"How should you know so much about the boys' home, Charlie?" Ida meekly asked.

"I have a friend, is all," I answered hesitantly. Then I repeated my statement to myself, listening for some slipup in my choice of words to account for the stunned look on both of their faces. "From school," I nervously added. "We talk some at school, is all." Then, regrettably, I added his name. "Dewar," I said. I wished I could have sucked it out of the air back inside me. I felt as if I'd betrayed something of our relationship, of Dewar and me together, by sharing just his name with Fay and Ida.

"Well, ain't that nice, Ida?" Fay Rose said, in a musical tone, brushing the cigarette ash from her shiny polyester pants. "Charley, that's so nice of you to be friendly with one of those poor orphan boys."

"He's not one of those hoodlums they lock up over there, is he?" Ida asked.

"No," I answered, trying not to sound insulted or insulting, defensive or offensive. "He's just a friend without a family." I clamped my jaw shut to keep from adding anything more personal.

"Well, some of them boys is terrible delinquents, you know, not even orphans, just disowned and put in the Home until they're big enough for jail," Fay Rose explained to Ida, for I was too disinterested in any aspersions she might cast on Dewar and turned my face again to the window, searching the gray drizzly landscape for anything distinctive to focus on.

There, across the blacktop, as if timed for my astonishment, a flock of maybe twenty cardinals swept down from the sky like a scattered flapping jigsaw of red and, with synchronized uniformity, alighted upon the leafless skeleton of a stunted tree, all alone in the foreground of the flatly stretched landscape. The cardinals were dazzling in their scarlet repose upon the gray twigs of the tree against the tin-colored sheet of sky. Twenty vibrant red birds perched in a bouquet of branches, now all atwitter with twitching wings, pivoting pointy heads, jerky tail feathers.

"Look at the red birds," I said, pointing my finger at the vision through the window.

Fay and Ida slowly dragged their attention from one another and heavily drew it past my extended finger and toward the window.

"What?" Fay Rose asked with mild distraction.

"They're gone, now," I said, retracting my arm to my lap. "Red birds. A flock of them. They all landed at once for a minute on that dead tree out there," I halfheartedly explained. "Then flew off again."

"Oh," Fay nodded. "They're pretty, but they are mean. Like bluejays. You ever seen a bluejay torment a dog?"

Neither Ida nor I responded. As the ensuing silence grew awkward, Fay Rose fiddled with her brassiere straps, Ida turned her head in sharp profile, staring toward the back door, and I said, "Anyway, I was thinking."

Both sets of eyes were suddenly back on me. "About Dewar. I was thinking of asking him over to the house for the weekend." Sensing no reaction, I waded on into cautious detail. "Just Friday after school and Saturday. He'd have to be back at the Home Sunday morning in time for church. They make them all go to church every week. In a bus. Unless they're really sick."

"What church do they go to?" Fay Rose asked.

"Strang Baptist, I think."

"Oh, Baptist!" she said enthusiastically with lifted brows.

"But, what would you two be doing all that time?" Ida asked. "I can't let Fay work alone all weekend. There'd be nobody at home."

"Good night, Ida. They're not babies. Two big boys don't need you to baby-sit them. Charlie's been taking care of hisself for years. I imagine," Fay Rose winked at me and conjectured, "they'll find some girls to tease on the telephone or watch TV till it goes fuzzy."

"Nothing," I interrupted. "Dewar's awful unhappy at the Home. I thought it'd be," I couldn't think of a neutral word to defend my motive, "fun, I mean, you know, nice to just get him out of there for a while. Besides, I never have company. Everybody does. It was just an idea." I gave up in frustration and lit another cigarette just to keep myself from storming out the door, mad.

"Well," Ida conceded, "I reckon so." She began thinking aloud, "I could cook up some meals for the icebox."

"Ida, I can cook," I said.

"Y'all could make some cookies," Fay Rose suggested excitedly, then burst into her familiar cackle. "Listen to me!" She shook her head. "Make some cookies! Honey, I was just thinking about when

I was a girl and we used to bake cookies and curl our hair. Course, we didn't have phone service then in Knotty Pine, but—"

"I'll have to make up the bed in your old room," Ida continued, cutting into Fay's girlhood memories.

"That's OK. I mean, it's not a big deal, Ida. All you really have to do is sign this form," I said, pulling the folded paper out of my back pocket and ironing out its creases against the bar.

"Oh," Ida whined worriedly. "I hate to sign papers I don't understand." She and Fay Rose craned their necks to inspect the paper.

"What kind of form is that?" Fay asked.

"It's a general information kind of thing," I explained, turning it around on the bartop so that they could read it. "It's just how they do it at the Home. They want to know your name and address and phone number, and the dates you're talking about, here," I pointed, "and where you work and—"

"Work?" Ida exclaimed.

"Yes," I said, "it's no big deal, Ida. You don't have to say Chick's Beer Joint."

"Why not?" Fay piped in. "Ain't nothin' wrong with that, is there?"

"I know, Fay Rose, but," I carefully picked my phrasing, "but it's an orphanage, after all, and they've got to be strict, I guess." To Ida, I suggested, "We could just write 'self-employed' or even something like 'housewife.' "

"I don't know," Ida began, wringing her hands. "What if this friend of yours gets sick or has an accident in the house and I'm not there? I can't afford no doctors' bills for some Strang boy."

"You most certainly can!" Fay Rose declared.

"Christ!" I yelled. "It's just a lousy piece of paper. It's like checking out a library book. You take it out, you take it back in time, nobody pays anything! Forget it," I said, snatching the form off the bar. "Everybody in the world has friends, but me. Just forget it, Ida. Don't have a fit. Just fizzlin' forget it!"

"Well, for pity's sake!" Fay Rose gasped, one hand over her heart, as if soothing a rising pain.

"I've got to go," I declared, moving in a clouded, blinded anger. I grabbed the car keys off the stool next to me, stood and spun toward the back door.

"Honey?" Fay called, while Ida simultaneously said my name.

I froze impatiently, waiting for whatever was to follow, embarrassed by the whole exchange and the fuss it'd turned into, feeling certain that it had something to do with her discernment of my hidden motive.

"Give me that paper," Ida said, "and let me find a pen."

Throughout the rest of that spring, Ida Hope's name was signed with a progressive casualness on as many Strang Home sleep-out slips as there were weekends in the remainder of the school year. Between Dewar's second and third visit, there was a solicitous phone call to Ida at the house early one afternoon from a General Newton of the Strang Home for Boys. Later, at the bar, Ida complained that he spoke so loudly she had to cushion her ear from the telephone receiver with nearly six inches of distance.

"Probably deaf as a rock," Fay Rose interjected. She was obviously bored with Ida's reenactment of the event to me, for she had inevitably heard the news told and pondered all day long at the bar. Ida's attitude toward telephones was still an odd one. When she did manage to calm herself enough from the disturbance of a ringing phone to actually answer it, she concentrated and reacted to the voice and its message with worried attention, grave seriousness and a tinge of awe, as if the transmission of voices through distance was too complex a miracle to be the result of man-made technology, and consequently, could be the work of the devil. Even at the bar, when forced to make or receive a phone call as mundane as a beer order to a distributor or jukebox repairman, my mother treated the act like a reverent ritual. A dazed expression engulfed her face; her voice dropped an octave in volume and depth; her speech was reduced to basic short syllables, affirmative or negative responses, as if giving her soul's attention to the annunciations of angels, maybe fallen from afar.

"You know how the hard of hearing shout like no one else can hear," Fay complained while carefully brushing her nails with a burgundy lacquer from an Avon bottle on the bar.

"What did he want?" I asked. My throat had tightened, making me almost choke on the question. Ida filled a beer mug with Coke from the fountain gun and set the heavy glass in front of me.

"Said he was just confirming—I think that's how he put it— confirming Dewar Akins's visits," Ida answered. "I told him, yes, I'd given my permission for my son's friend to come over anytime at all. 'Is there any trouble with that?' I asked him. 'Cause he was talkin' so loud and danged official, he was worrying me, and he says, no, there's no problem at all. Says, 'I'm only checking out the paperwork, Mrs. Hope, 'cause some of them orphan boys forge those slips I sign,' he says."

"Isn't that pitiful?" Fay Rose quietly commented, without breaking her attention from her wet nails. "Them poor little boys trying to get out of that orphanage with made-up names." She shook her head sadly.

" 'Well, I sure signed those forms for Dewar,' I told him. And I told him I'd keep signing for as long as Dewar wanted to come visit. Told him what well-mannered and behaved company he was, and this general says it must be the Hope family influence, and then I felt half-ashamed."

"Why?" I asked.

" 'Cause you know I'm not no family influence," she looked away, guiltily, self-accused. "Certainly not on your friend Dewar. I only see him at the breakfast table for the amount of time it takes to set down a plate."

"Honey," Fay said, pausing to blow gently at her fingertips, "he is Charlie's boyfriend, not yours. You have to find your own boy- friend to sleep over and influence." She laughed so hard she shook and had to anchor her spread fingers against the bar to keep from smudging the fresh polish.

"Abomination, Fay Savory!" Ida cried out, cupping her aghast face in her hands, perhaps trying to squeeze back the blood that had risen up to blush it an obvious bright pink. "I swear, you think about nothing but S - E - X and sin! Sometimes I'd like to rinse out your chatterbox mouth with a good bar of lye!"

Fay Rose slapped the counter with both stiff-fingered hands, tickled to near convulsions with her own good humor and my mother's predictable lack of.

"Sweetheart," Fay declared, "there's nothing funnier in this world than sex and sin. Anything else is enough to make you old, grouchy, or weepy."

I did not wish to share my recent familiarity with sex and sin by so much as a knowledgeable glance at Fay Rose, so I sipped the Coke to cover any expression at all on my reflection in the bar mirror.

"Stop chompin' that ice. You're making my skin crawl," Fay Rose scolded as she snatched the mug from my hand, literally prying it from my lips.

A few shards of cracked ice melted and slid around my tongue, numbing the feel of the words I tried to say. "Never mind, Fay Rose. I need to go."

"Already?" she asked disappointedly, turning with the soda gun carefully wedged between her freshly painted fingertips.

Ida was wiping down the bar at the far end.

"Momma," I called out. She looked up from the damp circular strokes of her towel. "I'm going," I said.

"Is Dewar coming?" she asked worriedly.

"Supposed to," I answered honestly, digging into my pocket for the car keys.

"There's beans on the stove," she said, "and cornbread on the counter."

I nodded.

"Potatoes in the bin, if you want to peel 'em."

"OK," I said, drawing nearer to her on my walk toward the back door. "But we might just drive over to Claud's or somewhere for cheeseburgers instead."

"Suit yourselves," she said dryly.

"Is he still making 'em so drippy?" Fay Rose piped up. "On those steamed buns?"

"I reckon," I answered, pausing in front of Ida.

"Um-um. Y'all swing by and pick me up if you go."

"All right, Fay Rose," I said with a smile.

Ida was frowning in profile at Fay Rose. I leaned awkwardly across the wide bar and kissed her lightly, surprising her turned cheek.

"Thanks, Ida," I said quietly.

Her face turned back down to the bar towel that she unfolded and refolded in her hands. "For what?" she asked absently.

"For talking to the General. For letting Dewar out."

"Drive careful," she responded, working the towel across the bar where she'd left off. "Put those beans up if y'all don't eat 'em."

"Uh-oh," Fay Rose called out from the front, chuckling as she blew across the rim of her coffee cup. Ida looked up from her vigorous cleaning. I stopped and turned with one hand on the back doorknob. "Here comes Owen," Fay Rose announced.

The Turtle Man was striding by the front window with a bulky burlap sack slung over one shoulder and a plastic shower cap pulled ridiculously over his head, down to his ears. His tall lanky figure paused outside the door as he gave the cap a snug pull downward—front, sides and back—before pushing open the door. I heard the bells tinkle against the inside of the swinging front door as I opened the back one to the graveled lot.

"Ha! Why're you wearin' that bathing hat, Owen?" I heard Fay Rose cackle from up front and then a nearer, guttural "humph," from my mother.

ONCE WE HAD CRACKED THE SAFE OF OUR SEXUAL ATTRACTION, WE were surprisingly conservative in the divvying up and doling out of its illicit fortune.

Given the vigor of our youth and the uncensored privacy of the house where we hid out, we were not gluttonous lovers. As we stripped down and climbed into bed each night at our disposal, sex was an awkward kind of chore, difficult to initiate. Each time was wobbly and clumsy, slightly embarrassing but respectful and never regretted. Our queerness was quite contained to the weekends, to the house, to what we sometimes did in bed, when not sleeping soundly side by side.

There was a kind of domesticity to our days and nights in the house. It evolved a weekend at a time. Dewar liked the house itself, the shelter of its drawn window shades, the quiet of its multiple rooms. The mundane comforts of Esther's abandoned furnishings, Chick's garage-sale taste for whatever was convenient, and Ida's compulsion for cleanliness and the habit of making do, had coalesced into the clutter that was common and acceptable for a home in Pryor.

The rooms had all petrified into what they were long before my birth, and I knew them backward with my eyes closed. For me, the place was haunted by boring ghosts. I followed my paths to and fro, from door to doorway. My roof was thatched with the hair on my head; my sense of home confined within the dome of my skull;

this house was only a place whose front steps were as mutable with Pryor as Pryor's town limits with Purley or Strang.

But Dewar made it his home, where we played a kind of House. Things like TV trays, an unlocked kitchen, a single shower head instead of a row, electric fans like personal breezes, and a bed twice the width of his shoulders without the grid of bunk springs sagging in his face, made him happy, like a child at play in the grown-ups' rooms.

We would come in the back door from school, into the quiet and cool rooms Ida had left straightened and sealed at noon, dump our books on the kitchen table long enough to raid the refrigerator for Cokes, maybe some pie, and smoke cigarettes that Dewar could not afford to buy, that I stingily never offered to buy for him, attached as I was to his bumming and to his "Got a fag?" inquiry and my affirmative response that had led us this far, this close together.

As I stewed and stirred up food like a wife in the kitchen, Dewar sat like the idea of a daddy in the living room, his feet propped up on an ottoman, a textbook uselessly open across his lap, mesmerized by the television, smoking sensuously, often dozing off for short naps that added up to hours of wakefulness at the end of the night as we slipped into bed. He'd start babbling then. He talked a lot about the routine of the Home.

"Half of the boys jerk the other half off under the sheets, all night long. In a room of a dozen bunked boys, if you can't hear what's going on, man alive, you can sure smell it."

I laughed quietly in the dark. "What's it smell like, Dewar?"

"You should know by now," he said.

I laughed again. "What do I smell like?"

"Eggnog," he said.

"Well, you smell like flat beer," I countered.

Then we started an exchange of such examples.

"The Home boys smell like hot wax," Dewar declared. "The younger ones, anyway. Little beaded drops of wax. The older ones are full of sulfur."

I tried to top that with, "Pryor boys smell like molasses, except the redheads. They're maple syrup."

Dewar snickered. "They ain't that sweet." He thought for a moment. "A room of Purley boys smells like a bushel of stewed turnips."

I laughed harder. "No," Dewar changed his mind, "a pot of beets."

"I hate beets!" I rasped.

"Yea," he agreed.

The spontaneity seemed to evaporate with the laughter. In the quiet, I asked, "Do they really all smell so different?"

"You think I'd know?" he immediately responded.

"I thought you'd lie if you didn't."

"You're the only one. I told you," he said, as if ashamed to confess it again.

"How come?" I pried. "If everybody at the Home does it all the time, how come you never did it with any of them?"

"How come you didn't?" he asked, rolling over to face me, wadding the pillow beneath his cheek. "I'm not the first orphan they ever let out, you know."

I thought about it, quietly piecing together Dewar's form in the shadows of the bed.

"I first knew a long time ago," I told him. "Fay Rose's nephew or something. She showed me his picture. He was older, about your age now, I guess. I fell in love with him, with the way he looked, I mean. And I just knew that that's how it was." The headboard creaked and I froze, waiting for any other sounds throughout the house that might indicate my mother's return from work. There was nothing else to hear but the ticking of the clock on the nightstand. "He's a grown man, now," I said as an afterthought. "Hunter. Married, I would reckon, without the slightest thought ever of what he meant." I let my thoughts drop like loose reins to the ground.

Dewar picked them up gently and said, "I had this one foster daddy when I was littler. He wasn't really so bad. He didn't ignore me like some or treat me like a new dog that needed trainin'. But I didn't feel nothin' for him. I didn't feel too much for any of 'em, to tell the truth.

"I wasn't a baby, but still too little to know anything about sex.

"I don't even remember that house or his wife. I don't think they kept me very long. There were so many when I was little. But I remember one night in a room, my room, I guess. The light from the other side of the closed door woke me when the door opened. And I remember the man comin' in, closing the door, just standing next to the bed. This tall man next to the bed. I just laid there, lookin' up at him. I couldn't see his face, so I knew he couldn't see me lookin' back at him.

"Then, finally, he knelt down like he was goin' to say bedtime prayers or somethin' and he started touchin' me. He just kinda patted and stroked me. But I just laid there like I was still asleep and waited for what he was goin' to do.

"He got around to it—you know—my peter, down there, through my pajamas. Through the covers even. It seemed weird, but I didn't really mind it. It felt nice. Not sexy or anything. It just felt good. It didn't scare me.

"I don't know. It was dark. He was kneeled down. He was quiet and it was all real slow and careful, even his risin' up and walkin' out the door.

"It was just that one time and nothin' was different after that." Dewar rose and recrushed the pillow, then fell back into it.

The clock ticked in the intervening silence. Its hands glowed faintly in the dark, both straight up twelve, maybe fifteen minutes till Fay Rose's car door would slam shut in the driveway and Ida would let herself in the front door.

I reached out for him under the covers, hooked my fingers in the waistband of his underwear. "What did he smell like?"

"Like wood polish on a church pew," he said with a grin.

The school year ended and Dewar was graduated, not because he'd done or passed any of his final work, but because he was a boy

from the Home, he was the age, and it was time to pass him on
to Pryor Rendering.

He had a third of a summer until he turned eighteen, and his
union apprenticeship was to begin. General Nuisance counseled
him on his privileged place in the rendering plant the night before
the graduation ceremony at Strang High.

The old military bachelor had a more or less public office attached to private quarters off the main hall of the Home, and
Dewar said he was always barking at the matrons to fetch him one
boy or the other for counseling.

"He's most in the mood about an hour after supper," Dewar had
dryly explained to me the next day across the front seat of the Impala as we hunkered over cheeseburgers the size of hubcaps in the
parking lot of Claud's. We'd cut school at noon on Dewar's last day
of classes forever; my last day before summer and one more year.

"Effie or Mrs. Sterling skitters around, stalkin' whichever boy's
been named and delivers the sentence so close to your ear you can
smell the tapioca she had for supper. 'General Newton wants you
in his office, Dewar.' Everybody within sight or earshot starts
razzin' you about bein' wanted in the General's office. They hoot
and catcall and work up a chant. 'Counseling. Counseling. Counseling,' until the matron slaps her hands and stomps her feet and
hisses 'Shhhhhh!' tryin' to put out the wildfire before it spreads
downstairs to the old goat's office. He's hard of hearin',", Dewar
said, "but he's got a nose for attitudes."

Dewar held his cheeseburger over the waxed paper spread over
his lap and dived into it with every tooth. A few stringy onions,
some mustard and grease splattered onto the paper as he lifted his
head and began chewing. I swallowed my own bite and washed it
down with a slurp of Coke.

"What does he counsel you about?" I was curious.

"Bullshit anything," Dewar mumbled with his mouth still full,
"or bullshit nothin'. So long as it's for your own good."

"What's that mean?"

"His board, Charlie," he cleared his mouth with a forced swallow. "He has this oak plank with a leather-wrapped grip, like a baseball bat that's been beaten out half a foot wide and an inch or so thick. All along the paddle, deep in the wood, is carved out real professional, 'FOR YOUR OWN GOOD.' All capitals. He swats that thing across your ass and it leaves a headline of welts." He cleaned the corners of his mouth with a wad of napkins.

I returned my sandwich to the paper it'd come out of and wrapped it into a warm ball of trash. I rolled down the car window and turned my head for a breath of air, hoping for a breeze strong enough to blow away the taste of onions and sour pickles that was overpowering my breath, the car, my ability to digest. But Claud's was situated in the draft of Pryor Rendering and the processing stench I inhaled caused a rise of food into the base of my throat that gagged me. I opened the door and leaned out over the gravel lot to retch.

I hung my hands around the window opening of the door with my eyes pinched. Dewar's hand eased up my sweaty back, and I heard a squad of cheerleaders squeal in disgust as they rolled their windows and started their car in a huff.

"You all right?" Dewar asked, patting his hand against my back.

After a few moments of hanging my head in quiet, I felt the up-heaval settle and I collapsed back behind the wheel. I opened my eyes and a couple of welled-up tears spilled down my face, which felt cool against my fevered skin.

"I'm sorry," I said, rolling my head against the seat toward Dewar. "I couldn't help it. I just felt so sick all of a sudden."

Dewar grabbed up all the remaining food and trash and hurled it out his window. A stray dog, all rib bones and mangy black coat, galloped up to the fresh spoils. "Can you drive?" Dewar asked.

"Yea," I assured him weakly and turned the ignition. "I'm burning up, though," I stated, shifting the car out of park.

"Just go. Just drive," Dewar directed and the wheels lurched across the popping gravel.

I unbuttoned and fanned my shirt. Once we hit the highway and picked up enough speed to somehow sift the rendering stench

from the wind, the driving air pried the fabric away from my skin
and cooled me down.

I sighed with relief. "We going back to school?" I asked.

"Hell, no," Dewar said, slouching down in the seat, shifting his
back to the door and unfolding his long legs across the width of
the car until his heavy boots landed in my lap between the steering
wheel and my bare stomach. "I've got seniors' privilege."

"Nice," I replied and smiled. "What've I got?"

"Some kind of sickness. My feet goin' to make you vomit?" he
asked with seeming concern.

"They never have before," I joked, "but your heel's about to
give me a rupture."

He uncrossed his ankles and resettled his feet. "Thanks," I said,
"you're a gentleman."

"And a high-school graduate," he added with a heavy emphasis.

"Yes, and praise God!" I shouted against the wind.

It was a bright, hot Friday in the first week of June. Dewar was
signed out of the Home into Ida's custody, which meant Dewar
was mine. We sped by Strang High and cheered loudly at the emptiness of the parking lot. Clearly three quarters of the seniors had
cut out for lunch and not bothered to return.

Traditionally, on the last day of school they could be found at
the lake, stripped down in the water and sun, sitting on the tail-
gates of trucks or hoods of cars with radios blasting competitions
of country-western and rock 'n' roll. Sweethearts would slow
dance and smooch the afternoon away, interrupted three or four
times by spats as spontaneous as static on the ratio station. In the
spirit of the occasion, some virgin would attempt to smoke a cigarette, the girl most prissy about her hairdo would inevitably be
chased down and heaved into the lake by a pair of the most popular boys. Her teary horror and outrage would be taken up by all
the other girls, who would surround her on the lakeshore in a circular battalion. The guys would all laugh in a male conspiracy as
if the ensuing mass exit of angry girlfriends had been plotted all
along. Once the girls had squealed off in a trail of gas fumes and

dust, with threats of prom night break-ups screamed from car windows, one of the guys would unlock his trunk or glove compartment and pull out the whiskey bottle imported all the way from Tulsa by some sympathetic older brother or cousin. They'd pass and pull hungrily on the bottle until it was drained and tossed to the lake bottom.

The teasing taste of the liquor would inspire some disagreements. A few tussels and pushes would flare up and peter out. Some big plans would be made for a drive to Tulsa after the cap and gown show. An hour of cock bragging and boasting about who would get laid that night or just diddled in the back seat would result in a few condoms passing hands, inspected and reinspected, then bought and bartered like surplus cigarettes.

Eventually, around suppertime, the same kind of boredom would strike as the waiting for the final school bell to ring when the clock hands clearly indicated the day was through and the desk chair outgrown, and they'd divvy up a pack of Sen-Sen to overpower the scent of whiskey and slide into their trucks to go home long enough to wash and put on a hot and heavy gown. They'd eat, probably a special meal of their liking all in their honor, the rest of the day and night, all in their honor; the rest of their lives from that day onward, at least in their own minds at that moment, all in their honor.

I had never witnessed this yearly ritual, of course. It was conjecture from common knowledge, overheard talk in the smokehole, between hall lockers, and the lunch counter of Claud's and such. My supposition about graduation day was tainted with an air of indifference; my judgments were always to the left or the right of those of the people in whose midst I mingled.

For years, I had longed to be graduated from school myself. Not because I projected myself from Strang to the rendering line in Pryor or the slaughterhouse in Purley or even behind the bar of Chick's joint. I loved the sound of the word *graduation*, its stair-stepped syllables, the hard climb of its tone and the soft inward resonance of its closure. The closure of that word for me would be my Pryor life itself, for I'd felt the call to distant lands when I was just a child.

All my years of school were just a prison, a penance for my age, and though Ida talked of my college education and I knew I had the mind suited for a lifetime of reading and writing, a whole career of thoughts, it somehow lacked the value of the only wisdom I craved, which was the yearning of my heart for its education.

Dewar was my first attachment in all my years at home, and his graduation was causing sudden swerves in the vision of my own future.

Greedily, I was looking for him to stay on in town, to take up the wages of rendering, his only opportunity, until I could refuse the same future for myself and unthinkingly abandon him along with it. That's how I'd always seen it and rehearsed it: my back ungratefully turned on the whole place and all it contained; my feet or, if fortunate, my wheels to the highway. Either direction, east or west, mattered little. Next year, at eighteen, I was vowed to leave, determined to find another life anywhere out of the middleness I'd been smacked into.

Dewar's graduation was not really that day; it was his eighteenth birthday, a month away. The oversized box of cap and gown in the backseat was no honor for him. It was his literal birthday suit in a month's time that would qualify his independence from the Home, cut the state ribbons that had kept him hogtied in the custody of one home after another since he was young enough to remember, then old enough to make himself not remember.

Still, that day was a celebration of limited freedom. We may have been too much the outsiders to follow the pack to the lake for close dancing and nips of hootch before a night of the same at a crepe-papered prom, but we were happy enough to be renegades on the road out of town, certain not to be missed at any prom or party in all of Strang, Pryor, or Purley.

"Got gas?" Dewar asked, lighting a cigarette off the red coils of the dashboard lighter.

"Half a tank," I told him after a glance at the gauge, "and money for more. Where you want to go, Arkansas?"

The wind pulled the smoke out of his lips and out the open window above his head, giving his face an eerie sheathed quality for the second I turned to him for a suggestion.

"Choteau," he said matter of factly, as if it were a place we went everyday at this time, as if it were a place on the map.

"Where?" I laughed.

"Follow the highway to Lawton. Right past Lawton there's a turnoff."

"What the hell is there?" I asked.

Dewar answered, "I used to be. Just a couple of years ago, right before the Home got me. I was with a foster couple for a while. Institutions are cheaper than foster payments, I guess. I don't know. I was there for about a year or so and then I was gone. Pauline promised she'd dance at my graduation." Dewar shrugged his shoulders and made a deliberately pitiful plea with his face. "It's my graduation," he half whined. "You got somethin' better to do than watch Pauline Tucker dance?"

"I reckon not," I smiled and pressed the gas pedal with the added weight of a destination.

We pulled into a dirt driveway, wide enough for three lanes of traffic, that was indistinguishable from what there was of a treeless, grassless yard. I knew it was the right place without Dewar's assurance because a painted board across the width and over the top of the screened front porch said PAULINE'S RESALE COME ON. I assumed Pauline ran out of board before she finished the IN, but the sentiment was just the same, if not more inviting.

Dewar raised his legs from my lap and sat up. He smiled at the house through the windshield, while I rubbed at the numbness of my empty thighs. "Watch," he grinned, leaning over to the wheel. He honked the horn repeatedly and then held it for a few ear-shattering moments.

"What's goin' on?" a woman scowled, coming out the screen

door and making her way carefully, with much body shrugging down the three concrete steps. She stood; then stooped, squinting at the car. "Well," she hollered, "who is it? Either git out or go away." Dewar opened the door and stepped out into full sunlight.

Pauline's scowl reversed instantly to a pleasurable shock. "Well, bless Bess! Look who's here. I don't believe it. Fred! I don't believe my eyes. Fred, git out here now, it's Dewar! Dewar's here and I just can't believe it." She held her wide-open and disbelieving face between both hands.

Dewar laughed as happily as I'd ever heard him laugh and until I stepped shyly out of the car myself, I was jealous of his show of affection. The minute I stood within her sightline though, she hollered at me, "Child, don't you dare be bashful, now! Come here and git some huggin', the two of y'all." She turned her head around and screamed for Fred once more through the darkness of the screened porch, as I let Dewar lead the way to the porch steps where she had rooted herself since the climb down and she now stood in a sleeveless print dress, her arms thin, lean, and widespread as frogs' legs in midleap.

Dewar squatted a bit to wrap his arms gently around her stooped back. She immediately fastened her own around his shoulders where her bejeweled hands roamed all around, searching for the tightest leverage. Beneath her thick white-rimmed glasses I saw her crying freely, the whole time emitting a nervous, joyful hum into Dewar's ear. When he finally pulled away, she opened her arms to me and flapped her hands to motion me into them. I was hesitant and embarrassed, but Pauline wouldn't abide it. "I'm so glad to see you, so glad y'all came all this way," she said, pulling my head to her shoulder as soon as I was within grabbing distance. "Thank you for what you've brought me," she whispered.

"I'm Charlie," I said with my cheek next to hers, "Dewar's friend."

She pushed me out arms length in front of her. "Um-hm," she acknowledged with a grin. "Now, I'm Pauline, if you didn't know and my other half is Fred. Lord knows where he's wandered off to."

She took each of us by a hand and started moving up the steps again. "Praise Jehovah, it's hot as hell, ain't it? Y'all want some pop or lemonade? I got ice tea." She kicked the screen door with her house-slippered toe, so as not to let go of our hands. She pulled us into the resale like a truck towing a wide load through a narrow tunnel. Dewar and I laughed, caught nose to nose in the doorway, and he surprised me with what felt like a spontaneous kiss of gratitude on the nose.

I almost raptured in the doorway of Pauline's Resale from that eager kiss. On my nose, of all places, and in Choteau, and by Dewar, whose lips until then hadn't kissed me at all since they landed on my hand, just as unexpectedly, that first sunrise at the lake. Straight through the front porch resale and into the dark, cool, open doorway of the house, I was dragged along by my hand. The numbness of my lap had spread downward to my feet, as if I were legless, bodiless but for the tender gleam of the kiss on the tip of my nose. It was the first time I had truly felt the impact of an unconditional expression of love.

Pauline dragged us all the way to the kitchen, the final room in the deep house. It was a more or less straight path from the front door to the kitchen's back door, which, I could see through its window, led out onto another screened porch and then a sprawling backyard as grassy as the front was bald, unfenced for the lack of neighbors on either side. The yard was littered with every kind of metal junk collectable: a few old car bodies on blocks, bicycles, and what could've been a unicycle frame, the wheels plus extras to most of the previous, piled in a heap of rust, plumbing of every configuration, sheets of tin, ovens, tailpipes, antennas, and clothesline poles. The junk gave the lawn with its two huge magnolia trees the sculptural air of a dreamscape. But even the junkyard out the window could not match the interior of the house for incongruous imagery.

The living and dining rooms through which we'd been towed were cluttered to the extreme with decoration. Two full sets of furniture filled the living area with roomy seating for ten. Then there were mismatched chairs of every style as additional seating for six more, providing you felt like settling down in the middle of a doorway or in a corner facing the wall. Where there was floor space, there were furniture legs standing on it. The three sets of double windows, each on separate walls of patterned paper, badly peeled and revealing other papers or shades of blue paint or bare spots of plaster in places, were each elaborately draped and curtained.

The north windows were hung like a small auditorium stage with red velvet fringed with gold rope.

On the wall opposite hung mustard colored satin, parted and held back with gilted medallions the size of saucers. The satin was water stained from top to bottom with irregular vertical stripes, but a pristine white lace shaded the panes between the pulled back panels. The front windows, looking out onto the resale, were covered from the middle down, with blue checkered café curtains. A short ruffled skirt was gathered tightly across the window tops, obstructing the view of business no more than the bill of a prairie bonnet would block the sight of a Sunday sermon.

Pauline's flair for window dressing had darkened her house from all but the most filtered of sunlight, and so it was a jungle of the most unusual lamps: huge gnarly table lamps, shades of distorted drum and cone shapes; floor lamps with milk glass shades; night lights in ceramic shapes of Aladdin, a panther, and such; a few stained-glass swags; and one quite beautiful bronze figure of a nymph or fairy whose leaded glass wings concealed the glare of its bulb with diffuse blues, violets, and greens.

To top everything off, there were doilies and coasters, draped shawls, quilts and afghans and coverlets with bric-a-brac, whatnots, figurines, dishes, and porcelain things indescribable, except that Pauline thought they were just plain pretty.

The dining room was more of the same excess, but for the theme of table and food. It was dominated by a crystal chandelier so oversized for the room its lowest shards tinkled across the center leaf of the mahogany table as we breezed by. It was spectacular. I'd never seen a crystal chandelier before and had never in my life expected to see one so close I could make music on four of its five tiers. It must have come out of a movie palace or some old variety house or maybe some black and white movie itself where such grand fixtures cut and refracted their sharpest light.

Pauline came to a sudden stop in the kitchen and released our fingers. With the back of her small frail figure to us, her hands frantically searched the large deep pockets on the front of her dress. The nervous energy of her hands traveled up her bare arms, shoulders, and neck where it was absorbed by the dozen pink sponge rollers tightly clamped around the rim of her limp salty black hair. The plastic curlers swung and bobbed and clicked dully against one another as she raised a handkerchief from her pocket to her nose and raised a free hand in the position of an oath and waved it in a manner to say, "Never mind, just a minute, everything is all right." She blew her nose fiercely, stuffed the hanky away, and swung around to face us.

"Y'all sit down, or are your rear ends sore from driving?"

"All right, Pauline," Dewar said agreeably as we pulled two heavy chairs out from the table. The table was decked with all the condiments and fixtures of a truck stop booth.

A large bowl of snap peas, soaking in water, sat beneath the spout that bent over one side of the shallow tin sink. The curtains over the window above the sink were white and patterned with colorful teapots that drew my attention to the shelf encircling the room over the window, cabinets, and doorways. Teapots of every description were crowded onto that high ledge, all coated with a dull film of dust on grease.

My God, I thought, this is the strangest place I've ever seen, while my heart felt this was the most wonderful place I'd ever been.

While there was no evidence. the musty and used smell of the house gave a first impression of uncleanliness and yet it was such an insignificance to the livability of the rooms and the combined characters and histories of everything in them. Everything overwhelmed at once: the colors, the patterns, the weights and smells of old-fashioned homeyness as well as slightly damaged, forsaken homeliness.

Pauline made us two large mixtures of iced tea and lemonade. "Teamonades!" she laughed, plunking down the tall glasses in front of us. "You want some fried pies?" she asked before sitting. "Got 'em at the day old just yesterday? Blueberry or gooseberry?" she tried to tempt as Dewar and I both shook our heads no. "Me, neither," she sighed, settling in a chair at the head of the table. "Fred likes 'em."

"I'm sick he's not here, Dewar. "Child," her voice sobered as she took Dewar's hands into her lap. She squeezed his hands emphatically with each of her words. "How are you gettin' along?"

Her small head with the dangling curlers and man-sized white framed eyeglasses made her cute rather than comical. Her dark and warmly prying eyes, brought forward by the lenses, and the tanned line-weathered skin of her face, so youthfully attached to the fine bones of her brow, cheeks and chin, made her look beautiful rather than cronish. Her voice was somewhat strained in its high register; it snapped and cracked in places like an old 78 phonograph.

"Fine, Pauline," Dewar said with a squirm against the chair. "How you've been is what I came to hear."

"Oh, baloney!" she said. "You know I'm as awnry as I was made and always will be. Now, tell me about that home, goddammit, before I tan that hide of yours."

"You're embarrassing me in front of my friend, Pauline," Dewar grinned.

Pauline reached for one of my hands and squeezed it. "I ain't never hurt him, Charlie. He's probably needed it but he was too big for it by the time he walked through this door. I sure threatened it though, didn't I, Child? I'm like one of them runty little dogs, the bald ones is so ugly?"

She was looking to me for help, so I suggested, "A chihuahua?"

"That's me," she said, letting go of my hand to slap the tabletop. "I just like to hear myself yap, like a chi-hua-hua, don't phase no-

body, but I just keep yappin'." She threw back her head and
laughed. She had false teeth that were too large for her mouth.
They seemed as enormous and unnaturally white as her glasses, exposed to the gum as she virtually jiggled with a hoarse and raspy
laugh reminding me of Chick's. But instead of Chick's rickety
cough, Pauline's hard laughter brought on tears that streamed freely
down her face. "Ain't I a chi-hua-hua, Dewar?" she barely managed to get out between her wheezy breaths. "I can just see one
of those ugly little ol' dogs with my glasses and my hair all up in
rollers," she slapped the table again and reached for her ribs with
the other hand. Dewar and I were smiling at one another and then
I couldn't help myself from bursting out, too. Dewar followed and
we each urged the other on with our unblended howls. Each time
I tried to get a hold on myself, I pictured Pauline as a chihuahua
with eyeglasses and a bob of bouncing pink sponge rollers as she
yapped and the laughter spilled out of me like a tapped spring.

Finally we pulled ourselves together with much exhaling and in-
haling and the wiping of Pauline's eyes. "I'm sorry, Pauline," I
apologized sincerely, despite my tenuous sobriety. "I don't mean to
be rude, ma'am. Please forgive me."

"Oh, baloney!" she answered, "If you can't laugh at yourself,
laugh at me, that's what I say. But I swear you have the sweetest
manners! You must've had a very nice and pretty upbringing."

"Yes, ma'am," I lied, although a part of me wished to confess
the opposite and by so doing, win even more of Pauline's sympathy
and affection. But I deferred to Dewar's claim on her. Foster
mother or not, he had more doting from her than I'd felt from Ida
in a lifetime. I did not want to ruin anybody's percentage of that.
I took a sip of my teamonade and asked Pauline if she minded if
I smoked.

"Well, hell, no!" she declared. "I love cigarette smoke. I think
it's sexy. Fred smokes like a yard fire. My Daddy and Mommy both
smoked. Everybody I know smokes, Child. I thrive on it. I sure do
wish you would, Charlie."

I smiled at her exuberance and when she had retrieved an ashtray for me and returned to her seat, I offered my open pack in her direction.

"Thanks, Child," she said sweetly, "I don't smoke."

Dewar made a flatulent noise as another burst of laughter exploded through the tense chewing habit of his lips. Pauline wheezed and crackled with her own sounds. The two of them leaned together and hugged in their shared convulsion while I lit a Winston, drank more teamonade, and tried to appear less baffled than I was.

"Child, never you mind," Pauline said, squeezing my knee. "Y'all should go over to the Reservation store and buy some cartons while you're here. Save yourselves some money."

"In the meantime," she said confidentially, as if Dewar could not hear her every breath, "I'll give you one of mine, later. I do smoke occasionally, after supper."

With a somewhat cunning grin, Dewar reached across the table and confiscated the cigarette from my fingers as his own.

"So," Pauline said, "you still ain't said word one about that home, Dewar."

"Ahh, Pauline, what do you want to hear? I've been real happy?"

"Oh, that would be so nice," she said.

Dewar stared at his fingers grinding the butt in the ashtray. "All right," he said, his head still lowered.

"All right what, Child? Do they treat you right or not? You get along with a houseful of boys? Is the cookin' good? Is it clean enough or too clean? Child, it's been two years without a word. Don't you think I've wondered and worried and prayed about you? Did you git my letters?"

Dewar looked up. "No," he said emptily.

Pauline bit back a word. "Well," she said rubbing her arm, "they weren't the best letters. Got lost, I reckon. But, we wrote. Me and Fred together wrote several times."

"Pauline, it *has* been all right," Dewar tried to assure her. "Honest. Come July, it's over anyway."

"Well, bless Bess!" Pauline exclaimed, clapping her palms to her chest.

"I graduated today, Pauline."

"Oh, my word! Child, it slipped my mind that you'd gotten any older than the day you left here. Ain't that just grand!" She slapped her hands to her chest once more and turned her face to me with an expression of such genuine and unselfish pride, it made me flush.

"Yes, ma'am," I said softly.

Pauline toned down her smile and rubbed my upper arm. "You graduated, too, Charlie?"

"Next year," I told her.

"That must feel so far off today," she seemed to voice my own mind. Her hand left my arm with a reassuring pat and then flew back to Dewar's. "Show me your pretty paper, Child. Whatchacall-it? Your diploma. You know how I love pretty things."

"I didn't get it yet, Pauline. It's still in Strang."

"But why, Dewar? What's the matter?"

"Nothin'," Dewar leaned forward to assure her, once more. "I just got to thinkin' about you, is all. It's my graduation, ain't it? I made Charlie drive me here, instead. I was hopin' we'd have a better time in Choteau than at the Strang Prom. See," he said confidingly, "Charlie's my date, Pauline." He cast a look at me and grinned at the confirmation of my enflamed cheeks, then hoarsely whispered, "He don't know how to dance, and we didn't have no fancy dresses."

Pauline threw her head back and screamed till her lungs were empty. Then she doubled over for a refill, threw back her head, and did it again—only the sound was all burned off the top of the scream and her dangling rollers trembled as her hands shook in front of her. She gasped once more and found the power of speech hoarsely returned. "Oh, Child!" she rasped unsteadily into Dewar's patiently still but amused face, "I boarded your scrawny butt for two years and you still think you can shock Pauline Tucker with that kind of talk?" She fanned at her neck and face with both hands, snatched a napkin from the dispenser to dab under her glasses. "I know I look like some ol' hillbilly woman—ha!—I reckon I am, but, Child, I know a few things about lovin'.

"That foster care was always sending me letters on raisin' and teachin' younguns. They burned up real good with the other rubbish. The thing with children is they already are what they're goin' to be, and that don't need nobody's meddlin'.

"Listen at me, now Charlie Honey, I'm an ordained minister with the pretty diploma to prove it, somewhere. I'm happy for you, Dewar, and you, too," she said to me. "I could see in y'alls faces when you stepped out in the sun, you was special friends. No reason for tiptoeing. I only read the pretty parts of the Bible and that's all I'll ever preach.

"So," she slapped the napkin in her hand flat against the table, "y'all come to Choteau for a prom night, we better git supper goin'."

Just as Pauline had settled against the sink and begun sorting through the bowl of peas, Dewar scooted his chair back from the table far enough to cross his legs and lit a fresh cigarette. I was about to offer Pauline any help she might need with supper, when the back door opened with a wobble and in walked two characters with rifles and two handsful of skinned squirrels.

All eyes turned immediately to the racket of the entrance. "Fred Tucker!" Pauline scolded in a high pitch. "I've been hollerin' my head off for you! Where've you been?"

Fred raised the two pink-fleshed creatures he held by the hind legs up toward Pauline's face. "Me and Rae got a hankerin' for some squirrel, Pauline." His companion stood impassively behind him, holding her squirrels down low, almost touching the linoleum with their front leg stubs.

"Well, bless Bess!" Pauline exclaimed, grabbing the squirrels out of his hand and taking Rae's also, once they were silently held out. "You must've divined it was prom night!" Pauline laughed, wiping her hands on the apron she'd tied around her loose dress. "Well, Fred, look who it is. It's Dewar!"

"Yes, I know it, Sweetheart," Fred said gently, leaning his rifle against the door, behind him. "I recognize him, but I been skinnin' meat and don't want to mess him up."

Dewar stood at the table, "I ain't as clean as I look, Fred. How ya doin'?"

"Fine, Son, fine and good. I swear you look good." With that, the two men seemed to gravitate into one another, their arms raising and lowering like windmill blades till they found the right fit of their shoulders above and below one another and held each other tight for several minutes. When Dewar loosened his grip and stepped back, Fred grabbed hold of one of Dewar's hands and raised it to his lips. He kissed the back, before gently releasing it. I was almost embarrassed by the unexpected tenderness.

"This is my buddy, Charlie, Fred."

I stood, as if cued for some moment on a stage I felt unprepared for. "Hello, Charlie," Fred said, stepping closer in my direction. "I apologize for my hands," he added, while extending one toward me. I took in a firm but comforting grip, wondering if he might kiss it, too, in the same courtly manner. But we just shook, rather sincerely, I felt. "We got plenty of soap and free well water," Fred offered.

"Hi, Rae." Dewar acknowledged the woman for the first time who loomed in front of the door with a shotgun braced against one shoulder.

"Dewar," she spoke curtly with a brisk nod.

"Charlie, this is Racine," Pauline motioned. I moved forward and offered my hand.

"Rae," she said with direct eye contact, taking my hand for one solid shake that was twice as strong as Fred's. "Ludy," she added, as she dropped my hand and retreated back to her space near the door.

"What finally brung you back this way, Dewar?" Fred asked,

shedding his hunting jacket as he kissed Pauline on the neck with both arms trapped behind him in the stiff brown coat.

"I finished school today, Fred, for good," Dewar explained, returning to his chair. "I'm almost a free man."

"Congratulations," Fred smiled, "that's the best kind to be."

"Fred," Pauline said bossily, "we're having a prom."

"Oh, good," Fred replied, as unphased as if he'd been told we were having squirrel for supper. "I don't think we ever had one of those, have we?"

Pauline laughed. "Rae Ludy, take your coat off and stay awhile!"

Rae complied, picking up Fred's rifle, still cradling her shotgun and ducking off to a small passthrough to the right of the door where there were hooks for coats and a rack for the guns, while Pauline slapped one of the squirrels across a large cutting board and raised what looked to be a short handled hatchet high above her head.

A few hours later, the Tuckers, Rae Ludy, Dewar, and I were sitting back from the dining room table, staring at the leftovers of fried squirrel, mashed potatoes, snap peas with bacon, wild onion biscuits, and buttermilk cinnamon rolls. But mostly we were staring into the tiers of the lit chandelier, which shattered the view of the person across the table into a dizzying number of beveled diamond and teardrop crystal images, while bathing the person to the right or left with the softest, most ethereal glow since fire must first have been lit in the darkness.

To my right was Mr. Tucker, calmly smoking a cigarette, wearing a plaid flannel shirt, though it was June and warm and a good month beyond the need for anything like flannel. At that moment, I was still sorting out the emotions I felt toward Fred, the confusing feeling that had grown since he'd taken Dewar's hand and kissed it in the kitchen. It felt like a crush. I didn't figure out till later that it was admiration, something I'd never felt and something that enriched those qualities in me that were most certainly good and appropriate but not always allowed the warmth and encouragement of daylight. Fred seemed to be the kindest, gentlest, and calmest man I'd ever encountered. He had no stories to tell or prove. He seemed satisfied. There was no regret in any of the fine lines of his complexion. His quiet comments and observations were all based on a sense of acceptance, but an acceptance that went far beyond what he'd personally seen or done.

He was a plainly handsome older man, built on the stocky side of average with short, stand-up hair, thick and gray as a barber's lathering brush and brown eyes that looked casually but deeply into things, and seemed to appreciate what they saw. He may have been the only happy man I'd ever met. The closest to God, but far from a missionary, he was the nearest I ever came to my own ideal daddy, though too late, I sadly thought. Too late.

To my left was Dewar, looking eager and engaged, a little anxious on the edge of his seat, the heels of his boots nervously tapping against the carpet, wearing down the nap of the bank logo that richly patterned the dining room rug. He had the palms of his hands pressed together between his knees. I guessed he was trying to squeeze them still. I saw him in the light of the chandelier, and it lit him up for me like the first time. It showed me his pecan brown hair, so well combed and behaved in its length that his forehead without the usual fallen locks was like a new part of him I hadn't seen before, fresh and vulnerable despite its strong, handsome definition. Everything had become so distinctive about him, the slight hollows where his shaving line met his sideburns, his thick eyelashes, almost transparent in profile in the crystal light. While making him pretty in a handsome way, it also matured him. His arms appeared harder, muscular in the bareness of his sleeveless T-shirt, and though his shoulders were slumped forward by his position, they seemed so much broader than the memory of my arms' last encircling measurement.

Like the light, the conversation around the table all bounced toward Dewar and was refracted by his smile, his dry wit, his compulsion for storytelling and listening. I retrieved a cigarette of my own and leaned into the match fire that Fred silently offered at my side.

"Fred," Pauline's voice came at us as if from the crystal fountain itself.

"Um-hm?" he answered.

"Did you hear? Dewar's got a job at a rendering plant in Pryor. Right after his birthday next month."

"What kind of job is it, Son?"

"Rendering," Dewar cleared his throat to answer.

"What do they render?" Fred asked, interested.

"Cattle. Cattle scraps."

"How'd you fall into that? I recall you being kind of squeamish about huntin' and skinnin' and such."

"Just one more boys' home privilege, Fred," Dewar replied. "I guess I'm not so squeamish, anymore."

"Well, you think you'll like the work?" Fred asked.

"I don't have another offer, Fred," Dewar stated bluntly, but with a smile. "Another month, I don't even have a home."

"Child, you got this home!" Pauline declared through the light.

"You need help with the resale, Pauline?" Dewar laughed.

"I always need help with the resale. I got boxes I ain't even opened yet, some of 'em older than you. Probably full of weevils, by now.

"You come and stay with us, Dewar. I need a load of help. I got competition in the town, now. Some kind of fancy resale. Called the Baggage Claim. Ain't it, Rae?"

Rae was the only one still eating. She'd set the chandelier to swaying and tinkling a couple times as she reached for squirrel or more biscuits. She was behind the light, too, next to Pauline, so we only heard her grunt of agreement and then the word, *airlines*.

"Couple of lady friends in Choteau, Dewar," Fred explained. "They go to the auctions in Tulsa where the airlines sell off their unclaimed baggage. They've opened up a resale where they sell off the clothes and such and the luggage, too, of course. I think the name's kind of clever, but Pauline's insulted," he grinned.

"Well, Child, you should see what they're chargin' for resale in

Choteau! Even if it is a little newer. Resale is resale. It's still somebody else's dirty laundry, ain't it?"

"Well, I don't think they've hurt the trade here any, Baby." Fred
soothed Pauline's agitation through the gentle sway of the crystal
fixture.

After a moment of quiet, the spirits of everyone seemed soothed
and sated. Even Rae had pushed her plate back to rest her elbows
on the edge of the table.

We each helped to clear the table until the plates were stacked
in an order of size and similarity on the sink counter. Pauline was
running cool well water into the sink as a bucketful heated on the
stove. She insisted on no help in the kitchen and shooed us all out
of her way with the suggestion that we walk over to the Reservation store and get some smokes. "Get me a box, too, Child," she
ordered Rae, and Rae donned her hunting jacket in the tight space
of the cloakroom, even though the sun was still bright, if low, in
the sky and the temperature was no less than eighty. Pauline pulled
out a drawer from the kitchen counter and peeled a five off the top
of one of the neat stacks of bills divided into compartments of de-
nominations where knives, forks, and spoons would have been expected. Rae stuffed the bill into one of her deep denim pockets
and strode silently out the back door as Dewar and I stumbled
against one another to catch up.

Fred was sitting on the front steps, his big hands cradling a delicate teacup. He took a slow two-handed sip, smiled, and nodded
as we crossed the front yard of packed dirt to the road of the same,
then he returned his calm thoughts and eyes to the sunset before him.

A few yards beyond the Tuckers' house, the wild greenery of the
countryside mobbed the edges of the narrow roadway in a riot of
shrubs, ivies, trees, and wobbly saplings so that after a short hike
we were engulfed in a long shady tunnel of vegetation that reached
out with great leafy hands, swatting at us from all sides as we
passed.

The overhanging brush was alive with the hum of wasps, flies,

gnats, crickets, birds, rattlers, and toads, a combined invisible chorus that put a ravenous voice to the countryside. It seemed capable
of swallowing us whole with one rolling flick of its parched
tonguelike road.

Rae Ludy matched us in height and both of us combined in
width. Her gait was heavy and intense. She outpaced us by ten
strides and bore herself slightly forward at the shoulders, head
down, like a yoked mule plowing the land.

She had been a strangely quiet and ominous presence all afternoon, a presence no one had seemed obligated to explain beyond
introduction, a presence like my own in that respect. But for the
softly rounder edges of her large figure, she appeared quite masculine in her loose bell-bottomed jeans, stretched out navy T-shirt,
and baggy hunting jacket. She burrowed into the roominess of the
jacket. Its stiffness afforded her a private fortress to move around
within. Her braless breasts beneath the soft T-shirt were widely set
and shapeless like a fat adolescent boy's. But her sex was neutral inside her jacket, whose patch pockets she kept her hands plunged
into and busy, as if mauling their stock of contents.

Her features were petite and finely rendered, close set in the
middle of a large round face, and so she seemed to have an abundance of forehead, cheeks, and chin like a plump round pillow in-
tricately quilted at its center, expanding to a plush blankness. Her
hair crept all around her pie-face like the wild vegetation that
threatened the passability of the road beneath our feet.

As her weight rose and sank on her feet pounding out the pace
between us, Rae's hair did not so much bounce with the shock
waves of her rhythm as shift about and fling its body against it. Rae
Ludy's hair was an amazing conduit of independent energy. If it
were straightened out from root to end, it would surely have
reached the missing waistline across her back, but Rae's hair was
curly and kinked, as tightly coiled as a porch door spring, and so
there was no line of length to it. It just spilled down as a mass and
prowled about her shoulders like a live critter with no place to
settle.

Bear brown and huge as a feather war bonnet, her hair reached up and out in a ragged thicket, swatting the air out of its way. Even indoors, it was never still, always on the move for a better configuration.

She was a freakish young woman. Just how young or old was difficult to determine. Her hair was somewhat mesmerizing in its utter wildness and like a royal crown, it radiated an off-putting dignity of sorts. It was not matted or unclean, and its thick texture and deep auburn color were curiously attractive. Her blue eyes revealed an intelligent mind that wandered over the entirety of a scene, taking in each detail while not loitering on the importance of one thing over another. I interpreted her silence as akin to my own. It was not the sound of rudeness or disdain, nor shyness exactly. She was just an open listener to the racket of others, but perhaps more attentive to the racket of her own thoughts and so familiar with the uselessness of their ever-changing nature and uncompelled to put the credence of voice to too many of them.

"Rae, rae, Ludy, ludy," Dewar hollered, exaggerating the distance between us by cupping his hands like a megaphone around his mouth and mimicking an echo.

Rae stopped instantly and turned with a blank expression, but for the tight, grim slit of her lips.

"We ain't talked none," Dewar said as we caught up to her. A wedge of her hair folded horizontally across her face, although I felt no breeze that could have placed it there. She shoved it to the side with the back of her hand and started walking again, but at a slower, if not lighter, pace. We picked up our feet beside her, Dewar in the middle, Rae and I on either side.

"Well, what do you have to say, Dewar?" she asked the distance in front of her, reaching out for a long thin branch of a tree as we passed and pulling off a leafy stem, which she absentmindedly began to pluck clean of leaves as we walked on.

"I'm glad to see you, for starters," Dewar said.

"You heard I graduated," he went on after a breath. "You, too?"

Rae kept her eyes straight ahead, plucking the leaves of the branch like a blind person. "I quit," she stated. "Last year. It don't mean beans around here.

"You really goin' to render?" she turned and set her blue eyes right on Dewar.

I looked to the other side of his profile, more curious about his answer than Rae Ludy after their two-year separation.

"I reckon. I don't know," he said, turning his face from me so that I could only judge from the redness of his ear the temperature of how he was feeling rather than the expression of what he was saying to Rae. "It's a job, a good one. I mean, it pays a lot, more that I could make doin'—I don't know what else. You think I shouldn't, Rae?"

She turned her head calmly back to its neutral, straight-ahead position. She finished stripping the branch, ran her hand up and down the nubbed switch, then whipped the air ahead of her with a few slashing sideways strokes, before tossing it back into the lattice of branches and leaves it'd been stolen from. "It stinks, don't it?"

"Like the dead come home to roost," I offered.

Rae laughed emphatically as if switching the air again, this time with her breath.

"What kind of job don't?" Dewar asked seriously. "Jobs for plain people, like us, I mean?"

"Yea," Rae agreed dryly, as if resigned to the sentiment from previous contemplation, "it all stinks to heaven." She kicked a rock out of her way, and it tumbled off into the ditch with a ratlike scramble. "But, then again, Dewar, I don't think we're such plain people."

Something from their unspoken history sparked between them. I sensed it, like static after close lightning. Dewar bit his lower lip and slid his hands into the rear pockets of his jeans. Rae ground her fists like pestles into the deep mortars of her jacket pockets, and my freely swinging arms suddenly felt reckless and frivolous in the darkening leafy tunnel. I crossed them in front of me, pinning my hands in the damp pits of my arms.

"Mary run off," Rae stated. "Last year."

There was a pause, as if the statement were soaking in deeply, before Dewar quietly commented, "She always was a wild cat."

"With Joe Turner, of course!" Rae added with disdain.

"And the baby?" Dewar asked quietly.

"She left him with her grandmama. On the Reservation."

We'd come to a turnoff in the road, so obscured by the high brush and overhanging trees, it only seemed to appear as we were upon it, as if the plant life had parted like a drawn curtain at the moment we arrived. Rae charged into the turn instinctively, Dewar followed at her side as if a memory of the way were returning to him with each step. I doubled my strides to keep up.

This road was even rougher and narrower—more like a trail. The three of us, side by side, filled its width, and Rae and I dodged and swayed inward toward Dewar to avoid the face slaps of the reaching branches.

"It was a boy, then?" Dewar wondered softly.

"Joe Deer," Rae said. "Least the last name's worth something."

"We're talkin' about this girl from here," Dewar suddenly turned to me and offered. It was the first time since we'd left Pauline's that I'd felt acknowledged by their swift exchange of information, and the truth is, my attention had wandered a bit. I'd heard everything they'd said but had applied no real reaction to it. So I more or less faked some curiosity by restating what I'd already gathered in the form of a question.

"She had a baby and then left it?"

"Not right away," Rae corrected, defensively. "She was too young to be wagging a baby around anywhere."

"She wasn't too young to have one," Dewar said, as if picking up the flip side of a familiar argument with Rae.

"It was that bastard Joe Turner!" Rae viciously cursed. "He was too lazy and helpless to walk away from here by hisself. If it weren't for his whining and begging, Mary would've stayed. That baby could've helped her grow up, and I would've helped 'em both."

"I don't know, Rae," Dewar argued. "She was always wild and

restless and about five years ahead of herself. I can't see her stayin' around here too much longer than she did, considerin' she'd had a bite of everything there was to swallow in Choteau."

Dewar turned to me again. "She was only about fourteen when Rae and I were sixteen, but Mary Deer was never underage a day in her life."

"She was pretty," Rae challenged with a nod that unsettled her hairs' arrangement and shifted it forward around her face.

"She was handsome," Dewar said. "Joe was the *pretty* one."

Rae spit. "He's a worthless turd."

Dewar laughed, and from Rae's hateful glare in his direction, I feared she might knock him down for it. She grinned instead, somewhat reluctantly, by the tension of her mouth.

"Is his nose still silver?" Dewar asked.

"Was when he left," Rae answered, "and Mary's was startin' to get shiny, too."

"What does that mean?" I asked.

"Oh," Dewar explained, "you see, Turner was this local bad boy, a bit on the scrawny side of good lookin', a little less bright than average. . . ." Rae snorted, muttered something under her breath. Dewar smiled and went on.

"He had a piece of family somewhere, drunk stepfather or somethin', but mostly he just loitered around alone, lookin' for trouble. I never knew him to go to school, but he hung out around the school, pickin' fights with the Indians, bummin' cigarettes and change, flirtin' with the girls."

"Like Mary Deer," Rae added.

"Nobody made her like him," Dewar said. "Rae was like a mother hen to Mary Deer."

"Eat me," Rae declared from the other side of the road.

Dewar smiled and restated, "Rae was like an older sister to Mary." He and I both leaned forward, heads turned to Rae for another disagreement. Her expression plowed ahead through the darkness for a moment, then she asked me, "Are you and Dewar like brothers?"

I searched out Dewar's eyes in the shadows, looking for permission, I guess, to respond. He nodded slightly, still smiling.

"Twins," I told her, marveling at the flexibility of words to bend what they mean to the way we say them.

She seemed to digest my answer and ponder whether she liked the flavor or not. Her silence acted as an affirmative permission for Dewar to go on.

He said, "Rae and Mary were like twins, you see, only Rae was a bigger twin than Mary, if you know what I mean."

Rae said, "I think he knows what you mean, Dewar."

Indeed, I thought I did. I thought the two of them, Dewar and Rae, were conspiring with this game of words to let me know that Dewar and I were not the only two queers in Oklahoma. We were at least three, and maybe Mary Deer, wherever she'd run off to with Joe Turner, made us three and a half.

Truth is, I was shocked by the revelation, without showing it, despite the sensible way that the news suddenly glued together all my hanging impressions of Rae Ludy. I had never in my life heard any words for such women, neither did I hear any that night in Choteau. Dictionaries are silently uninformative unless you know exactly what you're looking for. Continuing the walk on the ditch-edge of the dark road, my head reeled, as if blindsided, with a triggered mix of newborn understanding and inbred prejudice.

Because I was conditioned from the day I was born to be heterosexual and everywhere I had to look I was provided with its examples, both explicit and implied, I could and always had accepted it as normal, even though the acceptance was one of fact and not heart. I didn't recoil at the idea. I didn't feel sullied or insulted by its pictures. I just felt objective and unphased as any outsider, unlinked from its chain of lifelong assumptions. Within a dozen strides on down the road, I had unsorted myself again from one more of those rigid links and found a distance from perverse judgements. I couldn't relate to a naked Rae Ludy and any soft-breasted wildcat lover I pictured within her arms. There was no reward for me in the effort, and no business either. But I calmed down with the only connection I could make between us in this respect: the way love always seems to find its fit somewhere and somehow, regardless of its looseness or pinch.

I was suddenly a greater admirer of Rae Ludy, with no deepening of our acquaintance but the knowledge that she was in love with Mary Deer.

"He was a thief!" Rae scowled.

"Naw, Rae, he was a mooch," Dewar objected.

"He was a crazy paint sniffer," she tried again.

"Yea," Dewar agreed. "That's why his nose was always silver, and his clothes and fingers," he explained to me. "He had his charms though, I guess," he said to Rae.

"Shit!" she replied in disgust. "In his pants, maybe, if you care for charmin' grass snakes. Or worms!"

Dewar laughed. "Some people like handlin' snakes, Rae."

"Well, hell, Dewar, some people eat dirt, too, but that don't exactly make it appetizin'!"

Turning back to me, he said, "When Mary started up with Joe Turner, Rae and I kind of got dragged along for a while. Hangin' around, killin' time, mostly.

"Remember that time we went cleanin' bricks?" Dewar asked Rae eagerly.

"Shit, I'll never forget."

"Joe found this guy was goin' to pay him and any friends he could muster to clean the cement off the bricks of this building he'd knocked down. So Joe drags me and Rae and Mary out one freezing morning at like five o'clock."

"Four," Rae corrected.

"Pitch black out anyway and fuckin' freezin'. We were all goin' to make like a hundred dollars each by noon, chiselin' cement off bricks at two cents apiece."

To Rae, he said, "We must have been high on spray paint to think that." She grunted.

"We had to bring our own chisels and hammers," Dewar remembered. "We got there and there was a whole building's worth of bricks in a rubbish pile that filled the entire lot. You couldn't walk without climbin' a brick heap. And there's at least twenty others crawlin' and scavengin' all over the place, stakin' out claims on huge piles. We were about the only white people there, probably the only sober ones, too, and penniless as we were, the richest to begin with.

"Mary whacked maybe two bricks before she split a nail or somethin', threw a fit and had a seat for the rest of the mornin'. Joe went at those bricks with gusto for about an hour, and Rae and I tried our best with frozen fingers and feet and covered in dust. If you didn't hit the cement clot just so, the whole brick would shatter in your hand and this guy paid for reusable bricks. So after a hundred cigarette breaks and a pile of maybe 75 bricks between us, we just walked away at about six-thirty. I think the sun was just up."

Rae cut in, "We couldn't even pay for coffee at the truck stop with our lousy earnings."

"Then Joe got us all to sniffin' paint with him," Dewar picked up. "He bought, or stole, the metallic silver kind of spray paint. It was the best, he said. And he had this tent way back in the sticks where he kinda lived some of the time, but where he sniffed paint all the time. Just crawlin' into that little two sleeper hut was enough to get you sick or high. They were the same to me as far as paint sniffin' went."

Rae grunted again, seemingly in agreement.

"So the four of us are just wedged into this tent, so tight our heads were bulgin' out the sides and strainin' the stakes, all hovered in a circle. Joe had this pile of old rags, all wadded and stiff with dried silver paint.

"First he rattles the can, then presses the nozzle right into the wad of rag till a little pool of silver appears all runny in the cup of it, then plunges his head over the rag and breathes deep—I mean deep—until his head kinda floats up real slow with this ridiculous expression."

"Like a moron," Rae added, with a dull-witted slack-jawed demonstration.

"Yea, pretty stupid lookin' and he started gigglin' and slurrin' whatever he tried to say, which cracked him up more. Then finally he just falls back and the paint can rolls out of one hand and the rag falls somewhere, smearin' silver paint on whatever it touched.

"So Mary picks up the can and another rag like she ain't afraid of nothin'. Then the two of 'em are out side by side, not passed out exactly, but worthless as if they were. So Rae and I decide to give it a go."

"What happened?" I asked.

Dewar laughed. "Oh man! I barfed, just barely gettin' my head outside the tent. Got a headache that lasted the whole day."

"What happened to you, Rae?" I asked.

She assessed Dewar with a doubtful expression, rummaged her hands inside her pockets and said, "Nothin'."

"What do you mean, nothin'?" Dewar questioned. "When I pulled my head back inside, you was passed out like a fallen tree across Mary Deer, cooin' and groanin' like a baby."

"I didn't sniff no goddamned paint," she declared. "After watchin' two fools in a row fall down dead and you start pukin' your toenails, I didn't sniff no goddamned paint!"

"You are a two-faced prude, Rae Ludy," Dewar said. "You were just tryin' to take advantage of Mary Deer while she was out of it."

"I sure as hell was keepin' Joe Turner off her while I could," Rae stated.

"Rae," Dewar said, taking in a deep breath of nerve, "Mary Deer liked you, there's no dispute, but she did not like you like she liked Joe."

Rae stopped on the side of the dark road, as suddenly and as still as a doe who's sensed the snap of a twig. Dewar stopped a few steps ahead and turned back to face her. I stopped at his side, searching for the physical stance of neutrality. A negative and hateful energy was palpable in the air.

"You don't know nothin'," Rae declared.

"I know she liked boys and I know she liked men," Dewar said. "She may not have been the whore half of Choteau thought her to be, but she liked to flirt and she liked to tease, and more than once she did do more than that and liked it fine. She said so all the time, most of the time, just for your benefit."

"How was that supposed to benefit me?"

"She knew how you felt. Hell, anybody with sense could see how you felt about Mary Deer. She liked you, but she was usin' you. Usin' the way you felt about her to satisfy her own greed, I guess. If you'd ever once told her straight out you loved her, she'd have laughed and run scared."

"So what if I didn't. I didn't have to," Rae admitted, sternly anchored in place, hands turning things over in her pockets.

"But, she knew anyway and teased you, flirted the way she did with every guy whose head she turned."

"And maybe that was fine with me, Dewar. Maybe that was just fine. What business of yours is it anyway? Who asked your damned opinion anyway? You tryin' to impress somebody with your carryin's-on in Choteau?"

"I wasn't no kind of threat to you and Mary," Dewar said, a little more calmly.

"Who said you was?" Rae responded in kind.

"Nobody said it, but you knew it. Me with Mary didn't hurt your chances, no matter how slim, like Joe Turner with Mary. You just hated Joe 'cause he was in love with her and she loved him back. I can appreciate that. But I didn't appreciate the way you pushed me in the middle of it."

"Bullshit," Rae said.

"That night in Joe's tent?" Dewar continued. "That night Joe was off somewhere, high on paint, and Mary was stoned and giggly on her own can of paint, and you'd sneaked off with me and one of Fred's brandy bottles. Hell, I'd never been drunk before and you kept feedin' me more and laughin' and swearin' you was just as drunk. But, I'll bet you wasn't, Rae. I'll just bet you wasn't nearly so drunk as me and Mary that night in Joe's tent. You couldn't have slept through the two of us doin' it an inch away.

"It was a blur to me. I believed that you were asleep and when you never mentioned it and Mary never mentioned it, I thought it was just a drunk dream." I swallowed with an audible gulp and nervously shuffled around in a circle. I was embarrassed and strangely shocked and I don't know what else, but everything was tinged with a bit of jealousy as well. My jealousy disturbed me the most, the awareness that it sprang from a once only and long ago time and place and with a girl who was a year gone from here, two years gone from Dewar's touch. But, of course, it was the sex itself and not the girl that upset me. It somehow changed Dewar; he was different to me now, even from just one time with her, he was somehow different from me than I thought he was. Embarrassingly, I thought he was somehow better than me, a little bit redeemed from pure queerness, now. And even though I felt this, I was shocked at the narrow limits of my own self-esteem that allowed this. So, I shuffled aimlessly away, on down the road, my mind wandering in zigzags while my feet carried me the only direction available, ahead instead of back.

"I put you in the tent," Rae said, "I didn't put you in her."

Dewar had started after me and then Rae had followed from behind, talking even louder to be heard. "Even if it was like that, Dewar," she half admitted, "it didn't do no good, did it? First you got taken away, then she ran off with Joe."

"She had a baby first," Dewar said.

"Well, you can't blame me for that, too," Rae yelled.

"Well, I might blame myself, then," Dewar screamed back.

I stopped and listened to the confessions settle to quiet.

"It was Joe's baby," Rae declared.

"How do you know that?" Dewar asked.

"She said so."

"To who?"

"Me. Anybody who asked. It was Joe's baby, Dewar."

"She wouldn't say it was mine! Not if it could have been Joe's. She just wouldn't say it was mine, even if it was."

"So what's your problem, Dewar? What are you so mad about? You want a baby?"

We stopped in a staggered line along the road. They were speaking loudly to be heard by one another and were clearly overheard by me.

"Hell, no," Dewar said with earnest conviction. "Are you crazy? I wouldn't know up from down on a baby. I don't know why anybody wants babies."

"I want a baby," I said, surprised by the strange admission. "Someday," I qualified myself.

We all looked at one another, petered out and confused.

"You want to see it, Dewar?" Rae finally asked. "Mrs. Deer's still on the Reservation. The baby's the spittin' image of Joe Turner, God help it."

"Naw." Dewar shook his head definitely. "I trust your word on that.

"You want to see it?" Dewar asked me. I thought he was kidding at first, but he waited patiently for my response.

"Not like it means something to me," I said.

So we walked three abreast in silence another fifty yards, turned and passed through the gates of the Choteau Indian Reservation.

Just inside the gate was a cluster of wooden buildings. The biggest and nearest was the general store. Next to that, a liquor store and beyond that, a meetinghouse. Across a street of packed dirt was a church, a one-room office marked "U.S. Government" across its dusty window, and then a burned-out shell of a barn-sized place, with a saloon-style bar still intact and visible through the glassless windows and fire holes of its charred half-collapsed walls.

There were a few pickups pulled up to the plank sidewalks that lined the storefronts on both sides of the road. A twenty-foot streetlamp spotlit the entire scene from its northern sentinel next to the general store. Its light was alien with a bright yellow hue. It cast an unearthly glow on the ghost town look of the place.

We entered the store in a row, Rae leading, Dewar, and then me. I closed the wooden door behind me, turned and found myself one of a small crowd inside the close room. The bare bulb dangling in its center illuminated the room from the center outward, the center being the only blank spot in the room. The walls were shelved and stocked with an array of general goods—cornmeal, beans, canned foods, hardware, toiletry items, some utilitarian apparel. A slow look around couldn't take it all in, most of it was only visible as lumpy shapes in the dimness of the bulb's light, but it seemed that probably anything of true necessity was just waiting here for the asking.

There was an old but sturdy table, counter high, with a roll of butcher paper mounted at one end, ready to be yanked out by the yard across the table, ripped and wrapped around the bulkiest of purchases. Behind the table was a handsome young Indian man, shirtless but for the bib of his overalls, cut off at the thigh.

His hair was black and gleamed, parted down the center and just long enough to be held off his face by his ears. "Howdy, Rae," he greeted as soon as we'd settled ourselves inside.

"Hey," she nodded in return. Then she turned in the opposite direction and said it twice more to the men seated against the wall, next to the door we'd just entered. They sat in homemade-looking chairs on each side of a wood burning stove. The black iron potbelly was cold, but memory, imagination, or old-fashioned conditioning made the two seem more warmly contented than they might have been. They both wore cowboy hats of straw that they tipped in response to Rae. They were elderly Indians, dressed for farmwork. One had gray hair in symmetrical braids that frazzle-ended below each breast, like suspender straps that had busted loose from their front buttons. They each presented a kind, gentlemanly face and sat patiently still and silent, only mildly interested in our business, but private enough about their own that they seemed graciously willing to wait for us to go before carrying on with it.

"Jack," Rae said, turning back to the young man at the counter, "this is Dewar. You know him?"

Jack studied Dewar intently from top to toe.

Rae added, "He stayed with Fred and Pauline for a while a few years back."

"Nope," Jack said.

Rae said, "Maybe you was in jail then."

One of the old men chuckled in a soft high-pitched way as if he were trying to keep it to himself.

"Could be, Rae," Jack said. "Howdy," he said to Dewar.

"This is Charlie," Rae added. "He's from Pryor or somewhere."

"Nice to meet you," I said, stepping forward and offering a hand, which Jack clasped like a hand wrestler, so we shook with bent elbows and raised locked fists. In the grip of his greeting, my eyes wandered to the tattoo on his tightened arm muscle, an Indian head silhouette, apparently the profile from a buffalo nickel.

"Well," Rae said, "they need cigarettes and Pauline wants a box, too."

"All right," Jack said agreeably, letting go of my hand. "What's your brand?"

I told him.

"Good brand," he said, moving to the shelves behind and to his left. "How many cartons?"

"Just one I reckon."

"That's three eighty," he said, laying the box upon the counter. I laid my money beside it and picked up the carton. "And five for Pauline," he said to Rae, putting a single unwrapped pack of Kools directly in her hand.

Rae put the pack into one of her cavernous front pockets and pulled a five out of the other. "Mrs. Deer all right?" she asked, handing Jack the bill.

"She's fine, yea."

"Baby doin' good?"

"Far as I know, he's good, yea."

"Any word from Mary?"

"Yea," Jack said casually. "She called up a few weeks back. Wouldn't give me time to go get her grandmother—she was on a pay phone—said to just tell her she was in Ponca City, I think she said. She and Joe. Said Joe was doing some paintin' work and she was workin', but she didn't say where. Said they's movin' to Oklahoma City soon as they had the money saved. And, let me think. I might've been on a binge then, or in jail since then, and not remember everything." He winked boldly in my direction, but it may have been Dewar he was toying with. One of the old men chortled once more. Dewar grinned at Rae's pissed-off change of demeanor.

"Oh, yea," Jack remembered, "she said they was sendin' Mrs. Deer a money order, but then it hasn't arrived yet. And I think she asked somethin' about you."

"Well," Rae asked, "what'd she want to know?"

"I think she said, 'Is Rae Ludy still mad at me?' "

Rae grunted. "What'd you say?"

"I told her far as I knew, Rae Ludy was mad at everybody." Jack grinned, showing even white teeth. "Well," he said, "ain't it the truth?"

"You're sure as hell pissin' me off," she told him.

"All right," he said, laughing. "She said if you wasn't still mad and wanted to write, I should give you her address."

"Well?" Rae waited.

"Well, I think you're still mad, and I told Mary I wouldn't give it to you unless you weren't mad anymore."

Rae's round face puffed up like she was holding her breath. She stood on one side of the table facing Jack, her shoulders so tense they hugged her neck. Jack leaned back casually against the wooden shelves, his black eyes teasing, his bare arms and legs crossed.

"You look tense, Rae," he said. "You want a drink? Why don't we all have some drinks. The liquor store's open. I'll git us a quart and we can get drunk. Fine evenin' for it."

"Pauline's planning somethin'," Rae said, "we got to go." She turned and stomped out the door before Dewar could say, "Wait a minute."

"I tease her too hard," Jack sighed, unfolding his arms and legs and approaching the table once more. He pulled out a sheet of butcher paper and ripped it from the roll. It was about a yard square and in one corner he wrote an address, referring to a scrap of paper from his register. He tore off the addressed corner and held it out over the table. Dewar reached for it.

"Ain't love grand?" Jack asked Dewar with a sarcastic sigh.

"Ain't it?" Dewar replied, shyly, accepting the piece of paper while avoiding Jack's direct eye contact.

"Y'all take care," Jack said, bending down over the table, his square chin coming to rest on his fists, as we pulled the door closed behind us.

The walk back was brisk, with Rae leading Dewar and me by the length of six horses and about the same amount of fury. It was so dark by then, we could only see her ahead of us by the snatches of moonlight that flashed through the bald spots in the canopy of branches vaulting the sky from the road.

Since our arrival in Choteau, I had had the sensation of having fallen through a hole in my own place and time. Pryor seemed as distant from the moment as the hidden moon, and I felt like a stranger on the coattails of Dewar's past.

Dewar still carried the address Jack had given him. I carried the cheap carton of Winstons like a cumbersome piece of wood, good for nothing but fire. I also carried within me the bold dark wink of an eye and a greenish-black Indian head tattoo on a strong brown arm. If I let it, my memory would've slipped out of its arm-wrestling grip, further down to a crossed pair of hairless legs and bare feet. I was as shocked by the strength of my attraction to that storekeeper, as if I'd been bitten by a snake and as fearful of its poison. These feelings shamed me a bit, exclusive as my experience with Dewar was.

"He used to drive a truck," Dewar said quietly and spookily, as if he were sensing my wandering thoughts. "Jack," he added for emphasis. "A semitruck.

"He wrecked it though, drivin' drunk. Lost his license and went to jail for a short while.

"He remembers me," he said.

"I had a big crush on Jack Stillwater, when I lived here.

"I saw how you looked at him and how he was playin' with you, like he used to play with me. That's why Rae and I hung out at Jerry's Truck Stop. Everytime we knew Jack was comin' in. Wasn't nothin' to Rae, of course, you saw how she gets along with Jack. But she'd go with me and we'd drink coffee for hours waitin' for Jack to come in off the road, just so I could stare at him if not sit next to him.

"Hell, he doesn't even like boys! Might let you do him if he was drunk enough. He sure as hell don't care none. But, he's got girls everywhere."

"Like Mary Deer?"

"I imagine that's why Rae's so mad at him," Dewar said.

"Sounds like you don't like her much. Mary Deer."

"I like her fine. She's honest, in her way. She's not an orphan, really, but her grandma's very old, full-blood, and very old-fashioned. Strict. Mary's just wild spirited and couldn't be held back. She had white blood, too, and didn't want to be fenced on either side of the Reservation. She was always achin' for somethin' different. Jack Stillwater, Joe Turner, me, even Rae, I reckon. It didn't matter to Mary Deer. Just fillin' up that longing, was all. Everybody's a little drunk at the wheel in that respect, I guess."

"You think Jack could see how I, you know, felt, just by look-ing?" I asked.

"Charlie," Dewar laughed, cupping his hand on the back of my neck, "I think those grandfathers could see how you felt about Jack Stillwater, right through the back of your head."

* * *

Rae had come to a stop in the road, outlined on one side by the beam of the resale's light. She stood straight, her head erect, hands in her pockets, waiting for us to catch up to her.

"Whoa, Nellie! Whoa!" Dewar hollered, pulling back on invisible reins as we slowed to a standstill before her.

"You need a good brushing down, Rae, after that gallop," Dewar kidded her.

Rae intensified her grim expression. "I'm goin' now," she said. She pulled the box of Kools from her pocket and held it out for Dewar to take. "Give this to Pauline. Tell 'em I'll see 'em soon."

Dewar refused to take the cigarettes and asked, "Where you stayin' these days, anyway, Rae?"

"Depends on the weather," she answered impatiently. "Sometimes here with Fred and Pauline, but I've been usin' Joe's tent for nights like tonight." She shook the Kools as if they were stuck to her hand and she wanted them off.

"Well, I think you should deliver it yourself," Dewar said, "and not be so rude."

Rae huffed and reinserted the pack into her pocket.

"And here," Dewar said, tapping her on the shoulder that she had turned toward us on her way into the house. Her eyes swung around to Dewar's hand on her shoulder, suddenly overgrown with the mass of her own hair. A piece of white butcher paper poked through the curls and tendrils, practically brushing her nose.

"Jack wrote this down for you," Dewar said. Rae locked her blue eyes with Dewar's. They trembled in the porch light, or maybe it was just the light itself and the moths fluttering about it.

She took the paper, held it down, tilted against the light, staring at it for a moment. She lifted her face. "I can't help it, Dewar."

"I know it," he replied, sliding his hand gently down her back.

. "I don't like bein' a fool," she said. "I know that's what everybody thinks."

"Since when did you give a shit what anybody thought," he answered with a grin.

"I don't," I told her from my distance on the road, my toes just on the edge of the light. She turned toward the house and began walking, her hands and the address slipping back into her pockets, Dewar's arm draped across her bouncing back.

Pauline was seated at the head of the table in the dining room, concealed behind the dazzle of the chandelier.

"Well, bless Bess!" she declared as the screen door of the resale slammed hollowly on our return.

As we followed the light and her voice into the dining room, she rose and stepped into view. "Child," she said loudly, "I thought the hogs had ate y'all. What took so long?"

She had removed the rollers from her hair, which was now combed smoothly against her scalp into short straight bangs above her eyebrows and a tight springy flip beneath the lobes of her ears. Her brown eyes sparkled behind the magnifying frames of her eyeglasses, which reflected the dancing light as if tiny stars were reeling from the lenses.

She did a smiling turn in her white beaded tube dress and high-heeled yellow pumps, like a floor-lamp model of the tinkling crystal fixture hanging above and beside her.

Dewar put his fingers to his lips and whistled shrilly as I applauded, one hand against the carton of cigarettes. Rae grinned soundlessly, shaking her slow-to-catch-up mass of hair in disbelief.

Pauline beamed and curtsied like a flapper, as if forcing flexibility into her joints. "Fred," she yelled, "they're back. Hurry up!"

"Sit, y'all," she pushed down at the air with her hands and slid gently back into her chair. "Well, let's have us a smoke and then a prom."

Rae slid the pack of Kools to Pauline, who dumped its loose tobacco directly onto the smooth mahogany table. Fred entered the room from the back of the house through the kitchen doorway wafting a scent of mothballs. He carried a hammer in one hand and carried himself with impressive distinction in a satin-lapeled tuxedo, bowtie, and heavy-soled work boots that were at least semiformally black.

Pauline cackled lovingly at the sight of him. She reached out and grabbed his empty hand. "Once upon a time," she told us, "this was called the bee's knees.

"Sugar," she said to Fred, "I need my papers." Fred felt the pockets of his jacket as if he were hunting for the pockets themselves but eventually found a pack of rolling papers and placed them affectionately in his wife's hand.

He put the hammer down upon a crowded sideboard and took a seat at the table. Rae pulled her arms out of her jacket, beat the coat back against a chair, and slumped down heavily upon it.

Pauline proceeded to roll a cigarette the size and shape of a healthy green bean and not until the unfamiliar odor formed a pungent fog around the chandelier and the cigarette began a patient hand to hand circle around the table, did the nature of this after-supper smoke dawn on me.

First Pauline, then Rae, then Fred, then Dewar, then I pinched the limp, ashy joint at the moist mouth-end and sucked long, loudly, and painfully deep on its harsh smoke. The weed had an anesthetic secondhand menthol flavor from the Kool pack that helped me to hold the smoke and steep my lungs with it for as long as the obvious veterans at the table, whose repeated ritual I'd carefully studied.

My exhalation stirred the dangling crystals with a few tinkling notes as I passed the short hot butt to Pauline. I studied the bejewelled fingers of her hand as she attempted with difficulty to tweeze the joint from my own fingertips.

"I smoke for my arthritis, Child, and as you see, the medicine's all in my head," Pauline said confidentially to me. She pulled a bobby pin from the hair somewhere behind her ear, handed it to me with a smile and asked if I'd clip the cigarette for her. I was able to accomplish her request nimbly and quickly, considering my ignorance about what I was doing.

The marijuana barely survived its second circle around the table. I was self-conscious about even attempting a second draw on such a short bit of paper and ember by the time it reached me again, but out of an obliging sense of politeness, I did, and inhaled the remains out of the bobby pin and sucked it directly down my throat with the reflexive gulp-and-wince of having swallowed a fly.

Rae snickered audibly, while everyone else just smiled. Pauline clapped her hands joyfully. "Child, the last hit's always the Lord's sacrament round here, so I reckon the Lord's where He wants to be tonight." Her pupils had enlarged to the size of dimes behind the thick lenses of her glasses. Her entire little face beamed adoringly at my red-hot embarrassment. But the flushed heat drained quickly from my head, and I felt myself reclined into my chair as if coddled by a cloud.

Each sensation from that moment on was alien in its enhancement. Every vision, odor, sound, and feeling was amplified. Even Pauline's commentary that the Lord was within me became a somewhat obsessive fixation, and as I drifted about the house and yard that night, bouncing my consciousness off the smallest of occurrences until I was nearly disembodied of consciousness, I kept reminding myself and perhaps everyone else that the Lord was within me and I was therefore shepherded from all danger. I was therefore well protected and could relax with abandon. I felt love, both passively and assertively, and therefore, I grinned obnoxiously the rest of the night.

Pauline ordered us to the resale to find ourselves some fancy dress outfits. She and Fred had some finishing touches to put on the prom out back. Rae's eyes rolled with a glassy half-hearted attempt to scoff at the suggestion, but she rose with everyone else, staring down at her jacket like a soul being forced from its beloved body.

Pauline's Resale was a bin-lined front porch of heaped clothing. An indiscriminate selection had arisen from the unsorted piles to the status of display. Hangers hooked through the screened walls on three sides featured everything from folded drapery panels to a Halloween vampire cape.

Stoned and charged with our mission, we attacked the trove with the mindlessness of moths just following some blind instinct to know what was ours when we found it.

Rae found a pair of fat-sized tuxedo pants that fit, gave up on the hunt for a shirt or matching jacket and slipped on a dressy pin-striped vest over her T-shirt. She resembled a gangster and then took possession of the role by ordering Dewar and I to wear this or that as she dug through the bins, yanking up torn and ragged dresses of older and older vintage.

"We're not your doll babies, Rae," Dewar finally objected, while inspecting a pair of brown suede chaps of his own discovery.

"It ain't fair!" Rae bitched. "All of 'em fit y'all." She held up another long slinky dress of torn lace and battered sequins. "Charlie," she commanded, "just this one. Just for a minute."

"We don't want to outshine Pauline," Dewar said, buckling the chaps around his waist.

"Cain't be done," Rae said, rolling the dress into a hoop as she forced it over my head.

I wormed the thing over my arms and shoulders and with a few tugs from Rae, it spilled down me until the hemline hit my boots.

Rae took a step back and squinted. Dewar glanced up from his chap buckling and shook his head at me, then Rae with a wordless rejection of the vision.

"I know it," Rae said disappointedly. "He ain't got the hips to fill it out."

"Then help me out," I laughed, raising my arms over my head. Rae ignored me and began rooting vengefully through the heaps again. Dewar secured the last buckle around his ankle and rose to my defense, lifting the gown from the bottom up till I was free of lace and sequins.

"How about this?" Rae turned with a heavier, bustled two-arm load of black crinoline and crepe.

"That looks old as the prairie," Dewar said, picking through a box of clanking junk.

"A black dress is always in style," Rae informed him. "Didn't Pauline teach you nothin' while you lived here?"

"I might as well wear Dewar's gown as that thing," I said, perching my hipless body on the rim of a clothing bin.

"Go ahead," Dewar said, still rooting through tangles of beads and tiaras.

"You brought your own gown, Dewar?" Rae asked snidely.

"My cap and gown, from school," he said. "It's in the car. Charlie, go on. I ain't wearin' it. It'd hide my beads." He turned, holding up a woven bib of horn and silver tube beads strung on latticed straps of leather from a collar of turquoise and silver buttons.

The suggestion pleased me, and I ran out to the car for the large box on the back seat.

We paraded through the house single file, with extroverted chatter, stirring a breeze—what with the flapping of Rae's vest and hair, the leather fringe of Dewar's chaps, and the full-blown sweep of my sleeves and robe. The chandelier swayed and rattled in our wake.

In my dreamy swirl, the house and its decor came alive in a cartoonish dimension, each color and shape animated with an amusing personality. Everything danced and sang and jostled for the attention of my eye. The stranger my perception, the more hilarious my interpretation, and I laughed in appreciation of Pauline's marijuana-inspired homemaking.

I laughed a lot that evening. We all did. Of the hats we found, we laughed hardest at the beaver skin silo that Dewar strapped precariously atop his head from beneath his chin with an elastic band so padded to support its towering heft that he appeared to be in traction for a busted jaw. It had been hijacked from some marching band leader, but Rae said it looked like a beaver torpedo and that if he snapped his teeth just right he could launch it all the way to Little Rock.

Rae's gold-braided sombrero was laughable for its width, which was comparable to an open umbrella inverted upon her head. Her head itself seemed to shrink to the size of a grapefruit beneath the massive brim, but the most laughable thing was that despite its diameter and weight, it could not be crushed tightly enough over her hair to hug her skull. It was merely balanced upon the coils of her thick curls and slipped and slid and flapped its brim like vulture wings as she moved, so she moved slowly and bridelike, artificially level-headed and erect to keep the Mexican souvenir aloft.

The bulls-eye tasseled square of satin I wore was quite modest in comparison, and reputable, but it was its hilarious impracticality that inspired the hat hunt for the other two to begin with. Dewar insisted it was a crashed kite with a misplaced tail, but Rae said it reminded her of a tilted dance floor on my head.

With each of us uniquely adorned, we made our way through the kitchen, where the teapots and kettles encircling the ceiling whistled and waved their spouts like miniature elephants for my sole amusement.

We passed through the sleeping porch off the kitchen with some delay. Rae's hat was too wide for the doorway and Dewar's, too tall. But with vertical and horizontal adjustments we made it down the porch steps and into the backyard.

Pauline screamed through her multiringed fingers, squeezing her cheeks into the cavity of her open mouth. Fred laughed like a good sport at her side.

"Bless Bess!" she cried out once she could speak. "Y'all sure look pretty. Look!" She spread her arms to indicate the whole wide, deep area of the yard. Various chairs from the house had been dragged out between the twin magnolias at the furthest end, although there was no fence to define any end at all to the yard. It just rolled on into woods so thick they could not be seen into from the house.

Lanterns, candles, and oil lamps had been hung and strewn upon the metal heaps throughout the yard. Strands of Christmas lights were strung haphazardly from the detached garage through the branches of a nearby oak where they flashed like multicolored, hyphenated lightning.

In a rational mind, I'm not sure the yard would have appeared nearly so enchanting. Nevertheless, the three of us froze dumbstruck in the midst of the yard, transformed in the flickering live light into a garden of primal beauty. Rae audibly gasped and

Dewar softly sighed, the way I'd heard him sometimes in bed, after sex, when all such sounds of pleasure were presumed drained from his body. I was as moved by the surprising atmosphere as they, but I was ashamed of the sounds I might release if I allowed my lips to part at all. For I felt a strong urge to weep. It rose instantly through all the joy that was still there in me, too. It rose up with a grabbing force, like a hand rising up through the earth from a grave I did not even know I was standing upon.

What had been triggered was the time when I so strongly believed in this kind of enchantment and the magical atmosphere I now breathed again. As a boy, I called my capacity for wonderment God, and it gave me the security of faith and hope, naive as it might have been.

In the strangest experience of my mother's stern knowledge of what God truly was and her regard of the discovery from my ear, from within my small body's exploration of itself, as wrong, as blasphemy, as of the devil not God, as small and worthless as a bug hull, my very desire to hope and my hopes to desire anything, anyone, as faithfully as her approval had died.

The element of religion evident to me in the vast sense of countryside and this clearing of firelight and human affection would have shocked and disgusted Ida as heathen and savage. Such disgust made me want to cry with shame, despite the years of silent truce between us.

Seeing Fred and Pauline across the yard in their black and white fancy dress, arm in arm, I wanted to cry for the fact that I was seventeen and not four, not six, and that they were not Ida and my father.

Dewar's graduation robe swallowed me up as its fit was supposed to, made me small, wrapped me in the past. I was seized with the zeal of my childhood game of missionary. I was so appropriately robed for the part, in the firelit jungle, in the midst of heathens. Pauline in her flapper dress, Rae as a Mexican and a man, and Dewar with his half-naked, beaded torso and that fur phallus upon his head, were obvious sinners whose demons I would have cast out of them as a child and flushed their souls with the blood of Christ in my fantasy of converting God's graceless ones into my selfish little church of love-me-first.

Fred was above reproach from my vision, calm and elegant in his tuxedo, masculine and soft at once. Fred was a fatherly figure I'd never had.

Through the thick waxy leaves of one of the towering magnolia trees, high above Fred and Pauline, Bub's black fingers, arms, then smiling childlike face appeared, aglow in its dark skin's absorption of the lantern light.

"Bub!" I mumbled, alarmed and shocked to see him so robust and resurrected from his crucifixion.

"Yes," he acknowledged my shock. "Like in the Bible, Charlie," he laughed. "I am everlasting, now." His legs swung out from their hidden perch and he jumped, feet first, in an arch from the high limbs to the grass immediately before my feet. Still buck naked, dusty, perfectly pungent, and utterly challenging in our private tongue, he rose from his squatted landing to my full-grown height and nibbled at my ear.

"Preacher boy," he said, "I've been waiting for you to catch up." Following my own eyes with a turn of his head, he slowly surveyed the yard. His eyes roamed appraisingly down Dewar then returned upward with a slight tilt of his head and lingered on the tall beaver hat. He smiled in his teeth-baring, nothing-to-hide way.

"Did you make him up?" he asked with a nod and sly grin in Dewar's direction. Before I could voice a denial, Bub responded, "He's so much like me. Flesh and blood, like I said you needed, remember?" He leaped catlike in front of Dewar and placed his ear against the hollowed place of his chest. I held my breath. I could not move, felt stuck behind a thick pane of glass. But no one else seemed able to see me in my invisible trap or to see the wild man, sprung from my boyhood, now cavorting in their midst. Returning to me with the same quick grace, he continued, "He has no scriptures around his heart like you," he accused, flattening and

pressing his hand against my heart. "I've heard and know yours, little soul saver." He laughed wickedly. "But, I covet his hat!"

I felt his hand up to his wrist pass through my chest, and wrap
around my heart, whose beating swelled and burned in the manip-
ulations of his fingers.

"I think he'll be leaving you, soon," Bub said as if reading tea
leaves in a drained cup.

"I think so, too," I whispered.

Bub withdrew his hand and brushed it against his other like two
crashing cymbals. My heart retained some of the warmth from his
hand still. "Will you throw him back to the lake?" he asked.

"No," I swore, "I'll keep him, if I can."

His dark eyes flashed with his devilish laughter. His body danced
erotically against mine, his shoulders and hips swiveling back and
forth. He rocked himself seductively against me, his eyes rolled upward as his lids fell in a trancelike, possessed expression. His lips approached my face blindly and slowly, dryly dabbing at the tears I felt
on my cheeks, toward my mouth, his feet nearly running in place,
pounding the grass rapidly, sending a vibratory hum throughout his
body which I absorbed through my own in wave after wave of vi-
bration. His teeth snapped into my lower lip, piercing and pulling as
if tearing off a bite.

Before the wail of the pain could make itself past the shocked
constriction of my throat, Bub was gone, and all the lanterns and
candles and tree lights flickered calmly in the still and starry night
of early summer.

The magnolia leaves rustled near the uppermost branches where
the large white blooms were most abundant and shed petals, as if
stirred by a rough high wind. Pauline ducked with a startled cower
against Fred's chest then laughed and grabbed at the light June
flurry of magnolia petals.

In the voice of the invisible rustling wind, Bub admonished that
love feels good and hurts. Helps but hurts. Love is savage and queer. He
laughed tauntingly, *No one's sin, all's salvation.*

* * *

The prom began instantly with a toast of Fred's homemade blackberry brandy, which he poured from a brown quart beer bottle
into dainty stemware and distributed ceremoniously.

"Young man," he announced quietly, lifting his glass to Dewar.
"Pauline and me couldn't be any prouder than we are if you were
our own son." He stumbled momentarily on an inner thought.
"Well," he went on, embarrassed, I think, by the respectful attention of so many eyes upon him, "I hope you'll always think of us
in that regard, if you can. So, we love you is all, and we're real
proud. That's it." He lifted his little glass with a flourish and took
a sip. We each did the same. The brandy was sweet, fruity, warm,
and extremely satisfying in its aftertaste. It caused everyone to lick
their teeth and smack their lips.

Then, Pauline raised her glass and tearfully proclaimed, "Child,
you've just growed up so fine. I know it ain't been easy, God bless
you. Oh, baloney meat!" she choked up. "Give me some huggin'."
She swung her arms wide apart, the brandy sloshed in its glass in
her hand, and Dewar moved into the openness of her body with
his arms around her narrow shoulders.

We drained our glasses and Fred uncorked his bottle to refill
them. As he walked, stopped, and poured his way around the circle, Pauline began tugging at Dewar's arm, which she had been
holding and rubbing since their embrace. They exchanged private
words into each other's ears; then Pauline called to me to join
them as they walked toward the rear of the garage.

I thanked Fred for the brandy as he filled my glass.

"Pauline wants to show you something," he said, motioning for
me to go.

The rear of the garage had been extended with three walls and
a slanted roof of salvaged windows, their varying sized frames fitted
together into a precision puzzle of square and rectangular panes of
glass. The functioning sills allowed the walls and even the roof to
be virtually opened up to the private woods behind the building.

"This is where Pauline raises her real children," Dewar said as we
followed her through a door in the center of the back wall.

None of the lantern light reached back behind the garage, but the slant of the windowed roof caught some of the moon-and-star light and poured it in a thin film over the interior. Except for the pitch black enclosure at the front end of the garage, the greenhouse evoked a disorienting feeling of the outdoors, rather exotic in its intensity. The smell of soil was rich, thick, and lusty in the warm and moist air. Until Pauline pulled the chain switch beneath the fringed shade of a ceiling lamp and lit the room with a soft parchment kind of light, my chief concern was the humidity that densely packed the little room with a sultry pressure against my skin, even through my heavy robe and the clothes beneath that. I blamed the seeping sensuality and the arousing aroma of the fertile soil on the effects of the pot still meandering through my bloodstream and the warm flash of the brandy in my hand as I poured it in sparing but frequent doses over my thickening, lazy tongue.

Pauline had been reverently silent since our approach to the greenhouse. Now, in the lamplight, she stood demurely against one wall and Dewar remained wordlessly composed against the door as if the two of them had stepped back in a passive agreement to let the orchids present themselves to me.

The greenhouse was a thicket of orchids. Clay pots lined narrow wooden benches, sprouting tall, gracefully arcing stems ladened with buds or blooms so ornately delicate and strangely removed from the kingdom of flowers as I knew it that they emitted an almost animalistic aura. Some of the potted orchids hung from ceiling hooks overhead and draped their large petaled heads, snakelike, over the rims into my face with a frightening open-jawed exposure of the wild beauty of their raw throats.

The soft but aggressive colors of the blooms evoked the furs of African tigers, leopards, and zebras or the skins of tropical fish and deep-sea creatures rather than any shades of rose, peony, or dahlia.

"They are awfully beautiful, Pauline," I managed to utter, for I was tongue-tied with awe. I couldn't move from the spot I'd shuffled into in the dark. The light and what it had illuminated had riveted me there. I was too afraid of the vision of the orchids to approach them physically. Their beauty was almost too blatant and, in a way, sexual for even my eyes to linger upon.

"Most of these babies are older than my daddy, who built this hothouse before I was even born. So, I guess I have an excuse for my love of unusual and pretty things," Pauline explained. "Child," she laughed, "these orchids were my doll babies, and this was my playhouse growin' up." She tenderly reached up and stroked a spotted bloom with her fingertips. Then she studied, as if noticing for the first time, the dozen or more jeweled rings spaced around her ten fingers. Holding up her hands with the diamonds, rubies, emeralds glittering in the overhead light, she smiled secretively and said, "I think anyone who really *loves* pretty things deserves to have them. Don't you, Charlie?"

"Of course," I agreed, though falsely so, for I was not on terms as personal and magical with the word *deserve*, as Pauline Tucker. Really loving may qualify as deserving, but I knew from repeated and disappointing experience it did not necessarily bring the pretty things of desire to one's fingers.

"Well, now," Pauline sighed dismissively, reaching for the pull-chain of the lamp, "I don't want to bore you with a bunch of potted flowers. And it's awful sticky in here, ain't it?" She plunged us into blue-gray moonlit silhouettes and made her way toward the door. "Dewar always liked it out here," she said, hooking her arm through his and opening the door. "He said you'd like it, too."

"Yes, thank you. He told me about it once," I called out over my shoulder, hanging behind alone in the near dark. I cupped my free hand beneath the gobletlike bloom of an orchid, bending its stem gently so that the flower's scalloped petals pressed against my face and the stamen brushed across the tip of my nose. I inhaled deeply, slowly, as if sipping another kind of brandy for the first time and wanting to savor the warm aftertaste all through my body. But as I released the flower to its upright position and closed up the greenhouse, I drained my glass of the blackberry liquor, accepting, if not satisfied, that that was the most intoxicating perfume at hand. As my craving senses wove their way around the corner of the garage back to the party, I felt deserving of euphoria and thirsty for a larger dose of company, pretty lights, a whole carton of Winstons, more liquor, more pot, more love from anyone. For a brightly lucid moment between the orchid and the prom, one puzzling question of my boyhood was answered by my own delicious drunkenness. I understood why Chick had drunk. I understood the compulsive seventy-five-mile drives to Tulsa and all the fifties spent.

It was this glorious cellular warmth, this laxative of thought from the mind to the tongue, this sexy, physical invincibility, this sloppy but sincere sentimentality in the heart, these faceted jewel lenses that the eyes became. This is surely why he drank, why bars were built, why paint was sniffed, weeds chopped and smoked, maybe even why the Holy Spirit was let into the soul when it knocked. It was because something was always lost for everybody, I lectured myself. Nothing was as whole as it should have been. Love felt good, but hurt. Helped, but hurt. And orchids had no perfume.

I was in the mind and mood for such revelations. In my graduation attire, I felt dressed for wisdom and everything that reeled through my head that night seemed relevant to the quality of the next morning and the mornings after that. I was a little drunk and still dreamily doped, and I trusted that euphoria was an angel, nested like a crown on my brain, who would transfigure, sort, and save these mystical sensations to memory as I slept and he alighted to the higher air. Yet, each moment of that evening was always filtering through me as fluidly as water, some of them being absorbed by the softer, thirstier parts of myself but most of them sliding right off my memory.

The rest of the night was one long blurry pleasure. We drank more brandy and Pauline insisted on another of her cigarettes, if she was to dance. Fred played an autoharp, making a simple, earthy kind of music I'd never heard before. Rae found some hardwood sticks somewhere and backed Fred's strumming songs with a metallic percussion beat out on the various piles of scrap metal.

Eventually, Pauline fulfilled her promise to dance, temporarily relieved of her arthritis, which evidently knotted some of her joints with a pain that accounted for the stiff and awkward movements I'd noticed earlier, like the way she'd climbed down and up the porch steps to greet us and eased slowly into and out of her various chairs.

She did a wild lindy hop/Charleston kind of twist between the giant magnolias, all kicking legs and loose-wristed swinging arms. The tight flip of her hair unwound and rewound like a yo-yo as she bobbed her head and pecked the air with her sharp chin.

She was a joy and a delight to watch. Dewar and I bounced rapidly in place, smiling and encouraging her with our clapping hands. Rae beat out the fast rhythm of Pauline's feet against the steel ribs of a radiator, while Fred's warm and appreciative eyes seemed caught in a web spun by the shimmering shimmy of his wife alone.

"Child!" she panted at Dewar, fanning the neckline of her flashy dress, gasping for breath as we all applauded raucously around her. "It's a blessing . . . you . . . ain't goin' . . . to no vo-tech," she paused for air, " 'cause, Child, this is all she wrote! Whew! Hear me Fred? I'm retirin' my dancin' pumps back to the resale. There ain't another after-supper smoke big enough to make these old feet boogie-woogie another step!"

"But, what about Charlie, Pauline?" Dewar asked, throwing his naked arm around my shoulder. "He don't finish till next year. You got to dance for Charlie's graduation, too!"

"Oh, my Lord!" she groaned, half fallen with exhaustion. She opened her arms to me and fell into me with a tight hug. "Racine!" she hollered past my shoulder. "God bless you, Child, for droppin' out."

"Pauline," I said, "if you could stand it right now, while your motor's still running, I'd settle for a waltz and I'd be so honored."

Her lean arms radiated heat and a vibrant pulse upon my back.

"You are the prettiest thing on earth, Child." She squeezed me closer. "Racine, get us a radio, Hon, 'cause you know Fred can't strum slower than sixty and, Child, my speed limit is lowered for good."

Rae hauled an old Bakelite Philco from out of the house, and Fred plugged it into an extension cord from the garage. The two of them fiddled with the volume and tuning until a slow ballad, popular at the time, even though it was soul music, seemed to clear its throat over the static and find its gospel timbred voice.

The large square pattern of a waltz, the only dance I knew, did not fit the looser, rounded shape of the radio music. In my hesitation to improvise, Pauline began to lead and I gratefully followed.

She led me in a loose-hipped, S-curved tango around the yard space that seemed to clear our pathway of junk with the mere intention of our feet. I think our dancing may have appeared unseemly to more sober eyes, what with my clumsy, unbalanced, and nervous staggers toward synch and intimacy, but eventually Pauline's exuberance and flair seemed to rub off on me, like some of the beads and sequins of her dress with each close brush and shake of her chest against mine. Soon I was emboldened by her taming of my awkward dance style to bow gratefully to Mrs. Tucker, who curtsied graciously, if with fatigue and relief, and I offered my hand to the heathen brave in the tall fur hat.

Dewar took my hand and, at first, our dance was a serious joke. He grinned and skipped broadly, rigidly leading with his tense grip on my hand and around my waist, but neither of us had the presence of wit to sustain such an intentional gag and quickly, by default as sweet as the blackberry brandy, his grip slackened. We slipped loosely into one another's hold and our bodies relaxed and slowed into a mutual rhythm that was easy, jazzy, and almost natural.

The music had segued into another soul singer. This time a woman, trumpeting a blues in a voice high then low, sublime and raunchy as the lost good man her song missed and mourned. Such black market music was virtually unaired and so relatively unheard on the radio waves at that time and place. Rock and roll, in its most watered-down rhythms had just barely cut into the tame,

mildly bucking ride of country, bluegrass, and hymnals on the lo-
cally transmitted broadcasts.

I'd heard snatches of soul on jukeboxes in Tulsa bars as a boy
where it might have been occasionally tolerated for a while in preference to silence, like the scattered blacks themselves in such bars,
especially the women whose dark good looks might suddenly ap-
peal to a hopped-up red neck who'd been rejected by one too
many white girls.

I danced with Dewar in Choteau beneath the stars in a clearing
surrounded by untouched wild country, next to a hothouse of
plantlife primordially beautiful and rare, amidst piles of metal rubbish as bent and twisted as bones of some extinct awesome species,
to the rhythm of blues rendered from a soul as foreign to me as Af-
rica. The scene of our dancing was spinning through my blood
with the alcohol, and I held on to Dewar with both arms around
his neck, and though he had no insight into the emotions that the
liquor and the pot had flushed from my heart, he held me in turn.
The holding calmed me a bit, though the pulse of the music still
moved our feet in place as if we'd found a ritualistic motion. We
softly stamped back and forth and hugged tight in the middle of
the yard with its scattering of small, contained bonfires, the Christmas lights, lazy in the warmth of June, blinking at slow intervals in
the tree branches. Pauline cooled herself with a turkey feather fan
in a plastic webbed lawn chair between the magnolias. Rae and
Fred rhythmlessly two-stepped around the metal heaps, oblivious
to the slow humping bass time of the actual music. At least, I
thought, they hear the same music and I tightened my grip around
Dewar's neck until his beaver hat toppled and knocked the cap off
my own head as it barreled to the ground.

Do you hear it, Dewar? I was silently asking him. Do you hear
it, too? The calling? The radio, like a transmission from some far-
off jungle. These woods, so full of voices calling. Calling out for
the spiritual work to be done, a mission of the soul to be erected,
lives to be saved and changed. Something savage and primitive is
calling still, but now, I thought as I pressed him even closer, now

I can't hear the difference in the voice. Is it the Lord's call? Is it
Bub? Is it for me? Am I God's vessel or the godless heathen, the
missionary or the unwashed? Who's converted whom, here? Who's
being called away here? If my sins are washed away, what's left of
the sinner? If you go away . . . when I go away, I won't know how
to love anyone else; I can't remember the way we did it to do it
again. I came to you out of a dense jungle. Surely I was strangling
him with my greedy arms, but he rocked on his feet and returned
my grasp inch by gradual inch. It's all closing in. The calling gets
closer and deeper and the jungle crawls nearer. Can you feel it at
all? Smell it? Hear the leaves brushing, fronds stretching to reclaim
the clearing?

The music abruptly ended or was cut off by a loud static. Fred
casually turned off the radio, and Pauline suggested maybe it was
time for bed. "Before y'all squeeze the peewaddin' out of one another," she yelled to us.

Dewar convulsed against me with a choked laugh, and our arms
loosened and slid off one another like tangled vines strategically
clipped.

"What's a . . ." Dewar tried to ask with a grin, rubbing the back
of his wrist against one pink-rimmed eye.

"If you don't know what a peewaddin' is, child," Pauline told
him, rising awkwardly from her lounger with fan in hand, "then
don't ask."

It had been a long day and evening. While dancing with Dewar,
I had already grown as silent as sleep, but inside I wasn't quite
ready to let go of this night. It seemed that the day and night, and
in many ways all the days and nights preceding, had funneled down
to the tip of privacy of whatever the hour now was. I wanted to
be alone with Dewar now, reclaim him from the others and hold
him like he was mine alone.

He held me in turn and guided me affectionately toward the
house, as tenderly and protectively as a guardian angel. I heard the
unraveling of an argument in the yard behind us as Rae announced

she was going to sleep in her tent in the woods and Pauline insisted she was going to spend the night in the house. Rae's conviction was not too strong against the willfulness of Pauline's raised
voice, and I was peripherally aware of Rae's heavy stomping and
Pauline's careful high-heeled steps behind us.

Inside the back door, there was a brief exchange of information
and arrangements were quickly resolved. Pauline and Rae passed
on through the kitchen as Dewar lowered me onto a springy, quilt-
covered mattress on the sleeping porch. I smacked my lips dryly for
more of something.

Dewar seemed at peace with himself and amazingly at home as
he began pulling the clothes away from my body. It felt wonderful
to let him have me in this way. I didn't assist with the project in
any way. In fact, I hindered it where I could with a bit more dead-
ness to my weight.

While Dewar lifted me here and there, unbuttoned, tugged, un-
did, and removed everything that I wore, I watched Fred through
the porch screen, putting out the multiple flames, unplugging the
various cords of things, moving the radio and the autoharp into the
storage end of the garage, then gathering up the stemware as if on
an egg hunt throughout the yard.

The vision of Fred in the starlight in his tuxedo, tidying up after
the party like an elegant butler returning things to their order was
endearing. Walking toward the house, the crystal goblets hanging
from between the fingers of both hands, he managed to open the
screen door without so much as a clink. He paused inside and
smiled matter-of-factly at the bed, as if one young man stripping
down another on his back porch was an average sort of sight to his
eyes. He moved and the door came to behind him.

"Good night," he offered, making his way through the open
kitchen door.

"Night, Fred," Dewar responded, not removing his attention
from my half-completed peeling.

"Good night, Fred," I attempted to speak, but only a sweetly in-
toned mumble made it past my lips. A moment later, the kitchen

door closed, setting the screened-in porch adrift from the huge dock of the house like a raft on a lulling course down a river.

In the privacy of the closed-off porch, I stretched across the full length and width of the narrow mattress pushing Dewar into a standing position next to it. He laughed quietly, looking down on me.

It was the first time we'd been alone together since our arrival at the resale, and so much seemed to have happened, within me anyway, I couldn't wait for morning or sobriety to feel out what might have changed between us.

Dewar stood beside the bed, bent forward and worked at undoing the small buckles of his chaps. His hands moved up his legs to his waist and with one firm tug at the belt surrounding it, the heavy suede dropped to the floorboards with a soft thud. I watched him lazily from my sprawled position, my head turned heavily against one cheek.

Unbuttoning, then stepping out of his jeans, he said, "Charlie, I . . ." He seemed to pull the words back between his teeth and sat down on the edge of the mattress at the foot of the bed. I managed to lift one bare leg and then the other and slide my feet into his warm lap. That heavy fur hat had steamed the neatness out of his hair and it fell familiarly forward now over his eyes as he bowed his head and picked at the leather knot behind his neck. The bib of horn and silver rattled loose from his collar and collapsed into his lap, over my feet like a cool heavy net as his hands moved to the small of his back, untying the straps there that secured it to his waist.

"What?" I asked, transfixed by every nuance of his undressing.

He slipped one hand under the pile of beads and cupped it around my ankle, smoothed back his hair with the other. "Thanks, is all," he said, "for comin' here. For gettin' me here."

He picked up the beaded piece and tossed it onto a wicker chair beside the bed.

"I like Pauline and Fred," I told him, though every word felt like a jagged stone in the tumbler of my mouth that was worn down and smooth by the time I spit it out. I wasn't sure if I was speaking English anymore.

"Yea," Dewar agreed.

"And Rae Ludy, too," I added.

Dewar looked at me and smiled, probably at the slurred nonsense I'd just uttered. But he nodded, anyway, as if he were at least familiar with the same language. His hand moved up my shin and down again.

"Are you all right?" he asked.

"Oh, yes," I admitted, "aren't you?"

"Sure."

"You said we'd do it, a while ago, remember? You said sometime we'd smoke some grass and you said it'd be like the smell of orchids. I know what you meant by that. How come you tell me all these things about yourself, Dewar, but tell them in disguises? Jack Stillwater, the trucker, the greenhouse, and everything?"

"Are you mad?" he asked.

"No," I told him, "just a little high." We both laughed.

He began rubbing my leg again, the way one unconsciously strokes a cat just because of the way it feels.

"I've had to move a lot. You can't leave behind as much of yourself as the truth, everywhere you've been."

"Why not?" I asked.

"You ask too many questions. And I always tell. Before I even realize it, I've told you everything. Even if I start out lyin', I end up confessin'. You should be a minister or a policeman."

I groaned in disagreement. "What should you be?"

"How 'bout a renderer?"

"Yea," I nodded against the quilt, "good pay and union benefits."

"Yea," he agreed halfheartedly. "Everybody needs a union." He slid out from beneath my feet and rose from the bed in a long, tall stretch. "Could you spare an inch of space in that bed, Charlie Hope?"

I shifted obligingly toward the wall, while my eyes remained dazed and fixed on his backside. He slid his shorts below his hips and lifted one foot, then the other out of them. Even in the shadowy, screened light of the porch I saw the wicked welts and marks across the extra-pale flesh of his buttocks. He reseated himself and then fell back into the mattress alongside me, easing his near shoulder beneath my head, curling his arm to rest his hand lightly across my staring eyes.

"Too late," I said. "I saw."

He slid the blindfold of his hand from my eyes to my mouth. I was too stunned by the quick sight of those bruises to speak out again immediately, so I rested my lips against his palm and let the hot-branded sensation in my mind burn down a bit.

After a few moments of stillness, I pulled his hand down to my chest where I pinned it flat beneath my own two hands.

"Dewar," I said soberly, raising my face from his cradling neck and shoulder up to the level of his own eyes staring blankly at the wood-slatted ceiling. "What is that? What happened to you?"

"Nothin'," he said.

"What happened?" I persisted.

"Nothin'," he repeated with annoyance.

"It was the General, wasn't it?"

"It was for my own good," he said dryly.

"Goddammit! I'm serious. I mean it. That's got to be killing you and has been all day."

"Do I look like a dyin' man?"

"Why would he do that, Dewar? It's not right."

"I told you, he likes to counsel a boy along with his buttermilk and cornbread. It wasn't the first time. I wasn't the first one."

"Goddammit!" I swore again.

"You're too hopped up," he said calmly.

"Somebody should do something," I declared, the bed and the porch stormily pitching and rocking with my agitation.

"Oh yea? Like what? Like who?" he impatiently asked.

"Go to the sheriff, go to the doctor, maybe the principal. I don't know. Somebody should know, somebody could fire him or stop him or kill him."

"Calm down," he told me. "I'm doin' somethin'. All of us are."

"What?"

"Waitin'," he said.

"For what? Those bruises to heal?"

"For eighteen," he calmly answered.

I was too angry to debate any more about it, even though I thought maybe Fred or Pauline could do something if they knew. I let that idea settle somewhere in the sloshy waves of my mind, thinking maybe I would tell them in the morning, privately without Dewar even knowing. Or, in another flash, I thought maybe I could do something myself, somehow. Hurt the old bastard personally, cut him up, beat him with his own board.

"Roll over," I told Dewar.

He retrieved his arm from under me and willingly rolled himself onto his stomach, his arms and hands folded up neatly under him. I rubbed my hand through his hair, combed the short stubbly ones at his nape with my fingers and then tried to smooth away all the troubles that could be reached through the surface of his skin. I thought only of soothing and healing and the focus itself seemed to do something orderly to my own chaos, funneled my thinking into the smooth glide of my palms and fingers across his tensed shoulders and back.

The muscles of his ass tensed at the approach of my touch, but I was concentrating on tenderness and the cushy flesh soon relaxed beneath my strokes. The welts were blistered and smooth from one hip to the other, a braille impossible to read by touch, too horrible to study by sight. They were surrounded by bruises like a spilled ink that had run, then seeped, into the skin with indefinite fuzzy outlines.

I continued rubbing him down his legs to his feet, deeply massaging his tough soles with my thumbs.

I finished at the foot-end of the bed, my hands achingly empty and itchy resting on the quilt. "I wish you were bigger," I said, "so there'd be more of you to touch."

He twisted his torso front side up, raising his shoulders and head off the pillow with the support of his elbows.

"There is some more," he hoarsely said with his familiar grin, his messed hair across his sleepy eyes.

I stared at him intently, thinking, "I love you," but unable to trust the voice that could say it aloud, afraid it would not be heard in the significant tone in which it was felt.

"Well?" he asked, arching the dimpled edges of his grin a little higher.

"What?" I asked innocently.

He stretched both arms, reaching for me with spread fingers as he fell back into the pillow. "Come here," he said.

I was awakened by the heat of the sunlight through the sieve of the screen walls. My nostrils were filled with the woodiness of the house wall they faced and the musty old cotton of the quilt bundled beneath my chin. I pushed the covers off me and sat up, feeling chilled all over as the air hit my damp skin. My head swam a bit as I raised it from the pillow and my mouth was so dry, thirsty, and foul tasting I thought I might gag on the spittle I managed to draw out of it and swallow. I took an inventory of every detail around me: the chipped paint of the porch, the minute weave of the screening, the fly crawling on the ceiling, the amazing brightly shadowed depth and dimension of the yard and woods beyond the screen. A similarly clear focus existed inside my head, once the dizziness of rising had drained away. It was like the brandy and all had stirred up every heavy, encrusted feeling within me and somehow expelled it into the night. I woke up feeling connected and engaged with the morning light and heat and the birdsong coming from as far away as the twin magnolias. I woke up with a rejuvenated skin, the old one having been shed in the gentle friction and clean sweat of sex.

I picked through the pile of costumes on the chair and floor until I found my clothes and dressed.

"Sit down, child," Pauline said quietly as I opened the kitchen door from the porch. "I'll git you some coffee."

"Morning, Pauline. Thanks," I said, seating myself at the dinette as she rose in a flowered housecoat, her hair rewound in rollers, and poured me a cup of coffee from a percolator on the counter.

"It's a beautiful day, isn't it?" I commented pleasantly as she eased herself back into the chair opposite me.

I drank carefully from the hot thick mug. "Where is everybody?"

She looked into my eyes and said, "I hoped you might know, Child."

I asked her what she meant.

"They're gone."

I asked who she meant.

"Racine. And Dewar, too, if you don't know where he is."

Her meaning was still unclear. I drank another sip of coffee.

"It's almost noon," she said nervously. "I been up since seven. Rae was gone then, though her bed was slept in for a while and then I peeked onto the porch and you was the only one out there. I think they've run off, Charlie."

"But, why, Pauline? Why do you think that? Maybe they just went somewhere together, for a while. Maybe to the Reservation store, or Rae's tent, or to the truck stop for breakfast. They were talking about those places last night. Places they used to go. They're just out visiting or something."

"Oh, Child," she said, swinging the rollers of her shaking head, and capturing my hand beneath her own against the table. "I have a bad feeling. I know those foolish children have run off and, OK, they're big enough to know theirselves and where they want to be, but . . . Charlie, I have the sickest feeling."

I did not accept Pauline's premonition, but I sympathized with her conviction to it and I could feel the heaviness of the concern it caused her.

I asked where Fred was. She said he'd gone out looking hours ago to all the places I'd just mentioned.

"Well, there you go, Pauline. He'll be back any minute with the two of them in the truck, as innocent as anything, probably bitching and arguing the whole way back." I smiled in an effort to cheer her with my own strange optimism. He couldn't have left, I thought, not yet.

Pauline patted my hand instead of returning my smile. "Did I say you are the sweetest thing I ever met?"

"I think so," I assured her.

"I mean it, Charlie. I'm an ordained minister. I can read people from a mile away." She pushed her glasses up her nose. "Well," she grinned, "half a mile away.

"I don't know your story, Child, or the whole story of you two boys together, but I could see right away you was good for him and him for you. He'd growed up a little. Taller, yes. Still too skinny, of course, the both of y'all, but he'd growed up inside since leavin' here. Less angry and a little less hurt. Is he still the biggest liar in the state?"

I laughed. "Yea, he is."

"Charlie," she went on, looking up from our hands on the table, staring at nothing else but the space in the room it seemed. "He was the wildest little man. You just wouldn't believe. Foul mouthed, mean, cold, and sharp as an icicle when the foster care brought him here. Brought him here 'cause nobody else would have him by that time. But, of course, that's what Fred and me wanted. I said, 'Fred, if we're goin' to take in a youngun, for Pete's sake, let's take one that really needs us.'

"He 'bout wore me out at first. But, Child, I've got patience. Once he saw he couldn't shock us, hard as he tried, 'cause I was a wildcat myself and I probably should be in a nuthouse now or out in California somewhere. I'm as weird as the Lord makes 'em, and I know it.

"Dewar only needed that. Somebody to let him blow off his steam, somebody he couldn't shock into an anger as mean as his own. Finally, one day, he says to me, 'Pauline, I'm in love,' and I said, 'Child, that's so wonderful.' But he squints up his eyes and goes, 'I ain't in love with no girl, Pauline. I don't like 'em much.'

"I said, 'Child, ain't nothin' wrong with girls. You ought to re-consider your opinion on that, but if you're in love, that's what counts.' And he got all frustrated like kids do when they ain't gettin' the goat of somebody like they want to.

" 'I'm in love with Jack Stillwater,' he says. 'I love him like a fag-got.' That's just what he said, spit it out like the filthiest thing there was to spit.

"I grabbed him up in my arms and said, 'No you don't, Child. You love him like Dewar Akins and there ain't nothin' the least bit ugly or awful about that. But, I got to tell you what's awful about Jack. I know him, Child, and he ain't ever goin' to love you back. I know Jack is a pretty man, and I think people who really love pretty things deserve to have them. I think you deserve to be loved back.' Course," she turned away from the vision of her memory, looking squarely at me again, "I had the same heartbreakin' talk with Racine Ludy about that Mary Deer. Guess you heard about that?"

I nodded.

"Children got to learn," she concluded sadly.

"I do love him, Pauline," I confessed.

"Me, too," she said, rising slowly, rubbing her shoulders, walk-ing to the window. "But, Honey, he's gone for good, I can feel it."

Pauline made enough ham, eggs, grits, biscuits, and gravy for five people, probably wishing for that number to appear around the ta-ble and eat it all. I felt a nearly bottomless emptiness and ate all that I could hold.

I moved back a bit from the table and was thinking of finding a cigarette when I was suddenly electrocuted with a thought. "Je-sus Christ!" I said, causing Pauline to jump in her chair where she'd sat watching me eat, not touching a morsel herself.

"Pauline, what time is it? What day is it?"

"Child, it's Saturday, almost one."

"I have to use the phone. Jesus Christ! I can't believe I never thought to call."

"Who?" she asked with my same urgency.

"My momma," I told her. "I've got to call Pryor."

"It's in the dining room," she pointed.

On the ninth ring, Ida answered. "Praise God, Charlie, where are you? Are you all right? Is Dewar with you? I've been a nervous wreck. Fay Rose wouldn't let me call the sheriff and that General Newton has been calling every hour since yesterday. Dewar didn't graduate, or something. Where is he? What's wrong with you?" She said more words, asked more questions, expressed more emotion, talked longer on the phone than she ever had in her entire life. I couldn't even begin an explanation for three or four minutes.

"Charlie, where are you?" she demanded.

"I'm sorry I forgot to call. I'm fine. With Dewar," I lied. "We went for a drive and ended up sleeping in the woods."

"Why on earth?"

"Some trouble with the car, Ida. We got stuck quite a ways out of town . . ."

"Did you eat?" she interrupted.

"Eat? Yes, we ate," I responded angrily. There was a familiar silence on the line. "In a café," I added. "I'm sorry, Ida. Everything is fine, really."

"I just don't understand it, Charlie. Why would you just drive off into the wild?"

"We just did."

"You don't know what that general has put me through," she complained. "The fuss he's made, the things he thinks about me."

"Well," I said, "if he calls again . . ."

"He's been callin' every hour since last night. Dewar was supposed to graduate."

"I know."

"And I was supposed to know why he didn't." She sighed heavily into the phone. "I don't understand this, Charlie."

"Yes, I know," I told her. "I'm sorry, Ida. Good-bye."

"Well, I don't think she had much there to begin with," Fred explained, "but it looked cleaned out to me." He was talking about Rae's tent in the woods.

He went on with his detailed explanation of everywhere he'd been. "Mrs. Deer said Rae came by before sunrise, alone, woke her up, just to see the baby. Said she just studied the child sleeping in its crib and left.

"Jack said the two of them were sitting on the store step when he opened up at seven. They bought a carton of cigarettes and left.

"Lucille said they had breakfast at the truck stop a little past seven. Fried eggs and sausage. Then, one of the gas boys said he saw them getting into a semi that pulled out around eight."

"Where to?" I asked, disoriented by the trail of facts that led to nothing. Pauline sat quietly with her hands crossed over her mouth.

"Oklahoma City, he thought," Fred answered.

"Oh, I felt it," Pauline cried, "I just knew it." Fred approached her from behind her kitchen chair, bent and hugged her with both arms across her chest. He rubbed his face against hers and whispered calming words into her ear.

"They're old enough to get by," he said. "They're good kids. They're smart. They have their own ideas. They'll be fine. It's nobody's fault," he told Pauline.

She whimpered quietly, nodding her head in agreement against Fred's cheek.

I sat at the table feeling drained of blood, feeling a hum in my head and a waving motion in my stomach. "Excuse me, please," I mumbled, rising from the chair and moving quickly through the house to the bathroom, closing the door securely. I threw up breakfast and then some vinegared blackberry brandy. It was a long while until I was certain of my complete emptiness.

* * *

I couldn't stay any longer with Fred and Pauline, despite their sincere invitation to do so. Dewar's running off had left a gap between us. The affection was still there, but the channel for it was missing.

"Stay on a while, Son," Fred had advised with his fatherly arm around my shoulders. "It's a long drive back, all by yourself."

"I'm all right, Fred. The drive'll do me good. I have to go. There's already a commotion about our leaving."

"There's going to be questions," he said, "a lot of questions, I imagine. You want me to go with you?"

"Thank you, Fred, but don't worry. I won't take any blame." I did take his hand though and shook it at the resale door, then kissed the back of it quickly and headed toward the car.

Pauline came skipping out after me, across the dust yard.

"Child," she panted at the open car door, "take these things with you." She shoved the bulky cap and gown box into my arms. "I'm sure it was just borrowed, but the rest is for you." She grabbed me by the shoulders and practically climbed over the box I held between us to kiss me good-bye.

"Thanks, Pauline," I said, feeling so sad I couldn't really feel the gratitude, which I knew to be somewhere within me.

"I hope you'll come back, sometime. You don't need no invite. The resale's always open." She waved while clutching her housecoat together at the collar. Fred raised an open hand at the screen door. I backed the Impala into the road.

Maybe Bub was the one who took the wheel of the car and turned it off the highway into the Reservation parking lot. I knew it was a devious desire that pushed me out of the car and into the store with enough nerve to risk what I was about to attempt.

Thankfully, Jack was the only one inside. He was sprawled in a chair next to the cold stove, one leg hooked over the chair's arm, the other propped across the seat of its twin. I think he was asleep when I walked in. His head raised from his fist with a jerk as I closed the door behind me. He peered up with his black, wet-

looking hair in his face, then sat up a bit and parted it back behind
his ears.

"Mornin'," he said neutrally.

"Afternoon," I said.

"Yea," he sighed with boredom, "whatever."

He did not adjust his legs or rise to take up business behind the
counter. He just sat, patiently waiting for the transaction to come
to him. He was shirtless again and barefooted, but his spread legs
were covered with faded jeans. The tattoo on his bicep was in
clearer focus in the daylight pouring through the store windows
and I noticed that, except for the hair feathers, it resembled an
early president's profile as much as an Indian, but either way, it was
green as money and made a connection of commerce and skin.

"Pauline asked for another pack," I said, meeting his gaze
directly.

His eyes locked onto mine for a few doubtful moments like one
liar is prone to challenge another, then pulled his feet, one at a
time, to the floor and rose from his seat to walk heavily behind the
selling table.

"Pauline must be hurtin' extra-bad," he commented nonchalantly as he squatted behind the register, making the sounds of
rummaging and rearranging. "Or else," he said, rising up and tossing the cigarette pack, this time an unwrapped hard pack of Winstons, over the counter into my lucky catch, "y'all partied real
good all night."

I pulled a five from my pocket and laid it on the side of the register in reply.

Jack took a step backward, crossed his legs, folded his arms over
his chest, and leaned back against the shelves of thermoses, pipes,
cowboy hats, and fishing caps.

"I was wondering if I could also get a bottle," I said.

He grinned and turned his head to the left. "Liquor store's next
door," he said.

"I was wondering if you'd maybe get it for me," I trudged on.

Maintaining his grin, he asked, "What made you wonder that? It's a short stroll. You look healthy to me."

"Yea, well, see, I don't have any ID on me. I thought since you kind of know me, you'd do me the favor."

"I don't know you," he said, running his hands through his hair.

"Charlie," I told him, "Dewar's friend. We were in here yesterday."

"Yea," he said, "but I hear Dewar's gone, since early this mornin'. So whose friend does that make you, today?"

"Seems you're right," I agreed and turned to leave.

"Wait a minute," Jack called. I turned around. He was leaning over the table. "What's in this favor for me, Charlie?" he asked.

"I thought I'd pay you for your effort, of course," I answered.

"How?" he challenged.

A nervousness infused the intuition that began to dawn within me. But I was starting to feel impatient with his toying around and my mood was one of impulse; I didn't feel like thinking so hard about anything as unknowable as what was on someone else's mind. I bluntly asked, "How would you like, Jack?"

We didn't exchange many words after those. We negotiated with some hard stares, some brusk motioning and following. He led me behind an Indian blanket covering the doorway to a crammed storage room, hot and dank once the heavy blanket closed it off from the empty store.

Once there, he exposed himself eagerly to my touch and then my taste. I felt my way through to the finish without really feeling a thing. It took him forever, or so it seemed, at least in comparison to Dewar. The comparison to Dewar is where I tried not to let my mind wander in the back closet, but, of course, doing Jack Stillwater for a bottle of whiskey was such a different kind of exercise, my mind did nothing but compare.

Jack was bigger, and his configuration inside my mouth was intrusive and quickly tiresome. There was not a single hair on his thick legs and yet his skin lacked a smooth invitation to my hands.

He was also rigidly stationary and quiet; all the sound and motion came from my strenuous, mechanical effort.

The bargain was half over with his abrupt expulsion and quick buttoning up. Jack parted the blanket and was out of the store before I could get up off my knees. Just a minute after stepping out into the store and what felt and tasted like the freshest air I'd ever breathed, he came back in carrying a sack twisted around the neck of a quart bottle.

He shoved it at me and I took it in both hands. Jack settled into the same chair with the same sprawled leg posture I'd interrupted less than twenty minutes earlier.

"How much was it?" I asked.

"Why don't you just keep it," he said, his large brown hand hiding half his face which rested in it at a tilt away from me.

"Thanks," I said, not quite able to walk away yet.

"Can I ask you something that's none of my business?" He remained sullen and silent. "Did you ever know someone named Dean?"

Jack slowly lifted his head from his hand and turned his handsome face directly to mine. "Who the hell are you?" he asked, full of hate.

"Nobody. Just a friend of Dewar's," I said.

"Did he tell you I used to know someone named Dean? More likely, Rae Ludy did. But what's it to you, punk?"

"It's important to me to figure out something Dewar said once about you and someone he called Dean. He lies a lot, you know?"

"If he told you anything about Dean, he lied. Dewar doesn't know anyone by that name and Dewar doesn't know me, either."

"He never did?" I asked, despite his anger. "Know you—I mean like we . . . I just . . . ?"

"No," he said, "and you don't know shit, either. Why don't you take your bottle and your smoke and get out of here? You seem to have gotten everything you came for."

I persisted. "I don't care about you or who Dean was to you. I care about Dewar. It's important."

"Well, I told you, Dewar didn't know nobody named Dean. Maybe he should have. Maybe you should've too. Y'all have something in common."

"What's that?"

"Cocksuckers," he said with a squint of his black brows over his dark eyes.

I was ready to take that word and leave with it, but something kept my feet in place and my eyes focused narrowly on Jack's.

"He tell you I was in jail?"

"Yea," I answered.

"For turning a semi on the highway?"

I nodded.

"He tell you somebody was in the truck with me, passing a bottle?"

"Yea," I said.

"That was Dean, OK? Just a hitchhiker. That's against the law, you know, just like drunk drivin'."

"That's all?" I asked. "Just somebody you picked up once while trucking?"

"No, that ain't all," Jack said, putting his face back into his propped hand. "He died. That's all."

I twisted the sack tighter around the bottle in my hands. Finally, I raised it a bit, out toward Jack, though he was still turned away and couldn't read the gesture. "Thanks," I told him and left the Reservation store, as well as Choteau, with what seemed then more than I wanted to know after all and the means to maybe help me forget some of it for a while.

· Part Five ·

■

I GOT INTO PRYOR LATE IN THE AFTERNOON, GREETED BY THE SMELL of the rendering plant, which preceded its sight by more than a mile.

Slowing the car from highway speed to the town limit felt like entering another atmosphere where the air was thicker, the gravity stronger, and motion nonexistent. As numb as I felt inside, I still felt like a glaring and conspicuous life-form in comparison to the bolted-down stillness of Pryor.

The lot in front of Chick's joint was crowded with the trucks and cars of Saturday afternoon, business as usual. I crept on past the bar with an indifferent glance, aware that Ida or Fay could easily identify the Impala with a coincidental gaze out the window. There was too much time ahead, staring me in the face, in which to deal with them and their hand-wringing questions.

I drove to the house and parked, but I couldn't force myself to go inside those deserted quiet rooms for a while. Instead, I sat on the front porch steps and stared at the long driveway, Mrs. Mosley's plots of geraniums edged with half-buried tractor tires, and the blue of the unending sky.

Eventually, I retrieved the box from the front seat of the car and returned with it to the porch. It was close in size to a suitcase, and taking it out of the car felt too much like unloading from a long trip, which meant that it was over and any souvenirs had to be incorporated into the same life the vacation had reprieved.

I sat with the box on my lap, lifted the lid, and studied what Pauline had packed. The gown was folded up professionally, wrapped in tissue just as it had come. The mortarboard was flattened atop it next to the horn and silver beads Dewar had dug out of the resale junk box. My fingers strummed across them, and they clicked against themselves.

Atop everything was a stem of miniature orchids, five violet and white blooms that had wilted at the tips in the heat of the box, melted from the edges inward like dark grapey flaps of skin. I knew it was futile, but I sniffed at them anyway.

I opened the front door and carried the box through the house into my room in the back where I lifted the beads and the flowers, closed up the cap and gown on the bed and stood blankly for a moment in the middle of the room with each hand awkwardly occupied.

Confused by what I was trying, but not managing, to do, I put the things down again and searched through one of my drawers for my old cigar box of money and treasures. Having found it, I first took out one of Chick's old briarwood pipes, which I had snatched for its familiar smell from Fay Rose as she'd packed the others up for basement storage, and then I took the switchblade that had lain there, only occasionally handled, for almost four years and pocketed it. Despite their looseness, the beads would not fold or fit into the box. I spent a good deal of time trying to change this fact, before accepting it.

In addition to their personal, private value, I considered the beads evidence of a chain of events I was determined to cover up, so I hid them beneath a pillow on the bed for the time being and reburied the cardboard safety deposit box in the vault of my underwear drawer. I searched the room for flat weight with which to press the orchids.

The Bible was heavier and bigger than my dictionary, I decided, and Ida never touched it anymore anyway, so I carried the stem into the living room.

I placed them into one of the latter books toward the bottom and closed the Old and most of the New Testaments atop them on the floor. For good measure, I stood on the book, giving it a good heavy jump, before putting it back atop the TV.

With the pipe in my back pocket, I closed up the house and returned once more to the car. I took the Winston box from the glove compartment, plus a new pack of cigarettes from the carton, grabbed the whiskey bottle from under the seat, and took off on foot for a private place on the lake from which to watch some time pass.

My spot on the lake was quiet though desecrated by empty beer bottles, exploded fireworks, and other trash from the previous night's celebrating seniors. This intrusion upon what I considered my only piece of privacy stoked my anger at the stupidity of Pryor, and I kicked the bottles and cans with a vengeance until they were all out of sight of the elm tree I sat down beneath and settled back against.

The bourbon went down like gasoline in comparison to Fred's sweet brandy, but I got high quickly enough, and the swigs became comforting once the need to force them evaporated. I felt good again, or good enough, with the warmth of the whiskey filling the emptiness inside me.

The swirl of well-being took all the sharp edges off of everything I felt knocking against me from the inside. Even though drinking was just a day-old sensation to me, the bourbon's effect had a ring of recognition that seemed as old as my memory. It felt like a comfortable place that I had been looking for for a very long time with only a few clues and rumors to its existence. There at the lake, I found my place coming into 3-D focus like Disneyland in a Viewmaster, with the same kind of constructed depth and substance, mesmerizing, beautiful, just a trick of the eye, but a satisfying fantasy between me and the glaring light of the sinking sun.

I didn't know why I had brought the switchblade with me that afternoon, had even forgotten it was in my pocket until I was drunk and then it seemed like a coincidence too perfect to be accidental. I opened the sharp little blade and began whittling at the bark of the elm tree. I was claiming the tree and that spot on the lake as my own and as Dewar's, putting evidence, in our initials, that we had been there together, and I think, making an effort in my euphoria, to work some kind of magic spell, to call Dewar back to this tree where we had first come together and where the letters of our names in the naked wood would always call that out to us, or at least, to me.

I carved "CH" first, then "AND," then "DA," then "WERE HERE."

When I had finished, my hand was blistered and sore from the carving. I stepped back from the tree, took a drink from my bottle, and squinted at the cut letters in the yellowing light of the sunset. They were barely visible at all, too thinly chiseled with too small a blade. They stated nothing in the overwhelming thick bark of the tree. I spun around, reared back and threw the pearl-handled switchblade into the lake, whose surface it cut through blade first, with barely a ripple in its sink to the mud bottom.

For a moment, I regretted the angry impulse that had cast away Chick's last gift to me, but in a flash I recalled the pawnshop and the disgusting man who had sold it to us, how Chick himself had died with his body jackknifed in bed that very night, the overall uselessness of such a fancy little blade, and I took another swig of my bottle and decided I didn't care, decided to smoke some of Pauline's arthritis medicine so I would care even less.

Just as I was choking down the first bowlful, the Turtle Man stepped into my clearing rattling the contents of a burlap sack slung over his back. He stood calmly a few yards in front of me, his head turned toward the lake and the sun's mirrored image in its still surface.

My reflexes were too slowed by the liquor to even try to hide the pipe. Besides, the immediate air, which Owen was breathing, was thick with the ropey odor, and I passively accepted the fact that I had been caught. My only reaction was to drunkenly enjoy all the benefits of my crime I could before the privilege was confiscated for good. So I defiantly relit the pipe and sucked hard on its stem until my torso was puffed up with smoke and I felt light-headed to the point of blacking out from holding my breath. I exhaled a few deep coughs as Owen turned and walked over to where I sat.

He was a strange character in any light, but in the last dim rays of the day he was all shadows. He had the same plastic shower cap on his head as the last time I'd seen him at the bar. His shirt and pants were both gray and hung on him as Chick's clothes used to hang, on the same kind of lanky frame. As he set his bag down on the grass with a clatter, he leaned over, hands on knees, and his face approached mine, deeply marked with age lines, dry and shriveled around the lips, but surprisingly warm and engaging in the dark brown eyes that glistened with moisture and magnified clarity. Of course, his broken nose was blunt and downward bending, the most prominent feature about him. He licked his lips with a short pink tongue as if preparing to speak, but said nothing, just continued to lean down over me, as if studying my face.

Finally, I asked, "What's in your bag? Turtles?"

He twisted his neck, giving the burlap sack a careful once over, before turning his eyes back to mine. "Bottles and cans," he said gently. "The kids leave the lake a mess. I been pickin' up all day. Fourth load," he nodded toward the sack. "Piggly Wiggly'll refund two cents on the bottles."

"There's a mess of them under those bushes," I motioned with the pipe.

"Yep," he nodded. "I been watchin' for a while."

"What for?"

"No real reason," Owen answered assuringly. "Just an inkling that you maybe needed some watchin'."

"Thanks kindly," I told him, "but I come here to *not* be gawked at, to be alone if you don't mind."

"Naw, I don't mind," he said, lowering himself to a sitting position beside me and staring out across the dusky lake water.

Close as he was, he sat quietly and unobtrusively, so after a few minutes I decided to ignore him and relit my pipe. After several draws I began to feel the relaxing numbness of the smoke mingling with the glow of the whiskey and my mind began to unknot itself and cast its attention farther afield than my own personal anger and pain. The feeling was one of connectedness to everything that passed through my head even if that point of connection was the mere absurdity of one unrelated thing following another and how that conjures even another.

For instance, the Turtle Man's presence beside me suddenly seemed not just benign, but friendly, once I corraled my wandering attention upon him. I was convinced he meant me no harm, or he would have dragged me out of the woods by now or called the sheriff to do so.

With a teasing grin, I nudged Owen's knee with the pipe. He slowly looked down at my hand.

"Loco weed?" he asked.

"Naw," I told him, "Indian peace medicine."

"No, thanks," he replied, looking back toward the water, but continuing, "I tried that stuff before. It grows wild not too far from my boat. I was readin' up on that stuff—what do they call it these days?—in a magazine not long ago. You know, they're sayin' it expands the mind. Well," he licked his lips and nodded his head slightly as if lecturing the lake, "I reckon younguns might need that—in fact, I'd swear they do—but I think just livin' everyday to my age has expanded my mind enough. I don't feel a need to blow my mind out any farther than it's already been blowed.

"Now, for me, it's hard enough just walkin' from one place to another without gettin' distracted from where I'm goin'. I don't need the Milky Way swirling around in my head on top of everything else.

"Now, if there was somethin' to shrink the mind down some and git rid of some of the nonsense a-clutterin' it up, I'd try me some of that."

"There is such a thing," I said.

"What's that?" he looked me curiously in the eye.

"Pryor," I said.

He laughed quietly, but sincerely, then said, "Oh, I like it here, though." He extended an arm and swung it across the view in front of us. "This is nice, ain't it?"

I followed his motion across the lake and landscape with my eyes, taking in as much of the huge night sky as possible. It was beautiful and familiar, even out of focus. The stars seemed to rotate in their brightness.

I lifted the brown-bagged bottle from between my legs and took another drink, offering it to Owen when I'd finished. He took it wordlessly, smelled at the rim of its neck and took a huge swig.

"You seem pretty well stocked for a Saturday night," he commented. "You must've crossed a couple of county lines to get hold of a bottle of bourbon. You graduated last night?"

"No," I told him, "but I've been out of town."

"With that buddy of yours from the Home is what I heared at Chick's."

"Yea, we went for a drive. Had some car trouble. That's all."

"Your grandpa drove the wheels off that car. I reckon you got her fixed or you wouldn't be here now," Owen said casually. "The General sure don't like losin' track of one of his boys. Yes sir," he said, taking another swig of the bottle, "he was so riled last night, he come over to Chick's and was givin' your momma more grief than any righteous woman deserves."

"About Dewar?" I asked.

"Yep. And you, and where you two was and what you was doin', about your friend missin' the graduation at Strang, about your momma workin' a bar and not watchin' over y'all. Pardon my sayin', but he's got a itch up his ass so big a two by four wouldn't scratch it. Always has.

"I was raised there, you know," Owen said. "That general didn't take over till I was about your age. He beat the tar out of us boys. Mostly for being boys, if you know what I mean."

"Not exactly," I half-slurred.

"Well," Owen began, "you put a group of homeless boys together in one place, keep 'em fenced in as tight as you can, those kids is naturally goin' to stick to one another. Who else have they got?

"One thing the General wouldn't abide was suspicious friendship between his boys. The thing is, we was all of us suspicious friends at some time or another. Just plain growin' up curious, you know? Well, he was 'bout half his age then and strong—he broke my nose the way it still is today—accidentally to tell the truth—still, he swung that board of his too hard and freely. I felt like I had to swing back. That was my mistake then, but he's an older, weaker cuss now. I enjoyed pitchin' him out of the bar last night."

"Ida's letting you in the bar, now?"

"Fay Rose is, anyway, so long as I got some money." He motioned toward his sack of bottles and cans. "Your momma just kind of tolerates me for the time being. She's a fine lady, your momma. Too fine for me, I know, but she *is* a woman and needs someone to watch over her, like everybody else. One thing I got is patience."

I laughed aloud at the thought of Ida being courted by any man, but especially the Turtle Man.

Owen bashfully bowed his head as I continued to laugh, then he said apologetically, "Pardon if I'm out of line about your mother. I mean no disrespect."

"It's all right, Owen," I assured hm. "I just think you've got your work cut out for you, is all. Ida doesn't have much use for men, and excuse me for saying, for you in particular."

He smiled. "Oh, I know that. She's swatted me a few times with that broom. But, she's comin' around, slowly. Last night she gave me a draw and even thanked me for gettin' the General out of the joint before somethin' got broke."

"Maybe the next step, Owen, is taking that plastic bag off your head."

"Oh, I will. Believe me, I cain't wait, but I got another week of treatment to go yet."

"What kind of treatment are you doing?" I asked.

"It's experimental until I'm certain it cures, but," he lowered his voice confidentially, "I'm growin' hair with a turtle oil formula. The plastic keeps it cookin'."

"Oh," I said.

We sat quietly then, side by side. Owen took a few more drinks of bourbon, I smoked what was left in the pipe and tapped the ashes on the root of the tree.

"Owen, I don't know what to do," I finally said.

" 'Bout what?" he asked.

"Dewar's run off. I don't know where to, but I'm pretty sure he's not coming back," I confessed.

"Is he legal yet?" Owen calmly asked.

"Will be in a few weeks," I answered.

"Hmm," he thought for a moment. "Well, why do you have to do anything? He's the one who run away. A few weeks of bein' careful and he'll be legal. He'll be all right then."

I silently sulked on his unsentimental opinion.

"That ain't quite what you meant, is it?" Owen added. "But, I do admire your buddy's spirit, gittin' away clean from the General without any broken bones." He licked his lips.

"I seen the two of you out here together before. Don't worry," he said. "Voices carry over the water and my boat's not far. I was just checkin' on my own privacy, so to speak. Kids come out here for meanness all the time, to do damage to my boat, garden, whatever.

"I knew you was Chick's boy, and once I seen it was you and a friend skinnydippin' and all, I didn't hang around to see too much more.

"Don't you think the two of you is maybe too big to be playin' them kind of games, still?"

"I think we waited till we were just big enough," I told him. "I don't think either of us is ever going to outgrow it, Owen."

"Don't be so sure," Owen replied. "Like I said, most everybody goes through that—haven't you ever seen the way girls hold on to one another, dancin', kissin' like sweethearts? Well, boys are just more inclined to darkness for such things—but I've never known anybody who didn't shed it when the time comes along."

I sat sullenly and still, blocking out his philosophizing as surely as if he were quoting Leviticus.

Owen paused, seeming to assess my withdrawal and smacked his lips again. "Of course," he said, "in the meantime, a hankerin' is a hankerin'. Even I can recall the realness of that." He moved the bottle from between his legs and set it next to me. Then he shifted to his feet, brushing his behind with both hands. He reached into his pocket and pulled out a large pocketknife, the kind with four or five different blades inside its thick handle.

"Carvin' names into trees is pretty weak magic, really, but it can be an aid to a bigger spell," he began. "Don't tell your mamma, but I got her name cut into a couple of old pecan trees out front of my house," he winked. Folding out a broad, sturdy blade, he leaned into the tree trunk and began whittling away at the initials I had already carved there. "You've got to cut 'em in deep," he said, "so the tree feels 'em and will keep a high lookout for the one they belong to."

I rose to my feet and stood behind his shoulder, watching him widen and enlarge the lettering. "That piddlin' knife you was usin' is no good for carving. You was probably right to chuck it."

I smiled at the fact that he'd been spying on me, long before he announced himself with the rattle of his cans. Even in the dark, the letters were becoming more visible in the bark of the tree. Owen methodically carved, cut and chiseled at the trunk until the message that "CH AND DA WERE HERE" was emphatic and strongly anchored into the spirit of the lakewoods.

Folding up his knife and retrieving his burlap sack from the grass, he insisted I needed a love salve from his houseboat "to reinforce the spell and maybe a cup of coffee, just for the hell of it, while we're there."

Owen's houseboat was just a shack on a raft, but that one floating room was only where he slept.

"Till I found this boat, I never knew what real sleeping was," he explained. "Course I'm too old now to be a glutton about it. I don't need more'n a few hours a night anymore."

The boat was staked to the shore with steel cables and a sturdy covered walkway between it and a humpbacked trailer resembling an aluminum rolly-polly with a porthole. There was no well that I could see in the dark, but a small, orderly garden was plotted and fenced off between the trailer and a nearby outhouse.

There were no electric lines hooking the lake house to Pryor, so he lit the room with a couple of kerosene lamps and told me to have a seat. I took the one wooden chair at a small table and wondered where I should put my legs to allow Owen any standing room. I folded them up as best I could beneath the table and held onto my head, which was starting to spin in the closed-in, airless quarters, while Owen threw together a small fire in a wood-burning stove and some coffee and water into a pot on top of it.

"Is it kind of cramped in here, Owen, or has my mind just been expanded?" I asked with a sickly moan.

He smacked his lips and smiled. "Well," he said thoughtfully, "it's room enough for me when the weather's bad, a shell to duck my head under. If the weather's good, I'm outside. But I admit," he said, "it weren't designed for company." He stood, slightly stooped at the neck and shoulders to clear his plastic capped head from the curve of the ceiling, his hands in his pockets, his soulful brown eyes a little glossy from the whiskey slowly surveying the crammed interior. "Big houses is a luxury I've never known," he said. "In the Home, I only ever had as much place as a mattress to call my own, and I guess I got used to it and ain't never felt needy of much more space than that. Homes are for families," he stated, "and I ain't no family. But, here," he moved toward the plate-sized window, "you just need some air." He unlatched the porthole cover and opened it outward. Then he carefully carried a wash-bowl of water from a counter near the stove to the table. "Try some water on your face," he offered, handing me a clean hand towel that was stiff and scratchy from having dried in the sun.

The opened window, the water on my face, and Owen's re-boiled coffee were relatively effective in sobering me a notch more upright. I lit a cigarette and Owen reached into a box of turtle shells beneath the table and placed one before me as an ashtray. He'd dragged a crate up to the table as a seat.

I studied his face amidst the calm quiet that had settled between us since he put the coffee mugs on the table. The shower cap gave his head a smooth dome shape, and despite his kind eyes, he looked eerily like a six-foot turtle with arms withdrawn and folded and legs crossed inside his private hull.

I said, "Can I ask you something, Owen?"

"Sure."

"Why are you the Turtle Man?"

"Oh," he smiled, smacking his lips again, " 'cause I don't like fish, I reckon, never have." He continued after a beat of reflection. "Hate that oily texture and I never have understood the attraction of catchin' 'em."

"No," I agreed.

"Well, there you have it," Owen nodded. "What I'm sayin' is how most everybody else does. Now, if I loved fish, wouldn't be no reason for nobody to go callin' me the fish man. I'm just partial to turtles and that's not so common. I don't quite know why. They're as plentiful as perch or crappie, easier to catch, delicious to eat.

"I like 'em. They live long you know, by takin' everything slow and easy, pretty much inside their own shells. They live in two worlds, water and air. Imagine that. Then, there's the shells. Think about that. Houses on their backs.

"And of course," he said, coming out of his rumination, "they're magic. That reminds me." He rose from the upturned crate and wandered through the short, narrow walkway into the boat room.

I finished the coffee in my mug and rubbed my tired face. I wondered if I had passed the evening with a crazy man or had somehow encouraged an amusing old hermit out from his thick, invisible shell. I liked the man who liked turtles instead of fish, and his attention and conversation had distracted and comforted me for the time we'd been together. But the time was getting late, and with a sense of dread I felt the pull of my inevitable return home.

Owen reappeared through the archway, ducking his head to clear its frame.

"Here," he said, handing me a small blue glass jar with a screw-on lid whose label had been worn away to the bare tin. "It took me a minute to mix it up. See, there's a love salve for men and a love salve for women, but I ain't never figured on any salve for your kind of case."

"I reckon it's not too practical, from a business point of view," I said.

"No," he smiled. "Well, anyway, I mixed some of the women's with a little bit more of the men's and figure so long as lovesickness is lovesickness, this ought to help. I know it won't hurt."

"Help how, Owen?"

"Well, now, it's good you asked, 'cause one thing you ought to know about magic is that it don't always happen in a flash. Just 'cause results may take a while, sometimes a long while, don't mean they ain't results. That's why people don't believe in magic; they ain't got the patience for it.

"It's a lot like religion, but church people, they got to wait till they're dead to see if their believin' works. I can guarantee this'll work quicker than that.

"Now, this is private between you and me," he said. "I been wearing love salve for your mother for more than two years now. 'Cause we ain't married yet don't mean the potion's not working. 'Cause of the potion, she gave me a beer and a thank-you just last night. You know that's got to be magic! So I'll keep using the salve till it draws her in all the way."

I unscrewed the lid and peered into the jar. It seemed to contain nothing more exotic that petroleum jelly. "What am I supposed to do with this?" I asked, sniffing at the odorless stuff.

"Keep it rubbed on your peter," Owen bluntly instructed, "and in a circle around your heart. When it seeps in or washes off, rub on more. But rub it every day, one way or the other. It'll keep your prick stiff most of the time, but that's just a side effect. Now the important thing is to keep your friend in your heart. You got to direct the spell."

"I imagine so much rubbing would give anyone a hard-on, Owen," I said good-humoredly, tightening the lid on the blue jar.

"That's what I'm gettin' at," he said with a lick of his lips, re-seating himself on the crate. "I'm advising you to take this matter into your own hands." He studied my eyes. "You understand what I'm sayin'?"

I laughed nervously, uncomfortable with the situation of taking sexual advice from the Turtle Man. "Yes, sir," I nodded, averting my eyes to the table, to the small jar sitting there. "I think I do."

For a moment, I perversely pondered whether Owen ever took such matters in his own hands, with Ida in his heart.

"I've been away for two days, Owen," I announced, gathering up my half-drunk bottle of bourbon, pocketing my Winstons from the tabletop, and rising from my chair. "I have to get home."

Owen reached for the jar of salve, which I'd ignored on the table, and held it out to me. I said I couldn't take it unless I paid him for it. He continued to hold it out.

"That's only fair," he said. "A few swigs of pricey whiskey and an hour or so of company makes us even."

"Love is cheap," I told him, taking the jar from his hand.

"Oh, hell, no, son. It's the most expensive thing I sell. Let me give you a lift," he said, gathering up the bags of bottles and cans with quite a racket. "The Piggly's still open, and I can cash these in. It's on the way. Come on," he directed, bending over each kerosene lamp with a soft huff of air on his way toward the trailer door.

Owen's old truck was the noisiest vehicle in the county to begin with, but the roadless drive from the lakefront to the highway with four sacks of glass and cans rolling and rattling in the shockless steel bed shook me up to the point of senselessness. By the time those wheels reached pavement, my every tooth and hair felt loosened from its root.

My face must have revealed the jarred state of my wits, for Owen asked if I was able to hold my whiskey down.

"I'm not so sure, Owen," I slurred. "Just take me home, please. I'll call Ida from there."

The short hiking distance from the lake to home felt endless in the bouncing cab of Owen's truck. The racket of the motor in front and cargo in back made me stop up my ears and vow never to touch liquor again in exchange for an immediate moment of motionless peace.

That moment arrived as we pulled into the driveway behind the Impala and I stepped out of the truck, my whole body humming with the aftershock of the ride.

"You sure you're goin' to be all right?" Owen asked, leaning toward the open passenger door.

"Yes," I assured him, "thanks, Owen, for the ride and . . . everything."

He licked his lips, tipped his head in response, and straightened up behind the wheel. I slammed the door but poked my head through the open window. "Do you even know my name, Owen?"

"Well, sure," he said, shifting into reverse. "C. H., ain't it?" The truck pulled slowly away from my hands. "Come out and visit again, anytime," he called from the street.

I stooped slowly to pick up my bottle from the grass, waved, and walked unsteadily up the steps, into the house.

I was in no mood to answer the most obvious of questions, even though the state I'd been discovered in provoked nothing but questions.

It was a bit after midnight when Ida, driven by Fay Rose, had arrived home from the bar. I was passed out in my own bed when the overhead light and two hand-muffled gasps (Ida's an hysterical octave nearer to a shriek) startled me awake.

The inventory of time and situation took a few seconds and was still missing the few hours following my return to the house, before I closed my eyes to the painful light and growled a hoarse greeting from my parched throat.

"Charlie, what in the world has happened to you?" Ida nearly weeped from the doorway.

I rolled my head toward all the verbal fuss assaulting me from the doorway and peering through squinted lids, I saw my mother's back with Fay Rose's hand patting it briskly, the backs of their brassy and silver heads pressed together in low, soothing whispers of support.

Fay half-turned her eyes into the room. "Young man, you should not be sleeping. Not after the sleep that's been lost over you. And, Honey, for Pete's sake, cover yourself up!" she scolded.

I raised my head from the pillow and looked down at my stripped body sprawled atop the covers. I grabbed at the bedspread beneath me and flung it over myself, flushed with embarrassment and made aware by the cold and rattling sensation against my chest that I was tied into the beadpiece Pauline had given me. I realized just what kind of an indecent sight I had presented to Ida and Fay after a two-day absence.

But, in the glare of Ida's face, sympathetically doubled in Fay's eyes, I knew the truth to be too complicated to even attempt an honest defense. I said, "Would you believe I was kidnapped by a tribe of heathens?"

"By the look of you, I would," Ida snapped.

"Well, good," I sighed. "There you have it."

"Have you been drinking?" she asked. "I can smell it on you, Charlie." She stepped into the room and sniffed rudely over my bed, as if fumes were rising from my body up toward the ceiling.

"Oh-h-h-h," Fay Rose singsonged, "I do smell liquor."

"Bourbon, Fay Rose. Want a swig?" I asked.

"Listen to you!" Fay said. "Honey," she stepped toward Ida, "he's been drinkin'. He ain't goin' to make sense till he sleeps it off. He's just feelin' his oats, is all."

I smiled brazenly at the two of them, arm in arm, frowning back at me like I was too pitiful to behold.

"I knew that Dewar was going to be trouble," Ida whined. "Those boys are all hoodlums or they wouldn't be in a home."

"Nope," I said. "It was all my fault, Ida. Dewar didn't want to, 'cause it's against the Bible and all. But I put a knife to his throat and forced him to drink. I said, 'Dewar, let's get stinking pie-eyed and forget all about the shitholes we call home.' "

"In my born days I never in all my life!" Fay Rose gulped with her penciled brows nearly touching the gray roots of her hairline. Ida's eyes were closed, of course, her lips withdrawn between her teeth. With her fingers clasped at her belt buckle, she turned and walked out of the room, leaving Fay Rose stranded for a second next to my bed, her mouth half-opened, with nothing to say.

But she quickly regained her voice and, shaking a forefinger over me, declared, "Charlie, you are goin' to be so full of regret when you sober up. I pray you don't even remember what you've said here."

"I'm sorry," I interrupted. "Please, just turn off the light, Fay Rose. Wake me in the morning and I promise you I'll be just as full of regret as I deserve."

■

SUNDAY MORNING, AT THE SOUND OF CHURCH BELLS, I WALKED barefoot, but de-beaded and respectably robed, from my bed into the kitchen. I cleared my throat and asked, "Is there any coffee left?" even though I'd been awake since sunup, staring at the ceiling, and by that point in the morning my eyes were as wide open as they'd ever been. My thoughts were clear and alert, having outraced themselves several times over on one great circular track for the past few hours.

Fay Rose absently raised her attention from the diamond earrings she twirled between her fingers to my presence in the room. She sat at the table, as did Ida, whose back was to me, in the same clothes she'd worn last night.

The curl and ratted understructure of Fay's hairdo had lost its hard shape and collapsed nearer to her scalp. Or perhaps she'd merely slept on it without her usual precautions for the preservation of appearances. In fact, Fay Rose was rumpled all over, her manner as subdued as her faded makeup, her usual shine and luster worn dim. She looked very old; perhaps she simply looked her age for the first time as she turned her face from me to the coffee pot sitting over a low blue flame atop the stove.

As I poured my coffee, I did my best to suppress any sound. For the mood was so somber, I felt like a ghost having intruded upon my own wake. It seemed obvious as I sat myself at the table, that

I felt much better about my own drunken demise than my only two mourners.

"I am alive and well, you see." I said this calmly and with patience. I didn't feel up to any confrontations, but I knew some kind of explanation was inevitable. All morning in bed, I'd been rehearsing a litany of simple statements to satisfy their obvious questions, yet a sense of pride held me steadfast against relieving them of their disappointment. Disappointment in me is what I could taste in the air. My heart was hard set against an obligation to the self-righteous disappointment they seemed so worn down by. As far as I was concerned, any damage from disappointment was self-inflicted and rooted in false expectations.

Ida, too, was in the same clothes from the night before, but because they had been Chick's dark trousers and plaid short-sleeve shirt, they were threadbare and thin with age, too soft to any longer hold a wrinkle. Her thick, mercury-colored hair was pulled back smoothly from her always bare face, so she did not wear the same kind of up-all-night misery as Fay Rose. Still, sorrow weighed on her. She sat opposite me at the table with her eyes closed and lips as grimly tense as a loaded spring trap. Her stillness was like a deep meditation, and I found her prayerful pose personally insulting, but long familiar, and with another gulp of coffee I swallowed the urge to blast it wide open with a vengeful confession of the whole fizzlin' truth.

With her eyes still shut, without a twinge of extraneous movement, she asked, "Didn't Daddy's example learn you nothin'?"

Before I could honestly assure her that it had, there was a belligerent pounding against the front door.

Ida's lids snapped open, revealing large dilated pupils in the centers of her watery gray eyes, the white corners seemingly crackled with hairline pink veins. "Lord Jesus, what now?" she prayed right through me toward the living-room door and the second round of violent hammering.

Fay Rose gave my mother's hands a fluttery pat and rose from the table to dismiss the early caller.

"If that is that horrible general again, I may have to . . ." Before Ida could complete her threat, General Newton had pushed his way through the door past Fay Rose's weary protests.

"I am through pussyfootin' around," he bellowed, shaking the floorboards with each heavy step as he stormed into the kitchen. Fay Rose shook her head and shrugged her shoulders in a mumbled angry argument with herself as she trailed in behind him, then scurried around him, to take up a defensive stance behind Ida, who remained seated, offering the man nothing but her Christian cheek by turning her face toward the sink.

"Mrs. Hope," he growled in a deep snarl strained by a quality of hoarseness, as if the vocal chords were protesting the onslaught of so much wind. "I'll have you know, I have forsaken Sunday service to get to the bottom of this scandal. And if I do not get the satisfaction of some answers out of you, I am going straight to the sheriff with this matter. Where is Dewar Akins?"

I turned my chair around.

"Excuse me, sir," I said, "but isn't he at the Sunday service that you've forsaken?"

The General peered down a beaky nose at me. He was a man of considerable weight, not fat but thick; not muscled but solid. His ears sprouted patches of wiry hair as thick and untended as any other old man's underarm growth.

His bushy eyebrows bristled like a riled skunk. "I reckon you are the truant Charlie Hope."

"Yes," I responded, extending my hand. His spotted hands remained affixed to his sides. I withdrew mine. "I guess there's no need for introductions."

"There is a need for some hard explaining, boy."

"I'll tell you anything you want to hear, General, to get you back to church."

"I don't care for your smart-ass tone," the General threatened through clenched teeth.

Fay Rose interrupted, "For Pity's sake, Mr. Newton, why don't you just ask him what you've been badgering us to know?"

"Charlie," Ida pleaded, "tell the man where you and Dewar have been and where Dewar is now."

"Yes, ma'am," I said, turning back to the General. "I apologize for my tone. I'm just tired, you see. I've been on something of an adventure and it's a little confusing, the commotion it seems to have caused."

The General shifted impatiently in his spit-polished boots. The creak of the kitchen floor drew my attention to them. But for their thick, stiff combat soles, the high-laced, calf-hugging boots reminded me of wrestling gear, and for a moment I was deeply distracted from the kitchen and the tension around the small table.

Nuisance stomped his right boot sole against the linoleum. "Stop dreaming, boy!" he spewed with the volume of a gravel grinder. "I'm waiting for an accounting."

"Good night!" Fay exclaimed under her breath. Ida jerked her hand to her cheek, as if covering the sting of a hard smack.

"We went for a drive on Friday afternoon," I began. "Somewhere between Lawton and Tulsa, the car broke down. There wasn't a phone for miles. We were off the main highway. We tried flagging down a ride, but what few cars passed by just passed by like we weren't even there. By sundown, we decided to sleep in the car till daylight and walk the distance to the nearest truck stop.

"Well, that took all morning, sir. You can't believe how busy a Stuckey's can be on a Saturday morning. I mean, we needed a mechanic or a tow truck, and Stuckey's had only one of each until noon. And, believe it or not, the pay phone had been vandalized for its change and was out of order. We couldn't do anything but eat breakfast and wait."

The General's lips were as tight-laced as his military boots and seemed about to blister from the fuming pressure of his anger.

"Well, the spare mechanic showed up late but eventually showed up, and he drove us back to the car, which he couldn't fix on the road, so we towed it back to the station."

The General continued to stew with suspicions. Fay and Ida both looked satisfied, maybe relieved, with my orderly tale. Fay Rose remained standing, nodding her head in agreement. My mother's frown had softened. The concern in her eyes seemed to be begging me to go on, to give her at least a soft and clutchable conclusion with which to comfort the hard doubts in her own head that had cost her two nights' sleep already.

"The garage and the café both had working business phones, of course, but they had absolutely refused us to make a long-distance call from either, so we talked the tow-truck driver, an Indian named Jack," I said, antagonizing the General with another petty detail, "to stop and give us a minute to call home from a little bait shop on the highway that had been closed when we'd passed by it earlier on foot. That's when I called my mother and explained, General."

Ida and Fay Rose confirmed this fact with a synchronized nod at the old man, which made no obvious impression.

"Well," I said, "that's it. They fixed the car, of course. It cost me $47.00."

"Highway robbery!" Fay Rose whistled.

"Dewar was sick about having missed the graduation, but we drove home as fast as we could without breaking any laws. I let Dewar out at the Home gate yesterday. Right before sundown, General. I watched him wave from the back door as he walked inside."

Newton threw his bulk toward me with one lunging step, drew back his arm with a furious breath, and slapped me across the face. My head swung down and to the side with such a force I thought it might pull my body out of the chair after it. I grabbed the chair back to keep from falling to the floor.

Ida shrieked. Both of her hands tightly overlapped her mouth.

"Jesus Christ!" I moaned, cradling the lopsided throb of my face in my hands.

Fay Rose shouted, "Don't you . . ." digging her hands into my mother's shoulders as if her legs had gone dead and she were leaning onto canes for support.

No one quite regained their composure but me. Ida buried her face in her hands upon the table and continued to cry.

Fay Rose was torn between her godmothering duty to Ida and me and her obvious rage at the General.

"Git out of here, right now, you bullying old jackass," she barked at Newton. Ignoring her, he slid his hands down to his knees and bent into my face.

"Where is he?" he breathed all over me.

"I don't know," I said.

"He's not here, you thick-headed idiot!" Fay Rose yelled. "The boy's obviously run off—and from your action, who'd blame him!"

"If he has run away, General, I'm certain he's running for his own good," I said. Newton blinked and straightened his posture. "Considering the way his hind end's been branded, I don't think he'd be sitting too long in any one place. If you want to organize a manhunt between here and Arkansas, I could give a clear description of those identifying marks. I'm sure that would be helpful to any sheriff you care to call."

His face became so tightly drawn it seemed to restrict his ability to speak for a moment. His hands twitched at his sides, until he fumblingly inserted them into his trouser pockets.

"What's this?" Fay asked. "What in the world are you talkin' about?"

"I don't know, Mrs. Savory," the General answered with a mocking sweetness, unpocketing one hand to press the frayed brown strands of hair against his spotted scalp. "It seems like your boy here is babbling about somebody's hind end, by the sound of it."

Fay released a peeved breath that shot through her teeth with the sound of hissing steam. Ida raised her head from the table with both ears covered with her hands.

"Would you please get out of my house?" she pleaded with the man.

"Oh, it'd be my pleasure," the General nodded. "But, let me say this," he bent his thick neck forward to look down, once more, at me. His stiffly starched shirt collar seemed to saw into the over-hanging flesh of his throat.

"You can bet your sweet ass, sissy boy, that I'm going to find that friend of yours."

"Good luck," I told him, extending three of my own fingers up-ward in front of him. "You've got three whole weeks before he's legally free anyway."

He turned on one boot sole and stomped out of the house.

Fay Rose skittered out of the room to close the front door on his exit. I heard her chaining the lock for good measure.

Ida lowered her hand from her ears to her lap and raised the shirttail of my grandpa's shirt to her teary eyes.

"That is the meanest man I've ever met since Garl Hope," she stated absently as if she were alone in the room, merely airing thoughts.

"Maybe we should set him afire," I responded unthinkingly, just as wearily, and in the same spirit.

My mother's wide eyes peered above the plaid shirt hem, lock-ing onto me with a stunned, frightened, pained reaction. Their grayness overflowed beyond focus for a moment. "Oh, my God," she mumbled into the fabric. Her eyes snapped closed instantly. She rose and walked blindly out of the kitchen.

Fay Rose reentered the kitchen, having crossed Ida's path on the way. "What now?" she asked with exasperation, easing herself into a chair next to me.

"Something just slipped out, Fay. About a bonfire with Nui-sance as the fuel."

"Oh, Lordy!" she moaned. "Well, pardon my French," she sighed, "but he is a prick."

I met her eyes, but we were both too depressed to smile. "So was Garland Hope, Fay, but too many things are just unpardonable to Ida."

"An awful lot seems to be slippin' out of your mouth, lately," she commented.

"Fay, I don't know where he is. I wish I did. Truth is," I confessed, "I'd probably be there with him."

Her sealed lips stretched horizontally across her face, making deep dimples at each corner. She lifted her faint brows and eyes as she slightly lowered her head, as if looking over the rims of glasses she did not wear.

"Some things just might be most pardonable if they stay unspoken," she said carefully.

"Where do you think I've been keeping all of those unspeakable truths, Fay?"

I squeezed my head. "Here," I said. I placed my hands against my heart, "In here," I said.

She turned her face away and swallowed. "Charlie, I've never in my life seen a sad baby till the day you was born. Just sad, sad, sad the older you git."

"He more than pardoned me, Fay Rose," I said.

"All of us have loved you. And still do," she said.

"I loved him," I said.

"Your mother has worked hard for you, Charlie."

I said, "The only disappointment he ever caused me was leaving me behind, here."

She said, "You've got enough money to get away from here, if that's what all your gripin' is about. You can go to college next year anywhere you want, Honey. Be somebody. That's an opportunity that hasn't come easy."

"Fay Rose," I said, rising from the table, "I'm so full of disappointment I can't abide this one more."

General Nuisance didn't find Dewar. As far as I could tell, he never even looked. Neither he, nor any sheriff, nor police, nor highway patrolmen, nor local, state, or federal officials ever approached me again about when or where he was last seen.

On his birthday, I wrote Pauline and Fred in Choteau:

There was not too much of a ruckus here about his disappearance. No one cared enough even to try to track him down. I know you care and I do, too.

I'm happy to have met you. Thank you for the orchids and the Indian beads and Dewar's prom night. I think he planned on running off the way he did, with or without Rae Ludy. Our coming to Choteau was his way of saying to you good-bye and thank you. Knowing him the way I did, I'm sure he never said it himself, so on his behalf I'll say now I know he loved you.

Having known me for only a night, please realize that that night of me with Dewar is the best there is to know.

I hope that if you ever see or hear from him again, you'll say on my behalf that you know I loved him, too. Happy birthday to Dewar Akins.

Sincerely,
Charlie Hope

■

I HATED BEING AT HOME. ALONE OR WITH IDA, IT FELT JUST THE same. Vacant. There was not a single conversation between us after the General's violent intrusion. There were words here and there, simple utilitarian ones.

Being a Christian, she maintained her charitable work on my behalf. She continued to cook meals, to clean the house and my clothes, to leave her financial donations to my physical upkeep on the kitchen table each Saturday night. Ida was a failed missionary in the land of motherhood.

She'd lost her Pentecostal zeal years before by facing up to her own lost soul, but I suppose she'd assumed all along that mine was in the hands of the Lord by virtue of her backing off and letting go. The distance was no greater now, just colder.

I was used to misunderstanding her; had accepted her sadness, her weirdness, her distance as the unfathomable way she was. A long time ago I had shirked the responsibility for her mystery, and, I guess, that summer I began taking more responsibility for my own.

When our paths crossed in the house (she rising from bed, me collapsing into it; she cooking, me washing up; she leaving for the bar, me sunk into the couch chain-smoking), we related exactly as she and Chick had their whole Pryor lives together in that same house, on separate and silent never-touching tracks.

That summer in Pryor, like most, was shapeless, shiftless, lethargic. Time was as thick and sticky as a dough too heavy to rise.

I kept rubbing in the turtle salve, although it proved uninspiring. It became habitual, an unconscious act of faith, not in magic potions, but in Dewar's free will and well-being.

I rationed my bourbon into doses at the lake, drinking just enough to numb the sharp edges of abandonment that would not be smoothed any other way. Drink or dope got me through the days; both led me peacefully to sleep, which was my drug of deepest relief.

Owen said so much sleep was a waste of youth *and* liquor. He said this beneath the elm tree where I tended to sleep off my afternoon buzz before beginning my serious evening binge.

"What're you doin', C. H.? Storin' up dreams for your old age?" I partially lifted my eyelids to the blurry vision of him standing above me with his burlap sack slung over one shoulder, his scalp still bagged in its plastic beret, cloudy with the trapped humidity of his head.

"Maybe you ought to switch to beer," he suggested, toeing the almost empty bourbon bottle lying in the grass beside me. "It don't knock you over as hard as liquor, and it turns to piss so fast, it keeps you on your feet."

I stretched and propped myself against the tree, straddled by its forked roots.

Owen's was the only company I'd kept since the loss of Dewar's. It was a strange substitute but similar in some soothing ways.

They were each hermits after all: Dewar, reclusive in his layers of half-truths; Owen, withdrawn so far from normal he was barely tethered to land. Each was marked by the Strang Home. I seemed to be the rare exception to friendship they each generally shunned. I shared some unreasonable, unspoken, sudden understanding with each of them that had eliminated the need to really get to know them. We already knew something, something secret, some kind of key to company, and so, once we actually spoke, we didn't need to speak so much.

In a way, I came to love Owen, but only when he was there. If he wasn't with me, I rarely gave him a thought; when he was, I started regretting his departure. That's how I fell in love with Dewar, too, in the small doses of his company with no hangover in between. Once he was gone for good, I had nothing much but a swollen head with painful thoughts of little else.

The Turtle Man became my guardian of sorts. He was a busy, tinkering man who wandered as far on foot as in his truck. His preference for walking was another eccentricity in Pryor, where everyone drove the distance to all the nowheres there were to go. Owen's walking accounted for some of his reputation as simple or retarded.

I'd wake up on the grassy shore of the lake and Owen would be sitting next to me, contemplating the seasonal progression of the familiar view, and I knew he could have been sitting there for hours comfortably alone with my sleep.

Or he'd step suddenly from out of the trees and bushes with no more announcement than the rattle of bottles or turtles in his burlap sack, and I always felt that he'd been watching me awhile before joining me. He seemed to know, as well as respect, the difference between alone and lonely. He guarded the one and kindly eased the other.

Not too far into that summer, I found myself anticipating his company, and if I wasn't drunk enough to pass out cold beneath the elm, I'd close my eyes and struggle willfully against the heat of the day, the hardness of the ground, and the itch of chiggers to force myself to sleep with a single intention. So used to his guardianship of my unconscious and his appearance upon my waking, I ritualized the cause to the effect, invented a spell to call him near. He was there the way someone you loved should be, when you woke up.

I told Owen all about the General's visit to the house. He listened without comment but for a few smacks of his lips and an ex-

pression I couldn't interpret. Eventually I told him most of the
story of Choteau, Fred and Pauline and Rae. I told him of Mary
Deer and Joe Turner as if I knew them, the hothouse of orchids,
the prom, the Reservation store, everything but for Jack Stillwater's
tattoo and back room. And when it had grown very quiet because
I'd told and he'd listened to everything else, I told him how I'd
fallen asleep relatively happy in Dewar's arms, as if that night's sleep
were the threshold of a transfiguration that would be completed
by morning. "When I woke up, he was gone."

"Hmm," Owen sighed to let me know he'd heard.

"Need more love salve?" he asked, wiping his neck with a
folded handkerchief.

"Not yet."

"Well, how 'bout that beer?"

I followed him deep into the woods, along an uncertain path,
until we reached a shallow, narrow stream of clear running water.
He bent and lifted a chickenwire contraption out of a dugout in
the edge of the water's path, one of his homemade turtle traps. He
set the heavy crate on the shady bank and squatted to sort through
the contents. He retrieved two brown bottles of beer through the
hinged doors of his improvised water cooler, leaving a Coke, a few
eggs bundled in a tea towel, and a couple of sealed but labeless jars
of what looked like applesauce. I helped him replace the trap in the
stream, and we each carried a cool wet bottle wordlessly back to
his houseboat.

On the dock, Owen dumped four turtles from his burlap sack into
a washtub of water that was deep enough for them to swim around
in easily.

I took a seat as he busied himself with the preparation of his
catch. He had a metal drum next to the shack, which was full of
creek water. Every quarter hour he'd dump the turtle tub's water
into the lake and replenish it from the drum.

"To soften 'em up," he explained after the third such soaking, although I hadn't questioned the procedure.

I drank my beer slowly because it had already warmed in my hand. The tepid temperature enhanced the dry, malty taste.

"I heard a veteran once tell how overseas ice is so rare, for whatever reason, that beer is always warm, even in the bars." Owen tipped his bottle to his puckered lips. He swallowed, then smacked, then toasted. "Here's to foreign customs," he said.

"Owen," I asked, "how old does someone have to be to be a real drunk?"

He was poking sticks into the fire of his stone barbecue pit. He had a large cast iron pot of creek water heating on its grill. He answered casually without turning from his work.

"No age limits to it." He paused to study his flames from an upright perspective, brushing his hands against his pant legs. Momentarily satisfied, he turned and came over to the dock and took a seat on its edge next to me and his beer. "A real drunk has usually practiced at it quite a few years. But you could start drinkin' like a drunk around twelve I guess, maybe a little younger. Most drunkards take to it young, but not all. It's hooked up with misery of some kind, and that don't usually kick in till the voice has dropped."

I shrugged and drained the beer in my bottle.

"Also," he went on, "a drunkard has lost hope in everything but his drinkin'. It takes a while to lose all that. I'd say around eighteen, I guess, if I *had* to put a age on it.

"Hey, look at this," he said, yanking the shower cap off his head and tilting his scalp toward me. What he unveiled was an even scattering of hair stubble across his previously bald head.

"Jesus! It worked!" I put my palm on the pate of his head. The gravel-colored bristles needled the light touch of my hand. The new growth felt strong and sturdy, nothing wispy or newborn about it. My hand covered the prickly globe of his offered head, which radiated a fiery heat. When I withdrew it, my palm felt smooth, tingly, a little numbed, and so warm I shook it.

Owen lifted his face. "It's the potion," he said, then took another swig of his beer.

"It's unbelievable, Owen."

"It's the turtle potion," he stated again proudly.

"It's nearly a miracle," I told him. "You going to sell it?"

He smacked his lips, said, "I've given it thought. I'd like to bring it down to Chick's joint."

"Why?"

"Ain't you never noticed, C. H., how Chick's has more bald-headed men than any other place in town?"

After a moment, he stood and walked away. He removed each turtle from the soaking tub, scrubbed it thoroughly with a large cleaning brush, and gently set it aside, belly up on the dock so it wouldn't crawl away. When they were all cleaned, he piled them into a short-handled fishing net, which he swung over to the barbecue. He plunged the load into the kettle of boiling water, which bubbled over into the flames. The fire and water hissed and smoked as Owen remained near the pot, poking and stirring the scalded things with a boat oar.

My eyes had never been skittish like Ida's. I was not repelled by Owen's businesslike rendering of the turtles. I was a seasoned witness and had a quiet but insatiable craving to see what fizzlin' happened.

He'd dipped the scalded turtles out of the pot. The skin of their heads and feet had become white and easily peeled away with his rubbing with dry clean towels. The sight was sickening, and yet I passively watched. I wasn't heartsick for the dumb dead creatures themselves. I wasn't the least bit inclined to stop Owen from any of his further dismantling acts. They were quite dead and felt nothing. What happened next didn't matter at all.

As Owen tossed them, skinless, back into the boiling pot, all I could think about was how good another beer would taste, how good a swig of bourbon would feel, how magically sleep could black out the rest of the day's hours.

"How much longer for those turtles?" I asked.

"Oh," he smacked his lips as he turned to answer, " 'bout three quarters of an hour till the shells come off."

"Let's go get some more beer, then," I suggested. "I'll pay if you'll buy it."

He walked away from the boiling kettle toward the dock, leaned back against the planking next to me with his arms folded across his chest. "Where do you git your money, C. H.?"

"I have a stash from Chick when he was alive. Ida gives me more every Saturday night."

Owen seemed to think about my income for a moment. He said, "Let's drive by the joint for a minute."

"Why?" I wanted to know. "Ida won't sell me beer."

"She will me, if I got the change. I want to show off my hair and see what she says." My lack of enthusiasm caused him to add, "We'll stop at the Piggly Wig on the way back. We need beer to wash down the stew."

Around suppertime, we arrived at Chick's joint in Owen's roaring truck. The city fishermen had all headed back to town. All but two single locals at separate booths had already carried themselves home for dinner. Those with indifferent wives would return at around 8:00 to drink till closing. As Owen and I entered, the juke was silent and the hum of the window's neon lights was the only sound in the bar except for our bootsteps across the floor.

Fay Rose and Ida were seated on stools behind the bar, bent over meatloaf sandwiches and a tub of carrot salad, set out like a picnic on spread bar towels.

Their eyes rose from their meal to our entrance. They lowered their sandwiches as Owen and I took stools a slight distance away.

"Miss Ida, Miss Savory," Owen nodded.

Fay Rose chewed her meat slowly and mutely. Ida's jaw had slackened, and the food practically spilled out of her mouth as she and Fay continued to gaze wide-eyed at us. I propped myself forward over the bar. My face was passive and slightly dazed in the mirrored wall.

I looked like a slightly familiar stranger but was even more startled by the reflection of myself with the man beside me. There was something of Chick in Owen's physical build, craggy face and dark brown forearms crossed upon the bar. But I also saw some of Chick reflected in me.

"I'll have one very cold draw, Miss Ida, please," Owen requested of my dumbstruck mother. She and Fay forced the food in their mouths down their throats. Fay reached for her mug of coffee to help wash hers down. Ida rose from her seat, wiping her hands across the apron skirting her trousers, and approached us from the service side of the bar.

"Owen," she nodded, coming to a standstill, "you was helpful with the General a ways back. I'm thankful. I told you so at the time, but you still got no tab or credit here, you know."

"Oh, no," Owen deferred, shaking his head. "Your boy here." He tilted his head rather obviously toward me.

"I'm buying," I said and pushed a dollar across the bar toward her.

Ida took a deep breath and let it out. Rather gently, she asked, "Is this what you've been doin' with yourself lately? Buyin' beer for the Turtle Man?"

"If we'd been barhopping, Ida, you would have seen us before now. This is the only beer joint in Pryor."

"I know that well enough, Charlie," she countered with exasperation. "But you sure ain't been home much, and I've learned how you're prone to joyrides all over creation." Her eyes darted to Owen, uncertain of his involvement in her accusation, but she was obviously suspicious of our company.

"For pity's sake, sweetheart!" Fay said, climbing off her stool. "Sell the man a beer." She walked slowly toward the middle of the bar, dabbing the corners of her mouth with a bar towel, her eyes glued to the top of Owen's head. Ida turned with the huff of a scolded child and retrieved a frosted mug from the freezer.

"Owen, could that be hair on your bald head that you been coverin' up with that stupid shower hat for all these months now?" Fay Rose's nose was inches from Owen's forehead as she inspected the stubble of his new hairline. "I'll be damned if it ain't," she declared with a chuckle. "Ida, look at Owen's head," she ordered my mother, who pulled the filled mug from under the spout and set it in front of Owen's crossed arms. She ignored my dollar on the bar, crossed her own arms over her chest, and leaned slightly toward the object of Fay Rose's delight, frowning.

"Um-hm," she commented and turned her face toward me. "You want some coffee or somethin'?"

"Nothing," I replied and lit a cigarette. Owen drank deeply from his beer, savoring its frosty chill.

Fay Rose was mesmerized by the turtle man's head. Owen sat like a mannequin as she patted his new stubble. "It's almost a flat-top!" she exclaimed. "Ida, feel his head. It ain't bald no more!"

Ida cringed. "I can see he has some hair, Fay."

"But feel it, honey," Fay insisted. "It's a miracle."

"Oh, my Lord!" Ida muttered and took a step forward. She placed her hand atop Owen's head and patted his stubbly scalp lightly. Her eyelids lowered as her brow furrowed in concentration.

"It's a new potion Owen's made," I said, noticing in the mirror the attention of one of the middle-aged men we had roused.

"Some kind of hair potion, is it?" the man asked from the corner booth across the room.

The question disturbed Ida's entrancement, and she withdrew her hand self-consciously from Owen's head.

"Yes, sir," Owen responded to the mirror. "Turtle oils, some brewed plants mostly."

Within five minutes, half a deal was struck between Owen and the balding man for his first sale of hair potion. When it came to quoting a price, Owen deferred to my mother.

"Lord! I don't care what you can get for it," she said. Owen motioned her closer with a seductive wave of his hand. She leaned her head next to his, and he whispered into her ear. She straightened up, arms still folded, "This ain't no barbershop," she protested loudly.

"Well, it ain't no café, neither," Fay Rose replied, lighting a Chesterfield, "but, we serve chili and hushpuppies every Wednesday. And look," she pointed her cigarette next to the tackle box of cash, "we already sell pocket combs and nail clippers. And don't forget the you-know-what machine in the bathroom."

Ida blushed. I smiled at Fay's wink in my direction, and Owen obscured his poker face with a long swill from his mug. Finally, Ida announced to the customer across the room that the hair potion was ten dollars for the first bottle, eight dollars for each one thereafter.

He wanted to know how many bottles it would cost him. Owen swiveled around on his stool and measured the diameter of the man's bald spot with squinted eyes. He smacked his lips, blinked, and guessed such a small spot could be cultivated with one, maybe one and a half bottles.

That was how Owen and Ida's partnership in business was struck. With a vow to deliver a batch of hair potion the next day, Owen drained his mug, I stubbed out my cigarette, and we rose to go.

"But, where are y'all goin'?" Fay Rose asked with intense curiosity.

"We left something stewin' out at the boat," Owen answered honestly.

"Charlie," my mother called hesitantly, "when might you be comin' home?"

"I don't know," I answered. "I might stay out at the lake with Owen tonight." Owen blinked, silently startled. He turned to Ida and said, "I'll look out for him all right. I promise you that, Ida."

Owen was quietly pleased with himself. He didn't say a word in the truck all the way to the store for beer and back to the lake, but he was as smug as a wizard whose spells and predictions were all coming to life just because he'd willed it so, and waited.

When we got back to the lake, Owen removed the turtles from the boiling water, pinched their feet and determined that they had reached their cooking point. They were set aside to cool for the amount of time it took us to drink another beer and me to open a third.

"To foreign customs," I toasted the air with my bottle as Owen pulled the nails from the turtle feet with pliers, cut and pried open the undershells to carefully remove the flesh, separate and chop the feet. He emptied the upper shells and scraped them down to the white muscles of the insides. He sorted the various parts into buckets lined up along the dock: the feet, eggs, and livers; the hearts, intestines, gall bladders, and sandbags; the shell halves and pieces and even heads. The contents of some of the buckets Owen sprinkled heavily with salt, as he did the broth water, still roiling in the kettle.

I drank and smoked, quietly out of his way but within reach of the sharp, unsteady lantern light he worked by. I got up once and wandered a short ways into the dark woods to pee. When I returned, Owen was cutting carrots and onions from his garden over the kettle. I pulled another beer from the ice chest we'd brought outside from the houseboat. I opened it and held it out for Owen to accept, even though his back was several yards to me at the barbecue. He shook his head over the kettle and said, "I'm all right, C. H., thanks."

I put the bottle to my lips and drank. "How did you know I was offering?" I asked.

"Listenin'," he explained, dumping the bucket of turtle meat into the pot and covering it with a heavy lid, still not turning from his stew but stepping back from the fire with his empty bucket and wiping a handkerchief across his forehead and behind his neck.

I carried my beer around to the front of the shack and eased into the cocoon of a hammock stretched between two trees. I shifted and stretched myself within the swaddling web until my back was comfortably bowed enough for me to still drink and my body was gently swaying in a rhythm appropriate to the buoylike motion of my thoughts.

Lightning bugs filled the evening air between the grass and treetops like the constellations filled the sky farther above. Their tiny punctuations of light put a visual depth to the infinity of the sky. The illusion drew me into the vastness of the night like a graceful upward tumble.

The higher I rose from the hammock into the whispering specks of light, the safer I felt. The sensation of my own laughter was a very distant tickle in a throat miles behind. The glass bottle tipped against my lips felt as numb as my memory of yesterday because the beer had unlatched me from the cramped quarters of myself.

I liked this in-between place, between the pettiness of the heart and the purposeless spin of the mind. I felt like a late-show teenage werewolf; my corny, precious life sucked out of me by the night and the moon, transfused with a hot, rampant blood and the simplicity of dumb instinct. Alcohol let me howl and rant and lope into infinite wildness, then blotted my tracks and the forlorn echo of my own calling by wringing out the consequences of memory.

"You practicin' to be a drunk, C. H.?"

Owen was standing next to the tree at the end of my crossed legs. He held a beer bottle by the neck down against one thigh. His other hand rested on the hammock ropes looped around a stub in the tree trunk. His calm, even countenance flowed through his hand into the ropes and slowed my swinging body to a stillness suspended over the ground.

"It feels like a worthwhile thing to do," I answered.

"Oh, yea, it feels that way." He smacked his lips, took a swig of beer.

I tilted my head to steady my vision of him. "Owen," I asked, "do you think I'm sick?"

"Young is all. And that's a kind of plague." He patted the toe of my boot. "You really want to stay here tonight?" he asked suspiciously.

"I'd rather," I told him.

"Well, that's fine," he said. "You know I like you, don't you? You're welcome anytime?"

I answered with a sly, lazy smile.

"Soup's done," he announced with an emphatic blink.

We ate the soup on the dock. I had two shellfuls washed down with another beer. Owen consumed his dinner slowly, with gentlemanly manners, considering the lack of china or a table. I'd finished eating and had smoked a cigarette in silence before he blotted his lips with a towel and sighed with satisfaction.

Unlike hard liquor or weed, which would have ushered me into a sullen coma by then, the beer had hyped me up a bit and I felt compelled to jabber.

I stretched out on my back right on the ground and talked up at Owen, seated upon a crate. I must have asked a hundred opinions of him, most of which were just for the reassurance, by his response, that he was still there and willing to pay me any mind. But, more than meeting those selfish expectations, he was willing to talk through most of the night about anything at all I wanted to hear, and that was as satisfying to a still-hungry place in me as his peppered turtle stew.

Finally, I did drift off to sleep on the ground, lulled by a full stomach and Owen's recounting of his younger days out of the Home as a hobo, hopping all over the western states in freight cars on rails that didn't exist anymore. But he woke me almost immediately and half carried me to the cot in the houseboat. I mumbled objections to taking his bed and opted for the hammock with a rising, slurred volume.

"I don't sleep," he insisted, "more 'n a minute at a time, and I can do that sittin' up, sometimes standin'. I reckon you might be out for a good piece of time—no need to put a dent in your back while you're at it."

I had nothing but my time and presence to move into Owen's boat shack on the lake, so in a way, it probably never occurred to Ida that that's what I'd done from that night onward.

Just as Dewar had spent nearly a year, more at home in that house than I'd ever felt, without making the slightest wave in Ida's consciousness until he suddenly disappeared, now I was living in a hermit's wilderness, and the house was but a convenience station of a few luxuries in the primitive life I'd chosen.

I picked up free money every week off the kitchen table, dumped off dirty clothes and found them cleaned and pressed in drawers or on hangers faster than a commercial laundry service. I came and went, with or without the Impala, realizing that this evidence of my having been there was about the same as my actually being there to my mother.

Ida still cleaned and cooked and even paid the ghost of the boy who'd never really been there at all but was now gone for good.

I still saw her occasionally at the bar when I joined Owen to deliver hair tonic, which was selling well by the fact of so many men around town in shower caps and by the ironic fact that once Owen could actually afford to pay for his own draws, my mother wouldn't charge him by virtue of their profit-sharing arrangement.

With each icy mug she served him, the more she warmed to his kind manners, his humility, his quiet, gentle humor. During such visits, I tended to hover with Fay Rose over coffee and cigarettes at one end of the bar. She'd quietly tease me about my mother's "boyfriend" and how sweet of me she thought it was to help get them courting.

"It's not my doing, Fay Rose," I tried to correct her. "He's been using a love potion." I smiled.

Fay gasped, then chuckled, and choked on an inhalation of smoke. "Git out of here! Is he really?"

"I'm sure he'd sell you some, Fay," I kidded her.

"Hah! I'm too old for that kind of nonsense, Honey." She gulped her coffee and patted her puffy hairdo. "I was thinkin' of tryin' some of that hair tonic though. I'm thinnin' out on the top. It's gettin' to be a hell of an effort to look awake, let alone good, anymore." Her sparkling eyes made a quick span of the bar and its scattered male customers. "I don't know why I even bother."

"Because you're such a classy act, Fay Rose. You can't stop it any more than you can help it," I whispered sexily into her diamond-studded ear.

She slapped my hand. "Don't be fresh!"

"Do you think she actually likes him?" I asked, peering down the bar at Ida and Owen's seemingly relaxed conversation.

"Well, I'd never have predicted it," Fay shook her head, "but I can understand what she could see in him. It's not like she doesn't have a odd streak of her own." After a pause to light another cigarette, she exhaled, "What I can't quite figure is what you see in him, Charlie. Can't you find yourself a buddy even a little bit more your own age?"

"He ran off, remember?"

"Well," she responded, inspecting her nail polish, "I hope you've got that drinkin' out of your system, as well as that run-off hooligan."

"Nope," I said, "but you keep hoping, Fay Rose." I kissed her on the cheek, said a polite so long to my mother and Owen, and with no premeditation left town for a long, aimless drive. I think it was even a Sunday.

■

AN HOUR'S WORTH OF HIGHWAY SO STRAIGHT AND RIGID AND BOR-
ing that the potholes served as landmarks is all that separated Pryor
from Tulsa in distance.

There was no transition in the landscape from the green light at
the intersection of the Dairy Queen and the highway to the green
road sign announcing the Tulsa exit with a veering arrow toward
the city skyline.

Aside from its skyline's seductive impression, all I had ever
known of T-town was the skid row atmosphere of a few bars and
my one visit to the state fair.

I knew nothing of the city's layout or street patterns, hadn't been
within its limits in seven or eight years. Impulse drove me that day
in late July. I wasn't thinking of a destination more specific than the
sound of the city's Indian name and the glamorous hope its skyline
had once sparked but that Chick's passion for gloomy barlight and
unfamiliar women had dimmed.

I wanted to avoid the run-down outskirts of town I already
knew. Lighting a pipe full of weed, I held my breath and the steering wheel at the high, shiny business district, not even knowing
what directions to ask for, not really caring to know. My hope was
still ignited by the prospect of being dwarfed, swallowed up, and
rescued if really lost.

Something kept me circling the streets of downtown even

though the banks, office towers, and parking lots, as well as the streets themselves, were practically deserted of life.

It was all cleaner, prettier, and bigger than Purley, Strang, and Pryor stacked atop one another. All the grit and dust were paved over and sealed up with concrete, marble slabs, plate glass, and steel. The tall buildings shielded the glare of the setting sun with comfortable shadows, and the air, tinged with the fumes of gasoline and oil, was a pleasant perfume compared to the retched breath of rendering.

This change of scenery was satisfactory enough, considering my lack of purpose, but having memorized the alphabet of cities for which the streets were named, and having mastered the timing of the stoplights so that I had driven from Boston and Second to Cincinnati to Denver to Elgin, all the way to St. Louis and back to Atlanta and First without a single halting red or yellow warning, I still could not turn the car back toward home, where at least a chili or turtle supper would be waiting.

Truth is, I was too hungry to eat. I was bored to death with my own boredom. My loneliness was for something more than company. I was also stoned and almost hypnotized by the act of driving. I think I was looking desperately, if unconsciously, for my future, for its address.

After sundown, I was still cruising the empty streets. The lights came on gradually like stars appearing dimly in the blue sky, then shining brighter and brighter against the indigo and deep blue-black of night.

There were three particular structures I passed again and again, that kept me pointlessly looping the same city blocks for another shy and curious, almost flirtatious look.

On first sighting, the extravagant modernism of the library was impressive, but with each slow cruise around it, its futurism became more dated, clunky and old-fashioned, like a piece of Martian scenery in a science-fiction B movie.

As the sky darkened, the bright reading light inside the building displayed the smattering of people browsing the racks, calmly read-

ing, some just staring out the cool gray glass walls as I kept staring in.

It was like looking into a well-lit mausoleum at the ho-hum
world of the dead, and I could almost picture myself at home
there, browsing and loitering, fishlike among the maze of book-
shelves, researching the card files for answers to questions as alpha-
betically and numerically ordered as the streets I wandered instead.

Just a diagonal jaywalk up the street was an older, more
wholesome-looking structure with an entrance so discretely lit it
offered no clue to the exact nature of its business. The YMCA was
apparently a more cloistered and restrictive club.

Had I known that the building was an actual hotel of sorts, I
might have just abandoned my car to the street, my drunken summer days and hermit nights on the fishy lake of Pryor for the blue
swimming-pool waters and lifeguard lessons advertised on the
glass-cased posters outside the door; walked in, taken a bed, ordered up a room-service prayer circle of YCMs to help me exor-
cise the heathen spirit of which I felt so possessed and aimlessly
driven.

But who I was could not join in the power of Christian congregation without the spiritual amputation of a limb or more of my
soul. Naturally, I was a young white man with a ticket to the state
fair, to the Main Street library, the University of Tulsa, or even the
YMCA, but such attractions did not thrill me. Those games
seemed rigged against my winning any top-shelf prize, and I drove
on by finally, well past suppertime, down darker, grungier streets
where the pavement ran out of smoothness and bricks and abandoned trolley tracks emerged rugged against the tires, to where the
bus station stood amber-lit, alone and unshouldered by anything
but demolition and neglect for the past thirty years.

A low-slung structure for the rather low-life roustabouts loung-
ing on benches inside and out, the station had a towering aluminum facade at one corner that rose high enough into the night to
vertically spell Greyhound in yard-high letters of flickering red
light. The buses themselves lumbered into the wide, encircling lot

with none of the sleek grace of their namesake but more like snorting humpbacked mammoths nosing the asphalt for a watering hole, farting fumy black clouds till the moment their brakes hissed and engines were killed.

The grimy glass windows of the waiting station encased a platoon of civilians in a purgatorial light that harshly accentuated the drama of each face, the drama of waiting, of the moment between status quo and AWOL. I sat in the car in the parking lot for a long time just smoking and absorbing the shock of recognition of my own mother's silent, too-weary-to-think slump in the posture of a woman all alone on a bench more ornately carved than a church pew. Her fingers nervously picked at a loose button on her dress while her eyes stared through the plate glass into the parking lot as if it were just more highway scenery relentlessly blurring past a window seat.

I recognized two bars within sight of my parking space. Jewel's was half a block in one direction and the Beehive just a ways beyond. In fact, I knew the station itself from making the bar rounds with Chick. I'd sat at the counter of the diner inside more than once at an hour of the night when we were forced out of the closing bars up the street, and such a counter was one of the few places left open for sitting when Chick was sometimes a little too drunk to drive. I thought about the thick-skinned slices of lemon meringue pie I'd forced down a bellyful of Coke there, while Chick drank oil-black coffee, smoked, and flirted with a tired, bored waitress.

I wasn't the least bit hungry for nostalgia, for the flavor of going back or one more taste of any of my past. But I got out of the car and went into the bus station because I was stiff and sore from driving, because I didn't know exactly where else there was to go, and because this terminal of arrivals and departures called to me without intimidation. The smoky and littered atmosphere of waiting and the anonymous fellowship of strangers stuck together for a while between coming and going drew me inside.

I was propositioned for a quarter inside the door by a kid no older than myself in army surplus fatigues and a canvas duffel thicker and surely heavier than himself, which his head reclined against upon the dirty floor. I looked down questioningly at his outstretched olive-drab figure and his very long, unwashed, tangled hair.

Unused to panhandlers and such blunt requests, I was startled into searching my pockets for change. I poured maybe sixty or eighty cents into his upreached hand without a word, avoiding his eyes for fear of encountering his desperation or shame.

"Praise Jesus, man," he said like a blessing. I looked at him then with a nod and a guarded smile. His eyes were glassy and vacant.

As I started to step away, he called out again, "Got a butt, man?"

"No, sorry," I lied over my shoulder. He met my glance blankly with a spacey glare.

"The Lord loves you, man," he said. "Do you know my Lord?"

"No, sorry," I said once more, turning fully and walking away.

A poorly wired speaker system announced the loading of a bus headed for a list of unrecognizable destinations but evidently anticipated by the handful of people spread around the terminal. I found myself weaving a path through an exodus of gathered passengers, feeling as if my entrance were ill timed and against the flow of everyone else's agenda.

I entered the coffee shop and found it completely deserted but for a large waitress behind a barlike counter, her back to me as she stacked and counted change on a brown cafeteria-style tray.

The waitress's uniform was strained at the seams down each side of her broad back. Her hair was netted in a heavy bundle over her collar and seemed to weigh her neck down over the money she methodically arranged. She was unaware of my presence, and I almost turned to leave except for the stupid feeling that my footsteps out the door would be somehow as impolitely interrupting of her concentration as my footsteps to the counter.

I quietly took a seat on a low, wobbly stool, having decided to order just a cup of coffee instead of anything so troubling as a sandwich.

I sat, awkwardly and silently, until she finally turned her head, her lips still mouthing a tabulation of dollars and cents. Even with her face half obscured by her shoulder, I recognized the blue eyes. Rae Ludy turned around and grinned as widely as her narrow lips allowed without parting and baring anything so intimate as teeth.

"Holy shit! Did you miss a bus?" she asked. She stood as solidly as an icebox. Her eyes bore into mine from above that tense grin, which seemed frozen on her lips. I was too shocked to attempt any expression in return. The coincidence was awkward. The sight of her made me angry and happy at the same time.

"I just . . . I thought I . . . I just came in for coffee," I stuttered.

"Yea," she laughed with a snort, "me, too," lifting her bare arms away from her sides and then dropping them limply against her hips, indicating everything from the hair net and stained uniform down to her shiny hose and Keds. "Oh," she said, turning, and noisily assembled a cup to a saucer, overfilled it from an industrial-sized urn, and placed it before me.

I sat. Rae stood. The sloshed coffee ran on the counter. The overlit disarray of the deserted café exaggerated the nervous atmosphere. Tables needed clearing, chairs needed rearranging, some sort of conversation needed to be made. I felt a need to make order out of the situation, which grew more uncomfortable with each passing second of our silent standoff.

We each opened our mouths at the same time. "Well," I started. "So," Rae began.

Our stabs at the tension overlapped, and we each drew back into wordless waiting.

"I'm gay now," Rae finally blurted. Without a twitch, her stance took on a defensive posture, as if she were willfully tightening her flesh for a physical assault.

The word was new but not unknown to me. I'd seen it in print, heard it once or twice on television. It had embarrassed me, perhaps even more than the words it meant to replace and make less embarrassing. It felt contrived, too simple and short to mean much of anything relevant to me. It was a big-city sort of word, with a prissy social quality out of place even in Tulsa, certainly in Pryor. Perhaps in an international airport, maybe in New York or Hollywood, people could be gay. I'd never felt anything but queer.

I felt as though Rae was confessing more than the obvious, but the obvious was the surest thing to address.

"Yea," I nodded, "me, too, I guess." The stale air immediately lightened a bit. Rae's figure softened as she shifted her weight to the other leg.

"What about Dewar?" I asked. "Is he gay, now, too?"

"Beats me," she said, her eyes sweeping the floor. "I don't think he ever was."

I pretended to be untouched by her direct opinion. I sipped my coffee and lit a cigarette. I said, "He always was a good liar. Knew how to act a story, that's for sure."

"He's in the army," she said, leaning closer.

I looked away, out the window, at the empty parking lot, at the corner stoplight changing colors despite the absence of traffic.

"Enlisted on his birthday in Oklahoma City," she said to the back of my head. "He fell for that big-balls bullshit. Thinks they'll make a man out of him. Probably already have."

I met her face, "Is that where you all went, Oklahoma City?"

"No," she said, "we went to Ponca City."

"You must not have found what you were looking for."

"It wasn't planned, you know, the way it just happened. Once I had hold of Mary's address, I couldn't stay, not another night." She looked me in the eye. "I didn't ask Dewar to come along. He asked me."

"Pauline was sick about it," I told her.

"We've talked. They know."

"So, is Mary here now? Is she gay, too?" I asked, a little sarcastically.

"She's with Joe. That paint sniffer's gettin' paid to do it now." She shook her head, looked as though she wanted to spit. "They got a little house and everything. Common law married. We only sponged there about a week, is all. I never got close enough to

Mary to say what I came for. She and Dewar got tight though."
She made a doughnut with one hand and pierced it with a finger.
"Some kind of friend, huh?

"When I got fed up with that, Joe wasn't about to let Dewar stay
on by himself. As fucked up as Joe Turner is, he could sense what
was goin' on.

"So," she continued, straightening herself up, "we shared a ride
to Oklahoma City. Then I hitched here. I've met somebody." She
laughed and brushed a crumb off her chest. "Things are workin'
out all right."

"I'm glad for that," I said as Rae arched her back and stretched
with a self-involved groan.

"So, what are you doin' here, Charlie?" she asked.

"Just driving around since late afternoon. I guess I'm driving
back now. I've kind of moved out to the lake. For the summer at
least." I started to tell her about Owen, his love potions and hair
tonics, but it seemed like petty news compared to her own.

"Aren't you goin' to the bar?" she asked, turning back to her
stacks of change.

I glanced out the window once more, up the street at Jewel's
neon sign, wondering if she could possibly mean that old beer
joint with its spoiled smells, thick smoke, and juke music.

"I don't think they'd let me in, Rae. I'm not eight anymore and
still not eighteen."

"Dee'd let you in, with me. She's the one I met, you see. Dee."

I didn't see. I had fallen behind in the conversation, but playing
along seemed simpler and less aggravating than backtracking.

"I'm off, soon as I clear these tables," she said, dropping her
stacks of change into the register drawer and picking out bills in
exchange.

I offered to help, and by five after nine Rae had changed out of
her waitress uniform into a sleeveless sweatshirt, fleece side out,
and belled jeans that frayed at her boot tops, which seemed to have
lost none of the dust of Choteau by tromping city pavement.

I waited in the car while she punched a time card in the dispatcher's office and left the diner wide open and amply lit despite the absence of a cook or any late-night relief waitress in sight.

The hair net was wadded into a locker with the uniform, and as she eased herself through the passenger door of the car, her freed hair busily explored the upholstery of the car hood and crept over the headrest as if it might crawl into the backseat.

Rae Ludy took up a lot of space in the roomy car, but I was glad for her large companionship after so many hours of sealed-up solitude. Her substantial presence next to me soaked up all the excessive thoughts and reflections with which I'd filled the space and had left parked there in the headroom of the car. The news she'd delivered inside the bus station had put a sudden stop to the churning of my brain that had been set into a relentless overdrive by Dewar's disappearance. I hadn't processed the entirety of the story's ending yet, but I felt some of the relief that accompanies any solved mystery.

I was thankful for the abridged delivery of Rae's story, not yet certain of what its moral was. But the quick succession of facts and the editing out of all the feelings had allowed me to distance myself from the personal anguish I had invested in the tale.

I recognized a bit of my grandfather's succinct philosophy of "things just fizzlin' happen" in Rae's untangled telling and how that conclusion relieved everyone of blame to the degree, at least, that we can unburden ourselves enough to get on down the lane to the next fizzlin' thing.

I also recognized that this lifting within me was hanging on faith in Rae Ludy's version of what had really happened. I knew Dewar's version would've been different and different still for each soul he told it to. Mary Deer and Joe Turner would have their own versions for each other and themselves. But I felt freed enough then to buy just about anyone's version of his or her struggles with the disappointment of love.

★ ★ ★

The Queen of Hearts was the bar Rae directed us to. At 9:30 we took the last parking spot in the small lot, and, by the time I left alone at half past midnight for the highway back to Pryor, the streets for blocks around were lined with the overflow of the joint's customers.

Without Rae at my side and Dee at the door, I'm sure I would have been denied entrance for another three years of legal ripening, despite the illicit atmosphere. The foyer to the Queen of Hearts was as small as a closet. The street door swatted us up against a card table and nose to nose with a short-haired, plainfaced woman who grew fuller and wider from the neck down. Her hips spilled over the seat of the folding chair that anchored her behind the table of ink stamps, ashtray, and cash. Her breasts hovered between her arms over half the table, as flimsily contained as they were in the low-stretched elastic bodice of her granny dress. The laugh and squint lines in her sun-freckled complexion showed her to be at least in her thirties, and she rolled her eyes and whined as we entered the tight vestibule.

"Oh, buggar," she complained as Rae stepped around the table, bent and kissed her on the lips, "he's just a baby-doll."

"He's twenty-nine, Dee, I swear. Me and Charlie go way back to Choteau. This is Dee," she said to me, tossing her hair toward the woman, in fact, burying most of Dee's face in her hair.

Barely squeezed through the front door and against the vibrating jamb of an interior one, there was just enough excess room between the three of us and the table for me to extend my hand to Dee. She gripped it and held it tightly, eyeing me up and down.

"I been on my feet all night, Dee. Let us in," Rae said, mocking Dee's complaining tone.

Dee released my hand and turned her attention back to Rae. She suggestively lowered her voice. "You just keep your eye on this virgin piece.

"Miss Louise is counting heads tonight," she announced in a businesslike voice after clearing her throat. "I got to have the two-dollar cover."

Rae dug into her front pocket and gallantly peeled some singles off the folded wad of bills she withdrew before I could figure out what a cover was. We got the backs of our hands stamped with a black ink "PAID," and after a moment for Rae and Dee to kiss once more and exchange some nuzzling, whispered messages, an electric buzz unlocked the real bar door.

I pushed that heavy door against the pounding bass line of deafening music. Rae crowded in behind and pressed me through a thick crowd of men and some women. Without locking eyes on a single overt act, the innuendo and angle of queer relationships was so evident I felt it like a current through my skin.

Many beautiful eyes, some not so kind, some quite jealously cutting, many glancing and indifferent, passed over me as we squeezed forward through the bodies, touching, rubbing, and brushing intimately through a dark sea of shoulders, necks, profiles, and upheld cigarettes.

My belt buckle suddenly struck an islandlike bar, and Rae slid around from behind me, edged against the rounded lip of wood, and shouted a friendly order at the aged but athletically handsome woman who posed with the calm of an all-knowing matriarch in the middle of it all.

The drink was something tart and citrus with a clean bite, something small and light in my hand compared to the heft of a beer mug or the pendulous weight of a quart of whiskey. We paused at the bar for a few moments, sipping our drinks.

The Queen of Hearts was a dark, lush hothouse of queer orchids, nightmarish and gorgeous, varied and thriving. The tunnellike room throbbed with a tribal pulse that shook the blood-colored walls and floor. A neurological connection ignited over and over in the eyes glinting in the darkness like gems in a coal mine.

The music was like the oxygen of the place. It enveloped everything in its viscous rhythm like a rocking lake. My every gesture suddenly had an air of self-conscious performance. The bar was a strobing, clicking camera. It shot me from the inside out. Its walls were red with a strange, developing passion.

There was no space for talk, only shouting or a sign language of the face and body.

With our drinks in hand, I followed Rae to the back of the club, losing and regaining sight of her back as the bodies parted and closed between us. To move through the crowd was to wade through it. Each of my steps after her caused a wave of motion that moved everyone else like links in a heavy chain: drinks tilted, smoke swirled, a neck lowered, hips shifted and swayed. Each contact made me want to linger and meld to its warm sensual pulse, as faceless as it might be in the dim light.

The edge of a dance floor in the very back of the room, where Rae's trail came to a clearing of sorts, was a hypnotic hive of more bodies, more music, more light. A zone of stripped down, eye-clenched, frenetic abandon. The flooring vibrated with the pounding of an unleashed physicality, a full possession by the music. Hair lashed, sweat flew, backbones snapped, and hands rose aflutter like tambourines of jewelry.

I looked at Rae draining ice cubes from the bottom of her glass and was reminded of the drink in my own hand. Her knees bobbed with a stationary approximation of the dance before us. Her hair expanded and contracted as she nodded and rocked her head. I grinned at her unique rhythm and the odd kinship I felt, the serious traders that we were and how our hunter's instinct had led us here separately but together.

She caught my stare and slyly, probably knowingly, returned my grin with a smile warm enough to melt her mouthful of ice. I was still full of questions for her about Dewar and Mary, about Dee, about me: cold, crackling, hard questions that would never have survived the high heat and noise level of the bar, that would have been too exhausting to shout and whose answers would have been lost anyway in this roaring bonfire.

Rae snatched the empty glass from my hand and dipped her

head in the direction of the bar before charging through the tangle
of bodies for refills, which left me alone and a little less rooted on
the tremoring edge of the dance floor.

Adoringly, enviously, I stood there with the other half-initiated:
watching, learning, waiting for the dance to lay its sensuous hands
upon us and heal our reticence.

The longer I was left there, the stronger the spirit of the place
grew, until it was fully upon me and I couldn't resist the pull of the
dance itself and, without moving, imagined myself letting go of
something, urged on by the spirit in unexpected ways to join in
the primitive, innate jumping, shaking, loosening.

The thundering beat poured down like rain on the orchid-faced,
lanky-stemmed boys. Partnerless, my heart danced in the crush of
the entire bouquet until my hair and clothes and skin were
drenched with its perfume.

Rae Ludy's elbow nudged my arm. She offered another drink,
which I took with a grateful smile and a silent toast and sip.

When my eyes turned from her back to the dance, my spirit had
been swallowed up by the throng or ascended so far above it, it was
soaring beyond the ceiling, so far into the sky it was perhaps but
a shooting star falling over Pryor now and Purley Slaughter. It was
falling hard: a dazzling, unidentifiable falling spirit of flames, reflected in the calm lake's surface, perhaps glimpsed out the window
of Chick's place by Ida or Fay or Owen as a flash over the highway,
gone before anyone else could turn to see.

I was following Rae—for real this time—into the jungle of music and dance. The roaming eyes and sexy smiles made way for us.
We planted ourselves there with glasses raised and tentatively began
to make our dance. Rae's body ticked and swayed. Mine began to
climb into the motions of sex itself until I reached a certain vision.
The photographic image of Fay Rose's great nephew slowly developed in the dancing chemicals of my mind. I grinned at the re-
union with Hunter and felt awash in the texture of his turned
cheek, his taut, straight smile. The watercolor blue of his eyes fell

upon mine until it was a memento of my own immediate future looking through me on the verge of eighteen now, through me on the verge of a higher education, into a heart rendered hopeful and fit for love.

℗ PLUME

ON BEING GAY

☐ **THE HOUSE ON BROOKE STREET by Neil Bartlett.** Evoking the glamor of London's gay subculture of the 1920s and the terror caused by the repression of the 50s, this dark, erotic novel tells the story of two men joined in passion, yet desperately afraid to reveal their love. "Harrowingly, weirdly sexy, compulsively readable . . . nearly mythic."—Edmund White   (942734—$21.95)

☐ **READY TO CATCH HIM SHOULD HE FALL by Neil Bartlett.** A deeply romantic evocation of gay life and love. A tender, erotic, and brutally explicit portrayal of love between men.   (268737—$11.95)

☐ **BOYS OF LIFE by Paul Russell.** Teenager Tony Blair is ripe for adventure and is easily seduced by Carlos Reichart, a filmmaker who draws Tony to a secret region of passion and human corruption . . . "The great American novel of gay male experience."—*Booklist*   (268370—$11.95)

☐ **FAG HAG by Robert Rodi.** Brash, outrageous, and hilariously "incorrect" this is a novel that redefines "the war between the sexes", a comedy that takes no prisoners, from an irresistibly irreverent new voice. "A hilarious tale—bitchy without being savage. I adored every word."—Quentin Crisp

(269407—$11.95)

Prices slightly higher in Canada.

Visa and Mastercard holders can order Plume, Meridian, and Dutton books by calling.
1-800-253-6476.
They are also available at your local bookstore. Allow 4-6 weeks for delivery.
This offer is subject to change without notice.

PL165